THE BINDING OF THE HALO

The Binding of the Halo
<u>Copyright</u> Ⓒ 2017 Shea Swain

Warning: The Binding of the Halo is for 18 years and older.

ISBN-13:978-1546906537
ISBN-10:1546906533

Cover Designed: Sanja Balan of Sanja's Covers
Edited: Pam Howard
Proofreader: D. Swain, Kim Bey, Kelly Bey-Borden
Format: Shea Swain

Other Books Written By:

What Lilly Wants
previously known as Lascivious
An Erotic Novella

INVIDIOUS Betrayal
A Full-Length Paranormal-Sci Romance

ABSOLVE
A Short Romantic New Adult Drama

The Changing of the Seasons
Winter's Icy Heart
A Taste of Spring
Contemporary Romance

Chained to the Devil's Son
A Full-Length Dark Romance

The Binding of the Halo Series
Four Full-Length Paranormal Romance Series
The Binding of the Halo Book I
The Awakening of the Halo Book II
The Descent of the Halo III
The Battle for the Halo IIII
&
The Coesen-Origins

Heaven on Hell Island
A Contemporary Romance with Sci-fi undertones

Dedicated to my inspirations…
Sonserae
Daniel III
Daniel IV
Cianne

Prologue

Kayla closed the trunk of the car then looked over at her daughter who was waiting by the rear passenger door. The pain on her young one's face was enough to drive her to tears. But she held her sadness back and approached her daughter.

"Zaria, we can't stay here," Kayla told her.

"Because I did something bad. Because I scared people," Zaria mumbled. She glanced over at the house across the street where she'd spent many fun hours then looked down at her small shoes.

"No sweetie," Kayla said. Squatting down, she gently grasped Zaria's tiny face and kissed her forehead. Kayla brushed one of her daughter's long plait aside and peered into large blue-green eyes that were welling with tears. Eyes similar to *his*. Eyes that conjured such wonderful and horrible memories. "You did nothing bad. You are perfect in every way."

Zaria sniffed then said, "If I am perfect mommy, why do we have to move and I have to have a new name? Why are all my friends scared of me?"

"Baby, I know things are confusing right now but I promise that you will love the new house and you will make so many friends."

Zaria smiled. "You promise?"

Kayla smiled as she thought, *I swear on my life…* "You will be the happiest little queen in the entire world." She wiped Zaria's tears off her face then pinched her nose. "So, how about we use your new name from now on, okay?"

"Ok," Zaria said, then she sniffed again. "But will daddy remember to call me by my new name?"

"I sure will, Buttercup!" Joseph said as he walked up, lifted Zaria in his arms, and spun her around. When he put her back down, he winked at Kayla.

"Thank you", she mouthed. Kayla watched as Joseph pulled open the back passenger side door and strapped their daughter in the car. The love he felt for her and her daughter gave Kayla the strength to do all of what she needed to do to keep Zaria safe. Most men would think it was crazy to move across the country just because their wife claimed to have had a vision. Some may have even filed for divorce. But not Joseph, who married her knowing that she could never give him a child of his own and that she and her daughter came with 'special effects'. Joseph even knew about *him*.

If only she could forget *him*.

Kayla shut down her thoughts. It was better not to think of him at all.

"How about we grab some pancakes from the diner before we set out?" Joseph suggested.

Kayla forced a smile. "We can, but my homemade pancakes are ten times better," she bragged as she walked around the car and pulled open the front passenger door, and slid inside.

"True," Joseph said as he rested his arms on the roof of the car, "but we won't judge them."

Chapter One
Present, August 12th,

Cianne's *steps faltered as she entered the main doors of her high school. As she focused on the image in the mirrored trophy case in the entrance foyer, she realized the grotesque sight reflected in the mirror was her.*

An unnerving feeling tugged at Cianne as she walked through the main doors of West Hills High school. Last night's nightmare was still fresh in her mind. She swallowed the lump in her throat and averted her eyes when she passed the trophy case and moved toward the busy hallway that led to her locker.

Remaining calm was her top priority because…if she lost her composure, bad things could happen, so Cianne immediately changed the direction of her thoughts. Instead of focusing on the dream, she hummed a tune in her head. Only, that did little to distract her. Her nightmares always nourished the seeds of her fears, and those fears were branching out just like…

Cianne took a small step toward the mirrored trophy case, then another. She could hear the whispers of those who gathered around her, but it didn't distract her from the image. It was her, only her veins were as black as coal and very visible just beneath her paper-thin, pale skin as they branched outward. That image, in itself, was enough to warrant fear, but the vision of the blood red eyes that hauntingly looked back at her could have easily evoked madness.

There was something different about last night's nightmare that made her skin crawl. *He* had been there.

Stress and the constant fear of being discovered were things Cianne (Sahy-an) had to live with every day, but she usually kept them under control. Albeit, a shaky form of control. Her only solace was in thinking that as long as she didn't allow herself to get distracted or involved, everything would be alright.

Everything will be fine.

Cianne continued through the hall, avoiding other students and faculty as she went. She kept her head low as she walked. When she reached her locker, she let out a sigh of relief.

No distractions. No complications.

She started chanting those two phrases to an upbeat tune in her head when an intoxicating fragrance brought her mantra to a halt. The scent circulated around her like an invisible smoke cloud.

Cianne closed her eyes as she slid closer to her locker. She inhaled the scent that was as familiar to her as her own, allowing herself to enjoy the clean pleasurable aroma that never failed to announce *his* presence.

She gave in to temptation and sniffed the air again, then opened her eyes and quickened her pace of taking what she needed from her locker. Tristan Bertram was the one person in the entire world who was capable of distracting her, so she needed to be gone before he spoke to her.

Grabbing a couple of thin binders out of her locker, Cianne then dug into her bag and pulled out a folder she didn't need, and placed it inside. As she did, her attention was drawn to the bottom of her locker, where she spotted the book she needed under a pile of loose papers. Cianne crouched down, pulled the book out, and placed it inside her shoulder bag then stuffed the loose papers that spilled out onto the floor back inside her locker.

Before she pushed the metal door closed, she fumbled inside her bag for her cell phone. It only took her a moment to discover that it wasn't in her bag. Cianne patted the pockets of her fitted jeans only to come up empty.

"Where is it?" she asked herself, as she lifted and shuffled the cluttered chaos inside her locker. "Really?" she hissed as she stood.

Cianne smoothed her palm up over her forehead and down the back of her head until it rested on the nape of her neck, pinning her hair to her bare skin. She looked up at the ceiling and did a mental review of her morning in an attempt to remember where she saw her phone last.

It was on the kitchen table this morning when she ate breakfast. Right in the middle of enjoying her eggs and toast, she was responding to a text message when she experienced a vision.

Visions had a way of disrupting her day. Not because her visions were painful—because they didn't have to be. It was because her visions were preceded by a physical change.

In a way, she appreciated the physical changes that occurred before her visions. One would argue that she should be grateful for those fleeting moments just before the revelation of someone's pending misfortune was thrust upon her. She knew that if anyone witnessed her freak show warning signs, her life would be a series of needle pricks, lab tests, and doctors. But being helpless while in the throes of one of her ghastly visions was even worse. The visions could last from a few seconds up to twenty minutes or more. So, those little physical "alarms" gave her a chance to get to safety before the visions started.

Where is my cell phone?

"Are you looking for this?" Tristan's scent—diluted by the space between them before—was closer and was much more concentrated.

Cianne stilled as the sound of his voice vibrated through her, warming her in ways that caused her to blush. Annoyed, she grimaced at her reaction to Tristan before turning around to face him.

Tristan, in all his glory, stood directly in front of her, mere inches away. Their eyes met and…

Sadness, pain, death.

The words were just a whisper in her mind now, but still, she heard them loud and clear. Cianne dismissed the three words she heard following every first look into his eyes, as usual. She lowered her eyes before they revealed how he made her feel. What she didn't consider was her eyes settling on his lips.

Not his lips, she thought as she moved her gaze to his chest.

Worse idea ever. *Why not go for the gold and drop your gaze further south, Cianne,* she taunted herself. The thought had her eyes twitching with anticipation.

No! Cianne cringed, deciding his eyes were her best option.

With a lift of his hand, a wave of heat washed over Cianne's entire body. The reaction her body went through when Tristan was near, she explained away as nervous attraction. She was both nervous and attracted to him. Only she had a feeling that the heat she felt was no more normal than she was.

Cianne took a step back to widen the space between them. While hot, this level of heat didn't compare to the heat she felt at their first meeting a few years ago in middle school. On that day, the heat that assaulted her was intense. She feared that her skin had burned that day as she fled to the girl's bathroom.

The mirror revealed that she was perfectly fine. Needless to say, her little freak out had been the talk of the school. Well, it was the talk until one of the teachers fell in the gym. Cianne had made sure she kept her distance from Tristan Bertram the rest of that day and every day that followed.

That was why being near Tristan was so unsettling to her.

She continued to back away from him until she felt the cold steel of her locker door through the thin shirt she wore. Cianne embraced the chill that seeped into her skin as her eyes lowered to the palm of his outstretched hand. In it was her cell phone. Relieved, she stretched her lips into a rare smile. If she lost another phone, it would be the third one this year.

But her relief at the sight of the phone didn't ease her anxiety. Tristan's attention was on her and he was standing too close.

Cianne didn't reach for her phone right away nor did she look up at him. To be honest, she didn't need too to look at Tristan. She knew his face like she knew her own. His tanned skin was impeccable, except for a barely noticeable two-inch scar that began at the lobe of his left ear and trailed under his chin. His eyes were blue, remarkable, and depending on the light, could transform from a light Carolina blue to a dark royal blue.

He stood about six foot two, taller than her five foot eight. He had the body of a professional athlete, with sculpted streamlined muscles that made her want to stop and stare. His dark brown hair was cut close now, but for a couple of years, he wore it longer, so she knew it had a little curl to it. Cianne liked the curls but short was a good look for him too.

Today, he wore a fitted gray T-shirt, black cargo shorts, and a pair of black and white running shoes. As always, he was a mix of what she called comfortable-perfection. Everything about him was perfect, though nothing compared to Tristan's most incredible asset, his smile. Cianne had a mental meltdown whenever she saw it.

Seemingly confused by her reluctance to take her phone, Tristan extended his hand more. "I found this on the floor over there." He motioned to the hallway she walked through earlier.

Cianne tried to stay calm as she focused on his outstretched hand and was relieved that the familiar warmth he always ignited inside her had decreased to a mild annoyance.

Tristan sighed as he lowered his hand.

Cianne knew that he wanted some kind of response from her so she went over several in her head. *Don't say something stupid...and try to sound normal.* She decided on, "Thank you. I thought I lost another one."

That wouldn't win "the best response ever" award but it was all she could manage.

Ignoring the urge to caress his palm, Cianne took the phone from Tristan's hand without touching his skin. She glanced back up at his smiling eyes and almost sighed before turning her back to him and facing her locker.

"I...uh, I'm glad I found it then."

She fidgeted with stuff in her locker to look busy but she was certain she just looked ridiculous. In Tristan's presence, Cianne found it virtually impossible to relax. He was the kind of guy who got a girl's blood racing...or boiling. Especially when she felt his eyes on her.

Cianne nervously glanced at her hand. *No dark veins.*

Somewhat comforted, she tried to think of why he was still there, staring at her. *Is my hair out of place? Does he hate my new shirt?* Calm...nope, she was failing at staying calm. She launched into a self-conscious breakdown, picking apart everything she could think of that could be wrong.

Tristan cleared his throat. "I was thinking," he began, "there's a back to school party in Phoenix this weekend and-"

"Hey, Tristan," a chorus of passing girls sang out, interrupting him.

Cianne saw them pass by out of the corner of her eye.

They giggled, waved at Tristan, and jostled one another as they walked by.

"Hey," Tristan said, as he tilted his head slightly in their direction. He followed with a halfhearted smile and waved.

With her appearance forgotten, Cianne thought that his voice sounded automatic, almost empty. She dismissed it as the sound of the girls arguing over which of them were the intended recipient of Tristan's greeting amped up in volume even though they were moving away.

Cianne looked over at Tristan then passed him to the group of girls as they made their way down the hallway. The girls erupted in a single inharmonious scream when they looked back and saw Tristan watching them too. Cianne shook her head at the high-frequency giggles of her classmates and focused back on her locker.

The clicking sound of Tristan opening his locker was almost deafening. She had to get away from him. How they had been assigned lockers next to each other was still a mystery to her. Not just to her—it seemed that every girl in their graduating class openly questioned their locker assignments. His homeroom was on the north side of the building so his locker should be located in the north hallway, not next to hers which was in the east hall.

Cianne had no clue how it happened, but she refused several bribes from his admirers to switch with her. She wasn't about to give her assigned locker to anyone. At least that was what she told herself before Tristan started a regular campaign to engage her in conversation. It was already difficult ignoring the pull of his magnetism but now that he was her locker neighbor, avoiding him was almost impossible.

The sound of ruffled papers coming from Tristan's locker was a hopeful sign that maybe he forgot what he was about to say about the party. Cianne was reveling in her reprieve when his hand gripped the side of her locker door. He slowly eased the door she often used as a barrier between them back until he had a clear view of her profile.

"So, about the party—,"

"I don't go to parties," Cianne said, without hesitating. She leaned forward, using her long dark hair to hide her face.

"Dude?"

Cianne glanced up when she heard the familiar voice and saw Brian, Tristan's best friend, walking up. Relief washed over her, but she kept her head lowered.

Tristan tapped her locker a few times. "Right." He sighed as he moved her locker door back the way it was.

When he closed his locker, she felt rather than witnessed him turn and walk away.

Tristan glanced over his shoulder at Cianne before stepping in pace with Brian. "What's up?"

"I thought I would jump in and save you from embarrassing yourself. Damn dude, tell me you weren't about to do what I think you were about to do." Brian chuckled.

His friend's loud laughter never bothered Tristan before but today he felt it like coarse sand moving over his exposed nerves. Cianne brushed him off again and even though he never let it trouble him before, this time, it did.

"What are you talking about?" Tristan thought it best to pretend not to know what he was being accused of as they walked into their homeroom.

Brian sat down at the desk next to Tristan and blatantly stared at him, while Tristan stared blankly straight ahead. Tristan wondered how long it would take his friend to realize he was being ignored. After a few students passed between their desks, Brian finally spoke up.

"You know what I'm talking about. Cianne? Don't think so playa." Brian snorted. "She only dates college guys, remember?"

"Maybe," Tristan murmured. He waved hello to a couple of girls who touched his shoulder as they made their way to their seats in the back of the room.

"Yeah, ok." Brian shook his head. "If the fact that she's never dated anyone here at West Hills doesn't drive it home for you, as far as I know, she's never dated anyone at Westbrook either. Believe me, I've asked around."

Tristan's brows wrinkled as he returned Brian's famous stare-down. There was so much he wanted to say but all he could get out was, "Really?"

"What? I was curious," Brian explained with a crooked smile.

"Curious?" Tristan laughed. "So, you've resorted to interrogating her friends?" This amused Tristan because he had done the very same thing. Well, he wouldn't call what he did interrogation. Cianne's name may have come up on occasion when he was talking to some people who knew her.

For Brian to ask around, now that was interesting. His closest friend wasn't the kind of guy who researched a girl. Brian approached dating as a numbers game. He simply saw a girl he liked and asked her out. Brian once told Tristan that it wasn't a big deal if a girl turned him down because he would just move on to the next one. The more he asked, the more chances he had to secure a date. The strategy worked well for him.

"I'm a guy. I would have to be either dead or into you to not get worked up over Cianne Baxter." Brian broke eye contact to speak to a cute brunette whose name Tristan hadn't memorized yet, then met Tristan's gaze again. "Look," he whispered, "Brenda is wearing my new favorite shirt."

As discreet as possible, Tristan looked toward the classroom door but didn't focus on the voluptuous Brenda, who was rumored to buy her shirts a size too small to emphasize her shapely look. Instead, he thought about how Cianne looked in the new top she wore today. The sudden shift from the image of Cianne standing by her locker just minutes ago to images of her hugging on some random college guy made him pulse with anger.

In the four years they've known each other, Cianne had never even given him a second glance. He was aware that he was just as good as any college guy; he just needed a chance to prove it. Tristan frowned as he realized that his teeth and palms ached. He pushed the thought of Cianne with some other guy out of his mind as a wave of awareness hit him. He felt the rumble of his laughter bubble up out of him as he contemplated his feelings of jealousy.

Tristan ignored the questioning look Brian gave him and gave himself a mental scolding. Jealousy was a foreign emotion for him, and right then he decided that it was one he could do without.

Tristan was gone. Cianne pursed her lips, slowly exhaled, and rested her shaking hands on the frame of her locker. She tried to disregard the looming presence behind her but even when silent, Tranae was hard to ignore.

"Don't give me that look," Cianne said, as she closed her locker door. She turned to face her best friend who happened to be wearing her patented 'What is wrong with you?' expression.

"How did you know I was behind you?" Instead of waiting for an answer, Tranae just rolled her eyes and waved her hand in a dismissive gesture. "Why didn't you talk to him? You could be a little friendlier since you guys share the same space this year."

"I had nothing to say. Or would you have preferred, 'Thanks for finding my phone Tristan and uh, I've been aching, just plain aching to kiss you for all of four years, do you mind?'" Cianne said sarcastically.

Tranae rolled her eyes. "That would have been better than turning your back on him day after day."

"Yeah, well." Cianne shrugged, as she slipped her fingers under the strap of her bag and lifted it higher on her shoulder. They walked down the corridor side by side, instinctively avoiding a large number of students that filled the hall around them.

"Don't you think it's time you've gotten to know the opposite sex a little better?" Tranae asked. The two hurried down a set of stairs and into their homeroom. "…and I don't mean tutoring them either."

"I know the opposite sex," Cianne countered with a smirk. The room was almost full, but they managed to find seats next to each other.

"I mean up close and personal. Spending time alone, kissing, touching, faking orgasms." Tranae wiggled her brows. "You know…the normal things girls our age do when we like a guy."

"I'm pretty sure none of that is going to make me normal, and why don't the guys I tutor count? Aren't they the opposite sex?" Cianne pouted playfully.

"You know what I mean Cianne. Aren't you even a little bit curious about dating? The only guys you spend time with are those college idiots you tutor," Tranae paused and raised a finger. "…and no, they don't count."

"No, not curious in the least." If she was entirely truthful, dating was an interest of hers, but Cianne decided long ago that it wasn't an option. Especially with someone like Tristan. "I'm shy I guess."

"Bullshit! You…are not shy." Tranae laughed as she leaned her upper body closer to Cianne. "The only guy you freeze up around is Tristan. You act totally normal around other guys. Look chick, you're too beautiful…" Tranae sighed when Cianne exhaled forcefully. "Well, you are. Is it so bad that you were blessed with beauty? Just accept it already, I have." She popped her collar. "Now, like I was saying. You're beautiful, and smart, and the nicest person I know. Doesn't all that cancel out that little issue you think is so bad that you don't deserve love?"

"I can live without that kind of love, Tranae. Mother Teresa did. I just want to focus on my education." Love is overrated. "What you need to do is stop focusing on me and worry about yourself. What are you going to tell your father about your cell phone?"

Tranae rolled her eyes as she reached inside her purse. "So, you want to be a nun now," she continued, "and what are you talking about? My baby is just fine." She gave Cianne a suspicious look as she held up her colorfully bejeweled lifeline.

The homeroom bell rang out just as their homeroom teacher, Mrs. Franklin, slowly pulled the door closed. She allowed a few more stragglers in before shutting it softly. All conversation ceased as the morning announcements went out over the intercom.

Cianne watched Tranae unpack her books. Homeroom was the only classroom time they shared in the last seven years. When the bell rang, Cianne would go to the third floor which was exclusive to AEA students.

West Hills High School was one of the ten schools in the State that offered the program. AEA or Academic Enrichment Academy was a program that was offered only to those students who excelled in academics, which was Tranae's weakness. One of her few as it were.

Chapter Two

Throughout her morning, Cianne did her best to focus on her classes, but lunch couldn't get there fast enough. She was starving. When lunch time eventually rolled around, she went to her favorite burger spot, Crimpy's Burgers.

Crimpy's was located two blocks from West Hills High and it was Cianne's lunchtime hangout three days a week. It was a well-known spot but the place hadn't gained hot status yet. Most of her peers stayed on campus or went to the pizza shop that was directly across the street from the school. The great burgers and her peers' lack of interest made Crimpy's the perfect place for Cianne, who hated crowds and was a burger girl to her core.

She glanced at the time as she sat at her usual table, which was located in the rear of the restaurant, and played on her cell as she waited. After sitting for a few more minutes, Cianne checked the time again. Tranae being late was something she would never get used to. It was moments like this that made Cianne wish she had more than one real friend in the world.

Overall, Cianne found it easy to make friends. She just didn't care for the problems that went along with having them. The "he said/she said" games and petty arguments were not the price she wanted to pay for companionship. Besides, having friends meant sharing your secrets, along with the good, bad, and the ugly times. Cianne preferred to keep her good and bad to herself, with an emphasis on keeping the ugly a secret.

An unearthly grumble that came from her stomach provoked a sigh. Tired of waiting and fearful that her stomach would soon eat her from the inside out, Cianne decided to order her food. With a bounce in her step, she made for the cashier.

Happy she hadn't waited another second; she returned to her seat with her usual, a number three combo meal. The setup was simple: ketchup mountain, remove the pickles from the burger, and set the drink aside for later so the ice can dilute the sugar. Set and ready, Cianne dipped a fry into the ketchup on the side of her plate then put the hot crisped-to-perfection treat into her mouth.

"*Mmm.*" She mumbled with satisfaction as she pulled the book she was reading from her bag.

Books had always been a mainstay of Cianne's life. They were her introduction to the world and not just her small corner of it. They introduced her to people imaginary and real she otherwise could never meet. They were her travel guide and companion, taking her all around the world in a matter of days without her ever leaving the safety of her home. They taught her languages, cultures, and customs that she may never experience but would always respect and appreciate. Most of all, books were a great way to give people she didn't want to engage an indirect brush off. It worked 90% of the time.

But…

Before Cianne was able to find the dog-eared page she folded yesterday, three familiar words of warning whispered in her mind.

Sadness, Pain, Death.

For just a second, Cianne lost control and her entire body went rigid before she forced herself to relax.

"Hi."

Tristan's deep, smooth voice caused her body to involuntarily shudder. Cianne was hesitant to look up to confirm that it was him standing on the other side of the round table, one of the few physical barriers between them.

Though the need to respond was automatic, she couldn't because she was still dealing with the fact that Tristan was standing in front of her outside of school.

...and, where was the warmth that usually warned her of his approach? What happened to the broadcast of his pleasant aroma before he appeared? How was it that all of the necessary signs failed? She didn't even have to look at him to hear those haunting words this time.

"You mind if I sit here?" Tristan asked.

Cianne took her time raising her head to see exactly who she expected to see. Tristan held a tray with just a plate of overflowing fries and a cola on it. She had to clear her throat because he looked amazing as usual. Her hand that held the book sort of fell limply to the side, exposing some of her face.

"I'm waiting for someone."

When he smiled, her heart skipped a beat.

"No problem," Tristan said, "I'll leave when your *someone* gets here."

Seriously? Cianne frowned. *Why isn't he leaving? Fine, I'll just ignore him like I always do.*

She shrugged but didn't fail to notice that he bypassed the chair he stood behind and moved to the seat beside her and sat down. Cianne side-eyed him briefly before reaching for her drink and taking a much-needed sip to ease her dry throat.

Tristan grabbed the bottle of ketchup from the middle of the table and squeezed it, covering his fries completely. She felt him watching her, somehow feeling him smiling. Cianne didn't even realize that she was flipping the pages of her book as she wondered why he was sitting with her. Hadn't she been clear about not going to that party?

Maybe this isn't about the party. He may need help with a school project or something. Doubtful, but it could be the case.

Maybe Crimpy's was crowded, and there were no seats left. Cianne glanced around the restaurant. There were several empty tables.

Why didn't he sit at any of them?

Maybe he didn't like eating alone.

Not a big deal, him sitting here.

It wasn't as if they hadn't gone to the same school for four years. All she needed to do was relax. That's all. *I can relax around him*, she told herself. As casually as she could, Cianne placed a fry in her mouth.

Tristan openly watched Cianne while he ate his fries. She held the book up to her face, blocking his view, but that did nothing to suppress his imagination. His thoughts were all over the place.

Images of her biting into succulent fruit, wrapping her lips around lollipops, and yes…kissing him, clouded his vision.

In an effort to control his *growing* interest, Tristan focused on the book, but her dainty fingers caught his attention. They should be adorned with elegant and expensive rings. Not with the odd plain metallic ring she wore.

What the hell I am thinking? I want a date, not a wife.

He silently counted to ten, hoping to focus on what was happening now. "So…" When she didn't look up from her book, he decided to continue anyway. "You still run every day at Ridgeview Park? I haven't seen you there in awhile."

Tristan had seen her running a few times while he shot hoops at Ridgeview, a large community park with a jogging trail. He never saw her driving so he assumed she must live close by.

Cianne peeked over the top of the book, at him. "Sometimes…" she answered, then lowered the book a little more, "but I've been going after dinner lately. Why?"

Bingo!

Never had Cianne asked him a question or said anything other than an occasional greeting, prompted by him of course.

Tristan held her gaze for a moment. This time, she was waiting for a response from him and he saw no reason to answer right away. The fact that he had her attention and that she was looking directly into his eyes, excited him.

He watched her as she tilted her head down then to the side, allowing her long dark hair to spill over her shoulder and down toward the table. Before the silky looking mane made contact with her plate, Cianne's hand swept her hair over to the other side exposing her delicate neck and the small tattoo she had just behind her left ear. The urge to trace her bare neck with his tongue then lay a gentle kiss on her ink was strong. Then she blinked, pulling his attention to her long dark eyelashes that made him want to brush his thumb across them. He had never seen natural lashes that long before.

Tristan's mind slowed down her movements, frame by frame, as her stunning almond shaped eyes of the purest green stared back at him. He inadvertently dropped his gaze to her lips. Cianne's full peach toned lips parted slightly, causing aches in places he didn't want to acknowledge at the moment. He wondered if they were as soft and tasted as sweet as they looked.

Cianne focused back on her book then lowered her head so that her hair shielded some of her profile. Tristan didn't seem offended by her closing him out. She saw him smiling out of the corner of her eye.

Why is he staring at me? As if he was interested in whatever she had to say.

"Would you like some company?"

Cianne tilted her head and creased her brows. "Company?" she repeated.

"Yeah, when you run," he smiled.

That smile. Cianne's heart fluttered, again.

"See, I want to stay in shape and running seems to work for you."

Wait. She lowered her book then glared at him. Cianne had to close her gaped open mouth. "What?"

Tristan turned to face her, "I'd like to run with you."

"I don't think that would be a good idea."

Tristan chuckled, but his laugh had little humor to it. He sat back in the chair letting one arm fall to his side while the other remained on the table beside his tray where his fingers fidgeted with the edge of a napkin. "Have I done something to you that caused you to dislike me?"

Cianne brows creased and, as she wondered what had him saying such nonsense, her frown deepened.

"No?" he questioned. "Well, you never talk to me unless you have to. Even then, you brush me off. I smile, you run. Did I do something to you that I don't remember? Perhaps I said something. Or is it just me in general, you detest?" he asked calmly.

"I don't...not like you." Her words came out much quicker than she had intended. *Oh, if he only knew.*

For the first time in four years, Tristan saw Cianne Baxter's eyes clearly. He was amazed that they weren't green like he thought they were. Her eyes were a mixture of green and blue that reminded him of beautiful untouched waters in the tropics. They were dazzling, hypnotic even, but he needed to focus and not be swayed by her exquisiteness.

"Then why are you so put off by me?" he asked her.

"Put off..." She frowned again, seemingly confused by the question. "I never meant for you to interpret my actions, or lack of, that way. I apologize."

Tristan watched as she scraped her teeth over her plump lower lip. He pictured them kissing again, imagining how sweet her lip gloss would taste. He wondered if she knew how sexy biting her lip was, and if she did, was she doing it on purpose to distract him. Playful or nervous biting did sidetrack him.

Cianne was watching him, watching her. He never had her full attention as he did now. Her attention had his heartbeat throbbing inside his chest, and all he wanted was to touch her face, to see if her shimmering olive-toned skin felt as satiny as it looked.

Cianne smoothed her hand over her hair then touched her jaw. She lowered her eyes then looked directly back at him with a raised eyebrow. "What?" she asked impatiently.

"Um…" Tristan had to close his eyes and looked away. He took a moment to get his thoughts together and back to the conversation.

Focus…she's actually talking to you, idiot.

"There's no need to apologize. You can hate me if you like. I just want to know what I did and if I can fix it?"

"I…," Cianne started but stopped. "You… I just don't…" She hesitated again.

He had her tongue tied. "Was the question that hard?" he chuckled.

"No." She looked away. "It's just that you caught me off guard."

Tristan realized that Cianne was nervous. Extremely so, by the way she stumbled over her words and she was still biting her lip. Definitely a nervous thing for her. "What are you guarding?" he asked, playfully.

"Nothing," she said quickly, her voice cracking as she spoke.

Tristan watched as Cianne's cheeks reddened. Had he hit on something? She basically avoided him, but she did admit that she "didn't…not like" him. She was blushing because he accused her of guarding something.

She avoids me.
She never looks me in the eyes.
She's blushing.

He'd seen this before. In fact, he'd seen this type of behavior often enough to know what it was. The confusing part was that this was Cianne. Yet all the signs were clear. How did he miss all the signs?

Tristan scooted to the edge of his seat. He couldn't help the way his lips spread out into a wide grin. He felt like the cat who swallowed the canary.

"Did I say something funny?" Cianne asked. Her tone held a hint of irritation and that amused Tristan more.

The semi-smile, or maybe it was a partial frown, on her face made Tristan laugh. Or maybe he was laughing at himself for being so stupid.

"What?" Cianne pinned him with a hard stare.

"You like me," Tristan said, then grinned. The smile he displayed and the conviction in his voice showed no hint of doubt.

"WHAT?" Cianne demanded loudly. "What?" she hissed, her tone lower.

"You like me, and I don't mean as a friend. You're into me." He sat back in the chair. His smile was broad; exposing two rows of what he knew were perfectly white teeth. He watched Cianne as her mouth gaped open then closed a few times.

Tristan continued to look at her for thirty seconds as she tried to verbalize a response. "Cat got your tongue?" he teased. "Words can be hard to find for a situation such as this," he said, with mock sympathy. "A simple response would be 'Yes, I do like you, Tristan.' Or you may go in another direction entirely if you like a little flare. You can declare your desires loud and proud for everyone to hear. If silent and sexy is more your thing, which I so hope it is, you can write your number on my hand and seal it with a kiss." Tristan winked at her. "Either of those works for me, though I prefer that you kiss my palm right now. I don't want our first kiss to be in a fast food spot and…I don't want you to think I'm easy."

Cianne sat silently while he spoke, but she did gasp when he winked at her. When she did speak, she didn't whisper.

"I know lots of words," she said, sounding annoyed. Cianne put her book inside her bag, picked up her tray, steadied it, then stood up. "These are the words that come to mind right now: overconfident, self-centered, and egotistical." Her hair cascaded around her face then swayed with the breeze as she walked around him. She threw the contents on her tray into the garbage can a few yards away then walked toward the exit doors.

"Or, you can do that." Tristan laughed as he watched her leave.

He almost thought that he had deciphered the signs wrong due to her initial stunned silence, but then she spoke and what he heard in her shaky tone only confirmed his suspicions. There was too much emotion in her little speech for him to be wrong.

"She likes me," he announced, directing his words at all the onlookers. Tristan popped another fry in his mouth and smiled.

As Cianne walked home, she thought of several worthy comebacks for the pompous oaf. It was too late of course but wasn't that how it usually worked out. There was no use harping on it. Only she had done nothing but harp to herself since leaving him at *her* table.

Tristan had invaded her space, then accused her of…of the truth.

Cianne moaned. *How am I going to deal with Tristan now?*

In a split second every thought, every care in her world, disappeared. Cianne winced as the dizzy spell hit her. She frantically searched her surroundings and noticed she was close to the park in her neighborhood. The park had a public bathroom with privacy stalls.

She ran to the bathroom as if her life depended on it…and it did.

Drained emotionally and physically, Cianne unlocked the stall door and trudged over to the sink. Thankful that her community and the Parks and Recreation Department took pride in the park, she didn't worry about the cleanliness of the sink when she turned on the faucet and splashed cool water on her face. She all but dismissed the vision she had just minutes ago in the bathroom stall. There was little she could do about it now, anyways.

Deal with what you can. Her father's words always put things in perspective.

So, as she dried her face with the coarse paper towel, Cianne thought of the three words that came to mind whenever Tristan was near. *Sadness, Pain, Death.* What did the words mean? Were they for her to try and help Tristan, or were they a warning? Based on her past experiences, if the warning was for him, something was going to cause him harm. If they were a warning for her, which would be her first personal warning, he was going to cause her harm. Whatever the case, those words confirmed that Tristan Bertram was off limits.

She glanced at her reflection in the mirror long enough to confirm that her appearance was back to normal then walked out into the sunlit day. She followed her usual path through the park to get to her house. When Cianne saw the large sign that read "Homes at West Valley", she pulled her cell out of her bag and sighed.

The walk home after lunch which typically took under twenty minutes had taken her just about an hour today. She could blame the vision for the headache that mercilessly beat at her temples, or she could admit the real cause of both her headache and her delay.

Tristan.

She was letting what happened at Crimpy's get to her.

Cianne increased her pace when she saw her house come into view. It was a lovely three-story starter home nestled a block from the entrance of a family-friendly neighborhood. The brown and tan exterior of the house and the xeriscaping, a type of gardening that reduced the need for irrigation, were chosen because of the warm Arizona climate. Cianne loved the neighborhood and her house.

Inside the house, the air was filled with a delicious aroma that teased her senses, so Cianne placed her shoulder bag on the console table a few feet from the front door and headed for the kitchen. The sound of her rumbling stomach reminded her that both her attempts to eat today had been interrupted: breakfast by a vision and lunch by an egomaniac.

"Hey, dad." Cianne walked over to the counter and grabbed a carrot before taking a seat at the table. Just seeing her father had her headache easing off a bit.

Joseph Baxter, who stood in front of the stove stirring something in a pot, looked up at her. "How was your morning, princess?"

"I lived." She tried to push what happened at Crimpy's out of her head altogether. She was home, and home was safe.

"I'm elated that you've managed to survive another day in that horrid war zone they call a school," he teased.

Cianne's frown caused her father to chuckle, and her mind went right back to what will forever be known as The Crimpy's Incident. In an attempt to move past it, she asked, "What's cooking?"

He shook his head then motioned to the pot. "You are having grilled chicken with vegetables and rice."

"Why are you cooking so early?" She bit into the crisp carrot.

"Going in early," Joseph answered. He stopped stirring, turned the stove off, then washed his hands. Then he wiped the countertop. "How are you enjoying your half days?"

"The truth…" Cianne said, "they're boring. I'm home while Tranae is stuck in school all day."

Her father crossed the space between them and gently tapped her on the head. "Tranae should have worked harder on her studies instead of lollygagging."

Cianne leaned back to avoid another of her father's playful taps then quickly jolted forward to bite at his hand. Joseph was quicker, pulling his fingers away before she could get them then grabbed at her nose. She snapped at his hand again before he called it quits—but not before he grabbed at her nose one more time and pinched it.

"Alright, I'm done." He straightened his tie as he watched her, wearing a huge smile on his face. "You got some mail today." It was the kind of smile that had big expectations behind it. Joseph opened the drawer they kept mail in and pulled out two large white booklet envelopes.

Cianne watched as he placed the envelopes in front of her. She peered at the mail while she continued to bite off little bites of the carrot.

"I thought you would be more excited," he said when she didn't pick them up.

Cianne put the half-eaten carrot on the table beside the envelopes. "I'm excited," she lied. "I'm just a little nervous." She picked up her mail, read the sender on each envelope then placed them back on the table, unopened. When her eyes met her father's concerned gaze, she offered a nervous smile.

"Alright," he said, then sighed. The disappointed look on his face only lasted a second before he recovered. "I'll be home late tonight."

Joseph turned and walked out of the kitchen toward the living room. When he returned to the entryway of the kitchen, he had his briefcase in his hand. Cianne got to her feet and dragged behind him as he led the way to the front door.

"You're what we adults refer to as a teenager, right?" Joseph asked as he opened the front door.

"Yeah," Cianne answered, with apprehension.

"Shouldn't you be out hanging at the mall and spending my hard-earned money or something?"

The ends of Cianne's lips curled up in a partial smile. She would have rolled her eyes, but he hated when she did.

He turned back, facing Cianne, and stared at her for a moment before kissing her on the forehead. Joseph chuckled as he shook his head at her then opened the door and walked down the porch steps to his car.

Cianne felt like she should say something to ease his worries. But she could think of nothing so she chose deflection. "I'm not the only one who needs a life," she said. "You're the workaholic."

Joseph looked up at her as she stood in the doorway with the screen door open. His eyes were full of…everything. Love, expectation, pride, concern…

Why is he concerned?

He sighed. "I'll eat out tonight so put the food away." He opened his car door and slid into the driver's seat before sticking his head out of the window. "Tell Tranae to leave some leftovers, though."

"I'll try, but I can't make any promises, Mr. Baxter." Tranae tapped the hood of the car as she walked past his sedan. She jogged up the porch stairs and leaned on the railing.

Cianne acknowledged her friend with a halfhearted smile then turned to watch as her father slowly backed the car out onto the street.

Wait.

"Dad," she yelled, as she stepped onto the porch. "Tell Mrs. Pollard,"—she paused, "Tell her that I am sorry for her loss."

The sedan jerked to a stop, indicating that her father floored the brake pedal. His expression was grave because he must have sensed what was coming next but asked anyway.

Joseph stuck his head out of the driver's window. "What happened?"

Cianne heard Tranae whisper a curse. She glanced at her friend and saw Tranae shaking her head as she mouthed the word 'don't'.

"Never mind," Cianne yelled to her father. "Hurry or you'll get caught in traffic."

Joseph seemed as if he wasn't going to listen to her advice but he nodded and continued backing onto the street. She let Tranae inside the house as she watched her father drive out of sight before she backed inside the house and closed the door.

Upstairs in Cianne's bedroom, Tranae sat on the window seat looking out over the empty backyard. "You know you can't tell him stuff like that right when he's leaving," Tranae said, looking over her shoulder.

Cianne dropped her shoulder bag on the floor beside one of two large bookcases that covered a section of her wall. A desk with a task chair, a window seat, and a full-size bed completed the furnishings in her space. Each piece of furniture was made of a Birchwood finish that she assembled herself.

Nothing in the space screamed teenager. There were no posters of men with hairless torsos, no abundance of perky or goth colors, cutesy décor, or tons of stuffed animals. Yet, even without the pictures of teenage heartthrobs littering the walls, Cianne knew that Tranae preferred this room over her own.

"I know." It was all Cianne could say.

Tranae offered her a sympathetic smile before her eyes lit up. "I bet that party in Phoenix is going to be epic." Tranae beamed.

Cianne watched as the excitement in Tranae's eyes dimmed.

"But I won't be going, will I?" Tranae pouted. "Nope, I'll be home playing scrabble with my landlords." A sobbing moan followed.

Cianne placed her mail on her desk. "You mean your parents. You don't pay rent Tranae."

"No," Tranae whined, "I meant my jailers."

"Don't be so dramatic. Did you do your homework?" Cianne sat on the floor beside her bed and stared up at her spinning ceiling fan.

"Not all of it but that's why I've been given a day pass. My hair started to melt from thinking too hard so Jailer #1 said I could come over and get help. I wish I was smart like you, but I don't think geek would look good on me." Tranae rubbed her forehead.

Cianne threw a pen at her. "Who are you calling a geek?" The projectile missed its mark by a few inches.

"Only a geek would get straight A's every year." Tranae slid from the window seat and spread out on the floor beside Cianne. They lay on their backs, head to toe.

"Not every year. I got a B in Spanish my first year at West Hills." If her visions hadn't caused her to leave class so much during freshman year, she would have gotten an A. Her nerves weren't as bad now so her visions had slowed. Except for today…because of *him*.

Cianne rolled over on her belly before pointing to her diary.

Tranae looked in the direction Cianne pointed. The diary sat on top of a small pile of books beside her arm. She grabbed it and tossed it to Cianne. "You should lock that up," Tranae said, referencing the diary.

"No need." Cianne wanted to log what happened at Crimpy's today, but she wanted to tell Tranae first.

"Your step-father is so…cool. My wardens go through everything. And let's not forget Jess the Mess. If he found my diary," she said, shuddering at the thought, "My secrets would be in West Hill Times. He's such an ass."

"I guess privacy is the upside of not having any siblings." Cianne reached for the pen that had landed under her bed when a wave of dizziness hit her. She froze for a split second, then jumped to her feet. Cianne ran out of her bedroom and down the hall as if a fire had been lit under her feet.

Inside the bathroom, she slammed the door closed, braced her hands on the sink, then stared at her reflection. Cianne watched her reflection in horror as the transformation took over. The tips of her fingers darkened and that blackness traveled slowly up her arms and through her body until the veins beneath her skin resembled the roots of a tree and her face looked like a roadmap of varicose veins.

She cursed as her pupils flickered, so fast that the average person wouldn't have noticed. Then the vision hit. She closed her eyes and tightened her grip on the sink.

Instinct had her trying to shut the vision down, to stop it. Unlike her physical transformation, which would traumatize anyone who witnessed it, the actual images that played out in her head had no physical effect. Unless…

A sharp pain struck Cianne, almost sending her to her knees. As much as she hated what happened when she tried to stop the visions, Cianne refused to accept them. She hated seeing the horrible scenes that played out in her mind.

Cianne tightened her eyelids as she concentrated on willing the images away. It felt as though her head was imploding, a feeling she could only describe as her brain being sucked out through a straw.

Six minutes later, Cianne was drained. She focused on the sound of the running water to calm her racing heart as she leaned over the sink. Cold water dripped from her unblemished reflection in the mirror. She survived another vision, and her attempt to stop it was useless.

One of her biggest worries was that the visions left her utterly defenseless for the entire duration, several seconds to twenty minutes or more. She didn't like the risk of zoning out anywhere at any time. The dizziness allowed time for her to seek immediate shelter.

When Cianne returned to her room, Tranae was still lying in the same spot. As she entered her room, her friend's look of concern questioned if she was alright, because Tranae knew not to ask.

Seven years ago, Tranae had witnessed what happened to Cianne before one of her visions. It took two days for Tranae's mother to calm her frightened child, telling her that what she thought she had seen was impossible, that the heat of the day had gotten to her. Almost two weeks passed before Tranae would even come outside. It took another before she would even wave back when Cianne waved to her from across the street.

Cianne sank to the floor next to her friend. "I'm good."

Tranae eyed her with suspicion but said, "I figured." She gave Cianne a sympathetic pat on the leg. "Hey," Tranae said, "can I ask you something personal?"

"Sure." Cianne picked up her diary and pen then gave Tranae her full attention. She watched as Tranae sat up and rested against the foot of her bed.

"Do you ever wonder about your bio dad?"

Cianne was relieved that Tranae's question wasn't about her vision. It was an odd vision anyway. She had only seen a single drop of blood splatter over the Roman numeral sixteen. The vision was too vague for her to give any consideration, and honestly, she wanted nothing more than to forget the cryptic image.

"Sometimes," Cianne admitted. "What he looks like if he's even alive. If I'm his only child or if I have brothers and sisters out there who look a little like me. I even wonder if he is a freak of nature like I am." Tranae rolled her eyes at the freak of nature comment, but Cianne continued. "But then I think of how blessed I am to have my dad. He loves me, and I wouldn't trade him for the world."

"Did your mom ever talk about him?" Tranae asked.

Cianne wondered why Tranae was interested in her paternal side now when it had never come up before. Whatever the case, she didn't mind talking about him. "Not really. I remember asking about him once."

Tranae's eyes widened, and she leaned forward. "What did your mom say?"

"She just said that he did some things, awful things. But she loved him a lot and it wasn't easy for her to leave him." The quiet tapping of the pen on the diary cover was the only sound in the room for a long moment. When Cianne realized she'd been lost in her thoughts, she held the pen still, sat up, then placed it on her nightstand.

"I wonder what happened between them," Tranae queried. "I mean…what could be so bad that they didn't stay together if they were in love?"

"Don't know."

"Did he know about you?"

"Don't know that either. I do know that she left him before I was born. I don't think she ever saw him after that. Sometimes, I'd find her alone in her room crying. When I asked her what was wrong, she just held me. I think I reminded her of him."

Cianne glanced at the picture of her mother on her nightstand. She missed her so much that sometimes she had to put the picture in her nightstand drawer. The action always proved to be foolish because she could never forget her mother's lovely face.

"Do you know anything about him, his name, anything?"

Cianne shrugged. "Not really. Whenever I found her crying, she would always have this in her hands." Cianne held up her right hand. On her index finger was a ring. "She gave this to me. Said that there are two of them, this one he gave her, and the other was his. They're both inscribed." She twisted the ring off her finger and handed it to Tranae.

Tranae took the ring. It was heavier than it looked and Cianne winced when her friend almost dropped it. Tranae held the ring up in the air, twisting it as she inspected it. "Wow, it kinda looks like bone, maybe ivory or something."

The ring did resemble ivory, but the hue had a grayish tint. It was smooth and had a thin blue strip around the center on the outside.

Tranae raised her shoulders when she discovered the inscription inside. "With You Always." She handed the ring back to Cianne. "You never showed this to me before."

"I didn't think it would interest you," Cianne told her. "Besides, I've never been able to wear it until now. It didn't fit."

Tranae glanced over at the photo of Cianne's mother on the nightstand. "You sort of look like her, a little." Tranae inspected Cianne's face.

"You think so." Cianne got up and walked over to her closet. She pulled open the door so she could see herself in the full-length mirror that hung on the back. She looked at her reflection. "You have the same shaped face." Tranae walked over and stood beside her. "We do know one thing about him, your bio dad," Tranae said as she lifted a small section of Cianne's hair in her hands.

"What's that?" Cianne asked.

"He isn't Black," Tranae said, assessing Cianne. "You didn't get your silky straight hair, those blue-green eyes, or that olive skin from your mom."

Cianne shrugged at her image then walked over to her bed and lay across it. After last night's nightmare, she wasn't too interested in her mirrored image. Plus, her curiosity concerning her ethnicity had faded over the years. She simply felt that everyone had their physical differences, and she was comfortable with hers.

"What happened to you at lunch today?" Cianne wanted to move on to the serious stuff so she could tell Tranae about The Crimpy's Incident.

Tranae's angry gaze sliced at her. "That's what I wanted to tell you. My cell phone was minding its business on the side of my desk in English Lit. Next thing I know, two jerks I don't even know decided that they wanted to fight right next to my desk. After the scuffle, I realized my phone wasn't on my desk where I left it. I'm freaking out now. So, I looked on the floor, and there it was, all the way across the room against the wall, screen cracked. My freak out amps up several notches now, and I told them that they were going to replace it! Things got a little loud, and we all had to go to the principal's office. During my lunch break, of course," Tranae hissed. "I treasure my personal time, which they ruined. Not to mention my cell is totaled. I was so worked up that they let me out of school early, but you saw that in a vision already, didn't you?"

"I didn't see all of that. I didn't see that you were going to miss lunch today." Cianne twisted her mouth into a smile that said she had a secret. "Which brings me to what happened to me today at Crimpy's."

"What happened?" Tranae was on the bed in a flash, bouncing with excitement.

Cianne shied away, holding her hands up to calm her friend.

"What, tell me?" Tranae begged.

It was uncommon for Cianne to have juicy information so she wanted to relish the feeling of having something interesting to say that had nothing to do with academics. "Well…" Cianne dragged out the word. "Tristan sat with me."

"He did what? Where? What did he say?" Tranae asked, with wide eyes. "Tell me dammit!"

"Calm down." Cianne sat up and took a deep breath. She saw Tranae's irritation so she came clean. "He sat with me at Crimpy's. He wanted to know why I've been so salty toward him." Cianne twisted her mouth when Tranae gave her the 'I told you so' look. "I apologized, but then he accused me of liking him." Cianne couldn't hide the horror that was reflected on her face.

"What?" Tranae placed her hands over her mouth to muffle what would have been a scream. "Oh my god, what did you say? What did you do?"

"I got up and walked out." Cianne shrugged. She knew that Tranae was expecting more, but there was nothing more.

"Got up and walked out…," Tranae repeated slowly then gasped with disappointment. "Why? Tristan is obviously h-h-h-hot for you, Cianne." She squealed as she jumped up and did their version of the happy dance which looked like a foot fight with the carpet. They'd choreographed the dance when they were kids, and it was laughable now, but Tranae still did it from time to time.

"I doubt it." Cianne shook her head as she stifled a giggle. "He was just being nice. It's probably because we're locker neighbors this year. Besides Tristan has a girlfriend."

"Had!" Tranae smacked Cianne's leg.

The sting was secondary to her surprise from Tranae's announcement.

"Not anymore. I hear it's over."

"Yeah, like how it was over that two other times last year. It doesn't matter anyway." Cianne fell back on her pillows. "I can't go out with him. I'm damaged goods."

Not to mention the guy came with his own personal 'warning whispers' every time she saw him. There was something dark and dangerous about Tristan Bertram. No matter how gorgeous, sexy, or rich he was. He alarmed her in more ways than one.

"Why do you always…" Tranae started but stopped, "You know what? I don't even want to get into that right now." She sat beside Cianne on the edge of the bed. "Just tell me again what happened at Crimpy's and don't leave anything out."

Cianne squinted at the clock on her nightstand when she heard the front door open. She expected her father home earlier and would have called him, but she lost track of time. Plus, Tranae ended up staying later than usual, wanting Cianne to retell the Tristan story a few more times before she was satisfied that she got all of it.

Cianne placed the book she was reading face down on her lap when her bedroom door slowly opened. The tip of her father's head appeared behind the slightly ajar door.

"You asleep?" he asked.

"Not yet." Cianne dogged-eared the page and closed the book before placing it on the nightstand. "How's Mrs. Pollard doing?"

"As well as can be expected, I imagine she's going through a rough time right now," Joseph said. "Her mother was the one who called and told her that her father died today. That's a big thing to cope with." He stepped inside the room. "You were trying to tell me when I was leaving for work earlier today, weren't you?"

"I saw it on my way home from school today. That was one of the reasons I took so long getting here. Had to run into a bathroom stall in the park." She winced at the memory of the park bathroom she had to retreat into. "It was as if I was standing in his yard with him when he fell, Dad. I could smell the fresh cut grass from the lawn mower he was pushing."

Cianne could tell that her father was attempting to veil his alarm.

"And you met Debra Pollard's father only once?" he asked.

"Yes, at the Christmas party last year."

"Your range is increasing." Joseph rubbed his head slowly from crown to nape. "Debra's father lives over two thousand miles away." He looked down as if trying to work something out in his head. "Are the headaches getting any better?" he asked, concerned.

"Not really, but they're not getting any worse." Cianne winced.

"And the nightmares?" he asked.

"The same." She sighed. "But I can handle them."

"And you still can't see anything that's connected to you?" he asked.

"I saw Tranae's cell phone break today. What I didn't see was that it would make her miss lunch with me. It wouldn't even warn me that I was going to make a fool of myself today."

"Would you like to try a different sleeping pill? Eventually, we'll find one that actually works."

"No." Cianne watched as her father lowered his head and continued to rub it. He looked stressed and tired like he had for months after her mother died. Because of this, she figured that there was no reason to tell him about the weird vision she had earlier today about the Roman numeral. "Goodnight dad."

At first, he seemed confused but then he forced a smile. He closed the distance and kissed Cianne on the head and said, "Good night Buttercup." He closed her door behind him.

Cianne relaxed back pulled her sheet up over her shoulders and closed her eyes. Tristan was her last thought before she fell asleep.

Chapter Three

Tristan listened to the sound of each baseball as it struck the net. *Swoosh*, 2, 3...then a low thud. *Swoosh*, 2, 3...another thud. Each noise came after Tristan swung his bat and missed.

Normally he was a pretty decent ball player. Hell, he was a natural at just about every sport he tried, football being the sport he focused on and excelled. But even though baseball wasn't his favorite, he never sucked this badly.

Tristan looked over at Brian, who sat in silence as he witnessed the sad scene. Remaining silent was so unlike Brian. If you sucked, he let you know in a big way.

"You're up." Tristan walked behind the protective net toward Brian, handing off the bat. As Brian moved into position over home plate, Tristan sat on the bench and rubbed his head. He watched his friend hit over half the balls the machine pitched. When he was done his set, Brian motioned to Tristan that it was his turn to bat again, but Tristan didn't move.

"What's up with you? You stink today, Tristan."

Tristan heard Brian say his name, but his mind was somewhere else. He had to reel in his thoughts and focused on his friend.

"What's the problem man?" Brian asked.

Cianne, of course. She'd been avoiding him since Crimpy's and that had been over two weeks ago. "It's nothing." Tristan lied.

"Oh it's something," Brian said. He put the bat down and leaned on the fence. "Well?"

"Well, what?" Tristan huffed.

"Are you going to tell me or do I have to beat it out of you?" Brian picked up the bat and tapped it on his palm a few times. Tristan rolled his eyes. "It's Bianca, isn't it? Haven't seen her around lately," Brian said. "What's the deal with you two?"

"We broke up," Tristan admitted, with little emotion.

"Broke up?" Brian threw his head back and said something that Tristan couldn't really make out. "When did this happen?" Brian finally asked. He sounded uninterested but probably felt it was his duty as a friend to ask.

Yet, Tristan knew Brian was smiling on the inside, and he couldn't blame him for it. It was common knowledge that Brian and Bianca weren't the best of friends. That was most likely the reason Brian hadn't noticed her absence. Those two argued almost as much as he and Bianca had.

"It was right before summer break," Tristan shrugged.

"Before she left for Europe? Why didn't you tell me, man?" Brian slowly shook his head from side to side. "Dude, if I had known you were single all damn summer... I guess I should say I'm sorry." He sighed. "Did she tell you why she dumped you?"

"It's a bit complicated." Tristan looked up at a passing group of people. One of the girls in the group winked at him so he shot her a friendly smile then broke eye contact before she took his gesture as an invitation.

"Damn," Brian cursed, pulling Tristan's attention back to him. He walked around the safety fence and sat down next to Tristan. His expression was full of understanding but whatever he saw on Tristan's face had him changing it to a look of confusion. "Wait. You dumped her, didn't you?"

To the outside world, Tristan and Bianca were the perfect couple: the wealthy good looking guy who dated the rich hot girl, but their close friends knew the relationship had been a sleeping minefield.

"I just think we're better suited as friends." Tristan pulled a couple bottles of water from his gym bag and offered one to Brian.

"What? No," Brian said, as he swatted the water bottle away.

It took a moment of juggling to keep hold of the bottle Brian almost knocked out of his hand. Tristan arched his brow. "Really?" he questioned, as he returned the unwanted bottle to his bag.

Brian just stared at him, mouthing some garbled words before he said, "Friends? Dude, are you sick?" He placed his hand on Tristan's forehead.

Tristan smacked Brian's hand away.

"Are you aware of what you just gave up? I mean…you know how I feel about the girl but damn. She's one of the hottest girls at West Hills. She has her own cash so you don't have to pay for everything and even though she has bitch-itis on the regular, she is really into you. You've invested two years in that relationship."

"You sound like her," Tristan said, then sighed.

"You just gave up regular, handed on a silver platter, sex," Brian whined. "Do you know how hard it is to find a girl who likes doing *it* as much as we do? Who you don't have to worry about doing everyone else?" Brian threw up air quotes and said, "It's like they all attend the same "did it once with some other dude, didn't like it so let's wait…okay" cult." His tone was high pitched and annoying.

Tristan couldn't help but laugh. "You do that a little too well. And as for sex, it isn't everything, and…it really isn't that hard to get either."

Brian placed a hand on Tristan's forehead again. Tristan smacked it again, this time harder.

"Ouch." Brian rubbed his hand. "Dude, it isn't hard for *you*." He shook the sting from his hand. "Can I ask why?"

"She wanted things I couldn't see myself doing with her."

"What, she wanted it in the ear or something? I had a feeling she was kinky."

"You need help." Tristan twisted the cap off his water bottle. The sound of cheers and laughter amplified around them. Tristan looked up to see a few kids at the eatery having a blast. He smirked, remembering being that carefree at one time.

Tristan's expression turned serious. "Bianca had my whole life planned out for me. It was a little freaky, you know? She worked out the number of kids we'd have, where we were going to live." He lifted the bottle of water to his mouth then said, "I just didn't think about us in the way she did. When I told her I wasn't in love with her, all she did was stare at me." Tristan took another drink before he placed the cap back on the bottle.

No longer interested in discussing the past, Tristan decided to change the subject. He smiled when a pair of captivating blue-green eyes came to mind. "Anyway, I want to see what's out there."

"You want to see what's out there," Brian repeated sarcastically. "Other than Bianca Prescott? Shit dude, she could have planned whatever future she wanted for us, if I were you and could stand to be around her for five minutes." Brian shrugged. "My mom is pretty set on having little black grandbabies, but for a girl who looks like Bianca, I'd mix a little vanilla in our family's chocolate gene bar." Brian chuckled at his quip. "Yeah, you're sick." He raised his hand to place on Tristan's head but thought better of it.

"I'm not sick,"—Tristan lingered over his thoughts. "Just interested in someone else."

"Like who?"

Tristan leaned forward, rolling the water bottle in his hands as he avoided Brian's hard gaze. "Cianne Baxter," he muttered. Just her name on his tongue had Tristan sitting taller as if infused with determination.

He knew from the grin on Brian's face that he was waiting for something more. After a minute or so, Brian groaned. "You can't be serious. Dude, you need to give that up." He clapped his hands together in rhythm with every syllable of each word he spoke. It was something he did to emphasize his point.

When Tristan didn't respond, Brian looked up at the ceiling as he loudly exhaled.

"Look, college guys are what she goes for. Jacob's girl Susan…she said she saw Cianne on campus with some guy, and they looked pretty cozy. You'd have more of a chance with Mr. Baxter." Brian giggled. "I'm just trying to save you from embarrassing yourself."

"Thanks for the support." Tristan stood up. "I have to get going."

"What, no rematch?"

"It's the last Sunday of the month." Tristan grabbed his bag off the bench, throwing the handle over his shoulder so he could pick up Brian's duffle bag. "I'll see you tomorrow."

"Yeah, with my laundry cleaned and pressed." Brian's grin was broad and teasing. "And no cheating either, you sucked today so *you* have to do my laundry and that means no help from Martha or Celia."

"I wouldn't dream of subjecting those lovely women to this smell," Tristan said, as tossed his water bottle in a recycle bin he passed. He walked toward the exit holding Brian's dirty laundry bag at arm's length.

The Bertram home was in the exclusive gated community of Mountain Ridge Estates, where large mansions were hidden from the main roads. The development was surrounded by large mountains and trees, so few people knew the homes were there unless they were looking for them. A little piece of heaven was what the website boasted when Tristan's mother found it four and a half years ago.

Tristan absolutely loved the house. *Though it actually never felt like home*, he thought as he wrote the words SAVE ME on the fogged mirror in his bathroom. He wondered if anyplace would ever feel like home.

Standing over the sink with a towel wrapped around his waist, Tristan glared at his warped reflection through the distorted letters he wrote. He thought of all the private schools, the summer homes, the vacation homes, and estates he had occupied at one time or another in his short life. Not one of those places felt warm, inviting, or homey. They were just luxury museums that held his possessions.

He stared vacantly at his image for a short while then dried himself off and dressed for dinner. Tristan loathed Bertram family dinner night, but he knew better than to be late. It was the one day of the month that his parents demanded his presence.

Because his parents did a lot of traveling, the monthly dinners were engineered to keep them connected. Tristan felt it was his mother's way of reminding his father he had a son. Whatever the case, he was going to be late if he didn't get moving.

"Ten minutes till the fireworks." He sighed as he grabbed Brian's bag of laundry and made his way downstairs.

"Tristan, honey can you come help me please," Melanie Bertram called from the kitchen when he walked by.

"I'll be right there, mom." Tristan hurried to the laundry room on the other side of the house and put the contents of Brian's bag in the washer, including the bag. He then closed the washer lid and vowed to keep his head in the game the next time because he hated washing another man's jock straps.

His face brightened when he saw his mother in the kitchen standing over the island countertop with an apron on. "What can I do to help?"

She tapped her cheek. "Kiss."

He walked over and kissed his mother on the cheek. He hadn't seen his mother a lot in the last six months, and he did miss her. Since the death of his grandfather, his mother spent more and more time away from home with his father.

"Where's Celia?" he asked, looking around.

"I gave her the evening off. She and Martha may have gone to a movie." She held out the bread. "Benjamin could have gone as well."

"I wonder what they went to see. I wish I had known they were going." Tristan took the bread his mother handed him. He also picked up a large casserole dish she motioned to. She carried a large plate full of pasta to the dining room, and Tristan followed.

"You know how your father feels about you spending leisure time with the staff," she whispered to him.

"They're my family," he whispered back.

"But your father sees it differently. He likes our roles…"

"Well defined," they said in unison, but Tristan's words sounded sarcastic.

She stopped and turned to face him. "At least when he is home please…try to remember that." Melanie smiled as she reached up and caressed his cheek with her lips. "We haven't seen you in two weeks. I want dinner to be nice."

They entered their large dining room. Tristan sat the bread and the casserole dish next to the large plate his mother placed on the table. He nodded to his father, who was already seated at the head of the table. Mr. Bertram nodded back then stood. He and his father seated themselves after his mother sat down in her chair.

"Isn't this nice?" Melanie's eyes danced from her husband to Tristan. "My two favorite men are together again," Tristan smiled back as she served the food. "Oh, sweetie, before I forget. Bianca called while you were in the shower."

Tristan acknowledged his mother with a nod.

"How is Bianca?" Leslie Bertram asked as he wiped the corners of his mouth with a crisp white napkin.

Tristan looked over at his father. For a moment, he just stared at the man who didn't even bother to look at him when he spoke to him. He thought hard whether he wanted to answer before he finally decided to respond to the question. "I'm not sure."

"Is something wrong Tristan?" Melanie's genuine concern always amazed him. She reached across the table and touched his hand.

Tristan relished the warmth his mother's touch offered. "We're just taking a break from each other. Everything's fine, really." He said in a matter of fact tone. He refused to give his mother details. Not tonight, and not with his father present.

"I'm sure things will work out for the best." His mother must have picked up on his mood because she immediately moved on to the next topic. "So, how's Brian?"

She knew him so well. "Brian's fine." He moved his noodles around his plate. "So, how was Houston?"

"I am going to assume you were the one who decided you needed the break?" His father broke in before his mother could answer him. "If she had, there wouldn't be so many messages from her on the notepad by the telephone."

Tristan looked over at his father, his smile gone. He opened his mouth to speak but felt his mother squeeze his hand. It wasn't a firm squeeze, but it had enough pressure to center him. Tristan closed his eyes and fought to hold in his biting response. He manufactured a smile then turned his attention to his mother. "How was the flight home?"

"It was tiresome, as usual." She released his hand and gave him a thankful nod. "How is school going, did your first day go well?"

Tristan chuckled. "School started six weeks ago, mother."

Melanie laughed. "I'm just teasing sweetheart. Your teachers speak very highly of you. Mr. Eggleston says you have one of the highest averages in the school. I am very proud of you, Tristan."

"Why on earth we allow you to go to that public school is still a mystery to me," Leslie grunted with disdain. "You could have chosen any private school in the entire U.S. and would have been accepted."

"West Hills High *is* one of the best schools in the state. Their AEA program has parents across the country trying to move into our school district so their children can attend. Not to mention, I'm staying out of trouble there. That public school," Tristan sneered, "is perfect for me." He knew his father didn't care about the AEA program or the other parents, but it needed to be said. His father only cared about him acquiring an excellent education at an exceptional school, the best money could buy.

"Is that so?" Leslie casually sighed. "You get kicked out of three private schools in Europe, just to go to a public school here in Arizona. I hardly think that going to school with future food service workers, gang members, and gas station attendants is perfect. Though I'm certain their academic effort must curve the grading average a bit, giving you an advantage."

Tristan rubbed his temples in an attempt to calm himself.

"Have you given more thought about my offer, Tristan?" Leslie used the same calm unenthusiastic tone he often used when he spoke to his son.

"I've been kind of busy doing drugs but lucky for me we have a zillion fast food places around here so my classmates, who work at them, can feed my high. And with all the gang initiations I'm doing while hanging out with my boys, it doesn't leave me with a lot of time to go over all my options for my future."

"This is your life Tristan and if you want it to mean something you will make time. Sarcasm isn't a lucrative profession for most. You need to prepare yourself." Leslie's tone reflected a man who was barely interested in the conversation. He laid his fork down and wiped his mouth with his napkin again.

"Do you really want to do this now?" Tristan asked as he leveled a glowering look at his father.

"Leslie, can't we have one meal together without discussing our son's future? One damn meal without any arguments," Melanie spat out through clenched teeth.

"I just think that he should start—"

"Leslie," she raised her tone then leveled it out, "later would be a better time to discuss this."

Tristan knew that when his mother called his father by his first name that she was very upset. He decided to dismiss the entire ordeal to see that his mother enjoyed her dinner.

The rest of dinner was more or less uneventful, and after it was over Tristan helped his mother clear then clean the dishes, while his father did what he does best—disappear.

"Thank you for saving me tonight." Tristan smiled. He took the dish she handed him and started to towel it dry.

"Tristan, your father is worried about you. He means well," Melanie told him, as she put the last dish in his hand. She outstretched her hand and touched his shoulder. "You can't blame him for being a little apprehensive about your transformation. Getting kicked out of those schools for fighting and for throwing a…"

"You can say sex party, Mom," he said, laughing.

She smacked him on the shoulder, pouting as if angry. "We just assumed you gave up all the womanizing, the fighting, and the wild parties when we moved here. That was the deal. Plus, with grandpa passing, we thought you would start thinking about your future."

Tristan thought back to how he used to be. How he felt incomplete and restless as if there was something more out in the world but he just couldn't grasp onto it. He was quick to anger then. His peers learned it was best not to be on the receiving end of that anger. The one thing he regretted most was that the antidote for all his unhinged emotions at that time was meaningless sex with girls he could barely remember.

"Your father and I really liked Bianca." His mother's words broke him free of the shameful memories. "You do realize that you are going to have to tell him something soon."

"I have given up all that stuff," Tristan told her. "Just because I don't want to be with Bianca doesn't mean I've gone back to my old ways. I also don't understand why me going to law school is such a big deal. I know what I have to do, and I'm going to be ready when the time comes. Look, mom, for some reason, it's different here. I'm different here. Besides, why is he so interested all of a sudden? It's not like he cares what I do." Tristan sat the dried dish on the counter.

"Of course he cares. If he didn't, he wouldn't have called on his friends to make certain you have this opportunity. He wants the best for you."

"If I wanted to go to a university right after graduation I would have started the process two years ago. I don't need dad's friends to help either. Believe me, I can handle that on my own. Did it even occur to anyone that I may have my own plans?"

Melanie shook her head as she put her arms around her son's waist. "You are just like him."

"That's what everyone keeps telling me," Tristan replied, as he hugged her back.

"Is that so bad?" she asked as she kissed him on the cheek.

Chapter Four

"**M**iss Baxter?" Mrs. Sheppard called across the crowded classroom. "Did you hear me, Miss Baxter?"

Today was already shaping up to be one of those days for the twelfth-grade instructor. Lisa Morgan, a pretentious little twit who was in Mrs. Sheppard's first-period class, decided that a phone call was more important than doing her class assignment. Mrs. Sheppard detested teenagers and would have had fewer problems teaching English as a second language to grizzly bears, she often relayed to her husband over dinner too many times to count.

Mrs. Sheppard sighed as she looked down at her desk calendar. The large bold print read September 3rd. "Seven weeks down," she said under her breath as she pushed away from her desk, "and my sanity to go." She walked from the front of the room to the desks in the rear of the room where Cianne sat.

"Miss Baxter, can you answer the question?" Mrs. Sheppard asked again.

Cianne, whose elbow rested on the desk with her chin placed in the palms of her hands, just stared ahead at the blackboard in front of the room. Mrs. Sheppard waved her hand in front of Cianne's face.

"Are you alright, Miss Baxter?" Mrs. Sheppard bent over and touched Cianne's shoulder. "Are you ok, Cianne?"

Cianne, startled, jumped to her feet causing Mrs. Sheppard to cry out and stumble backward into an unoccupied chair.

"Jesus," Mrs. Sheppard said, panting. The teacher covered her chest with her hands as if her heart was about to give out.

◉

Cianne's eyes darted from one classmate to the next as she tried to steady her breathing and calm down. Some of them looked amused while most looked scared. She immediately looked to her hands.

No blackened veins, no vision but…

But she'd been dreaming.

She'd been locked inside a nightmare, and this one was the worst, so realistic. Her eyes burned as she tried to hold back her tears. In front of her, Mrs. Sheppard stood still, clutching her chest, looking as if she had seen the devil himself. Only, her teacher was focused on her. In fact, everyone in the class seemed to be focused on her.

"What happened?" a tired voice called out.

"Miss goodie two shoes just freaked," a girl said, then giggled.

Ignoring the insult, Cianne grabbed her bag and quickly maneuvered through the desks and out the classroom door. The lockers were a blur as she ran down the empty hallway with tears streaming down her face. She turned a corner and collided with something hard. Cianne grunted when she hit the floor.

"Sorry," she winced, "I didn't see you." The collision had her on the floor with an aching backside and head. A pair of feet and the legs attached to them appeared in front of her as Cianne rubbed her head. It wasn't until the heat surrounded her that she looked at the hand that reached down in front of her.

"Are you all right?"

Cianne cursed to herself as she looked up and saw Tristan's concerned gorgeous face. She quickly pushed herself up off the floor, avoiding his hand and thinking that this day couldn't get any worse. Once on her feet, she lowered her face so Tristan couldn't see her tears and puffy red eyes. Tristan obviously had no problem invading a person's personal space because he moved closer, lowering his head to get a better view of her face.

"What's wrong?" he demanded.

Confused by Tristan's tone and the anger knotted through his question, Cianne backed up and glared at him. He stood rigid, his chest expanding and falling with every breath as if he just ran a mile. He was a tower of solid incredible strength.

Why does he look so angry? I surely couldn't have hurt him.

"I'm sorry I ran into you," Cianne apologized again. "I um…I have to go,"

Her avoidance of his question only made him move closer to her. Feeling cornered, with only a few inches from his face and staring into his eyes, Cianne mumbled her apologies a third time.

They stood there frozen for only seconds but it felt like an eternity. The penetrating blue of Tristan's eyes was uncompromising, his jaw set.

Was it anger? Or was it compassion, longing, and desire in those eyes? No, she saw none of those things so she dismissed the out-of-place thought immediately.

Cianne broke his mental hold on her and tried to turn and head in the opposite direction, but Tristan put out his arm, blocking her way.

"Wait," he said. Tristan grabbed her arm and spun her around to face him.

Once again, they were eye to eye. He seemed calm but the eye contact was becoming a problem for her. Though, being eye to eye wasn't that big of a deal when she compared it to being pressed against Tristan's chest. His hard, firm…

Oh God, the heat!

"You have to let go. Please." Cianne jerked and pulled as she tried to pull free of Tristan's hold. They were going to combust if she didn't separate from him. Only her struggles caused him to hold on tighter.

"Calm down, Cianne. I'm not trying to hurt you. I just want to know what's wrong."

After a few seconds, Cianne's fight faded. It took another second for her to realize they weren't on fire. She also realized that Tristan wasn't going to let her go. As she steadied her breathing, Cianne tried to calm her thoughts. While the heat she always felt when she was near Tristan was still there, it wasn't as intense.

So that was a plus.

"You're bleeding," Tristan told her as he lifted his hand. He brushed his thumb over her lips then used the back of his hand to wipe away a lone tear from her cheek.

Speechless, Cianne stared at his hand that now rested at his side. There *was* blood on his thumb. Her head was spinning but wasn't due to seeing her blood. Tristan had touched her. He touched her lip and her cheek.

"I'll take you to the nurse's office." It wasn't a request, which was evident by the way he pulled her along.

"I can walk on my own," Cianne said the words so quietly that she was a bit surprised when Tristan let go of her arm and nodded. She steadied herself, and at the same time, she tried to convince herself that Tristan's touch was just that and nothing more.

She followed Tristan, but not too close, as he led her to an office she had never been inside. The walls were bare except for the Norman Rockwell poster "Before the Shot", which was located directly behind a busy-looking desk that was unoccupied at the moment. A huge leaf from a big potted plant that sat near the entrance brushed her arm as she continued to follow Tristan's lead toward a pair of doors behind the lone desk. She wiped at her face with her hand so she wouldn't have to explain any stray tears to anyone else.

Thank god there seemed to be no one else around.

Tristan opened one of the doors. He pointed to one of two exam tables before he disappeared into a narrow closet. Cianne walked into the room and chose the table closest to her. It was the same one Tristan had pointed out, but she chose it because it was the one closest to the door.

Cianne took a moment to assess her surroundings. There was the exam table that she sat on and the other, a couple of glass jars filled with cotton balls and Q-tips that sat on the counter, tissue, plastic gloves, and hand sanitizer by the sink. She wondered if this nurse's office, which seemed elaborate, resembled others.

After Cianne got a feel of the room, she looked over at Tristan. She hadn't heard him come back in. His back was to her, but she could tell by his movements that he was busy with something.

Great…how will I avoid him now with him so close?

Cianne's eyes grew big when she became fully aware of the fact that she was alone with Tristan Bertram.

"Wait…," she said. "I'm fine. It's just—"

"It's just a little scrape, but I'll feel better putting something on it," Tristan said, cutting her off. He turned around to face her. In his hand, he held a cotton ball.

Cianne tensed as he closed the space between them in just two strides. Before she could protest, Tristan nudged her thighs apart to get closer and was lifting her chin with a tenderness she would have never imagined. He dabbed her cut lip with the wet gauze. The sting of her lip was a distant annoyance as she peered directly into his cobalt blue eyes.

"Looks like you bit into your lip when we collided."

The sound of his voice was so unusually gentle that it anchored her back to the here and now. "I'm sorry," Cianne mumbled. Her words were a little distorted with his hand on her chin and his fingers pushing down on her lip. She turned her head, refusing to look into his eyes a minute longer when he released her.

"You can relax." Tristan chuckled. "I'm not going to press charges."

Startled, Cianne lifted her gaze back to his enchanting eyes and blushed. She wasn't sure if it was more embarrassing that she missed his touch or that she feared he somehow knew that she did. She looked down at the floor.

"That was a joke Cianne," Tristan said as he tossed the soiled gauze over his shoulder to the waste basket in the corner. "Do you mind if I ask who you were running from?" He moved to touch her face again, but she pulled back. "I just want to see if the bleeding stopped."

Cianne relaxed enough to allow Tristan to touch her lips again. His thumb methodically traced her entire bottom lip from end to end. A tingling sensation ran down her chin to the pit of her stomach. All she could do was hold her breath. When he dropped his hand, she cleared her throat and took a shallow breath.

"I wasn't running from anyone," she whispered.

"Something had you in a hurry… and upset," Tristan said.

Something in Tristan's expression changed in an instant. The caring, helpful Tristan had disappeared. Cianne leaned back, not knowing if it was something she provoked or if he was having some kind of episode. Just when she slid off the exam table to leave, before she found out just how angry he was and why a short pleasant woman stuck her head into the room.

"Is everything ok, Tristan?"

◉

With a great degree of difficulty, Tristan pulled his attention from Cianne to look over his shoulder. "Everything is fine, Nurse Clemens. I was just about to get something for the cut on her lip, so it doesn't crack."

"Alright then," Nurse Clemens said, as she retreated, "I'll be doing inventory. It's only September, and we are already running low on the essentials."

When Tristan heard the supply closet door shut, he returned his attention to his patient only to find a confused look on her stunning face. He smiled and gave her a wink. "I volunteer here for my community service hours so I can graduate," he explained. He picked up the packet of petroleum he placed near her thigh and gently smoothed a little over her lower lip with his finger.

With her lips parted the way they were, Tristan fought the driving force to taste them. Instead of giving into to his base desires, he continued to circle her soft peach-tinted lips with his finger. "There, all better," he said hoarsely, as he let his hand fall.

He wondered how angry she would be if he kissed her right now. Studying her though, Tristan noted how steadily she breathed.

No response to my touch.

Plus, she turned away from him earlier when he thought they may have connected as if she had no interest in him at all. The problem was that her indifference only sparked his desire and fueled the need to kiss her more.

"Happy Birthday."

Cianne's small voice melted over him like warm honey. Tristan sighed in an attempt to hide the shudder her demure tone sent through him.

Keep it together or you'll scare her, again.

"Thank you," he said. Tristan smiled, as he crumpled the opened packet of petroleum and tossed it in the garbage can. "What tipped you off?"

"I don't know," she answered, her unusual green-blue eyes sparkled with irritation, "maybe it was all the balloons, streamers, and cards that happened to be blocking my locker this morning? And if that wasn't a clear indication, I think the lovely happy birthday song that your fan club sang over the intercom during the morning announcements sort of gave it away."

Sarcasm, how cute.

"Sorry about that." Tristan laughed as he turned to wash his hands. With his back to her, he took a deep, shaky breath. He had to regain his control because he didn't want Cianne to see that she had him tied in knots.

It's now or never.

With his back to her, Tristan grabbed a paper towel and dried his hands. "Cianne, I'd like to take you out," he said as he turned around to face her, "…and before you say no—" He balled up the paper towel he dried his hands with and threw it into the garbage can and cursed. "Awesome!" he growled.

Cianne had managed to sneak away, again.

The cafeteria was curiously crowded and that was sufficient reason for Cianne to retreat. If not for her promise not to back out of her lunch date today like she had for the past week, she would turn right around and leave.

But, here she was, trying to avoid bumping into her peers who hovered and hung lazily around the lunch tables. Her goal: Get to the table where Tranae and her two friends sat without causing a catastrophe. Technically, they were Cianne's friends too. Well, maybe they weren't per se, but Cianne had known Vanessa and Brenda for a few years. Only she hadn't embraced the two of them like Tranae had.

Invisibility meant keeping to herself.

When she made it to the table without incident, Cianne sat down in the seat Tranae always saved for her. She smiled at Tranae then waved.

"Hi," she said to Vanessa, who sat across from them. Vanessa greeted Cianne in the bubbly cute way she always did, with a smile and a warm hello. Brenda, their fourth, sashayed up to the table with a bounce that made her exposed cleavage ripple with each step. She sat next to Vanessa and pasted a fake smile on her face for Cianne, a smile that disappeared just as quickly as it appeared.

Cianne mentally shrugged, dismissing Brenda's halfhearted acknowledgment. She decided to focus on what was happening in front of her instead. Vanessa's attention was trained on Tranae, apparently awaiting an answer to a question that had been asked before Cianne arrived. Cianne pretty much knew what the question related to, or rather *who* the question related to.

"You can stop eyeballing me, Vanessa. How many times do I have to tell you the same thing?" Tranae pushed the large tray of fries toward Cianne. "I am not hooking you up with my brother."

"Why not, do you think he's too good for me?" Vanessa asked. Her arched brows furrowed over her doe-like brown eyes.

"Can you believe this chick?" Tranae asked, turning to Cianne. She ate a few of the fries that sat between them, ignoring Vanessa's question.

"Jessie *is* cute," Cianne said then shrugged, "gross at times, but cute."

Cianne picked up a fry from Tranae's tray and popped it into her mouth. As she nibbled on another fry she looked around the cafeteria. There were so many people here today. If she had one of her freak pre-vision episodes here, there would be so many witnesses. She looked over to the closest of several exits before returning her attention to Tranae, who was listing off all of her brother's faults for Vanessa to consider.

The list would be a long one.

Cianne anxiously waited for a chance to get Tranae's attention. She didn't want to be rude but she needed to say her goodbyes. She couldn't chance staying.

"What's wrong Princess?" Brenda asked, with a dash of venom lacing her saccharine tone. "You can't handle dining with your subjects?"

Cianne's eyes met Brenda's briefly before she looked away. She hated that it was obvious to Brenda how uncomfortable she was but it didn't mean she would indulge her in whatever her issues were. Tranae often said that Brenda was…well, she was just *Extra*. After experiencing Brenda for herself, Cianne agreed.

"I'd rather we eat at Crimpy's anyway, I like their food much better," Vanessa chimed in, as her eyes moved from Brenda to Cianne.

"First of all, Vanessa," Brenda said, looking at Cianne when she spoke. "We don't go to Crimpy's every day because Cianne likes it better when it's just her and Tranae. Secondly, Cianne needs to at least mingle with the common folk once or twice a week to stay relevant. She does this by showing up here." Brenda smirked as she looked around the crowded cafeteria. "Otherwise people would think she was completely stuck up."

"Versus partially stuck up." Cianne's voice cracked with emotions she didn't care to spend on Brenda.

Vanessa forced a laugh, her attempt to lighten the atmosphere, while Tranae shot Brenda a menacing look. "Just tell me if Jessie has a girlfriend," Vanessa asked, trying to change the subject. Confrontations always made Vanessa uneasy.

"You need to explore other options, Nessa." Tranae, who was scowling at Brenda, turned her attention back to Vanessa. "I wouldn't hook Jess up with my worst enemy."

"What's wrong with the guys here, Vanessa?" Cianne asked. She was truly curious to know.

"Yeah," Brenda agreed with false enthusiasm, "what's wrong with the guys here?" She had Cianne in her sights again. "There are a few cute ones that are still available, who don't stand a chance with me," she added. "You can attempt to find a guy our age who's worthy of your attention." Brenda offered her patented devilish grin. "What about Tristan? Isn't he single now? Though," she said as she flipped some of her long hair off of her shoulder, "I may want him for myself."

Cianne clenched her teeth together. No one could deny that Brenda was attractive, in a seductive Lolita kind of way. Why wouldn't Tristan go for her?

"Trick, you're beginning to piss me off," Tranae said, looking furious at Brenda.

Brenda, not fazed at all by the threat said, "Well, he is gorgeous."

Spitting on someone was one of the most disgusting things one person could do to another. So, when the urge to spit on Brenda surfaced, Cianne felt ashamed that she had even thought it. She shook the unusual aggressive urge away and stood up. "She's right Vanessa; I think he is single now." Cianne lifted her bag over her shoulder then walked toward the closest exit.

Tranae stood, flipping Brenda's diet soda to the floor before she went after Cianne. Brenda slid her chair away from the table before the cola could splash her pants or ruin her designer shoes. She glared angrily after Tranae while half the cafeteria looked in her direction.

"I am getting so tired of her shit," Brenda said through pursed lips, to no one in particular.

"Cianne, wait," Tranae called. She had to run to catch up with Cianne at the cafeteria door. "She's just jealous. Everyone knows Tristan is into you."

"Is that why she's been so nasty lately? Because she thinks Tristan likes me?" Cianne peered around Tranae to see Brenda checking herself for stains while Vanessa was fast at work wiping up the mess with napkins. "Why would she think that?"

They walked out of the cafeteria and down a hall.

"Because he isn't keeping it a secret; seriously, where have you been these past weeks? Oh yeah, you've been avoiding him since that day he nursed you to health." Tranae's eyes rolled skyward then she focused on Cianne. "Well, the last few weeks he's been asking everyone about you, even me. I told you this already."

Cianne didn't remember that conversation. In truth, she was having trouble remembering anything at all lately. Her mind has been clouded with more visions and nightmares than ever before. Plus, with the stressful prospect of leaving her father to attend college, Cianne felt overwhelmed.

"It doesn't matter. I don't date."

"Oh please, this again," Tranae whispered as she pulled Cianne to a stop, "Cianne, there is nothing wrong with you. So what, you have nightmares sometimes and you've got a little psychic thing going on, that..." she said, then shrugged, "presents a skin condition from time to time. That doesn't mean you have to ghost through life. You are a beautiful person, inside and out, and you deserve to be happy." Tranae took Cianne's hands in hers. "What are you so afraid of?"

The images of her as darkened veins took over her body and the reoccurring nightmare of being exposed publicly was a monumental deterrent. Then those pesky words of warning that called to her whenever she was near Tristan, the ones she didn't care to decipher that constantly ate at her.

She *was* afraid. Being rejected or abandoned because of her issues would hurt her deeply.

Tears burned behind Cianne's eyes as she stood face to face with her only friend in the entire world. How could she tell Tranae that the one thing she feared most in the world was Tristan seeing her for what she was, a monster who should be put down when Tranae couldn't see that truth for herself? That she was a danger to everyone around her but she put her selfish desperation to have a friend above her best friend's safety.

Ashamed, Cianne lowered her gaze.

"Cianne," Tranae tried to meet her eyes. "Are you ok?"

Cianne pinched the bridge of her nose. "I'm just tired that's all." The look on Tranae's face told Cianne she needed to be more convincing so she quickly thought of something more believable. "And I've been getting back some of the responses from the colleges I applied to. The thought of being so far from my dad is bothering me a little." She smiled. "I just need to talk to him about the big changes that are going to happen soon, that's all." She slowly pulled her hands-free from Tranae's hold. They started walking back toward the cafeteria.

"We'll come home all the time to visit our parents," Tranae promised. When Cianne gave her a worried look, Tranae added with conviction, "We're going to the same college, even if I have to kidnap the Dean's child and force him to let me in, like in that one movie." She grinned as if what she proclaimed was the "end all-be all" of the matter.

Cianne produced a smile as they arrived at the cafeteria doors.

"Come on back and finish my lunch with me. If Brenda continues to be a bitch, I'll lay her ass out flat."

"So…not ready for round two." Cianne looked over at the table she stormed away from. A janitor was busy mopping up the floor. "Besides, I don't need all these eyes on me if I flake out. It's way too crowded and it would take a while to get through them to reach the bathroom. I'd rather not be here."

Tranae regarded her for a moment. Her expression was one of concern but her gaze flickered away briefly. When she looked back, Cianne noticed that Tranae seemed perked up.

"Ok then, I'll see you tonight. I think I may get paroled soon. We can go see that new vamp movie, late show of course." Turning on her heels, Tranae took off for her lunch table as if she was late for a hair appointment.

Cianne stood there a moment, watching Tranae's energetic departure. She frowned when Tranae looked over her shoulder at her, with a larger than life grin.

What the deuce is she so happy about?

"Hello."

That sneaky little…

Cianne whipped around to see Tristan standing in front of her. *No warning or heat.* Well, there was heat but not the usual "Oh my God I'm Melting" heat. That *heat* was replaced by that pesky heat of attraction that Tristan ignited inside her. One she would never allow to burn hotter.

Cianne looked up at Tristan, noting everything that made him, well him. "How long have you been standing there?" she asked, a little alarmed.

"Not long." Tristan took a step toward her. "Look I wanted to ask you if you like sushi—"

Cianne moved around him. "Not really."

"You're not going to make this easy, are you?" Tristan followed, easily matching her strides.

Gosh, he smells so good. Clean, strong, sexy.

Cianne stopped and looked at him, "Not sure I understand."

"I'm trying to ask you out. Or was I completely wrong about your being into me?"

"I uh…" Cianne felt dizzy but wasn't sure if it was a vision or Tristan causing it. She took a step back, putting space between them. "I need to be somewhere." Cianne spun around and power-walked in the opposite direction.

Don't look back.

She wanted to look back but Tristan was a crush, a fantasy, a dream. Nothing more.

Relief washed over Cianne as the doors that led to the bathroom appeared ahead of her. At the same time, happy butterflies erupted inside her belly. Tristan wanted a date with her.

Oh God…he wants a date.

But she couldn't. With a new sense of urgency, Cianne sped up. She hoped he didn't wait for her because she wasn't sure if she was strong enough to deny him a second time.

◉

"Stings a little, don't it?" Brian appeared out of nowhere. He leaned against the entrance wall of the cafeteria.

Tristan sighed, somehow knowing that Brian was behind him before the comedic wannabe recited the obscure phrase from one of their favorite classic martial arts movie. He chose not to acknowledge Brian as the sting to his ego eased. He just stood there, looking confused.

However, he wasn't confused. Cianne Baxter was into him and Tristan knew it.

I know it.

If she wasn't, she was going to tell him so. Tristan started down the hallway after her.

"I thought you moved past this Baxter obsession. Didn't you go on a date with that girl, Minnie, last weekend?" Brian followed, trying to keep up with Tristan's pace.

"Maggie was her name, and yes I took her out." Tristan looked down the hall to his right. He then looked to his left, having to look around Brian to get a clear view. Tristan chose to go down the hallway to his right.

"Are you looking for her?" Brian asked, sounding amused. "Come on man, you're scaring me." Brian stopped walking. "You didn't seal the deal with Miggie, did you?" He asked loudly.

A teacher walking by gave Brian a warning look but raised his brow at Tristan.

"No, I didn't," Tristan hissed, "and lower your voice please."

"Why the hell not?" Brian demanded. He jogged to catch up to Tristan again.

"Because I didn't want to." Tristan continued down the hallway. "Besides, Miggie...I mean Maggie, isn't my type."

"When is a blonde with big boobs and long legs, not your type? Since when is that not your type?" Brian repeated.

"Since right now," Tristan said, sounding more annoyed.

"Let me guess, your type just walked down that hall." Brian pointed in the opposite direction. "Who by the way has just left you standing here looking stupid, and has never given you the time of day. Am I right?" Brian didn't wait for a response before he continued. "Did it ever cross your mind that she might not be into spoiled rich white boys? Her dad is black you know, I've seen him. I hear girls usually date men who look like their fathers…or something like that."

Tristan passed Brian but stopped. He gawked at his best friend, trying to remember why they were friends.

"I'm not saying that's why she's not all over you like the rest of these girls," Brian said, then shrugged, "but it's possible and explains a lot. All I know is, the college guy she was seen with is a brother—that's all I'm saying." He held his hands up in defense. As Tristan walked away Brian yelled, "Hey! Coach wanted to talk to you today."

"Tell him that I said I'm done," Tristan called out. He walked the hallway Cianne had used. Once he was outside, he had to walk halfway around the building to get to his truck. Cianne was gone.

Tristan climbed inside his truck and put his key in the ignition, but didn't start it up. Deflated, he sat back. His attempts to get Cianne to look at him as an option hadn't worked. This rejection thing was new to him and if he didn't want her so badly he would have given up by now.

He thought about every cute quirk she had that he memorized. How she twirled a piece of her hair when she was bored or how she bit her bottom lip when she's nervous or angry. It was either, he didn't know which, but he wanted to find out.

Every way she moved and everything she did was like watching living art.

Still, what was he doing? This wasn't him. He was confident and never had to work this hard for any girl's attention.

"What's wrong with me?" Tristan grabbed his head. "She's only a girl." Tristan laid his head on his steering wheel. "A girl I can't stop thinking about."

Chapter Five

Inside West Hills Public Library, Cianne found the book that she saw featured in a magazine, ordered a medium frappe and a blueberry muffin, and then took a seat at a small café table nestled in a quiet corner. She didn't want to think about what had happened in the cafeteria with Brenda or the fact that she just dismissed Tristan again. Her thoughts were divided between the two situations the entire time it took to walk to the library. Now that she was in the quiet sanctuary of the written word, she wanted to park all her problems at the door and read a little.

Her plan was to read a few chapters, drink her frappe' while eating her muffin, then go home and call Tranae because she needed help with the Tristan situation. Like it or not, she was going to have to talk to him. She was going to have to convince him that they were never going to date and she was going to have to look as though she meant it when she said it to him.

For now, she was going to read and relax.

Six enthralling chapters later, Cianne looked up and noticed that daylight had slipped away. Sure, time had gotten away from her but it shouldn't be that dark out yet and her cell phone confirmed it. It was only a quarter after five.

She threw the remnants of the frappe' and the muffin wrapper in a nearby waste basket and went to the register to check out the book she'd been reading. She glanced at the eReader sales display for the hundredth time but shook her head. She considered purchasing one another time. She loved her books with spines but she was intrigued by the ease of the eReader.

Cianne looked through the glass doors that led outside and discovered why it looked so dark. Technically, it was still monsoon season, a time when high winds and severe downpours plagued the area. Cianne stepped through one of the glass doors and looked up into the supercharged gray sky.

"Looks ominous, doesn't it?"

She glanced at the attractive guy standing next to her. He was a little taller than she was, young too, maybe early twenties. "It doesn't look good," she said to the stranger.

"I saw you inside." He motioned to the bookstore just behind them. "My name is Marvin."

"Cianne," she said. She smiled as she shook his hand. Her attention went back to the sky. "If I want to beat this rain I'd better start walking. Nice meeting you Marvin."

"I bet that if we go back inside, get an iced coffee…maybe a slice of cheesecake…that by the time we've gotten to know each other the storm will have passed us by."

He reminded her of Jesse, Tranae's older brother which meant a resounding NO.

"I'm sorry Marvin, but—,"

"Well at least let me drive you home. I'd hate to see you walking in this storm."

He was sweet and his smile was welcoming. Cianne tried to imagine him holding her, kissing her but the image wouldn't manifest in her mind. There was nothing there. There seldom was when she looked at a guy.

"Thanks, Marvin," Cianne began, "but I'll be fine."

He touched his chest as if an arrow had been shot through his heart. She laughed as she took a few steps toward the curb then looked back and waved. He waved back. Cianne turned and started her walk home.

Two blocks down with only twelve blocks to go, Cianne thought, as she strode down the walk. She passed a number of stores she considered taking shelter before the rain started but knew that she just wanted to get home.

The first dime sized drops fell from the sky while she waited for a traffic light to change. As Cianne hurried across the street, the rain began to pour. She spotted a bus stop shelter a few hundred feet away; it was her best bet so she made a dash for cover.

Protected from the rain, she took a minute to check her bag and books. Her things were a little moist but they were ok. She, on the other hand, was completely soaked. Cianne took a tissue from her bag and patted her face dry as she looked to the sky. The rain was coming down harder now. The sound of large drops hitting the various surfaces was so loud she barely heard her name being called.

Cianne searched for the source through the haze of water. An older gentleman seated on the bench behind her whistled for her attention. When she turned to look at him, the man pointed to a truck at the intersection, two lanes over. The rain was coming down so hard that she couldn't make out the person driving, let alone the vehicle.

She heard her name more clearly when the passenger door of the truck swung open and the driver beeped the horn. She still couldn't see the person behind the wheel but she knew she saw that truck before, only she couldn't remember where. Cianne realized she had to get wetter just to see if she wanted a ride from this person. She weighed her options—stay out in the storm with nowhere to run if a vision hit her or chance a ride with a possible serial killer.

There was no question in her mind. Cianne hugged her bag to her chest and maneuvered around the cars that were stopped at the light to get to the truck. This person knew her name so it stood to reason that she knew him or her as well. If a creeper was driving, she just wouldn't get inside.

"Get in." The person inside called out when she reached the vehicle. A large hand reached over the passenger seat for hers.

Cianne, at first sighed with relief when she saw that it was Tristan but fear quickly reared inside her.

A horn from the car behind them rang out. There was no time to work this out in her mind so she grabbed his hand and jumped inside the truck.

"Seat belt," Tristan advised. He ignored the impatient motorist behind them, moving only after she was secured.

A moment later thunder exploded outside and the sky lit up with lightning. She cringed as the thunder crackled away. Tristan only smiled as he reached for a knob on the dashboard. Cianne jerked her legs out of the way.

"Just turning up the heat," he told her, "you're soaked." Tristan glanced over at her. "I'm not a danger to you."

She ignored his reassurances. He didn't realize how dangerous he was to her.

"Can you see through this?" The rain was coming down so hard now that she couldn't see the lines that separated the lanes. She couldn't even tell where the road and the sky separated.

"I can."

"No, really," Cianne said, as she gripped the seat. "I can't see a thing out there." Tristan didn't respond. He continued to drive and though she was a little on edge, she quickly realized he could see. He seemed relaxed as he confidently peered through the heavy flow of rain even though she couldn't see at all. After a brief silence, Cianne spoke again. "Thank you for stopping."

He said nothing, just nodded.

The sound of the rain that had been drumming the roof of the truck transformed to a soothing series of taps. She wished that her pounding heart would slow. Tristan made her nervous and knowing that made her more nervous.

He doesn't feel he's a danger. She almost laughed at the thought.

Tristan asked Cianne out during lunch hour today and she blew him off. After reflecting on his lack of progress with her, he decided he was done. He felt that trying to get a date with Cianne was as useless as Brian had said. That was until he spotted her standing on the bus stop dripping wet and looking more beautiful than she ever had. There was something about a gorgeous woman drenched with water. It was so damn sexy.

It's only a ride, nothing more.

Tristan focused on the road. He planned to get her home then get on with his life. There was no need for small talk. It was just a ride.

He got her home fairly quickly. When he pulled his truck onto her parking pad, Cianne undid her seat belt.

"Thank you again for giving me a ride home."

Tristan didn't look at Cianne. He couldn't. "You're welcome," he said, keeping his eyes straight ahead. When she shifted in her seat he cursed to himself. He was raised to be a gentleman. "Let me get that for you." Tristan got out the car and pulled the passenger door open for her, thinking nothing of the raindrops that fell on him.

When Cianne got out of the truck she stood in front of him. He had the feeling she wanted to tell him something. There was really no need. "I got the message loud and clear earlier."

"I…" she began but paused.

The rain had slowed a little, but not much. He didn't want her to be out in this weather so he closed the door and tried to usher her toward her front door.

She dug in and said, "I… I would like it if you would come in for a moment, to dry off."

Tristan looked at her for a moment. Really? "Alright," he said finally. He ran to the driver's side of his truck and removed his keys from the ignition.

They ran to the house together. Cianne opened the door and Tristan entered behind her. She motioned for him to stay just inside the entryway, then she hurried up the stairs. Tristan looked around from where he stood, taking in the décor until Cianne returned carrying two towels.

He took the one she gave him and rubbed his face dry before rubbing the towel over his head. "Thank you," he said as he followed her.

Cianne led him down a hallway, past the stairs, and into the kitchen. He liked the way the house looked lived in, especially the kitchen. It definitely didn't resemble his kitchen, which looked like it belonged on a department store's showroom floor. He preferred the lived-in look.

"Would you like something to drink?" Cianne motioned for him to sit at the table.

"Am I going to be here long enough to finish a drink?" He sounded more abrupt than he had intended. He shifted his weight from one foot to the other as he wiped his neck with the towel.

Cianne turned to the fridge as if she hadn't noticed his tone. "Bottled water, cola, or fruit juice?"

"Water please." Tristan sat at the kitchen table as she placed a bottle of water in front of him. She sat on the opposite side of the table, but not directly across from him so he had to sit at an angle to watch her twist the cap off of her water.

"I haven't been very nice to you. I apologize," Cianne said. Their eyes met briefly before she looked down.

Dripping wet and looking unbelievably gorgeous, Cianne effectively melted Tristan's resolve away. Screw it. He couldn't lie to himself. He wanted Cianne Baxter and he wouldn't lie to her. "Look, you have to know by now that I like you. Wait…it's more than that." He leaned toward her, placing his arms on the table that divided them.

She pinned him with a look of bewilderment.

Did she not know?

"I think about you all the time," Tristan said. "When I don't see you at your locker in the morning, I worry." He hadn't planned to spill his heart out but he started, and even though she looked more frightened than flattered, he was going to finish. "I wonder what you like and what you don't. I think about what I should say to you or if I should say anything to you at all. I even managed to get my locker assigned right next to yours; just so you would notice me this year. I want to be near you, to know you."

Tristan watched as Cianne sucked her bottom lip into her mouth and nibbled on it as she stared at him impassively. When she stood and went to the counter, she said nothing.

"You see, it's that there. That look you just gave me comes first. Then you walk away," he said, then chuckled. Tristan leaned back in the chair, ignored the creaking noise, and lifted his water bottle off the table. He shook the bottle a few times then placed it back on the table. "You always give me that same look and as beautiful as it is, I've seen it enough times to know that..." His words faltered when she turned around to face him.

"I'm not like the girls you're used to dating," Cianne told him.

Tristan was taken aback by the fact that she hadn't shut him down. "Good," he fumbled out.

"No...you don't understand," she said.

Tristan got to his feet and walked over to her. Standing in front of her, he leaned closer and placed his hands on the countertop on either side of her waist, caging her in. He was so close he felt the water bottle she held, resting against his stomach. He leaned in closer and whispered in her ear, "All I need to know is..." Tristan lowered his gaze to her neck and inhaled her unique scent that resembled vanilla and something fresh. "Do you think of me as much as I think of you?"

He fought the urge to get closer, to brush his lips across her cheek.

Cianne shivered as Tristan's calm breaths caressed the side of her face. The warmth of his skin next to hers triggered every cell in her body to scream out for attention.

He admitted he liked her, that he had their lockers assigned next to each other. She honestly had no clue how she should feel about it all. Speechless, Cianne just stood there with only a water bottle and their wet shirts to separate them.

When Tristan raised his head, his lips were mere inches away from hers. She had no choice but to look into his eyes. There was where she saw the flames of determination, strength and…danger. If she was being honest with herself, all of what she saw in him excited her.

Scraping her teeth across her bottom lip, Cianne breathed, "More."

Unaware of where that had come from, she swallowed hard and closed her eyes. She just embarrassed herself and had every intention of taking back the four-letter word when Tristan leaned his head over her shoulder and brushed his lips across her birthmark just behind her left ear. His lips were fire on her overly sensitive skin and she couldn't stop the moan that escaped her parted lips or the shudder that went through her.

She unconsciously crushed the half empty water bottle she held in her hands.

"You're my first thought when I wake and my last thought when I close my eyes at night," he whispered in her ear.

He was so close that his breath tickled her earlobe. God, she wanted to pull him closer, to kiss him like she had so many times in her head. Only now it wouldn't be a fantasy. Cianne's heart raced just knowing that he wanted to kiss her too. She willed her trembling hand to move slowly toward his chest but stopped when his entire body stiffened.

Tristan raised his head as if something had distracted him. He suddenly stood up straight, gave her what seemed like a longing, pained look, then stepped away from her so fast that Cianne wanted to shout "NO" and pull him back. He was already seated at the table when she heard the front door shut.

"Buttercup, whose truck is that parked on the parking pad?" Her father's voice carried through the silent house. "I couldn't pull my car in. My feet are wet now."

Cianne cleared her throat. "It's uh, a friend's truck Dad. He drove me home." Her voice sounded normal enough so she went on. "I got caught in the rain today."

When she looked over at Tristan his head was low, his eyes were down, and he was busy wiping his head with the towel. As if he felt her gaze, he looked up and flashed a wicked smile. Cianne nearly burst into flames or at least thought she would. Only this time it had been motivated by desire and not the annoying heat she usually felt when Tristan was too close.

Awareness hit her then. That freakish warmth had been MIA and so had the warnings.

When Joseph entered the kitchen, he looked at Tristan then to Cianne, who was nervously chewing on her bottom lip. She raised her brows, widened her eyes, and stared hard at her father, pleadingly. The look only lasted a second but she hoped he got the message.

The "please don't embarrass me Dad" message.

Joseph raised his brows as if he got the hint but his grin said that he didn't plan to comply. "Ah, I'm guessing this is Tristan."

Tristan smiled as he glanced at her.

Cianne avoided looking at him, worried what her father would reveal next.

"It's good to finally meet you." Joseph extended his hand.

Tristan stood and they shook hands as he glanced sideways at her again, "It's nice to finally meet you as well Mr. Baxter."

Cianne wanted to crawl into her bed and hide under her sheets for the rest of forever. Tristan now knew that he was the topic of a few family discussions. She was going to kill her father.

Finally? Did he have to say finally? Was he totally clueless or was he trying to be funny?

"Will you be joining us for dinner Tristan?" Joseph asked.

"Uh, no sir, I actually need to get going."

Joseph nodded then said, "Maybe another time then." He stepped aside to let Tristan pass, giving Cianne an exaggerated wink as she followed.

She nudged her father in his side, making him chuckle.

Neither spoke as they moved down the hallway. When Tristan reached the front door, he turned around to face her. "Don't shut down on me Cianne. This," he said, motioning to her then to himself with his hand, "is going to happen. *We* are going to happen."

Cianne's stomach fluttered as she stared blankly at Tristan.

He flashed a confident smile then opened her front door and exited her home. Cianne watched Tristan as he jogged to his car. Once inside he waved to her then pulled off.

It was later that night, as Cianne sat in a warm bath, that she thought about the decision she made today. There was no way to fully understand the consequences of her actions. She had spent much of her life keeping her distance from people in order to keep her personal trials a secret.

She had limited her participation in school activities, never went to parties, didn't have many friends, and never dated. When in public, Cianne had always been careful. She had always made sure that she knew the location of every exit, every bathroom, and every dark corner in any establishment, in case she suffered a vision. The restrictions she had placed on herself were necessary all these years and she was pretty lucky thus far.

Was it so bad that she wanted a life now? That she wanted Tristan?

Cianne rinsed then stepped out of the tub. She dried off then put on a tank and panties. She was still riding her Tristan high when she hopped into bed. She planned to go over every word he had said for as long as it took her to fall asleep when her cell phone rang.

Crap! She had forgotten to call Tranae. She swiped her answer button.

"Did I wake you?"

Cianne didn't recognize the number but knew immediately whose low relaxed voice was on the other end of the phone. "Umm…no," she answered.

"I just wanted to hear your voice before I went to bed," Tristan said, "I like the sound of it."

Cianne tried to calm her excitement as she basked in what Tristan had said. "I like hearing your voice too, especially when you say my name." The end of Cianne's words trailed off to a soft whisper. She closed her eyes tight, astonished that she just said what she did, to Tristan.

It was in her haze of disbelief that something occurred to her. She was talking to Tristan Bertram on the phone. "Um…how did you get my number?"

"That day you dropped your phone at school I had to look at the personal info to find out the owner. I remembered the number."

"How did you bypass my security?"

"Those are useless. I promise, I only looked at the phone number."

"One look and you remembered my number?" she asked.

"Yeah, are you angry?"

"No," she said quickly. "I mean… I wish I could do that."

"So, are you ready for bed then?"

"I am. Are you in bed?" *Did I just ask him that?* Where the heck was all this coming from? Cianne squeezed her eyes shut again and prayed he hadn't heard her.

"I am," he said in a very seductive slightly amused tone. "I wanted you to know I didn't want to leave. I mean, I wanted to stay for dinner with you and your dad but—"

Cianne cut him off. "It was a spur of the moment thing. You don't have to explain."

"I know," he agreed. "Well, I don't want to keep you on the phone too long because I want you to be fully rested. I would like to spend some time with you tomorrow if possible."

"I…I don't know." Cianne was still very uncertain about getting closer to Tristan. She knew what she wanted but if things went wrong, if he found out about her she would…

Cianne's thoughts came to a halt when she heard manic laughter inside her head and it sounded like her. It *was* her laugh. *What the heck was that*?

"I want the chance to prove that I'm good enough for you but I can't if you say no."

Tristan's voice did two things to her. It calmed and distracted her, bringing her back to the subject at hand. "It's not that I don't want to, it's… Wait, good enough?"

"Don't analyze this Cianne. Just say yes."

"*Give him a chance*," she heard Tranae say in her head. Thank God it wasn't that freaky disembodied "Cianne" voice, the one who had just laughed.

"Alright," Cianne said with more worry than enthusiasm. "What time?"

"Would six be too early for you?"

"I can be ready by six."

"It's settled then, I'll be at your door at six p.m.," he confirmed. "Goodnight Cianne."

"Goodnight." She disconnected the call and placed her cell phone back on the dock.

Cianne couldn't help but feel she just agreed to something that was going to change her entire world. Whether it was for the better or for worse, only time would tell.

Chapter Six

The car glided around the curved road with a grace that only a beautiful machine could. It was modern, sleek, and very clean as if it had been just driven off the showroom floor. If Tristan meant to make an impression, he had.

Cianne loved the feel of the leather seats. Though to her, a car was just a way to get from point A to point B. The wealthy demanded more, but she was a simple girl. Tristan was one of the wealthy. The thought had Cianne shifting in her seat, suddenly feeling a bit generic.

"What?" Tristan asked as if sensing her unease.

"Nothing," she said, looking over at him then back to the pristine dashboard.

Tristan shifted gears with ease and increased the vehicle's speed. "You've been quiet since we left your house," he said glancing at her.

"Is this your father's car?"

"No." Tristan laughed. "My father prefers to be driven versus actually driving."

"It's nice…the car," Cianne told him. She ran her hand over the sleek dashboard down to the stereo knobs and pushed a button. A sports announcer's voice came through the speakers, giving the latest news in the athletic world. She quickly pressed the button again, turning the radio off.

"Don't you want to know where I'm taking you?"

Where is he taking me? Was it odd that she didn't ask?

"Alright, where are you taking me?" she asked.

"If you don't care…," he teased.

Did it matter? She was with Tristan and she felt safe so it really didn't. Then it occurred to her, what if he is taking her some place fancy? She hadn't dressed for fancy, and what if she had a vision.

"I do, where?" she asked, with concern.

Tristan must have heard the panic in her tone. "I'm taking you to a place where we can get to know each other without any interruptions. You have nothing to worry about, you know. I've told you before that I would never hurt you."

Cianne gave him a smile that she knew was uneasy. She wasn't thinking of him hurting her. What had caused her panic was the fact that there wouldn't be people around to buffer the conversation in case they ran out of things to talk about. Being completely alone with Tristan wasn't what she had expected.

She turned her head and looked out the passenger window. *Alone*, Cianne thought as the car turned off a busy main road onto an empty one lined by only grass and tall trees. She remembered that this particular area had been under massive construction in the last few years.

As they drove through a couple of traffic lights she could see that most of the construction had been completed. It wasn't far from her neighborhood but this area was so vastly different than her cozy middle-class section of town, that Cianne could easily believe that they were hundreds of miles away.

They drove past a property so beautiful she thought that nothing could possibly compare. That was until she saw the next one, then the next. Each house held her attention until she could no longer see it, and then another came into view.

When they turned onto a curved driveway, Cianne was surprised to see that this home was larger and more beautiful than the ones she had already seen. The home was set back about a quarter mile from the road and as they got closer to it, it took her breath away. The modern mansion looked like a picture taken from Luxurious Homes magazine or a television show, with its amazing landscape and view of the large mountains behind it.

Tristan parked next to a garage that looked larger than her house. He got out of the car and opened the door for her.

"Is this your house?" Cianne asked, amazed. When she stepped out of the car she was able to take in more of the house. The place was gigantic.

"It's where I live." He reached for her hand.

Cianne, without thinking, placed her hand in his. Their fingers interlocked perfectly. Warmth settled within her stomach, giving her an unfamiliar sense of completeness.

"This is my parent's house."

They strolled along a paved walkway to the large front door. "Your parents must have really good jobs," Cianne said. Tristan released her hand to unlock the door. She glanced at her hand, already missing his touch.

"Well my father, David Bertram, is acting CEO of Arlington Inc. My mother, Melanie, is his biggest fan."

Tristan pushed the door open and led Cianne into the vaulted foyer. She looked up at the high ceiling and the large shimmering chandelier that must have cost a fortune. After allowing her a few seconds to soak in the extravagance, Tristan gently placed his hand on the small of her back and led her further inside.

"David," she thought out loud. "David Bertram is your father?"

"Around here he's known as Leslie but yeah, that's him."

Had there been a hint of annoyance in his tone? Furthermore, how did she not know that Tristan's father was one of the most important men in the business world and also one of the wealthiest?

She knew that Tristan was well off. He drove a Mercedes G550 to school for goodness sakes! A good number of the kids at West Hills had wealthy parents. Even her father owned his own collection agency and it was doing well but David Bertram's wealthy was…

Tristan's life was a whole other world than hers. Again, Cianne felt less than worthy.

As he led her further into the house, their eyes met and he smiled. With that perfect image alone, her mind went blank. Everything that mattered prior to that smile was no longer an issue…for now anyway.

The tour of the house Tristan gave Cianne took a while because she lingered, taking in everything she saw. She was especially interested in the locations of the bathrooms. Eventually, they ended up in a brightly-lit elegant gourmet kitchen. Together they crossed the spacious room to a breakfast nook that offered an unobstructed view of the mountain landscape.

On a large round table sat two side by side place settings. There were three covered glass dishes and a basket of bread. In the center was a large vase full of calla lilies and beside it was a wine bottle in a bucket of ice.

Cianne was thoroughly impressed.

"I asked Celia to help me out tonight." Tristan pulled out a chair for her to sit. "I cook, but most of what I make she says isn't fit for human consumption."

"Then I suppose you should thank Celia for me," Cianne said playfully, then sat down.

"Celia is our cook," he explained, "and if…well, I'm guessing you'll be meeting her at some point so you can thank her yourself."

Cianne lowered her head to hide the fact that she was blushing. Tristan had just let on that he may want to see her again socially, but she refused to let it go to her head.

"It must be nice to have a cook." When she looked up he was seated in the chair beside her. She hadn't realized the place settings were that close. *It's nice*, she thought as she looked at him.

"Celia is an amazing cook." He lifted the lids off the containers, releasing a delicious aroma. "Tonight, we are having Watermelon and Feta Salad, Sauté Greco Shrimp Scampi, and Dark Chocolate Chambord Mousse for dessert. To drink we have a non-alcoholic apricot mist."

For years, she tried very hard to not look at Tristan for too long. Or rather, she didn't want him to catch her looking at him. But now, as he listed things she never even heard of…at that moment, Cianne felt she earned the right to gaze at him and she wasn't going to hide her curiosity as she eyed him boldly. Tristan was turning out to be more amazing than she dreamed and being this close to him was exhilarating and surprisingly comfortable.

"Everything looks great," Cianne said, glancing at their meal then focusing back on him.

Cianne was right, everything did look great. Celia had come through for him with an amazing meal, but Tristan knew she would.

"It does, doesn't it? Celia outdid herself." He poured them both a drink. "You're going to love Martha and Benjamin too. Martha is our housekeeper and Ben is our groundsman," he said, answering her question before she could ask.

"Should we ask them to join us?" Cianne looked over her shoulder to the kitchen entrance. "It looks like we have enough."

"Beautiful, and thoughtful." He grinned with pride as her cheeks reddened. Not many of the girls he knew would suggest eating with the help. "I'm sure Celia has left by now. She doesn't live on the property. And inviting Martha and Ben to join us would derail my plans of being alone with you." He served Cianne first. "If you don't like anything here we'll order something."

Cianne's face lit up with the first bite. "This is amazing," she said, covering her mouth as she spoke.

"I told you Celia is a great cook." Tristan smiled as he watched her for a moment.

Cianne returned his gaze, both of them caught in each other's pull before she looked down at her plate. She stabbed the fork at her salad. "You have a nice smile."

"So, it's my smile you think about," Tristan teased.

"Other things as well." Cianne lifted her eyes. They held each other's gaze again. "I think about the things you might like and what you don't. Sometimes I wonder what I should say to you or even if I should say anything at all."

He chuckled at her repeating his very own words. "Ah…and you're funny too."

"I'm not trying to be," she said. "What you said was exactly what I couldn't, plus I've always been curious about you."

"Ok," he mused, "My favorite color is greenish-blue. If you want to see the actual hue all you need to do is look in the mirror." He motioned to her eyes. "I'm an only child and I was a bit of a handful, my mother would say, until a few years ago. I enjoy taking bubble baths." He lifted his index finger to his lips. "With scented bubbles but that is for your ears only" he whispered.

Cianne rewarded him with her perfect smile. Tristan watched as she nervously played in her food. He cleared his throat. "Your turn," he said before he started to eat.

"I really don't have a favorite color, but my name was morphed from the color cyan. My mom liked how it sounded but didn't like the way it was spelled. Let's see… I was always a good kid. I love seafood but hate lobster. Oh," she said as she smiled, "and I use to think that Farrakhan was Chaka Khan's brother. My mom loved Chaka Khan."

Tristan laughed. Cianne hinted at a smile at first then she joined in. When Tristan composed himself, his expression had changed from a relaxed look to a solemn one when their eyes met again.

"That day in the hall, when you ran into me, what were you running from?" His question caused an immediate reaction from Cianne. Her entire body tensed and she nervously looked down. *Don't mess this up, Tristan.*

"You don't have to tell me," he said.

"I have nightmares," she whispered. "I guess I fell asleep in class."

"You looked pretty freaked. Can I ask what that one was about?" Tristan could tell from her reaction and hesitation that she was thinking whether she wanted to tell him or not.

"Usually they're about me," she finally said. "Well, I think it's me, but it isn't me like I am now." She closed her eyes and tilted her head up. "I looked different. Sometimes my eyes are completely red and I get the feeling I've hurt people but no one's around. I'm all alone."

Tristan was surprised how easily she shared something so personal with him. His voice was low when he asked, "Alone, as in everyone has left you?"

Cianne opened her eyes and looked at him. "No. I don't think anyone else is left. I mean…I feel…no, I *know* that I'm alone in the world."

Tristan sighed. "That's some nightmare alright. Did you have one last night?"

Cianne brows furrowed as she placed her finger on her chin. He thought it was cute how she pretended to think. She then gave him a grin and shook her head. "As a matter of fact, I didn't."

He smiled big. "I think my phone call was maybe exactly what you needed then."

"Really?" She cut her eyes at him.

"Seriously," he said then grinned. "My calling you last night distracted you, hence good thoughts and no nightmares. Meaning, it would be in your best interest to keep me around. Me being your very own dream catcher and all."

"Maybe." Cianne lifted her fork to her mouth.

They ate in silence for a while, each of them stealing glances at the other every so often.

"Do you like movies?" Tristan finally asked.

Her mouth was full of food so she held up a finger and swallowed before answering. "I do."

"What kinds of movies?"

"Old movies, the Technicolor ones though. I like comedies and action movies too. You?"

Tristan cleared his throat. "Any movie where the guy gets the girl," he told her.

Cianne wasn't looking but she could feel his eyes move over her as if he were caressing her with his hand. She felt lingering stares from men before. It didn't take much effort to imagine what they were thinking but she had always been indifferent, never feeling anger or pleasure from the attention they gave her.

That was until now. Now she felt flushed, overwhelmed, self-conscious, and God help her, on fire. She was the one with thoughts of how it would feel with his warm hands on her untouched skin.

She took a sip of apricot mist to ease her dry mouth but it did nothing for her thirst. "So, you're a romantic," she said after swallowing.

"I wasn't always but I guess you could say that I am now."

"Why the change?" she asked.

"You, I think." He hesitated for a moment but continued. "Yeah, I'm pretty sure it's you." They both continued to eat.

Cianne looked down at her plate. She traced small circles in her food. She was new to dating but she wasn't a fool. Not yet anyway. "I don't really know how I should take that. I mean, you were just with Bianca and now…now you're sitting here with me?"

"I *was* with Bianca. The key word is, *was*. Loving someone Cianne, and being in love with them is very different. Have you ever loved someone?"

Cianne felt the rush of blood spreading through her cheeks. It was the way he was looking at her, and not his question, that caused the unintended reaction. "No," she stared back at him.

"Never?" He sounded doubtful.

"Never." Cianne shook her head. She saw a twinkle in his eyes and could almost hear him telling himself that he would be her first. He was arrogant that way.

"Can I get you anything else?" He asked as he laid his napkin over his plate.

Cianne had eaten all she could too. She put her fork down and wiped her mouth with her napkin. "No, everything was great, thank you."

She watched him as he took a drink from his glass then placed it back on the table. Every move he made was so precise, from years of etiquette lessons she surmised.

"If you can stay a little longer that would be awesome, but if you want me to take you home…"

"I'd like to stay."

It was visible in his smile that her quick response surprised him. It had surprised them both.

"I was hoping you would." Tristan stood. He walked around the table and reached for her hand. Cianne stood, placing her hand in his for the second time, feeling like it was the most natural thing she ever did.

"Up these stairs is my sanctuary." He told her as he led the way to a staircase that was hidden behind a wall just beyond the kitchen.

She didn't speak as she followed him up the steps and down a hallway. He hadn't taken her to this section of the mansion during his tour. They'd stayed on the first level.

He stopped in front of a closed door. "The second floor is mine." He motioned down the hall to an open room through an archway, and at least one more door. "My office and this is…" Tristan pushed the door open to reveal a room that could easily pass for a large apartment—"is my room."

The first thing that caught her eye was the enormous picture that was positioned over the bed. It was a framed print of Blue Comes Through by Alice Dalton Brown. Underneath the print was a large dark cappuccino bed frame that sat against the wall directly in front of them. Cianne blushed, feeling uncomfortable about looking at his bed, so she looked away.

"The bathroom is there." He pointed to his left. He then led her toward four white columns aligned evenly apart that reached from floor to ceiling. The columns encased three curved steps that went from one side of the room to the other. The stairs led down into a sunken sitting area.

"Your room is amazing," Cianne said as they descended the steps.

Chapter Seven

Tristan and Cianne sat down at the same time, next to each other, still hand and hand. Tristan watched her as she turned her head in one direction then another, taking in her surroundings. He noticed the fall of her hair over her shoulder as her head moved.

"Your hair is lovely." He took a few strands in his fingers to examine them closer. When she turned to face him, their eyes met. "Forget not that the Earth delights to feel your bare feet and the winds long to play with your hair," he said softly. His fingers gently twisted her silky strands until each fell slowly to her shoulder and down the front of her blouse. He expected her to turn away but she didn't.

"That was beautiful. Do you write poetry?"

"No." He watched her pull her hair away from her face into one bundle then let the long tresses fall to her back. "I can only take credit for remembering it. A poet named Kahlil Gibran wrote it." Tristan moved closer. He wanted to kiss her so badly that every muscle in his body ached. "You are so beautiful," he told her, as he leaned into her very slowly, placing his finger under her chin.

She didn't attempt to pull away so he gently raised her face upwards and softly kissed her on the cheek. With no resistance from her, Tristan kissed her other cheek. He then slid his hand slowly around the back of her neck. Cianne's hair fell between his fingers as he secured his hold on the soft skin of the nape of her neck and pulled her to him, pausing only to look at her expression before gently kissing her on the lips.

It was a sample taste that kicked his heart into overdrive and he wanted, *no*, he *needed* more, but he pulled back to gauge her response. To him, she didn't appear to be upset. With her eyes closed and her looking relaxed, Tristan leaned forward and tasted her top lip and then her bottom lip. They tasted like sweet sin with a tinge of vanilla. Feeling comfortable enough to really kiss her now, he leaned into her again.

All time seemed to slow down as he kissed her, and when she opened her mouth for him, he moaned. He, Tristan Bertram, flipping moaned! The kiss was long and passionate and when he had no choice, his body's *reaction* to her being the deciding factor, he reluctantly pulled away. But not before gently kissing her bottom lip again then sucking it into his mouth before releasing her.

Cianne barely had time to take a breath when he moved toward her. When he touched her chin, she almost fainted. Her entire body was set ablaze when he kissed her and she had to remind herself to keep breathing.

It was over way too soon and now he was looking at her, waiting, and she didn't know what to do or say. She went over this possible scenario with Tranae earlier? She had, but all she could do now was bite on her lower lip.

"I'm sorry. I should have asked you if I could do that," Tristan said, filling the silence. He stood, patting his thighs on the way up. "I should take you home?"

Without thinking, Cianne took Tristan's hand. *Oh god,* she thought, *did he regret kissing me?* "Did I do something wrong?" Cianne heard the weakness in her voice but she didn't care.

"No, it's cool if you felt nothing," he said, "but to suffer through your silence is excruciating."

Cianne knew that she must look pathetic and when he sighed and looked away, he confirmed just that.

"Awesome," he said, rubbing his palm over his head. "That sympathetic look you're giving me now isn't helping either."

She looked down but held onto his hand. She was ruining this.

Don't ruin this.

"Look, I really like you Cianne. More than you know and it's driving me crazy. I know it shouldn't but it is…but I don't want you to feel bad about not feeling anything for me. It's all good, really."

Sympathetic look? Not feeling anything for him?

Was that what he thought? *Say something,* she urged herself. "I like you too and I don't want to leave," she managed. "I just need to wrap my head around all of this, that's all." She tried to relax by taking a deep breath. "I don't know what to say to you. You…this…it's all so surreal for me." She shrugged. "I've never had anyone kiss me before and—"

"No one has ever kissed you that way before," Tristan interrupted. He smiled, clearly full of himself as he sat back down beside her. "I can kiss you like that again."

Cianne knew Tristan was arrogant but his overconfidence still shocked her. He leaned into her again but she placed her hand on his chest, stopping him. It took a bit more strength than she thought it would and she tensed as his solid chest flexed against her palm and fingers.

She wanted him closer. She wanted to feel his lips on hers again but...

Suddenly, Cianne felt ashamed. With her hand on him and the thoughts that were flashing in her mind, it all felt wrong. Tristan wouldn't want her when he found out how inexperienced she really was. Not to mention her *issues.*

Cianne settled her hand on her lap. Embarrassed, she looked down at them. "I've never been kissed."

Tristan frowned as he sat back. "You've never been kissed? Ever? What about when you were in middle school or the college guys you've dated?

Cianne frowned. "I've never dated any college guys. I've never dated anyone."

His expression went from shock to Holy Hell before it seemed like he gained an understanding of the bigger picture. "You're a virgin."

The statement sounded vulgar and more like an accusation. Cianne felt her blood rush to her face. She went rigid and her hands fisted when she said, "I was being sincere when I told you that I wasn't like any of the girls you've dated."

"I apologize, that didn't come out right. I just… It's just…," he said, staring at her. "But you're so..." Tristan looked her over again and when their eyes met he must have seen the hurt look in her eyes. "Uh, being a virgin isn't something you should be ashamed of," he said quickly. "It's just that you are so very,"—he paused again, "enticing and that makes it kind of shocking."

"So, you thought I would be easy?" Cianne accused. She felt an ache in her chest that surprised her. It wasn't as if she thought that she meant anything to him. However, he was her dream guy, her fantasy, and honestly, Tristan meant something to her even if she hardly knew him.

Cianne lowered her head and rubbed the ring on her finger with her thumb. She almost didn't feel it when he moved closer to her. He gently lifted her chin and when his ocean eyes bore into hers, she felt a surge of emotion.

"Sex isn't what I want from you, Cianne."

"What do you want Tristan?" She couldn't find her voice so her words came out in a whisper.

Tristan's body strained as all the sexually charged images he had created of Cianne surfaced in his mind. "I would be lying if I said that being with you has never crossed my mind." The sultry images slowly faded but wouldn't vanish. "But sex isn't important to me." He wanted her mind, her soul, and her body. He wanted her trust, her passion; he wanted her to love him. "I want…" There was no way to express what he wanted without sounding like a complete psycho. So, he improvised. "I just want to be close to you."

Getting to know you will do for now.

"The kiss," she said, nibbling on her lip. "It was everything I dreamt it would be."

Tristan watched her teeth scraped slowly across her bottom lip. He exhaled then adjusted his position on the sofa so that a certain body part didn't bend in an odd position. It was definitely going to be a rough night.

"Good," he said, but on the inside, he groaned, "I don't want to disappoint."

Everything about Cianne was so damn desirable that Tristan knew it was going to take a great deal of effort to keep his desires in check. He looked away from those luscious lips he just kissed and honestly couldn't imagine not ever kissing them again.

He needed to focus on something else. "Um…" Tristan realized he was looking at her smooth neck. He saw himself tracing his tongue over her collarbone then kissing slowly down to her… He closed his eyes and shook his head. Stop it. "Uh," he said then swallowed, "who did your ink?"

Cianne touched her fingers to her neck. "I get asked that question a lot." She pulled her hair up and away from the brand then tilted her head slightly, exposing the delicate length of her neck. "It's not a tattoo, it's a birthmark."

Tristan looked at her holding her long hair high on top of her head and couldn't think of anything more erotic. Several strands fell loose, conjuring more stimulating thoughts. He closed his eyes again and tried counting. It was as if her neck was inviting his tongue to a taste test.

Tristan took in another calming breath then opened his eyes slowly. He shook off his lust again then moved closer to see the dark circle behind Cianne's left ear. He examined the solid black nickel-sized circle that was surrounded completely by a very thin outer ring.

"Wow." He ran his index finger over it. "It's two perfect circles."

Visibly caught off guard by his touch, Cianne dropped her hair and pulled away abruptly.

Oh hell, mistake.

"Sorry. I didn't mean to make you uneasy." Tristan eased back, allowing her a little space between them on the sofa. He hoped that he hadn't messed up things between them.

"You don't," she said, "well you do, but not in the way you think. You make me uneasy because I like it when you touch me."

Fantastic.

Only, restraint was the key with her and that meant they had to stay otherwise occupied. "So…" he said, leaning forward, "some movies were sent to me that I should have watched by now. Would you like to watch one with me?" He pulled out a drawer from the large coffee table in front of them. He then took out movie cases and handed them to her.

"I have never heard of any of these before, except for this one." She held a case up. "But I thought it was still being filmed."

"It's done filming and should be released soon. The others will be in theaters in a few months. Which would you like to watch?" Tristan reached for the remote that sat on the arm of the sofa and pushed the button for his television.

"I don't really like black market movies. The special effects aren't always complete, and it's sort of stealing," she said, as she handed them back to him. Cianne's attention was diverted to the large flat television that was lowered from the ceiling and rested over the low shelves lined against the wall in front of them.

"They're not bootleg movies, Cianne. They're perfectly legal, I promise." He clapped his hands together. "So, which would you like to see?"

"I guess we can watch the horror film?"

She gave in without much of a fight which meant she trusted him; either that or she was not all that interested. Whatever the reason, Tristan was just happy she decided to stay. He inserted the movie into a virtually invisible opening on the side of the large TV then returned to the sofa, sitting closer to her.

"Can I get you something…popcorn or some water? My arm perhaps? I hear this movie is very scary." Tristan raised his arm to wrap around her shoulders.

"I think I can handle it," Cianne said, as she pulled his arm down to her lap and placed her hand in his.

They settled into comfortable positions and watched the movie.

Two hours and fifteen minutes later, the end credit music rang out through the room as Cianne clung onto his arm. Even he had to admit that the movie had its frightening moments. Apparently, Cianne shared his opinion because she looked absolutely terrified.

Cianne sat up and released the death grip she had on his arm. "Sorry." She looked embarrassed.

"No problem." He chuckled. "What did you think?"

Cianne took a deep breath then exhaled. "I think I am going to avoid the train for a while."

With that, Tristan laughed, then he said, "It's getting late. I should probably get you home."

Cianne stood and said, "May I use your bathroom first?"

Tristan watched her walk to the bathroom. When she closed the door, he leaned back and relaxed, thinking to himself that it was a pretty good first date. Not his usual, but good nonetheless. He would have to take it slow with Cianne. Much slower than what he was used to. However, she was well worth it. He didn't know how he knew this, he just did.

Cianne Baxter was the one.

"Ready?" Tristan got to his feet when she returned.

"Ready." She smiled.

They drove to her house in virtual silence, just like they'd driven to Tristan's house. It seemed he didn't speak as much when he drove, so Cianne figured she shouldn't either. When he pulled his car in front of her house she decided to ask him something that had been bothering her.

"Why did you think I dated college guys?" she asked before he could exit the vehicle.

Tristan had taken his seat belt off and was opening his door. He sat back in the seat but left his door slightly open. "I guess everyone figured you were into older guys because you never said yes to any of us high school guys who've asked you on dates. You've been seen with some college guys too."

"Ah," she said as she nodded, "I used to tutor some of the students at Kennecott University for my volunteer credits." She took off her seatbelt and turned to face him.

"It's ok for us to sit here for a few minutes then?"

Cianne nodded so Tristan closed his car door. He reclined his seat then shifted his body to face her. Cianne reclined her seat as well so that they were face to face.

"If I had known you were a tutor I would have hired you a long time ago. That would have been much easier than following you around like a lost puppy," he said.

"You have never followed me around like a lost puppy. Plus, the tutor thing wouldn't have worked anyway. Your GPA is higher than mine," Cianne argued. "Besides, I don't tutor anymore." Her last statement sounded more solemn than she had intended. Her voice betrayed her and she hoped he hadn't picked up on it.

"What happened?"

He did. Cianne sighed. "One of the guys got really aggressive." Her tone was softer. "It was easier to just quit versus making trouble."

"What did he do?" Tristan's tone sounded curt but he looked calm.

Cianne knew that she was going to tell Tristan as soon as he asked. The thought of not telling him anything he wanted to know had never occurred to her. So, she took a deep breath and began.

"This guy was cut from his football team because of his grades so I began tutoring him. Eventually, he asked me out and I said no, in a nice way." She made that clear. "When his grades improved and he was back on the team he didn't need me as much, so I scaled back on our sessions and took on another student. That's when he started to change. During our sessions, instead of talking about the lessons, he wanted to talk about the other student I tutored. I told him that I was just tutoring the other student and that was it but even if we were dating, that it was none of his business.

"He seemed to let up for a while and things went back to normal. Then one day he asked me to meet him at his dorm room. I wouldn't normally do that but he said he had something to show me and it was too big to bring to the library. He promised that he would be on his best behavior and I believed him. Soon after I got there I knew I had made a big mistake. He cornered me immediately. He told me that he knew I wanted him. At first, I thought he was joking and when I realized he wasn't I told him that I didn't like him in the way he thought. That I was interested in someone else."

Tristan placed his hand over hers.

"He didn't listen. He pushed me on his bed and pinned my hands above my head. I screamed and yelled for him to get off me, but he wouldn't. He said that I'd been flirting with him for over a month and that he was tired of me playing hard to get. That some guys could take my flaunting 'it' in their faces and maybe wait until I decided to stop playing games but he wasn't like those guys." Cianne cringed as she thought back to that day. With a squeeze of Tristan's hand, she continued. "He started kissing me on my neck. My hands were pinned over my head and he was lying on top of me so I couldn't move." She closed her eyes. "I couldn't move when he started to unbutton my jeans and if…if it wasn't for his roommate walking into the room he would have…"

Tristan tried his best to keep calm. He had one hand over hers while the other was fisted but out of her view. He couldn't believe that a guy would ever force a woman into doing something she clearly didn't want, but the fact that some asshole did that to her, to *his* Cianne…

"Did you report him?" he asked, trying to keep his tone even.

"He didn't really do anything," she said. "Anything I could have reported anyway. I shouldn't have gone to his room." Cianne opened her eyes.

Behind the alluring shade of blue-green, Tristan saw acceptance and she confirmed it with what she said next.

"It was my fault. I shouldn't have gone to his room," she repeated.

"What's his name?" Tristan made sure that he sounded composed but anger raged inside of him. The street lamp lit up part of his car so he leaned back into the shadows to hide his eyes. His mother often said that his eyes always gave him away.

"I just want to forget it even happened. His name isn't important anymore."

Tristan traced his thumb over the back of her small hand. "Please don't blame yourself for what he did to you."

He needed just five minutes with the unnamed asshole that caused Cianne to blame herself for his transgression but Tristan knew that him being angry wasn't what she needed right now. Reluctantly, he forced his fist to relax. After counting to twenty in his head he was able to defuse some of his anger so he changed the subject.

"Is your father going to be alright with you being out so late?"

Cianne tipped her head back and smiled, wiping his angry thoughts clean. The effect she had on him achieved what thousands of dollars of therapy failed to do. She had the ability to calm the ever-present anxiousness and anger he tried so hard to suppress. Cianne was a breath of fresh air, air he seemed to need.

"Don't worry, my dad doesn't own a gun," she teased.

As much as he didn't want to end their time together, Tristan knew that there was a limit. "I really don't want to upset him. I'd like to spend more time with you so it would be to my benefit if your father likes me instead of hating me for keeping you out past your curfew." Tristan returned his seat to the upright position. "It's getting late. I better walk you to your door."

Tristan walked around the front of the car and opened the door for her. He trailed behind Cianne as she walked slowly to her door. Her pace was a good indication that she hadn't been ready to end the night as well.

Cianne stepped up on the first porch step then reluctantly turned around to face him. He stood in front of her with his hands clasped safely behind his back so he wouldn't do something he'd regret.

They looked into each other's eyes for a moment before Cianne moved hesitantly toward him. He shivered when her soft hands touched the back of his neck. Her eyes betrayed her, reflecting her fear of rejection as she moved into him until her full lips pressed against his.

Tristan wrapped his arms possessively around her waist and pulled her closer. He kissed her long and skillfully, hoping he could draw it out until…forever. She fisted his shirt as he deepened their connection. The sweetest sound escaped her lips before she pulled away.

As Tristan let his arms slowly fall from her waist, he felt her hand caress the nape of his neck. He relished her touch as he rode the sensation of tasting her again to its peak.

For the umpteenth time, he realized he didn't want this day to end. He would happily accept any consequence her father felt necessary for another kiss but Cianne had already turned from him and was opening her front door. He watched helplessly as she waved goodbye, feeling an unexplained sense of dread as she disappeared inside.

The thought that invaded his mind should have scared the hell out of him. It would have if it had been about any other woman. Instead of panic, Tristan felt stable, solid, and whole; and he agreed wholeheartedly with his inner self. The thought *'don't let her go'* wasn't a whisper like it was seconds ago. It was now a full out command.

Tristan smiled as he walked to his car. "Never," he said to himself, "I'll never let her go."

After arriving home and taking a long shower, Tristan grabbed his cell phone, scrolled to the newest most important number stored, then pressed the send button.

"Hello?" Cianne mumbled drowsily.

"I wanted to tell you to have only sweet dreams tonight," he said, "goodnight Cianne."

"Goodnight Tristan," she breathed.

He closed his eyes as she spoke the two syllables that made up his name, the second gift his mother had given him. The first was life, and he finally loved his life right now.

"I don't think I've ever heard you say my name before."

"Really?" she asked. He could tell she was smiling. "Goodnight, Tristan," she repeated slowly.

"Goodnight Cianne."

As he placed his cell phone on his nightstand Tristan experienced a feeling he would never be able to describe. It was unseen yet immediate and no one would ever believe it. In just one night, he had been brought to his knees. Cianne had and would always have his heart at her disposal, and that was just fine with him.

Chapter Eight

Bianca sat in the small car with the headlights off as the engine cooled. The lingering scent of some sweet flavored fruity air freshener wafted through the vents during the long drive, and it was starting to annoy her. It was a scent she couldn't wait to wash from her skin and hair.

She dragged her hawkish gaze from her destination and peered out of the driver's side window. The stretch of driveway where she was parked held many memories. Bianca grinned as she thought of how often she had driven up the winding road and parked in the exact spot she was parked in now. This was her spot and the house she had been watching was her home away from home.

"It's good to be home," she sang, as she looked in her purse and retrieved her favorite lipstick. Pulling the rear-view mirror down to see her reflection, she smoothed the frost pink color over her puckered lips. She wanted to look her best. Being gone for so long was unfortunate and in no way her choice, but she was home now and she knew Tristan wanted to see her as badly as she wanted to see him.

He would want to know where she was. He would want to know that the people his family employed were keeping her messages from him. That would be the only reason he hadn't returned her calls.

"Those damn domestic workers overstepped their boundaries for the last time," she said, to no one in particular. Bianca never liked Celia. The cook was way too opinionated for her taste, and Tristan, in his misguided ways, had encouraged Celia—all of them—too much. Her eyes lit with the knowledge that, that behavior was coming to an end.

Tears suddenly glistened in her eyes.

The entire situation was so upsetting and Bianca was fuming but she wouldn't show it. She was taught that a true lady never displayed her emotions and she was comforted by the fact that Tristan's staff would be dealt with. It didn't matter that they never really liked her because in the big scheme of things none of *them* mattered.

Tears forgotten, Bianca smiled as she took one more look in the mirror. "He's waiting," she said, as she exited the vehicle.

Inside, she walked slowly up the staircase. Ringing the doorbell would have definitely ruined the surprise and she relished the fact that she had gotten a key made last summer.

Bianca carefully pushed the bedroom door open, trying to make as little noise as possible. She then tip-toed over to the bed. Once there, she looked at the sleeping figure she would risk everything for. He was as she remembered, flawless and real.

Not a dream, she told herself with a smile.

Tristan was not a dream. Their relationship was real and not a figment of her imagination. Being away from him for so long, she feared she may have forgotten the smooth contours of his face. The curve of his lips, the strength of his chin, the angles that made him so perfect, only she hadn't, she couldn't. No matter what those fools had told her or how many pills they had given her, she would never forget Tristan's face or their love.

She let the long white lab coat slide down her arms and onto the floor. The rest of her clothing soon followed. In only her panties now, Bianca gently lifted the sheets and slid into the bed beside Tristan. She ran her fingers gently through his short hair, down the side of his face, and over his chest. His body stirred under her fingertips. Leaning over him, she kissed his lips.

Tristan unconsciously responded to the kiss and the closeness of the warm body beside him. Still asleep, he pulled the feminine form closer to him. Moaning whispered words under his breath, he willingly kissed her back. Feeling the warmth of her body, her lips, he didn't want to wake up.

He knew that he was dreaming. That his fantasies would be stronger tonight. He often dreamed of them like this, together. He squeezed her tighter, loving that she felt so real.

Real. It was because their date had only been a few hours ago.

"Ci," Tristan moaned, but the taste of her lips was all wrong. He tasted her gloss again.

Tristan's body went rigid and he stopped responding to the kiss. He slowly opened his eyes and focused on the figure that was surrounded by the dark of the night. His hands fell from the embrace and he quickly pushed himself away. As he tried to stand his leg tangled in his sheet and he fell to the floor with a thump. Managing to stand almost instantly he looked at the beautiful woman in his bed.

"I see that you've missed my touch." Bianca smiled. He saw the twinkle in her eyes as she took in his naked body.

Tristan picked up his shorts that were lying at the foot of his bed and pulled them on. "Jesus Bianca, what are you doing here?" He looked around his room as he pulled his shorts up his legs.

"I've missed you so much." She kneeled on his bed. "And I know you missed me too."

Bianca thought his arousal was for her. She raised her arms to him but Tristan shook his head as he took a few steps back. "How did you get in here?"

Bianca dropped her arms and gave him a confused look. "Why are you being so discourteous Tristan?" She pouted.

Tristan searched the floor around his bed and when he found her clothes he handed the garments to her. "You need to put your clothes on." He avoided looking at Bianca as he waited for her to reluctantly dress. When she was clothed, he sat on the bed next to her. "Bianca," he said then sighed. "You shouldn't be here."

"You don't want me here?" She looked up at him with sad questioning eyes.

"I want you to get better."

"I'm fine," she whined, "and I want to be with you."

Tristan didn't respond right away. He just looked at Bianca while she looked at him. "I'm sorry," he said finally.

Bianca began to cry as she leaned into him. Tristan wiped her tears away as he held her. She was hurting and there was nothing he could do to ease her pain. He rubbed her back as she laid her head on his shoulder. They sat like that for a long time and when she fell asleep he stood and gently placed her head down on his pillow. Then he covered her with his sheet and swiftly left the room.

This was a mess. Guilt consumed Tristan as he walked into his office down the hall from his room. He knew what he had to do; he just didn't want to do it. He gritted his teeth as he searched through the directory on his desk. After a few false starts, he forced himself to pick up his land line again. He took in a deep breath before dialing the number.

"Hello, Mrs. Prescott?" Tristan took another deep breath. "This is Tristan, I'm sorry about calling so late." He listened then spoke. "Yes, she's here." He wasn't surprised to know that Bianca's parents were already looking for her.

Tristan waited while Bianca's mother informed her family that Bianca had been located. "No, I've done what you've asked me to. I haven't been returning her calls. No contact at all just as you requested." He listened again. "In my room, she's sleeping now. She's a little confused and upset." Tristan hated telling Mrs. Prescott that her daughter, whom he had broken up with, was upset because of him again. "I'm truly sorry about this whole situation Mrs. Prescott." He listened again. "I will. If there is anything I can do to help…" he started. She broke in, silencing him. "Ok." He hung up the receiver.

Tristan waited near his front door for what seemed like an eternity, but in reality, it was only about twenty-five minutes. He opened the door before the bell could be rung. Mrs. Prescott walked in followed by her husband and a couple of men he had never seen before.

"Thank you again, Tristan," Mrs. Prescott hugged him tightly.

Tristan hugged her back. "Hello, Mrs. Prescott." He looked to Bianca's father. "Mr. Prescott."

Mr. Prescott ignored Tristan and nodded to the two gentlemen who entered with them. They returned the nod, but Mr. Prescott just gave Tristan an empty stare.

Looking at Bianca's father now, people would have a hard time believing this was Harvey Prescott, the Real Estate king who always greeted everyone with a handshake and a smile. That Harvey Prescott was long gone, and in his place was a man with the look of defeat.

Tristan quickly looked away from Mr. Prescott's accusing eyes.

Mrs. Prescott pulled Tristan aside. "These men are here to help take Bianca back to the hospital. We don't want to upset her more than what she already is so if I could make a small request of you?"

Mr. Prescott's face turned from as pale as a ghost to the color of hot lava. Tristan knew that Bianca's father partly blamed him for what was happening to his daughter. In some small way, Tristan understood. He could only imagine how hard it must be for Mr. Prescott to be here and not be able to express his feelings about the matter because of his wife.

Mrs. Prescott felt differently though, she held no ill feelings toward him. She treated him as she always had, with kindness and respect. She repeatedly told him he had done nothing wrong, that Bianca was ill and it was no one's fault.

"What do you need me to do?" Tristan asked, willing to do just about anything.

"Could you keep out of sight while we bring her down? After you direct us to your room of course," she requested graciously.

Tristan pointed up, "It's the first door up the stairs." He watched them ascend the stairs before disappearing into the hearth room.

Chapter Nine

Last night had been the best night of her life. It was true that Cianne didn't have many nights to compare, but if she had, she was sure that last night would still be the best.

With the date still fresh in her mind, Cianne found it hard to focus on the conversation that was going on without her. The high she still felt was probably why she allowed Tranae to talk her into hanging out with her and her friends, in public. Her mind was so consumed with Tristan that she wasn't thinking clearly.

In an effort to keep her mind occupied with him, Tristan had sent her a beautiful crystal vase filled with a dozen long stemmed roses. His choice of color had struck her as odd, but then she read the card.

Cianne,
The orange thorn-less roses are a symbol of my infatuation for you. The single white bud is for your pure heart that hasn't known love, yet. I enjoyed spending time with you and I hope we can do it again real soon,

Truly yours, Tristan

When the doorbell rang that morning, her father had opened the door. Cianne wanted to scream with excitement, but she just stood at the top of the stairs with a blank expression on her face.

"Must have been some date," her father had said teasingly.

"The best," she had admitted.

Cianne hadn't stopped smiling since. Even as she sat at an outdoor ice cream parlor in Belleview Plaza with Tranae, Vanessa, and Brenda, her smile broadened. Tranae suggested that she either stay busy or sit in the house and drive herself crazy thinking of Tristan. Because she hadn't had a nightmare or a vision in a couple of days, cold refreshments at Belleview Plaza had won.

Cianne glanced up from her cell phone and looked at Tranae. She'd been talking for ten minutes straight. Cianne smiled and pretended she was listening to the conversation but she continued to glance at her phone, noting for the hundredth time that there were no new calls or text messages.

She sighed and placed her phone on the table next to her smoothie.

"Right, Cianne?" Tranae asked.

Cianne looked up from the table. If she wanted in on the conversation she would need to pay better attention. The last thing she remembered hearing was something about Tom. Tom was Tranae's ex-boyfriend who'd failed to inform Tranae he was dating a sophomore from some Catholic school in his old neighborhood.

Tom broke it off with the girl when Tranae found out but she dumped him anyway. To Tranae, relationships were an investment she didn't take lightly. So, she followed her "warning signs rules of dating". Tranae's philosophy was that every bad relationship had warning signs.

Some of the signs:
*If you meet a guy and he asks for your number but doesn't offer his own, he most likely has a girlfriend checking his phone.
*If a guy is usually hard to reach and can only spare a minute or two in a three-day period, warning sign. It maybe another woman or he's just busy, either way, it's a warning.
*If you don't see or hear from a guy until after 11 p.m. each night and the reasons aren't related to work, this would be a warning sign.

The list went on and on but Cianne had to focus on the here and now.

"Sure." Cianne agreed with Tranae even though she hadn't heard the question. Again, she tried to listen to the spirited conversation that everyone sitting at the table was so involved in. She lifted her cup and took a sip of her smoothie as she listened in.

"You think you know everything," Brenda said, sneering at Tranae. "Just because you are the queen of breakups doesn't make you an expert on men. I would think that with your track record, you would be considered more like a trainee."

Tranae smiled bitterly. "I can't expect you to understand, Brenda. You're not even smart enough to get to know a guy before dropping your panties. And for you, that would just mean getting a full name. Hell, a first name would be an improvement. What was the name of the last guy you hooked up with? Gator was what you called him, right? What was his first name, Brenda?"

Brenda stuck up her middle finger as an answer to Tranae's question. It was apparent that she didn't know Gator's real name. It was common knowledge that Brenda rushed into sex with every guy she thought liked her.

Cianne didn't think Brenda was a slut like some said. She could tell that Brenda liked the guys she hooked up with; that Brenda thought she and the guy had a connection. They usually did, but it was often disconnected after she gave them what they wanted.

"What's Gator's name Cianne?" Tranae twisted one corner of her mouth up as she glared at Brenda.

Brenda turned from Tranae and threw a restrained look of shock at Cianne that immediately turned into a grimace. Cianne hated cosigning when it came to petty arguing, even when it made Brenda, her least favorite person, look like a fool.

"I don't remember," Cianne said then shrugged.

"Why would Miss Goodie know his name?" Brenda rolled her eyes at Cianne.

"What is your problem today?" Vanessa demanded as she glared at Brenda.

Cianne had planned to keep out of this particular conversation but Brenda had a way of scraping at her sores. "George Fletcher," Cianne tossed out easily. "Would you like his phone number, address, and work number?"

"George has been trying to get with Cianne since last summer. He's been the perfect gentleman for two reasons. Reason one: he knows quality when he sees it. Reason two: he respects her because she respects herself. Your only asset is sex Brenda, and that's out the window as soon as the burger and fries digest. You should really try not to waste your *ass-sets*, Brenda." Tranae rolled her eyes.

Brenda didn't say a word. All she did was gawk at Cianne. Tranae, who had finished making her point, quickly moved on and was now speaking to Vanessa.

Cianne met Brenda's gaze for several seconds then looked to her phone. It wasn't anger she saw in Brenda's eyes that caused her to look away so fast. She would have been able to handle anger; it was the hurt she saw. Cianne wished she stayed indifferent and kept her mouth shut.

Vanessa tapped the table as she stood, gaining everyone's attention. "Anyone want to split a slice of cake with me?"

Brenda cleared her throat. "I could use another diet soda."

"I'll split a piece with you," Tranae said, as she stood. "You want something Cianne?"

"I'm good," Cianne lifted her half-finished smoothie. She watched them walk into the ice cream parlor, hoping the air would be clear between her and Brenda when they returned.

Not being the type to dwell, Cianne stretched her legs out under the table and looked up at the sky. It was clear and the sun beamed refreshing rays of light over everything. The beautiful September day might be salvageable if she could avoid any more drama.

Cianne picked up her phone and typed 'symbolic meanings for roses' on her keypad. She scrolled over several sites before finding one that had what she was looking for. Cianne read silently as her friends returned to their seats and started conversing again. What she read verified what Tristan's note said about roses.

"Are we leaving soon?" Brenda asked. Several minutes had passed since they'd sat back down but she still seemed to be upset.

"We happen to be enjoying ourselves if you want to leave be our guest." Tranae smirked. She reached for the center of the table and took another bite of chocolate cake with her fork.

"After I'm done my half of the cake, we can go. Why don't you get something to munch on?" Vanessa suggested. She stuck her fork into the other side of the cake she and Tranae shared. She lifted the fork to her mouth and chewed slowly as she moaned her delight for the chocolate treat.

Cianne looked at Vanessa. She was adorable. Her long wavy hair complimented her round face. Cianne truly liked her and wished there was a way they could be closer.

"I'm watching my figure," Brenda replied, as she slid her hand down the side of her torso.

That couldn't be further from the truth. Brenda was the leanest one of the four and she ate any and everything she wanted and still didn't gain an ounce.

The sudden sound of loud voices carried over to their table. Distracted, the girls looked for the source. Everyone, except for Cianne, looked up at the approaching group of guys that were headed their way. Brenda instantly sat up straighter, heaved her chest out, and flipped her shoulder length blonde hair back.

"Desperate dear?" Tranae teased, noticing Brenda's actions.

"You got some kind of hard on for me or something? Why are you riding me today?" Brenda asked angrily, totally missing the guy parade.

"Maybe I am sick of the way you pick on people," Tranae said, with disgust. "Maybe the bully needs a bully."

Cianne tuned the drama out again. This time she would act like she wasn't there and let Vanessa play referee as usual. While the bickering continued, Cianne's phone vibrated. *Good*, she thought, a distraction.

Hey. How r u? – Tristan

☺ n u. Luv the flowers – Cianne

☺ need 2 talk 2 u – Tristan

Call me – Cianne

Face to face – Tristan

Cianne's heart pounded with excitement. She was just about to tell Tranae that she was heading home when she heard a deep voice above her.

"Hey teach."

That name always made her cringe. Startled, Cianne let her phone slip from her hands as she looked up. "Nick." Her eyes confirmed what her mind had already processed.

No words of warning came to her with Nick. She didn't expect any either. The whispers were new and worked just like the visions. They were random, but she knew a few words that described Nick perfectly.

Cianne stood up and took a few steps back. Tranae got to her feet as well.

"Who's your friend, Cianne?" Brenda asked, in the most alluring voice she had.

Vanessa looked from Cianne to Tranae and then to Nick. She must have picked up on the tension because she tapped Brenda on the knee and slightly shook her head in warning.

Nick bent down and picked up Cianne's cell phone, which landed near his feet. He held it up like he wanted to give it back but teasingly kept it close to his body.

Cianne looked at his slightly outstretched hand. It was obvious he wanted her to come closer to him to get her phone. She reached out but Nick pulled the phone back. She quickly retracted her hand. She ran her fingers through her hair at the top of her head and looked away.

With several feet between them, it was still too close for her. She felt sick when Nick put a big smile on his deceptively handsome face as he held the phone out to her again.

This time Tranae reached around her and took the phone from his hands before he could react. "We were just leaving," Tranae said as she hastily stepped between them, grabbed Cianne by the hand, and started to walk off.

Nick quickly grabbed Cianne's free arm, taking hold of her wrist. "Teach and I have some catching up to do. Don't we teach?" His grip tightened.

"Let go of me." Cianne attempted to pull her wrist free. She grimaced as he tightened his grip again.

Nick and Cianne stared at each other. Her expression was one of fear and anger, his was one of wicked determination. Cianne had seen this look on his face before. It was a look that she hoped to never see again.

Nick smiled as he slowly moved his gaze over Cianne from her head to her feet, holding her hostage with his eyes. "Damn girl, you look good. But you know that already, don't you?"

By this time, Vanessa and Brenda seemed to realize that something was wrong. They were standing now and had made their way over behind Cianne.

"She's not interested in catching up with you," Tranae said, trying to pry them apart. "So, let go of her arm now before—"

"Before what," Nick demanded? "Are you her bodyguard?" He turned his attention from Cianne and cut his eyes at Tranae.

"Does she need one?"

Relief washed over Cianne but only for a brief moment. Fear replaced her relief as she spun her head around to see Tristan walking toward them.

"Does she need a bodyguard?" Tristan repeated; his words were spoken slowly, punctuating every syllable. He stepped between Cianne and Nick.

Nick let go of Cianne's wrist and looked Tristan over with a crooked smile. Brian, who Cianne hadn't noticed walking with Tristan, corralled all four girls and gently moved them a few feet away from where Tristan and Nick were standing.

"Are you ok?" Vanessa whispered to Cianne.

Cianne didn't respond. She nervously watched Tristan and Nick, hoping that they would just back away from each other but she somehow knew that wasn't going to happen.

Nick chuckled. "Is this white boy with you?" He looked at Cianne as he gestured to Tristan.

Cianne winced. "Don't do this Nick. We don't want any trouble," she pleaded. She started toward them, but Brian put his arm in front of her, blocking her path.

"I wouldn't get too close," Brian advised her.

Tranae took Cianne's hand and gently pulled her back a few more steps. Cianne was in full panic mode now. She looked from Nick to Tristan again. They were about the same height but Nick was a little bigger in the shoulders and arms.

"Look here, Dude," Nick said, sarcastically, "This is between me and her." Nick started past Tristan, toward

Cianne. At the same time, Brian stepped in front of Cianne and Tranae while Tristan moved directly into Nick's path, pushing him so hard that Nick stumbled into a table behind him.

This can't happen. Cianne searched the area for police or security guards. *Never around when you need them.*

But people were starting to notice them. That could be good; security always came when a crowd formed. Cianne looked to Tristan again. It was subtle but she noticed him doing some sort of hand signal. Then Brian reacted, blocking her and Tranae with his body.

Nick had stumbled back a few feet from the push but quickly recovered. He rushed forward, swinging at Tristan's face.

"STOP!" Cianne yelled. She tried to move forward but Brian held her back.

Tristan took a step back, steering clear of the first blow and ducking the second. When he saw an opening, he threw a right punch that connected with Nick's jaw. The blow almost knocked Nick off his feet.

Cianne yelled stop again when she realized that Nick had been stunned by the blow. She had a small window of opportunity to stop this madness. While Nick struggled to steady himself, Cianne pushed Brian's arm away and jumped in front of Tristan.

Tristan never took his eyes off Nick as he quickly moved Cianne behind him. At the same time, a large man who was eating a few tables away jumped up and grabbed Nick. This wasn't hard to do because Nick seemed to be still trying to find his bearings. Another man, who was much smaller than the one who had grabbed Nick, stepped into the empty space in front of her and Tristan. He looked prepared to hold Tristan if he tried to get to Nick.

Cianne pulled at Tristan's arm. "Please Tristan, stop," she begged.

Tristan, who had been watching Nick, looked at her for the first time since he arrived. For a brief moment, it seemed as if he had been waiting for her to tell him what to do as if he was in a trance. Then Tristan blinked and noticeably relaxed.

"Please…let's go," Cianne begged, as she tugged on his arm again.

Tristan looked over at Nick and the man who was holding him up.

"We should probably get out of here." Tranae touched Cianne's shoulder.

Cianne saw the urgency in Tranae's eyes. Her friend didn't want to get caught in another altercation. She'd be grounded for a year instead of a few days. Cianne wasn't too comfortable with getting in trouble either, only she wasn't about to leave Tristan to take the fall alone. She just had to get him to go with them.

"She's right," Brian added.

Maybe it was Tristan's sense of self-preservation that had kicked in or maybe Brian had gotten through to him because he started walking away from the scene. As the six of them pushed through the gathering crowd, Nick began yelling threats at Tristan. Vanessa was the only one to turn around to look at him, her face pinched with concern. They all continued to walk until they didn't hear Nick's curses.

Vanessa was the first to speak. "My car is back there." She pointed back in the direction they'd come from. Everyone stopped, forming a distorted circle.

Tristan turned to Cianne. Taking hold of her wrist, he lifted it to inspect the bruise that was beginning to appear. "Are you alright?"

He sounded so calm that it was unsettling.

"I'm fine." Cianne pulled away from him. She took Tranae by the hand and tugged her over toward where Vanessa and Brenda were huddled. "Can you take us home now, Vanessa?"

"Uh, sure," Vanessa said, almost whispering.

Cianne noticed that Vanessa wasn't looking at her so she followed her gaze and saw that she was eyeing Tristan. When

Tristan met her gaze, Vanessa blushed then reached for Brenda's hand as he walked over to them. Brenda, who Cianne noticed was also staring at Tristan, began swatting Vanessa's hand away.

"I'll take you home Cianne," Tristan insisted, looking at her.

Cianne turned to glare at him then turned back to Vanessa who apparently was still under Tristan's spell. "Vanessa?" Cianne waved her hand in front of Vanessa's face.

"Oh…uh," Vanessa looked down at her watch. "I'm sorry Cianne. I can't. I was just about to leave before everything got crazy. I'm already late." She looked over at Tristan and blatantly winked an eye. "Won't you let Tristan take you home, Cianne?"

Were Vanessa and Tristan working together?

The world was against her and so was her potential friend.

Tristan still wasn't sure if Cianne was angry with him or why she might be. No one spoke during the brief ride to Cianne's house. So, he decided to wait until she spoke first so he would know what her mood was.

He pulled into her driveway but before he stopped the truck, Cianne opened the passenger door and was practically running to her house.

Tranae opened the rear passenger door and slowly got out of the truck. "Thanks for the ride, Tristan." She closed the door. "And thanks for earlier."

"Just glad I was there," he said, as he got out his truck. He looked to Cianne's front door but she had already gone inside.

"Tell Cianne to call me later," Tranae called over her shoulder as she walked in the opposite direction.

"Sure," Tristan said dismissively, as he shut his door. He took his time as he walked up the path to Cianne's house. She had left the door open, though he was uncertain whether she had for him or Tranae. Shrugging, he walked inside anyway and closed the door behind him. "Cianne," he called out.

Cianne appeared in a doorway that was directly across from the kitchen entrance; he figured it was either a bathroom or a basement. She glanced over at him before walking down the short hall toward the living room.

Tristan hurried to her side. He reached for her arm and pulled her gently to him. When he turned her around so that they were face to face, she avoided looking at him so he lifted her chin. Once again, he got lost as he gazed into her beautiful eyes.

"I'm so sorry," Cianne said before he could find his voice. "I didn't think he would still be..." She lowered her head again.

Tristan could hear the sadness in her voice and it caused a reaction in him he didn't expect. He felt his chest tighten as if someone was actually squeezing his heart. Tristan shut his eyes for a brief moment to attempt to calm whatever was happening to him. When he opened them, the feeling had not gone away, it only intensified. Somehow, he knew that her sadness was the reason for the aching pain he felt. Somehow, they were connected.

Maybe it was their sudden closeness or perhaps it had to do with kissing her before. Whatever the case, Tristan couldn't stand to see her hurting in any way. He sat her down on her living room sofa and positioned himself next to her. It should frighten him, this new sensation and development but for some reason, it didn't. Tristan decided then that he'd gladly accept whatever came his way, for her.

"What do you have to be sorry about?"

"For putting you in this situation, you could have gotten hurt. You don't know Nick like I do. I saw him really hurt a guy once," she said, as she looked at him. "We've only been on one date and already my crap is spilling over into your life." Her brows furrowed in frustration. "I don't think it's a good idea for you to get involved with me, Tristan. My life…I am so damaged."

Tristan searched her eyes to see if she was jesting but realized that Cianne was serious. "First of all, you didn't put me in any situation, I chose to get involved. Second, I'm pretty sure I am old enough to decide who I want to involve myself with." Tristan pushed himself back on the sofa. "My life isn't all sunshine and roses, Cianne. I'm just glad I was there because if I had heard about it later, I would have been very, very angry. I would have had to pay this Nick a visit."

"Right," Cianne said, her laugh was hollow, "because that wasn't you angry earlier?"

"No," Tristan said. He flashed his best smile, exposing his perfect white teeth. "That wasn't me angry." He pulled her back against the backrest of the sofa and put his arm around her shoulder. Cianne gasped from his sudden movement or their contact but she settled herself down. "Now would you like to tell me why this Nick felt it necessary to manhandle you?"

"Nick is the guy I used to tutor. The one I told you about last night," she admitted.

"That was *the* asshole?" Tristan tensed as he sucked in air through his clenched teeth. He wished he had known earlier that Nick was *the* guy. He looked at Cianne as she watched him. A tinge of heartache passed through him again. She was upset by his reaction. He needed to compose himself…for now. "Need a hug?" Tristan asked playfully.

"Actually," Cianne said, as she snuggled into his chest. "A hug would be perfect right now."

Tristan wrapped his arms around her.

Cianne felt so at ease in Tristan's firm—and to her relief—capable arms. She closed her eyes and listened to his beating heart while he gently combed his fingers through her hair. She could sit like this forever.

Of course, she thought, *this may not be what I think it is.* He could be just being nice to her, and not mean for his actions to seem so much like a relationship.

She promised herself that she wouldn't assume anything without him clearly stating what they were to each other.

What if he just wants to be friends?

Did she care? Tristan was here and he was with her. Nothing else mattered.

All Cianne wanted was for him to continue holding her.

She sat up and looked at him. "We have been so occupied with my mess that I forgot you wanted to talk to me about something"

Tristan almost forgot that he wanted to talk to her. "Yeah," he winced. With her snuggly fitted against him, Tristan felt so good that he was selfish enough to keep her there. To keep what he wanted to tell her to himself so that he could continue to hold her. He didn't want to let go just yet. They fit together perfectly.

Like we were made for one another, he thought, as he released her grudgingly.

"I want to say something to you first. I want this…" he said as he moved his hands between them, "us…to evolve into something more. Not saying that I want to rush things, because I don't. I just want to get to know you and I want you to get to know me. That being said, something happened last night that I wanted to talk to you about." Tristan sat on the edge of the sofa and turned to face her. "Bianca and I called it quits at the beginning of the year." He rubbed his hands together nervously. "I'm only telling you this because it wasn't a normal split."

"A normal split?" Cianne sat up. "I'm not an expert or anything but none of the split ups I've heard about over the last few years could be considered normal."

"Bianca is having trouble understanding that we aren't a couple anymore and that we will never be again."

"She loves you," Cianne surmised. Her eyes did that sheepish thing that women's eyes did when they learn of something beautifully sad.

Tristan shook his head. "It's not that simple, Cianne. We split up a few times before. We usually worked things out but this time it's different. As soon as she realized that, she sank into a deep depression. I assumed that she was just going through the breakup blues and that she would be fine in a few days. But a few months went by and she was still depressed, so I went to her house, to try and talk to her. I wanted to let her know that just because we weren't a couple anymore didn't mean we couldn't still be friends.

"Mr. Prescott, her father, answered the door and instantly started yelling and pushing me off their porch. Bianca, of course, heard the commotion and came to the door. When she saw me she immediately ran to my defense, telling her father that he couldn't talk to me that way. That she and I were going to be married and that he should apologize to me at once. I couldn't move or speak. As a matter of fact, her father was more shocked than I was. We just stared at her. She looked so different, not like the Bianca I knew. She was so much thinner and she had dark circles under her eyes.

"By the time her mother came outside, Bianca was holding on to me so tightly that I could barely breathe. Her father had stopped yelling and he had sat on their porch steps with his head buried in his hands, sobbing. After about ten minutes, Mrs. Prescott convinced Bianca to let go of me, and to go into the house to get herself presentable. Once Bianca had gone inside, Mrs. Prescott asked me to drive to a coffee shop up the road and wait for her. I did.

"When she arrived at the shop, she explained to me that Bianca wasn't doing so well. That they were going to have her evaluated at some hospital in Phoenix. She said that this was necessary because Bianca had experienced a few episodes of mental illness when she was younger but nothing this severe. Mrs. Prescott asked me not to correspond with Bianca at all until she is well again. She said that a clean break was best and this was the only way Bianca was going to get better."

Cianne remained silent for a good while after he finished his story. That made Tristan nervous, real nervous.

"How long has she been in the hospital?"

"I'm not sure. I think since the end of May." He continued to rub his hands together.

"I feel sad for her." Cianne sighed. "And for her family, but why tell me any of this?"

"Of course, this should be kept private but I want us to start off right. No lies, no secrets. I can't explain it but I feel something between us. Don't you?" he asked. Cianne waited a few heartbeats then nodded. Tristan smiled at her admission. "When I first saw you, I felt it but you didn't give me a second glance." Tristan's grin faded then he frowned. "I care about Bianca. She'll always be my friend and I want to be there for her when she needs me."

"I understand completely," Cianne said. She laid her head back on his chest and he wrapped his arms around her again.

Chapter Ten
December

"What about this?" Cianne asked. She held up a beige sweater with a high collar that zipped up the front. She twisted the hanger around to give Tranae a view of the sweater from all angles.

"I told you what to give him," Tranae said, as she typed something in her cell phone. She had been sitting on the round ottoman in front of the mirrors that lined the store's wall for so long people were beginning to ask her questions as if she worked there. Looking extremely bored, Tranae glanced at the sweater that swayed in front of her.

Cianne looked the sweater over again before she placed it back on the rack. She slid a few more items around the rack before moving to another. After a few moments more of searching, she looked over at Tranae and flashed a desperate look.

"Cianne," Tranae whined. "If you don't want to give him what I told you, then just get him the damn sweater. The first one you showed me is fine." Tranae tapped on her knees in frustration.

They had been to several stores and Cianne still couldn't decide on one measly item yet. "I don't remember the first one I showed you." Cianne sluggishly walked over to where Tranae sat. "Let's go to the food court, I'm hungry."

Maybe food would help her think. They had been out all day looking for the perfect Christmas gift for Tristan and neither of them had eaten. Besides, Tranae looked as if she could use a break.

Tranae stood, her expression one of relief and joy. Cianne took her friend by the hand and they walked through the mall to the food court where they ordered and sat.

"If you're not ready, then you're not ready. But it's been almost four months." Tranae lifted the gigantic burrito to her mouth and bit into it just as the last word came out.

Cianne pulled her attention away from a couple sitting a few tables away. Over the last ten minutes, she and Tranae discussed a book that had been turned into an HBO series, some school assignments Tranae needed help with and a very nice pair of boots that they had seen in the leather store. Yet, Cianne could only think of the comment Tranae had made when she showed her the last sweater in the extremely expensive store they were in.

When Tranae said it, Cianne had tried to ignore her. Not because she didn't want to talk to Tranae about it, she actually did. She ignored the comment because she didn't want to discuss it with strangers listening in. Even though they were still inside the mall, being seated at the small table seemed more intimate.

"It's not that I'm not ready," Cianne blurted out. She figured she might as well get it off her chest because it was driving her crazy and she needed the advice of her best friend. "*He's* not ready."

Tranae halted her assault on the burrito and looked curiously at Cianne. Her face wrinkled into a frown. "*He's* not ready?" Tranae repeated.

"We're just good friends, sort of." Cianne shrugged.

"Good friends," Tranae echoed, "really? Is that what you two are?"

"I guess so. I mean, yeah." Cianne was confused herself.

She and Tristan spent a lot of their time together. So much time that Tranae and Brian agreed to go on a double date just to hang out with the elusive pair. That date led to Brian and Tranae becoming a couple, more of a couple than Cianne and Tristan were. In the two months that Tranae and Brian have been dating, they went from first base to third and will soon be sliding into home plate.

"I don't think he's into me like that. Maybe he was at one point, but I guess he figures we make better friends now."

Cianne didn't know what she had done for Tristan to have changed the way he felt about her. In the beginning, the attraction between them was undeniable, and it still was for her. She still had trouble thinking straight when Tristan was around. However, as the days turned into weeks, things had cooled down considerably.

Tristan barely held her hand now. Aside from their lack of intimacy, everything had been so perfect for the past three months. Even her visions, the headaches, and nightmares were all but gone. Tristan had no knowledge of those issues so she couldn't blame them for his loss of interest. She was sure she hadn't in any way let her precious secrets out. Though, the fact remained, Tristan hadn't shown her nor told her that he was interested in being more than friends.

"Make the first move girl. He's crazy about you and you know it."

"I couldn't do that and embarrass myself. I like being around him and I don't want to risk our friendship by making him uncomfortable."

He hadn't made any advances toward her at all. Even when he kissed her now it was on the cheek, like a guy kissing his mother. It was nothing like the way he kissed her on their first date and yet the innocent strokes of his lips on her skin created the same reaction in her as the kiss on the lips had.

"Tristan is head over heels for you Cianne. Brian says so and he should know. What do you think? He stays and sits with all of us at lunch because he enjoys our conversations?"

Tranae laughed. "And he gets up early almost every day to drive us to school because he needs the company? You have one of the hottest guys in the world pining over you, well other than Brian of course."

"Of course," Cianne said as she smirked.

"So, let him know you're into him as much as he's into you. He's probably playing it safe because you're a virg-, uh, inexperienced." Tranae stopped before she said the word.

"A virgin," Cianne groaned.

A look of regret instantly covered Tranae's face. "Look, do you want me to ask Brian what his problem is?"

Cianne gasped. "God no!"

Tranae held up her hands in defense. "Calm down."

"Besides," Cianne said, "maybe getting involved right now wouldn't be a great idea anyway."

Tranae froze, her burrito was mere inches from her mouth. "It's not a big deal, Cianne. I'm a big girl you know." Tranae placed the half-eaten burrito back on the foil. "You think it's a bad idea because you're going away, right?"

Cianne would have kicked herself in the butt if it were possible. "Isn't it?"

"Not if he goes to a college close to you. Couples do it all the time." Tranae half smiled.

Cianne avoided talking about college because of all the denial letters that Tranae had received from their colleges of choice. She didn't like discussing sensitive subjects. She preferred to avoid them altogether and just deal with the results.

"Couples," Cianne said under her breath. "We're not a couple." The ringing of her cell phone had her lifting it out of her purse. "We've talked him up," she said, hitting the silence button.

"You're not going to talk to him?" Tranae asked, surprised.

Cianne had never silenced a call from Tristan before and Tranae probably knew it. "No. He will only distract me. We came all this way, to a Mall that is way too expensive, to get a gift for him, and I'm still not close to finding one. So no, I am not going to talk to him."

"Well, let's do this then." Tranae packed up her food. "It's only a few days left until Christmas and I can't do this again tomorrow."

They walked toward stores they hadn't checked yet. "What did you get Brian?" Cianne sipped her soda as they moved through the crowd.

"I'm giving Brian exactly what I told you to give Tristan," Tranae said with a grin. "It's the best gift he will ever receive—me."

Cianne covered her mouth to silence her gasp.

"A nice eight-by-ten photo," Tranae squealed as she bumped into Cianne. They laughed.

Cianne used her shoulder to nudge her front door open. She used her knee to hold and stabilize the box under her arm as she shimmied over the threshold. With her keys and a heavy bag in one hand, she dipped and lifted the three bags off the porch with her other hand, and placed them just inside the door. With everything inside, she dropped the bags and her keys to the floor and reached for her ringing cell phone.

"Hello," she said, winded and tired. She used her foot to slide the bags further inside so she could shut and lock the front door.

"Cianne, what's wrong?"

She smiled at Tristan's brotherly concern for her safety. "Nothing's wrong," she said, trying to slow her breathing. "How's New York?"

Tristan exhaled then said something under his breath.

Wow, she thought, *he must have really been worried.*

When Tristan spoke again the tension was gone in his voice. "Cold," he said, laughing. "I called you earlier. Did you get my message?"

"No, I'm sorry. I've been a little busy." She forgot to shut the door so she reached to close and lock it.

"You're just getting in?" he asked, sounding a little irritated.

He must have heard the door shut. "Yeah, Jess drove me and Tranae to that classy mall I've been dying to go to." She made her way to the living room and flopped down on the sofa, exhausted.

"You wouldn't need a ride from Jessie if you would have let me leave my truck with you."

"I'm not really comfortable driving your truck Tristan," she told him. Tristan fell silent. Cianne listened to him breathe for a while, wondering what he was thinking. Now it was her turn to ask if something was wrong. "Are you still there?" She chickened out.

"Yeah," he finally said. "I'm still here. I guess I assumed you were more comfortable with me than you really are." Before she could respond he sighed. "Uh, could you hold for a moment Cianne?"

Is he disappointed? Why? Cianne heard it in his voice.

"Sure," she said. She sat forward and was about to get up from the sofa to get a drink when she heard a female's voice through the line. Cianne sat back and pressed her phone closer to her ear. It *was* a female's voice all right, but Cianne couldn't hear what the woman was saying. Tristan must have covered his phone with his palm.

"I can't control the weather, Lela. If you want, I can take you out to dinner tonight. Some place fancy. Go ahead and get cleaned up," he said to the mystery voice, "I'll just be another second." Several seconds passed before he came back to the phone. "Cianne, can I call you back later?"

"Sure," Cianne said. Tristan hung up the phone before she could even say goodbye. Cianne looked at her phone, confused.

*I guess we **are** just good friends.*

She slowly placed her phone on the coffee table then walked absently into the kitchen. When she turned on the kitchen light, a yellow sticky note stuck to the refrigerator was the first thing she noticed in the room.

"I won't be home in time for dinner so start without me." She read. "Your grandmother sent you a package. I put it in your room. Love you, dad."

Awesome, Cianne stuck the note on her shirt sleeve and opened the refrigerator. She grabbed a bottle of water and closed the door. She then turned off the kitchen lights before grabbing the bags in the hallway and jogging up the stairs to her room. She would come down later for the box.

Eleven forty-eight p.m. was the time highlighted in blue on the face of Cianne's phone. She looked at the incoming number through squinted eyes. *Nine-one-eight area code*, Cianne rolled over on her side.

"Hello," she said drowsily.

"Hey you," a familiar voice said into the receiver. "Were you asleep?"

"I was...but I'm up now."

"I'm sorry to be calling so late, it's just that time means nothing here. I just wanted to see what you've decided." Tristan's voice was quiet, yet always sexy

"Decided about what?" she asked.

"Did you listen to the message? The one I left you earlier."

"No, I didn't. I'm sorry," she apologized. Cianne had come upstairs and wrapped all her last-minute gifts, played some games on her networking site, and fell asleep while watching "Sleepless in Seattle".

"Not a problem, I can just ask you now," he said. "I wanted to come over on Christmas and give you your gift and maybe hang out for a while if you're not busy."

"I thought you were going to be there until the 27th? Won't your parents miss you on Christmas Day?" Cianne grunted as she rose up on one arm.

"My parents aren't here in New York, they're in St. Thomas," he said. "I figure we can hang out. Maybe watch some of those movies you talk about, no biggie if you can't."

"I can," Cianne said quickly. She hoped he couldn't tell how excited she was.

It was cute how he would always ask permission to hang out with her. They hung out often enough that she figured he would just assume he could come over, but he always asked her permission.

"We can totally hang out," she said, trying to sound nonchalant.

Before Tristan could respond someone spoke in the background on his end. It sounded like the same voice she heard earlier. At first, the words were muffled but when the sugary voice spoke again the words were coherent.

"I thought you were staying here with me for Christmas?" the woman said.

"We can talk about it tomorrow Lela. Go back to bed," Tristan replied.

Cianne heard the subtle hint of agitation in his voice.

"Cianne," Tristan said. "I'll call you tomorrow if that's ok?"

Cianne didn't answer right away. The same woman who was in his room earlier was still there. "Uh huh," she said finally.

"Goodnight," he said. Tristan hung up before she could reply, again.

Chapter Eleven

It was finally Christmas day. Cianne had all but driven herself mad about Tristan's gift. *It's too late now. You have to live with your choice*, she said to herself as she got out of bed.

After she polished herself up for the day, she went to the kitchen and prepared a nice breakfast for her father. When he came downstairs the table was set and Cianne was placing their food on plates.

"Looks good," he smiled, then kissed her on the cheek, "Merry Christmas, Buttercup."

"Merry Christmas, Dad," she said as she leaned into him.

Cianne handed her father the syrup for his pancakes and sat down across from him. She watched as he took his first bite. When a smile lit across his face, she decided it was ok for her to eat. They ate in silence for a few minutes then her father cleared his throat.

"So how long has it been now since your last vision?"

Cianne noticed his body had stiffened as he waited for her response. "No nightmares since the end of September and no visions in two whole months." Her smile was bigger than it had been in years and her father noticed.

Relief washed over his concerned face then he smiled. "That's good sweetheart." His smile faltered a little. "But don't get too excited, alright."

She knew what he thought. That this reprieve of hers was only a remission that may not last. What Cianne hadn't failed to miss was the certainty in his tone.

Does he know something that he isn't telling me?

"What time is Tristan getting in?" Her father changed the subject.

Cianne shrugged off her suspicion. The thought of Tristan always overpowered her senses. "Umm, I don't know."

"I feel better when you have someone around when I'm gone."

"Don't worry, Dad. I'll be fine even if he doesn't show." Cianne picked at the remaining scraps on her plate as she scraped her teeth over her bottom lip. When she noticed that her father's eyes had narrowed, she quickly straightened up and placed a piece of cold pancake in her mouth.

"What's wrong?" he asked, as he pushed both their plates aside.

"I think Tristan has a girlfriend."

Cianne couldn't talk to Tranae about it because whatever she said to her friend would eventually get to Tristan, delivered special in a typhoon hell-storm of fire and accusations, courtesy of Tranae. Her friend wouldn't act out of malice but out of concern, and everything would be blown way out of proportion.

"But you don't know for sure." Joseph looked doubtful.

"No," she admitted. "I guess I don't."

"I think Tristan likes you just as much as you like him and I don't think he would mess that up," her father told her. "Believe me Buttercup; I'm a good judge of character. Tristan's one of the good ones."

What her father said wasn't all true. Cianne didn't *like* Tristan. She hadn't *liked* him since that first kiss. What she felt was more than just being fond of him. Liking would be less painful.

"I know he is but… I don't know dad," Cianne said.

"The best advice I can give you is to just talk to him. Let him know how you feel about him. That's about all you can do."

Cianne gave him a half smile.

"Now are you sure you don't want to go with me?" he asked her.

Cianne looked into her handsome father's gentle brown eyes. She couldn't count the number of times he held her tight when she woke up screaming for her mother in the middle of the night. He, who loved her no less than he could have loved his own child, was the best thing in her life. Yet, if she could avoid going to his family's holiday party, she would.

"Yup, I'm sure," she said, kissing his cheek before she stood.

"You will be missed," he told her. "You know that Brandon was hoping to see you. His mother told me that he has pulled out all the stops this year, just for you."

"No offense dad," she said, frowning, "but your nephew is a creeper."

Cianne shuddered at the thought of sitting at the dinner table beside Brandon Baxter. He was a gangly seventeen-year-old with all the afflictions a teen could have. She could deal with his abnormally tall stature, his braces, and the acne, but the squeal that was his voice could drive the biblical Job mad. Despite it all, Brandon was quite confident. He professed his love for her to whoever would listen, including Cianne herself.

Christmas dinner, every year, was a game of Cianne hide and Brandon sought.

"None taken, Buttercup," he said, laughing, "but what is a creeper?"

"He's a crazy stalker weirdo, Dad!" Cianne said. She stood and started clearing the table.

"Oh! I knew that," he said, jokingly. "I guess I'd better get going then." He stood up and left the kitchen.

When Cianne met him in the hall, he had on his jacket and hat.

Her father glanced at his watch. "I wanted to see Tristan before I left but—" Just then, a hard knock sounded at the door, cutting off Joseph's words.

Cianne felt excited for a moment but then realized that it couldn't be Tristan, he never knocked that hard. So, she let her father answer the door while she checked the bags to make sure he had all the gifts he was taking with him.

"Merry Christmas, Mr. Baxter!"

That is Tristan's voice.

Cianne's heart leaped with excitement again but she immediately calmed herself by silently counting. When she looked up, she saw Brian holding the end of a large wrapped box. Her father held the door open, and at the other end of the box, she saw Tristan. When Tristan saw her, he smiled, setting off the flighty butterflies in her stomach.

Cianne stepped aside as they carried the large box inside. Brian passed by, giving her a nod. When Tristan reached her, he stopped and kissed Cianne on her cheek. She blushed at the contact, as usual.

"Hey you," Tristan said.

"Where's it going?" Brian called out.

Cianne snapped out of her Tristan-induced haze to look at the box.

"Downstairs, in the family room," Tristan replied.

Cianne scooted past Brian and opened the basement door. She went down the steps first and directed Brian to place the large festive wrapped box in an empty area.

Joseph appeared just as the guys placed the box gently on the floor.

"Merry Christmas Mr. Baxter," Tristan said again as he motioned cheerfully to the box.

"This is for me?" Joseph stepped around Tristan and Brian to look at the box.

"Open it, Daddy!"

Her father hesitated for a moment, as if he wasn't going to, then he ripped the wrapping paper off to reveal a brown box with a large picture of a flat television on it. "Fifty-five inches," he said slowly. "Tristan, this is uh..." He opened his arms wide, sizing up the television. "I love it, man," he said. Joseph laughed. "But it's uh."

"It'll only take us a few minutes to hook it up," Tristan said as he waved to Brian.

Brian picked up on Tristan's urgency and began unplugging the cables from the thirty-two-inch box set that was on the TV stand.

"Yeah but—," Joseph started.

"It's no problem Mr. B," Brian said, unscrewing the last cable from the old TV. "I handle all installations of electronics in my house." He lifted the old TV off the stand and placed it out of the way. Tristan already had the new television box open and Cianne held the box still as Tristan and Brian pulled the television out. They gently placed it on the TV stand and Brian quickly got to work hooking up the cables.

"It looks really good, Dad," Cianne said as she stood by his side.

Joseph watched quietly as Tristan and Brian connected his gift. Cianne reached into the box and took out the remote from its protective package, inserted the batteries provided, and tuned it until a picture came in.

"The picture is so clear," Cianne said with awe. She looked at her father and could tell he was trying to figure out how he could refuse the gift. She flipped through the channels until she found something sports related.

"It really does have a crisp picture," Joseph said under his breath.

"You are going to be late if you don't leave now daddy." Cianne reminded him.

Her father glanced over at her. "Yeah," he said, rubbing the back of his head. "I almost forgot." He turned to Tristan who was now standing at his side. "I don't know what to say."

Tristan shrugged. "Merry Christmas will do." He extended his hand.

Her father shook Tristan's hand then pulled him into a man hug. "Merry Christmas," he said merrily. "I'm inviting you and Brian over for Super Bowl Sunday, to really break her in."

"We're going to hold you to that," Tristan said.

"I'm in." Brian walked over to the steps and followed Cianne's father up. "I'm outta here too. Tranae and I will be over in a few," he called down the stairs.

"Alright," Tristan called back.

Cianne felt Tristan watching her. She nervously rocked on her heels a couple of times before looking back at him. "I'm going to make sure the door is locked." Cianne hurried away. She bounced up the stairs thinking how she missed him while he was away. The desire to run to him, to wrap her arms around him, to kiss him as she slowly traced her fingers up and down his neck while inhaling his intoxicating scent, was almost unbearable.

She fought it though because they were just friends.

The problem was that Cianne always felt like jumping into Tristan's arms, especially when he returned from Houston with his father every now and then. The two days he was usually gone wasn't too bad and she still missed him, but this time he had been gone for five days, thousands of miles away...

She hadn't just missed Tristan. She felt lost without him.

Cianne realized as she checked the locks that she didn't care about the woman whose voice she heard in Tristan's room. He wasn't her boyfriend. He hadn't betrayed her in any way. In a weird twisted way, she couldn't fault anyone who fell under Tristan's spell.

Hadn't she fallen?

Tristan took a moment to look around the basement. Even though they'd been friends for months, he rarely spent time inside Cianne's home. He had only been in the basement twice and both times were mere fleeting moments.

The nice size room was split into three sections. The sitting area, located in the center of the room, was decorated with an oversized tan sectional and a wall unit entertainment system. To the left, was a pool table, a bar, and four stools. To the right of the bar was the sitting room. This was definitely a man cave and the new television fit nicely.

Tristan walked over to the pictures that hung on wall shelves by the stairs. The pictures showed Cianne at different ages of her life. One photo stood out from all the rest. In an 8 x 10 wooden beveled frame was a family portrait. Tristan studied the photo. Cianne looked about three or four years old, with two long ponytails that were tied with yellow ribbons. A younger Mr. Baxter and a beautiful Black woman, who had to be Cianne's mother, smiled as they sat beside Cianne.

Tristan could see a slight resemblance between Cianne and who he assumed was her mother but he was a little confused.

"Don't look at those," Cianne said, pulling him away by his arm.

"Wait," he teased as he halfheartedly resisted, "you were so cute." Cianne dragged him over to the couch and pulled him down so that they sat side by side. "So where is your dad off to?" Tristan asked.

"To his sister's house for Christmas dinner." Cianne smiled. "We usually go every year."

He loved the way her green eyes sparkled as she spoke. "Why didn't you say something? I would have gone with you if you wanted to go."

She shook her head. "It's no biggie. Besides my Dad's nephew has a crush on me. It used to be cute, now it's just weird." Cianne cringed.

"You mean your cousin has a crush on you," Tristan said. It was more of an inquiry than a statement. The picture he just viewed of her and her parents sparked a few questions.

"My Dad's family never really looked at me as his daughter even though he adopted me," Cianne told him. "I see us as cousins but Brandon doesn't," she added. "So, how was your Christmas morning?"

"Hmmm," Tristan said as he rubbed his chin, "a reluctant cousin with a crush. I would have loved to witness you guys at dinner. I think we can still catch up with your dad."

Cianne playfully smacked his shoulder. Tristan grabbed her hand, pulling her close. With barely an inch between them, they stared into each other's eyes. In hers, Tristan saw life, beauty, passion, and…fear, before she broke the connection and pulled back.

"So…how was your Christmas morning?" Cianne asked again.

Tristan half smiled, wondering if she pulled away to avoid a kiss. He dismissed her reaction and leaned back. "My parents and I haven't really celebrated Christmas since I was about ten. I exchanged gifts with Celia, Ben, and Martha though. We do it every year, so I always get something."

"Aww, poor baby." Cianne pouted teasingly. She got to her feet and walked over to the bar, reaching behind it. "I have something for you." When she came back to the sofa she carried a wide gift box. "Merry Christmas, Tristan." She extended her arms and the box to him.

Masking the pleasure he felt when she said his name, Tristan took the box and placed it on his lap. He pulled the top of the box up and was rewarded with the scent of leather. It swirled around him before he even pulled back the thin white paper. Lifting the leather jacket from the box, Tristan held it up.

"I love it," he said, but his voice suggested something else and he could tell she picked up on it.

"If you don't like it we can exchange it for something else."

"No," he said quickly, "I really like it. It's just…I would have rather you gotten me something a little less expensive."

"Don't do that Tristan," Cianne said. "You haven't let me pay for a single thing the entire time we've been hanging out, so please just accept my gift, *if* you like it."

"Honestly Ci, I love it." He kissed her on the cheek.

◉

It was the second time today Tristan had kissed her on the cheek. She watched as he stood up and tried the jacket on, hoping that her irritation didn't show on her face. Just five seconds ago it seemed like he wanted to kiss her. Really kiss her, but she moved away. Damn her nerves.

"It fits nice," Tristan said, as he zippered it up. He unzipped his new jacket and placed it on the arm of the sofa. When he sat back down he sat closer to her than he was before. "I need to tell you about something."

Tristan sounded more serious than she had ever heard before, but he looked calm. His calmness meant nothing because Tristan had the most stoic demeanor and facial expressions than any person she ever met, even when he was upset. Though, she was worried about what he wanted to say. Cianne turned her entire body around so they could be face to face.

"I've been thinking about us." He said plainly. "We've been hanging out for a little over three months now and it's been fun. I like hanging out with you."

Cianne listened to every word carefully as she felt her chest began to ache. She waited for him to say what she was expecting from the very beginning. She nervously nibbled on her bottom lip. He wanted to move on.

"I can't…wait," Tristan said. He stretched out his leg and pulled something from his pocket. "I know that we haven't really talked about it but I was hoping that..." He held what he took from his pocket up in front of her.

Cianne eyebrows crinkled inward and her eyes narrowed as she focused on the little white leather box that had black stitching around the edges. She lifted her gaze to his face again, focusing on his smiling eyes, then back to the box. She started to lift her hand to take it but nervously pulled her hand back.

◉

Her hesitation only strengthened his desire for her. Tristan wanted to pull Cianne to him and kiss her so passionately, so lovingly that his soul would imprint on hers. But, he just laughed as he pulled the top of the box back to reveal its contents.

Cianne blinked slowly as she looked blankly at the box. He saw every thick dark lash close over her eyes and watched as they lightly brushed the skin above her cheeks.

God, she drove him crazy.

"This ring, if you accept it, is my promise to you," he said. The beautiful sapphire and diamond ring set in a platinum band shimmered as the lights in the ceiling struck it. "It signifies my honesty, my dedication, my desire and," he paused, "my trust in you. I want to be more than just your friend, Cianne." Tristan lowered the box. "But if you feel that friendship is all you have to give me, then you should close this box and I will try very hard to be a good friend to you."

Tristan watched as Cianne closed her eyes again. She took a deep breath then let it slowly seep out. She looked at the small box he held then back to him. He imagined that she would be a little shocked, maybe even speechless, but what he didn't see coming were the tears that formed in her eyes.

"Please don't cry."

Tristan placed the box on the table then wiped her tears away with his fingers. He never felt the need to cry, couldn't quite understand why people did. But, the emotions he felt were threatening to overtake him as well. He felt confused and hurt, and he felt a good deal worse when her silent cry had transformed into a sob as she jumped up and ran for the bathroom.

"Great," he murmured, "not exactly how I pictured this moment."

Tristan glanced over at the bathroom door then at the ring box before he closed the lid. He stood and walked over to the bathroom and lightly tapped on the door a few times. "If I've spooked you, I'm sorry." He put one hand on the doorknob and laid his other hand flat on the door just above his head. Resting his forehead on the door, he wiggled the knob. Of course, it was locked. "But don't shut me out Cianne. Talk to me."

Chapter Twelve

Cianne wiped the tears from her face with a tissue. She sighed because she made up her mind. She unlocked the door and slowly stepped out as Tristan cautiously backed away. Her eyes were a little red and somewhat puffy, and she knew she looked a mess but she didn't care.

When Tristan started toward her with his beseeching eyes she lifted her hand to stop him.

"I can't accept the ring."

She wanted the ring. Cianne wanted nothing more than to put on that ring. It stood for everything she ever wanted from Tristan, but he didn't want her, not really. He wanted truth and she was full of secrets and deception.

When he had first pulled the ring out, she was so happy—until he had given that very sweet speech. Then she knew she couldn't accept it. Tristan wanted who he thought she was, a plain simple girl next door. He had been crystal clear about what wearing his ring required and that had instantly dissolved anything Cianne thought herself capable of. It wasn't about what she wanted anymore. What mattered most was Tristan and she knew he deserved the truth.

"I need for you to sit down and listen to me," Cianne said finally.

Tristan stepped toward her again but she shook her head and pointed to the sofa. Again, she saw a flicker of hurt in his eyes but he turned and walked to the sofa and sat. Cianne followed and took a seat on the sofa, allowing a gap of space between them. She didn't face him, she couldn't, but she knew he watched her as she pulled her hair back from her face and tied it in a knot.

Cianne stared at her fisted hands for several seconds then she placed them in her lap. She glanced over at Tristan again and was going to turn away but she wanted to…memorize his face.

He had let his head fall back on the cushion and was looking up at the ceiling. His entire body was rigid, hard, and so was his tone when he spoke. "Are you interested in someone else?"

She shook her head but also managed to speak. "No," she said quickly. "I—"

"You're just not into me," he interrupted, then turned his assessing gaze on her. The sadness she saw in his eyes echoed painfully through her very soul but Cianne pushed her own heartache away. This wasn't about her. "If you tell me that you're going to become a nun, this will be easier for me to handle," he said, then managed a strained smile.

His sudden humor made her giggle a little and in turn, Tristan gave her a genuine smile.

"You have to listen to me before I lose my nerve," she begged.

Tristan scooted to the edge of the sofa and turned toward her. He rested his elbows on his knees and held his hands together. "Alright," he said, "I'm listening."

Now or never.

"There's something you need to know about me. Something that I hope won't ruin our friendship." Tristan shook his head. "Don't shake your head no. You don't know what I am going to tell you."

"There's nothing that can change the way I feel about you," Tristan said with certainty.

Cianne hoped he meant that. "I can see things happen before they actually happen." She anchored her attention on his hands and waited.

Tristan cleared his throat, causing Cianne to look at him. "You…see things? Like a psychic or clairvoyant."

Cianne thought about it for a second. "I guess," she said, shrugging. "Sometimes the visions are clear and other times they're not so clear." Cianne knew how it sounded but she had to do this.

"Ok," he said, then sat back on the sofa.

"You don't believe me?"

"I didn't say that," he said, followed by a low giggle, but held his hands up defensively. "I said ok. I guess I don't see how that has anything to do with you accepting my ring."

Showing was better than telling. Determined to do just that, Cianne stood and walked to the bathroom. When she returned, she was holding a handful of tissue. As she sat back down beside Tristan she felt her stomach sour.

She didn't know how he was going to take what she planned to do but it was too late to turn back now. Cianne faced Tristan, who tried to match her intensive stare but couldn't because he let out another slight giggle.

Cianne didn't laugh, so he sat up straight and gave her a concerned look.

This had better work.

She inhaled deeply then just watched him for a moment. The possibility that this may be the last time that they were together, shredded her but she cleared her thoughts, looked into Tristan's eyes, and hoped for the best.

If Tristan hadn't been looking directly into Cianne's eyes, he wouldn't have noticed how her pupils shook rapidly for a few seconds before they took on a subtle glow. Just as quickly as it began, Cianne's eyes stilled. They seemed darker, almost clover green as they fixed on him.

"C-Cianne," he stuttered out. Tristan took her by the shoulders just as the veins at the corners of her eyes surfaced and turned black, trailing outward toward her hairline then disappearing.

What the hell was that?

"Cianne!" he said louder as he shook her, "Cianne, are you alright?"

Tristan worked hard to smother his worry, to keep his head. When she blinked once, then again, he relaxed enough that he realized he was holding her too tightly. He stared into Cianne's eyes. The color was now her normal hue and the darkness of her veins was gone as if what he just witnessed had never happened.

However, it had, he was certain of that.

Cianne was thankful that Tristan hadn't seen the full transformation her body experienced when the visions came. Because she had called for the sight and welcomed it, he witnessed the subtle, less frightening version. Still, what he had seen was enough to weaken the stomach of the strongest man.

She tried not to shrink under his questioning gaze and got to her explanation. "Forcing it always makes me a little sick, so I don't do it anymore. Plus, I don't even like what I see so..."

Cianne looked into Tristan's concerned, confused stare, trying to ignore it as she continued. "Ok then," she began, "Your mother is about to call you." She bravely went on with the details of the vision, trying not to think of the consequences. "She's going to ask you to join your father and her in St. Thomas. She already has your family's private jet on standby." Cianne tilted her head. "Your family has a private jet?"

As soon as the last word left Cianne's lips two things happened simultaneously. Blood dripped from her nose and

Tristan's cell phone rang. She lifted the tissue from her lap and pressed it to her nose.

"Bend your head back, it will slow the bleeding." Tristan picked up a few tissues from her lap and held them to her nose.

His phone rang again.

A bit dumbfounded by Tristan's continued concern and lack of hesitation, Cianne gave him a confused look.

Why isn't he running for the door?

"I'm fine, answer your phone," she insisted. Cianne wiped her nose and held the tissue out for him to view. "I'm fine. It's slowing, see. Answer your phone."

Tristan hadn't heard his phone ring. The only thing his mind registered was the blood coming from Cianne's nose and how he desperately wanted to stop it. Nothing else around him existed; he heard nothing, saw nothing, except the crimson fluid that sat stark against the white tissue.

"Tristan, answer your phone."

Cianne saying his name broke through to Tristan like an intense light slicing through the darkness. He closed his eyes and when he opened them again all the sounds and sights around him came flooding back at once. His breathing was steady but his heart raced as if he just ran a hundred-meter dash.

He watched Cianne's face to anchor him as she peered at his pocket where his cell phone was tucked away. Annoyed that it was even ringing, Tristan took the phone from his pocket and answered it as he picked up another tissue and wiped her nose to make sure the blood had really stopped.

"Merry Christmas," Tristan said mechanically, holding the phone to his ear. It was his mother. He listened while she spoke but he never took his eyes off of Cianne. "No I left early… I'm home and I'm kind of in the middle of something important here." Tristan smiled when Cianne gave him a frown as he listened to his mother. "Besides, I don't think it's a good idea to have someone leave their family on Christmas just to fly me there." He listened again. "Right, I will see you then. I love you too, bye." He pulled the phone from his ear and looked at it for a moment before turning it off. He looked back at Cianne.

She wiped her nose again before balling the bloody tissues up and sitting them on the table. "I can see more clearly when I force it but there are a few nasty side effects so I've only done it a few times."

Tristan placed his phone on the table next to the bloody tissues. He could see Cianne was trying to measure his reaction so he spoke. "That's some gift you got there. Are you sure all the bleeding has stopped?" He took her face in his hands and tilted her head back. He moved her face from one side to the other, checking for blood. Tristan was relieved when he didn't find any.

When he focused on Cianne, she looked angry. "What do you want me to say?" he asked quietly. "Am I not giving you the reaction you saw in your vision? Didn't you already see what I'd say?"

"It doesn't work like that," she said. "I can't see anything in connection with myself. Whenever I've tried I just pass out. I only saw what I did because it wasn't directly related to me. You would have said no to your mom anyway." Cianne focused on him again with questioning eyes.

"What do you want Cianne? Me to be frightened of you?" He shrugged. "I'm not. I'd be lying if I said what you just did wasn't…" He searched for the perfect word.

"Freaky?"

"Unusual," Tristan offered, correcting her, "Very unusual, but not at all freaky. Do you think you're a freak?" He studied her until she looked away. "So, this thing you can do is why you've never had a boyfriend. It's why you've always avoided me. You've let this dictate your life, haven't you?" Tristan frowned. "Is this why you won't accept my promise ring?" Cianne didn't answer so Tristan scooted closer to her. "So, you can see things before they happen. That isn't a bad thing, it's extraordinary."

"Extraordinary? Tell that to the kids at my first grammar school who were supposed to be my friends but called me a witch and a freak because I had an episode in front of them. Or their parents who kept their children away from me. Or the teachers who thought I was crazy and it might be contagious so they kept their distance too. It's a curse. A random curse that can happen anywhere at any time," Cianne said with irritation. "If I flake in front of anyone again I'm going to be carted off to some science lab in no man's land." She was visibly upset.

Tristan placed his hand on hers and instantly saw a change in Cianne. His touch relaxed her. That was an ego boost, but he didn't have time to relish it. "The world is full of ignorance Cianne. People fear what they can't explain but I'm not one of them." He lifted her hand to his mouth and kissed it. "Besides, I would never let anyone make you a lab rat."

Cianne looked at their entwined hands then back at him. "You still want me to have the ring?" she asked him.

"I guess you didn't understand what I said earlier." Tristan smiled, knowing how corny the things he was about to say would sound. Things he thought he'd never reveal, but Cianne needed convincing. "I went to a carnival near that old farm on Oxen drive during summer break four and a half years ago. You know the one?" When she nodded, he continued. "I'd only lived here for a few weeks so I didn't know anyone. Well, I heard this harmonious laugh above me so I looked up. You were on the Ferris wheel with your dad and when I saw you for the first time, with your feet dangling above me, all I could think of was that you were the most beautiful girl I had ever seen. I watched you that entire day.

"When I saw you smile, I smiled. When you laughed, I laughed. I was love-struck that very first day but I didn't know anything about you and for the first time in my life I was scared to approach a girl. I kicked myself because as I watched you and your father drive off, I just knew I would never see you again.

"When I saw you in school a month later I thought, how lucky am I. But you didn't pay me any mind. That motivated me at first. I joined the football team because I thought maybe you were into jocks but that didn't work. I found out you were smart so I put a little more effort into my school work," he said then laughed, "but you still didn't give me the time of day. You actually began to avoid me. I eventually gave up.

"Until this year. I figured that this was our last year and my last chance. So, I had my locker moved next to yours and freed up some of my time. These last four years, I've seen how sweet and gentle you are. You're smart and amazingly beautiful. Now, I find out that you come with special effects too." He teased. "I said before, nothing could ever change the way I feel about you. I've waited a long time for you Cianne and I want you to accept the ring and all that I've promised, but only if you feel the same." Tristan picked up the ring box and opened it, extending his arm out to her as he did before.

Cianne slowly lifted the ring from the box, then turned it from one side to the other. "It's beautiful," she told him.

"It's nothing compared to you. Nothing and no one can compare," he said, looking into her eyes.

Cianne blushed, "What finger do I wear it on?"

Tristan placed the empty box back on the table and motioned for her to give him her ring. When she gave it to him, he took her right hand and slowly placed it on her ring finger.

Tristan was taken aback when she slammed her body into his, almost knocking him back on the sofa. She squeezed him tight as she began to cry, her face burrowed into his chest.

"What's wrong?" He lifted her head to look at her as he wiped at the tears running down her face. If she understood how her tears tortured him, she would never cry again.

"My father and I have kept this from everyone except Tranae." Cianne looked at him with fearful yet oddly relieved eyes, as if she was happy to have someone else know her secret.

"You needn't worry." Tristan took her hand and covered his heart. "Your secret is safe with me. Cross my heart and hope to die." He kissed Cianne's wet cheek.

When she leaned back and looked at him in a way she never had before, it was clear that something had changed between them. He wondered what, exactly, and was about to ask when Cianne's arms wrapped around his neck and her mouth was on his. Her fingers gently stroked his neck as she passionately and slowly kissed him.

Tristan responded the only way he could. He gently cupped her head, tangled his fingers in her tied up hair, and tried to fuse them together.

While still locked in the kiss, Cianne raised her leg over Tristan's thighs, straddling him. However, before she could lower herself onto his lap, Tristan placed his hands on her hips and applied a little pressure to prevent her from sitting on him.

Discouraged, Cianne pulled back and peered down at him.

His body had reacted to the kiss more than he wanted to allow and if she sat on him she would know just how much he liked her touch. She felt so soft and smelled so delicious that it actually pained him that he had to stop her.

Winded, he took in a deep breath. Reaffirmed by his obvious reaction, Cianne smiled then leaned forward to reconnect with his lips again but Tristan applied more pressure to her waist.

Cianne tilted her head and frowned at him with confusion. "We're a couple, kissing is allowed now," she plainly stated.

Tristan's body ached beneath hers as he tried to focus. When he thought he had enough control, he said, "It's just that we haven't kissed like that since our first date. You caught me a little off-guard." He attempted to talk himself into relaxing as she lowered herself back on the sofa beside him.

He glanced at her then immediately shut his eyes again. After a few failed attempts to get his body under control

Tristan jumped to his feet. "I need something to drink." He had to retreat and regroup. "I uh, I'm going to go get something to drink," he repeated. "Want anything?"

"Water," Cianne said. She pouted as she fell back on the sofa.

Tristan watched as she undid the knot she placed in her hair, causing her long tresses to fall past her shoulders. The way her hair fell was so seductive that Tristan had to rush up the stairs. When he returned, he handed her a bottle of water and sat down beside her but not as close as before. He watched her open the bottle and take a long swig.

Cianne was finally his. He knew they were fated. Had known that he would always be hers and that he would do whatever it took to keep her.

"I almost forgot." He said pulling out his wallet. "Lela wanted me to give you this." Tristan took out the photo and handed it to Cianne. The image was of him kneeling next to a pretty young girl in front of the Prometheus statue in the background at Rockefeller Center.

"Lela?" Cianne asked.

"Lela's my little cousin. Whenever I go to New York, I stay with my Aunt Delia and Uncle Howard. They have three kids. Gerald is thirteen, Lela is eleven, and Steven is four." Tristan smiled, "Lela demands all my attention and was a little jealous of you at first."

"Of me?" Cianne asked.

"Yeah," he said, laughing. "Lela doesn't like competition. Do you know she actually hid my phone until it was time for me to leave?"

"She has nothing to worry about, I'm willing to share." Cianne smiled.

"I'm not." He said, winking. "I was never one for titles, but you do know that you officially have a boyfriend now." Tristan slid closer and took her hand. He turned the ring on her finger one full time.

Cianne leaned in and kissed him again but he pulled back almost instantly. It was hard enough to control his desires around her without her touching him, but when she touched him.

Tristan had urges like all men but he refused to rush Cianne. He wanted to kiss her, to touch her every minute of every day but if he did, he knew he would go too far. He also knew that Cianne wouldn't say no. She wasn't ready for that kind of relationship, even if she thought she was. That was the reason why he had always taken her out in public instead of being alone with her.

"Can I ask you something?" he said.

"About the thing I can do?" Cianne asked. He nodded. She placed the cap on the water bottle, sat it on the table, then brought her legs up to her chest and wrapped her arms around them.

"Is this something only you can do or did your mother-"

"No....no," Cianne said hastily. "She wasn't like me. My mother was perfect."

"You're perfect Ci." He truly meant it. "If your mom wasn't gifted, then what about her family or your father?"

"My mother was an only child and her mother, my grandmother, is my only living relative on that side. Apparently, she and my grandmother weren't too close. My mom was raised by my grandmother's close friends. As far as I know, my mother's side of the family was normal. If she had been like me my dad would have told me." Cianne looked down at her feet. "If my biological father was 'gifted'," Cianne said as she made quotation marks in the air, "my stepdad and I wouldn't know. We don't know anything about him and don't have any way of contacting him."

"I could help you find him if you'd like."

"I don't think that would be a good idea. Anyway, he's probably normal. It's possible I'm the only freak of nature in the family."

"Why do you say stuff like that? You are perfect, you're better than perfect." He touched her thigh and she smiled bashfully. Tristan quickly moved his hand. "I was wondering," he said, needing a distraction, "when did you know you could do it?"

"My father said that it started just before my mother's passing," Cianne told him. "I can remember only bits and pieces of my life then but nothing from the day the visions started or the days after…"

Chapter Thirteen

Fairfield Elementary
Ten years earlier,
field trip day

Zaria loved field trips and today her class was visiting the City Zoo. Teachers, their aides, and the parents who had volunteered moved the groups of children through the Zoo's front gate at a steady pace.

The grownups only allowed five to ten minutes at each exhibit so that there would be time to visit as many animals on display as possible. That worried Zaria. She was having a wonderful time seeing all the animals she learned about but the tigers were what she wanted to see most of all.

Particularly, the white tigers named Cotton and Sasha. Zaria was an eight-year-old animal enthusiast who was delighted that a private breeder had loaned his two white tigers to her local zoo.

When Zaria's group finally reached the beautiful creatures, their habitat was surrounded by children on all sides. Zaria lowered her head, distressed when she heard her teacher tell her group that they needed to come back later. Her teacher promised that when the crowd died down that her group would come back to see the tigers.

So, they had left with Zaria trailing behind her peers. Even though she was a little upset by the detour she forgot about the white tigers by the time lunch was over. By then, her head had started to hurt really bad.

The headache had started early that morning but had disappeared during her ride to school. However, it had returned and was now much worse than before. Zaria dragged behind her group as they viewed the rest of the animals.

As time got closer to her group leaving the zoo, Zaria's pain grew worse but she didn't tell her teacher. Her mother had given strict instructions to be contacted whenever Zaria had what her mom called migraines, and Zaria knew that she would be taken home so she did her best to manage the pain. That was until her class started to board the school bus to leave the zoo.

Zaria was quiet in line as she leaned against the bus while the other children talked loudly about their day and all they had seen. As the line inched forward she didn't move. Her head hurt too bad and all she could do was cover her ears as the horrible pain tore through her.

It was worse than it had ever been before.

When someone gave her a gentle push from behind, Zaria staggered forward a little, bumping into the side of the bus. Most of her classmates walked around her to board the bus as if she wasn't even there but others watched her with curiosity.

●

Mrs. Shuster didn't notice that some of the children hadn't boarded the bus but were instead gathered at the rear of it until she heard one of the students call her name.

"What's going on?" she asked as she made her way to the small gathering.

"It's Zaria!" a little girl yelled to the teacher. She pointed in the direction of the Zoo entrance. "She went back inside."

"Her face!" another girl yelled out. "Did you see her face?"

"I did," a boy staring in the direction of the entrance added. "She turned into a monster."

●

It hadn't taken long for Zaria to hear her name over the loudspeakers advising her to find anyone wearing a tan zoo employee's outfit or a teacher to return her to the bus depot. She ignored the instructions.

She sat alone, hidden in a corner next to the habitat containing the white tiger cubs she wanted to see earlier that day. Her headache was gone. It had been replaced by a flash of horrifying images that she would never forget.

Zaria looked down at her hands again. Just minutes ago, they looked like something from a horror movie but now they were her hands again.

She lifted her head. They were calling her name over the loudspeakers again, with instructions to find an employee but she ignored the request for the seventh time. She had counted. Zaria wiggled her fingers to make sure they were really back to normal, then hugged her legs to her chest and cried softly, never once noticing that she wasn't alone.

"Are you lost?"

Zaria didn't know how long the boy had been standing in front of her. She had heard his question but all she could do was look at him as he looked down at her. He couldn't have been any older than she was but something about him suggested he was. She was often told the same about herself.

The boy smiled at her and if she wasn't so upset she might have given him a smile in return. Though looking into his eyes, pretty ocean colored eyes, she almost forgot how upset she was.

When he dangled a handkerchief in front of her, Zaria took it and wiped her tears. She felt foolish crying in front of a stranger, no matter how nice he was, but she hadn't mastered her emotions yet. Her mother was still teaching her.

Zaria suddenly thought it strange that she had to learn to mask anything, let alone her emotions. Finished with the soft cloth that felt good on her face, she extended her hand to return it only to find that the boy had taken a seat beside her.

She was happy that he didn't want to talk. She didn't want to talk either, so they just sat there for several minutes in silence. Zaria winced when the people shouting her name got closer. She liked sitting with the pretty eyed boy.

"Zaria," the voices called out all around them.

"Over here. There are some children over here!" a woman yelled.

As teachers, staff, and parents surrounded them, the boy stood and wiped the dust from his pants. He extended a hand to Zaria and she took it to pull herself up. Only she didn't let his hand go when she got to her feet. She held on to him tightly as they peered at the group of excited adults.

Mrs. Shuster pushed through the crowd, grabbed Zaria into her arms, and held her tight. "Gracious young lady, what were you thinking, running off like that? You just about gave me a heart attack. What's wrong, did you hurt yourself?"

Zaria continued to hold on to the boy as her teacher felt her forehead and gave her a quick once over.

"Are you hurt? Why did you run off like that?" Mrs. Shuster looked at the boy when Zaria didn't answer. "What did she say?"

"She hasn't said anything at all, ma'am," the boy answered as he rubbed the back of Zaria's hand with his thumb.

It felt so nice, just as nice as it felt when her mom rubbed her head when it hurt. Zaria wanted him to never stop rubbing. His hand on hers was nicer than her mom's too. Just as that thought came to her, heat raced down her arm, through her hand, and into her fingers. She tensed, wondering if the boy had felt it too.

"I have to go." The boy told her.

He must have felt it, she thought as he gave her hand a gentle squeeze.

He let his hand slide from hers until they were only hanging on with their pinkies, then nothing. A feeling of loss, great loss, enveloped Zaria as she watched the boy walk away.

He can't be leaving. It is all wrong. He has to stay with me now.

Adults crowded around her but she heard none of their questions. Instead, Zaria focused on the boy who stood a few feet away. She watched as he talked with an older man who was dressed just as nicely as he was. After a minute or so the boy turned around and mouthed the word "Goodbye", then he waved to her. When Zaria waved back, he smiled before taking the man's hand and walking away.

"Zaria?" Mrs. Shuster kneeled and shook Zaria to get her full attention.

Zaria blankly looked at her teacher, wondering what the other kids had told her about what they had seen. She knew it must have been bad because of the looks on their faces. "What on earth has gotten into you, young lady? Why did you run off like that?"

Zaria said nothing. She was scared and felt totally alone since the boy had left her. She felt deep inside that he shouldn't have left, but she didn't know why.

Mrs. Shuster shook her head as if agitated then stood facing all the other adults that stood around them. "My aide said that she forgot to take the kids to see the tigers," she explained. "Zaria probably wanted to see them before we left." Mrs. Shuster took Zaria firmly by the hand. "Thank you all for helping me to locate her."

Zaria waited quietly while Mrs. Shuster spoke with some people who worked for the zoo, then they walked hand in hand to the exit.

Once Zaria realized they were going to the bus, her heart stilled and she started pulling and tugging, trying to free her arm from her teacher's hold. She couldn't get on that bus. No one should get on that bus. No one should get on any of the buses.

However, Mrs. Shuster tightened her grip and managed to get Zaria on the bus without making a big scene.

As soon as they got on, Zaria pulled her arm free and ran to the very back of the bus where there were several empty seats.

"I don't know what's gotten into her." Mrs. Shuster said to the bus driver and the teacher's aide that was staring at them as they entered the bus.

"Well I thanked the others for staying and helping with the search," the aide grimaced.

"You know we're probably gonna hit traffic now." The bus driver huffed, as he closed the door.

"She has never done anything remotely troublesome, ever." Mrs. Shuster said as she walked to the rear of the bus and sat next to Zaria.

Zaria sat with her legs pulled to her chest and her face buried in her knees. She felt her teacher's hand on her back, rubbing her gently as the bus pulled out of the parking lot.

School buses from several schools, including Zaria's, left the lot in an orderly fashion. As the buses pulled into traffic, Zaria felt a strange pull from outside of the bus. She lifted her head slowly and peeked out of the window.

A long black limousine had allowed her bus to pass. She watched the long car as her bus drove by, and when they were just about out of sight she saw the back window slide down. The little boy who had been nice to her was seated inside.

Zaria started to cry again. She buried her head into her knees and wondered what dying felt like.

Zaria's classmates watched her even after their teacher told them to turn around and sit with their eyes forward. A few had listened but most watched her rather than watch the driver go through the toll for the bridge.

As the bus driver inched the bus toward the bridge, Zaria's low sobbing became a loud wail. Mrs. Shuster tried to console her but by the time the bus inched a few feet onto the bridge, Zaria's crying had become a deafening scream.

The bus driver, alarmed by the terrifying sound, slammed on the brakes. Several motorists behind the bus beeped their horns in frustration when the bus came to a sudden stop. Undeterred by the honking but not the screeching sounds of Zaria's screams, the driver looked at her in his rear-view mirror with an irritated glare. Her screams also alerted the few children who hadn't noticed her before. The entire bus full of people was all focused on Zaria.

"What's wrong?" Mrs. Shuster repeatedly yelled over Zaria's cries.

With all eyes on her, Zaria couldn't speak but she slowly pointed to the front of the bus.

"What is it, child?" Mrs. Shuster looked to the front of the bus. "Is it the water you're frightened of? We drove over it to get here."

Zaria shook her head wildly as she looked up and pointed again. Everyone who had been watching her followed her instruction. One by one everyone on the bus turned and looked forward. Mrs. Shuster stood and strained her eyes to see out of the wide front window of the school bus.

●

Mrs. Shuster saw nothing but midday traffic through the large window from where she stood. She was bending to sit down when the bus started to shake, and a loud storm of noises rang out all around them. Some of the children laughed but the ones closest to the front of the bus started to cry out. No one cried louder than Zaria.

Mrs. Shuster grabbed onto the back of a seat to steady herself through the violent jolts. Once the shaking had stopped, she ran to the front of the bus. "What happened, did you hit something?" she yelled, looking to the driver whose face was stark white, his eyes forward.

The bus driver said very slowly, "I think the bridge just collapsed."

Mrs. Shuster glared out of the cracked front window. About 10 or so feet ahead, a large section of the bridge was gone, with the water below visible in its place. Cars that had fallen along with the section of the bridge could still be seen, slowly sinking into the waving water below. Some cars had landed on top of others while some hit the water and bobbed.

People flailed in the water, screaming for help. Mrs. Shuster was sure that most of them had been dragged under the water in their vehicles. On the bridge, motorists frantically exited their cars, moving toward the gaping section of missing concrete and steel, in an attempt to offer help to others.

●

Zaria rocked back in forth in her seat. She refused to look at what they saw. There was no need, she already saw it in her head.

"If we had left on time, we would have…" The driver's words died away as he looked at Mrs. Shuster. The two adults looked at each other and then they both turned and looked at a sobbing Zaria, who watched them from the back of the bus.

Present

Cianne looked at Tristan. "What I do remember is the way I was treated by everyone after the visions started. My mom changed my name and we moved here shortly after."

Tristan wrapped her in his arms and kissed her forehead. He was happy that she had no recollection of the painful incident that happened to her when she was a kid. He wished he could take the pain away for her as well. Tristan wanted to wipe all her sadness clean but the important thing was that he was here to do just that now. He would do everything in his power to protect her from any and everything that came their way.

"What was your name then?" he asked. He wasn't sure why he wanted to know. It didn't really matter but he just did?

"I don't remember." She frowned. Cianne looked at him and shrugged, "guess I didn't like very much."

Chapter Fourteen

Tristan thought of his grandfather as he drove past the "Welcome to Kennecott University" sign. It had been almost a year since his grandfather's passing and another three that he visited his grandfather's, Alma Mater.

Patrick T. Arlington, Tristan's grandfather, loved Kennecott University and had made sure that he did what he could for the college that he credited with his success. Four generations of Arlington graduates had attended Kennecott, including Tristan's mother. In truth, Tristan had seriously considered attending Kennecott as well. For that reason alone, he had convinced his mother to move to West Hills four years ago.

Tristan pulled into the crowded parking lot and eventually found a parking space. Time had been slowly healing the hole that his grandfather's death made in his life. With that healing also came the realization that he was no longer a boy. A man is what Tristan had to be and that meant he needed to continue his grandfather's work and generosity.

He parked, got out of his truck, and looked at his watch. If he hurried, he could surprise Cianne. They spent Christmas together but he flew back to New York the next day. She wasn't expecting him until the sixth but he wanted to surprise her by arriving two days early. He missed her so much more now that they were officially a couple.

It was something he couldn't explain, but it needed no explanation.

Inside the building, Tristan walked over to the large desk with a security guard stationed behind it. He nodded at the guard as he wrote his name on the sign-in sheet. He then glanced at the directory behind the guard before making his way to the elevators in the rear of the building.

"Could you hold the elevator please?" Tristan called, as he saw the doors closing. A hand appeared, retracting the doors. "Thank you."

"No problem," the guy in the elevator replied. Tristan and the guy acknowledge each other with a nod. "Hey," the guy said. He lifted his hand, slightly shaking his finger at Tristan. "Aren't you Tristan Bertram?"

Tristan didn't answer but instead asked, "You play?"

"Wow, you were All-State two years in a row." He grabbed Tristan's hand and shook it. "Yeah…yeah, I play, here man. You here to register, we could really use you?" He released Tristan's hand.

"No. I don't play anymore."

"What, why?" the guy asked.

"I don't know. I just woke up one day and football didn't seem so important anymore."

"You were good man; you should rethink that." A low ding sounded in the elevator signaling their arrival on the fourth floor. "This is my floor." The guy stepped closer to the door. "It was nice meeting you man. Tristan Bertram…small world." He shook Tristan's hand again before getting off the elevator.

Tristan smiled as he stepped off the elevator on the sixth floor and walked down the hallway. He wasn't the kind of guy who lived for recognition but it was nice to be known for something he once enjoyed.

He stopped at the door at the end of the hall and read the sign "The office of the Vice President of Advancement and

University Relations'. Tristan opened the door and stepped inside.

Tristan decided to continue the annual donation to the University under the same terms his grandfather had set before his passing. All parties involved were satisfied. With the meeting behind him, Tristan noted the time. It was quarter to one.

He walked swiftly toward the parking lot looking in the direction he had parked his truck. The meeting took less time than he allotted so his plan to surprise Cianne and take her to lunch was still in play.

As he closed the distance between him and the parking lot, he took notice of three figures standing near his truck but he maintained his pace. As he got closer, Tristan recognized one of the figures.

Nick, the idiot Cianne tutored, he already knew a bit about. The other two, he knew nothing about so he sized them up as he approached. One of the guys was about his height and build and wore glasses. The other was a bit shorter but a lot thicker, a muscle head to the core.

"Are you in the market for a truck, Nick?" Tristan stopped a few feet from them. "I see that you and your friends," he said, looking from one stranger to the other, "seem to like mine."

"No one's interested in your piece of shit truck," Nick smiled.

Tristan shrugged. "Then why are you here?"

"My man comes into the dorm talking about this real deal running back who's here visiting Kennecott. Imagine my shock when I found out he was talking about your ass. I knew I'd seen you somewhere before."

Nick snorted then spat close enough to Tristan's feet to cause him to look down. "I have a date so if you could get to what it is you want." Tristan grinned.

Nick sucked his teeth. "You thought I forgot about the ass whooping I owe you, boy. We're not in your neck of the woods now. There's no one here to help you." Nick stepped in front of Tristan. The other two boys positioned themselves as backup.

Tristan smile widened.

"Is something funny?" Nick asked then rushed Tristan.

Tristan somehow knew that Nick's intent was to lift him in the air before slamming him hard to the ground but Tristan took a few steps to the side and smacked Nick hard on the back of the head. Nick stood up straight and turned around to face Tristan, more furious than before.

Tristan chuckled as he glanced around to gauge the location of the other two. Neither of them had moved so he figured they were here to observe, at least for now.

When he looked back, Nick was bearing down on him again. They tousled for a moment then Nick punched at Tristan's face and neck before Tristan pushed him away and tagged him hard on his left side then quickly followed that with a left to the jaw. This knocked Nick off balance and Tristan saw his opportunity.

He stepped into Nick, bringing his fist up and connecting under Nick's chin. Nick swayed on his feet. Tristan was about to throw another solid blow to Nick's jaw when he was rammed from the side. The larger of the two strangers tackled him, causing them both to fall over a small car and into the street where a vehicle swerved to avoid hitting them.

Tristan hit the asphalt hard, with the largest of the trio falling on top of him. The muscle head attempted to straddle him but Tristan wasn't about to allow that. The guy had given up on pinning him but threw a few wild punches that stung Tristan on the head and ear.

Tristan pushed Muscles off with a sudden burst of strength, lifting the guy a few inches in the air. None of the onlookers who gathered seemed to notice the oddity of this, or that Tristan, with a new sense of energy, got to his feet before the big guy even hit the pavement. Tristan darted to the side of Muscles and kicked him while he was still on all fours trying to catch his breath. The boy seemed to go limp as his body lifted a couple feet in the air then landed on the pavement, flat on his back.

By this time, Nick had recovered and was running toward Tristan.

Tristan didn't appear to see him coming, his eyes were focused on Muscles. But surprisingly, Tristan turned to meet the charge. He grabbed Nick's right wrist with his right hand. Spinning inward, Tristan elbowed Nick in the face. He then flipped Nick over his shoulder so that Nick was seated on the ground in front of him. Tristan kneeled and locked his arm around Nick's neck and began to squeeze.

Tristan didn't feel Nick's friend, the one with the glasses, grabbing at his arms. Nor did he hear the words the boy was yelling at him. He was focused, in a trance of pure concentration. He couldn't hear the roar of the crowd that gathered or anything else for that matter.

It was as if his brain only sensed aggression, leaving him to focus on the real threats, which were Nick and his muscled friend. He could hear and see his aggressors clearly but everything else around him was just faded images and muffled sounds.

Nick struggled for air, clawing and hitting at him, but Tristan held on tight. As Nick's eyes began to close and his body relaxed, an image of Cianne flashed in Tristan's mind. She was smiling as her long lashes closed slowly over her beautiful eyes.

As if an alarm clock had gone off, Tristan suddenly heard the panicked yells of the crowd. He heard and felt Nick's friend, the one who wore the glasses, yelling and pulling at his arm.

Tristan released Nick and stepped back, aware that if he had wanted, he could have killed the prick. Nick flopped to the pavement coughing as he held on to his throat. Tristan, a little dazed, looked at his hands. There was no time to question what he just did because someone grabbed his arm and pulled him to a car that had "Campus Security" in large blue letters across the door.

Tristan was seated in a mid-sized office, at the end of a long table. Even though his head was a bit fogged he knew where he was and why. He'd been in a fight but at some point during that fight, he was moving on instinct alone, blocking out any sound or distraction other than his goal.

My goal, he thought to himself, *what was my goal*?

What was his goal?

Tristan lowered his head as he rubbed his head. He looked up when Nick came into the office with a security guard who followed close behind. Nick's friend with the glasses and another, much younger, security guard followed them. Nick, who looked somewhat worked over, glanced over at Tristan.

"This isn't over bitch," Nick hissed.

"Shut it up." The older guard said, pushing Nick toward another long table that was on the other side of the room.

"You want to be cuffed to that table?" the young guard asked Nick.

"That won't be necessary. Will it Nick?" The older security guard asked, looking sternly at Nick.

"No. Not necessary Mr. Ed." Nick sneered.

Tristan looked over at Ed, who motioned for Nick and his friend to sit down. Nick sat down but kept his eyes on Tristan. The guy with the glasses sat across from Nick.

"I need to see some ID from you fellows." The older guard looked from Tristan to the guy with the glasses. He then looked over at Nick. "Yours too Nicklaus, even though we are on first name basis."

The younger guard walked over to Tristan and sat on the table just to the side of him. He folded his arms over his chest and looked Tristan over slowly. "You don't look so tough to me. You hopped up on steroids or something?"

Tristan just looked at the guard as he pulled out a very thin leather wallet that was the size of a credit card. He noticed as the guard leaned forward, a very large tattoo that covered part of the officer's neck. He wondered what it was but his interest faded just as quickly as it appeared. Tristan flipped his little case open, exposing a driver's license and one credit card.

"You travel light, huh?" The young guard took the thin leather wallet and looked over it. "Tristan, is it? Well Tristan, do you attend school here?"

"No sir, I don't," Tristan said politely, even though the security guard looked only a few years older than him.

"Then what are you doing on my campus?" Ed asked, as he walked over and took the ID out of the younger guard's hands.

"I had a meeting to attend."

Ed eyed the ID, then he looked at Tristan. He did this twice before walking out of the room and into a small office with glass windows, near the entrance.

"So," the younger guard said to Tristan, "How did you manage to put JC down? He's on his way to the hospital. I mean you look pretty fit and you may have a bit of a sting to your punches but I've seen Jay take on three guys at once and they didn't get up so fast." He looked Tristan over again.

Tristan moved his gaze from the young guard's face to his name tag. It read: E. Patton. *E. Patton is a tool*, Tristan thought to himself.

"Bitch got lucky is all," Nick said from across the room.

Tristan looked at Nick and gave him a smug smile. Nick responded with a mouthed curse and threat.

"JC worked out pretty hard this morning," the kid with the glasses said, breaking his silence.

Tristan hadn't given the quiet unassuming guy with the glasses a second look, but he looked at him now. He didn't carry himself the way Nick did. Tristan found himself wondering how they were friends.

"Shut up Pete. Where were you anyway?" Nick asked the guy.

"Mr. Bertram," Security officer Ed said as he walked back into the room. He looked a little pale. "Do you need any medical attention?"

Everyone looked over at Ed as he went to the water cooler. Ed took a paper cup from the dispenser and flicked the blue tab. He carried the cup of water across the room and placed it in front of Tristan.

"Mr. Bertram?" Nick sneered, "Why you calling him Mr. and shit?"

"Sit down Nicklaus, NOW!" Ed pinned Nick with a hard look until Nick sat down then he turned his attention back to Tristan.

Tristan winked at Nick.

Infuriated, Nick stood again and this time he slammed his fist on the table. With another look from Ed and the younger guard who seemed anxious to use some force, Nick reluctantly sat down.

"Mr. Bertram, we have a Police Officer coming if you would like to press charges," Ed advised him.

"Press charges?" Nick yelled as he kicked the chair next to him, sending it flying across the room. "This is bullshit."

Ed looked at the young guard. "Remove him before he gets himself into more trouble." Ed turned his attention back to Tristan. "We have a witness that says you were attacked in the parking lot next to your car."

The young guard took Nick by the arm and led him to the office with the glass windows. Tristan was listening to the older guard Ed, but couldn't help looking past Ed to see Nick cursing and resisting the younger guard. Once the younger guard got Nick inside, he closed the door and stepped back into the room with Tristan, Ed, and a quiet Pete.

"I won't be pressing charges," Tristan said to Ed. He took his wallet that Ed handed him just as a nicely dressed silver-haired gentleman entered the room

"Mr. Bertram," the silver-haired man said, as he walked over to Tristan. "My name is Charles Hendrickson and I represent Kennecott University. When I say that I am deeply sorry and apologize for this situation, I say it with sincerity. I assure you that our Campus is very safe. This sort of thing never happens here. We will investigate this matter extensively and the assailants will be dealt with swiftly. If you would come with me, I have a car outside that will take you to the hospital." The man motioned toward the door.

"The hospital isn't necessary, but I could use a ride back to my truck if you don't mind." Tristan stood. "Am I free to go, Officer Ed?" Tristan looked up at the older guard who seemed to have shrunken just a little.

"Yes sir," Ed answered, looking a little embarrassed as he nervously glanced at Mr. Hendrickson. Something silent passed between the two men.

Tristan would have sworn that Ed paled a bit more as he walked by the seasoned guard and followed Mr. Hendrickson to the door.

What the hell was that about?" The young guard asked as he and Ed walked over to the doorway Tristan and Hendrickson had just exited.

"That kid is Tristan Bertram," Ed said.

"Ok?" The young guard shrugged.

"As in Bertram," he said emphasizing the name. When Patton hadn't put the obvious together, Ed said, "As in Arlington-Bertram Hall and the new Arlington-Bertram Library. Those are buildings his family had built. Apparently, his grandfather damn near made this place what it is today. He passed away last year. The Dean is desperate for Mr. Bertram to attend Kennecott, some kind of legacy or something. His family is very rich and very important to the University."

"How rich?" the young guard asked. He sounded unimpressed.

"Think of how rich you would want to be. Multiply that by one hundred, and you probably won't even scratch the surface of what he has."

The two guards stood outside the doorway looking at Tristan and Hendrickson as they drove away.

Chapter Fifteen

Nothing but darkness surrounded a speechless Cianne as she stood as still as a statue. She tried to gather her thoughts, to figure out how she had ended up here, wherever here was. What she did gather was that she was not in her bed where she lay only seconds ago.

It was somewhat difficult to remember what she was doing before, especially in the blackness; but she tried, hoping that by doing so she would uncover an explanation of what had just happened.

The last thing Cianne remembered was that she went for a run through the park across from her house. When she was done, she had gone home and showered. A nap was what she intended for the afternoon but when she couldn't get to sleep, she started looking through photos of her mother.

Cianne held her arms out in the darkness, partly because she wasn't sure she was alone, and if she wasn't she wanted to make sure that whatever or whoever was around wasn't too close. Though she was unable to see her fingers, she tried to feel for something…anything, near her.

What if there was something out there that she didn't want to touch? Cianne pulled her hand back suddenly.

Although she hadn't had one in months, this could be a nightmare. Terror wrapped its claws around Cianne as she chewed her bottom lip. Pain was the most effective way to bring her out of one of her nightmares so she bit down hard on her lip until she tasted the copper tang of her own blood.

Nothing happened. She was still consumed by darkness.

Confused, Cianne tried to soothe the sting of her bottom lip as it continued to throb. Either she wasn't asleep or she needed another way to wake herself. With no apparent solutions to her situation, Cianne searched for other possibilities. Unconsciousness was a possibility, but she was sure that being so usually meant limited awareness. Cianne knew that wasn't the case because she was fully aware and plenty scared.

Just when Cianne decided to move, out of nowhere a small light appeared and seemed to be floating toward her. Cianne took a step back but the light continued coming closer. The light grew bigger and brighter as she stood there with no place to go. After only a few seconds, the glow became so bright that Cianne had to lift her arm up to shield her eyes as the light took over the space around her. Soon the light enveloped Cianne completely, blinding her. Then without warning, the light rescinded.

When Cianne was able to slowly uncover her eyes, her vision adjusted and all she saw all around her was green. Her eyes were slow to focus but her other senses were unhindered. Cianne smelled and felt fresh outside air. She smelled fresh cut grass and heard the rustling of trees. Voices of people and the sounds of a day in motion surrounded her.

The first thing Cianne noticed when she was able to focus was that large full beautiful trees were everywhere. She stood in a courtyard with stone benches, trees, and sidewalk paths. There was even a glass-enclosed bulletin board nearby. Surrounding the courtyard were large buildings that varied in design.

People were everywhere, walking and talking. Some sat on benches or in the grass eating or reading, most just stood around talking. Cianne looked from one person to the next, actually enjoying the scene before her. There was something so very familiar about this place but she wasn't able to pinpoint what it was. She felt it though.

Why am I here?

Cianne glanced over at a woman who sat on a bench a few feet away. As she turned her head to look in another direction she froze. She'd know that smile anywhere. The beautiful brown skinned young woman looked about the same age as Cianne but there was no mistaking what she knew to be fact. Her heart almost jumped right through her chest as she slowly took a step toward the bench and the young woman who sat on it.

"Kayla."

Cianne stopped. She didn't know what to do as a young man with his back to her said her mother's name. She couldn't see his face, only that he was nicely built and had blond hair. He lifted a camera to his face as Cianne watched in stunned silence.

"Don't," Kayla said but her face lit up when she saw him, and despite her comment, she made no attempt to cover her face. The camera flashed, capturing the moment forever. "You came," Kayla said with excitement as he walked over to her.

Cianne watched as her mother took the guy's hand and pulled him a few feet away, behind some bushes. Cianne could see her mother's face but the guy's back was still to her. She heard both of them clearly though.

"Do you love me?" Kayla asked him. She nervously twirled a section of her black t-shirt that hung from the fluorescent pink clip it was knotted through. Cianne noticed her mother looking around as if searching for something or someone.

"If you insist on measuring my feelings with such a shallow phrase, then yes Kayla Harper, I love you with all that I am." Cianne saw the man's hand reach out and touch her mother's cheek. "Only it doesn't matter, does it?"

Is he my father?

The need to call to them was overwhelming. There was so much Cianne had to say, so much she wanted to tell them. Yet all words escaped her. She wanted to hold her mother one more time and to see the face of the man who may be her father.

"Run away with me," Kayla exclaimed as she excitedly bit at her lip.

Wait, run away from what?

"It isn't that simple, Kayla."

Cianne waited for him to continue but he said nothing else. He just lowered his head then turned it slightly in the opposite direction as if distracted by something. Cianne took a step toward them. She had to see his face. Her heart sped up when he started to turn his attention in her direction.

Excited, Cianne picked up her pace. He was her father and she was going to meet him. As soon as the thought surfaced, her movements became sluggish. Cianne looked down at her feet, noticing that each step was exaggerated and slower. She wasn't the only one moving in slow motion either. The man she thought to be her father was still turning to face her but his movements were slower than hers.

"Please," Cianne begged as she tried to push herself to move faster. *So close…just a little more.* Before she could see his face that all-encompassing bright unbearable light swallowed her up.

"Mom!" Cianne yelled.

Cianne was back inside her bedroom, spread out on her bed. On her chest, she clutched the photo of her mother sitting alone on a bench in the courtyard.

"The same courtyard," she said as she sat up. The photo dropped onto the floor.

Cianne swung her head around and looked at the time on her alarm clock. No time had passed since she laid on her bed and looked at the clock after showering. However, she felt as if she missed minutes, if not hours, of her day.

"I was dreaming. I fell asleep and dreamed of the last thing I saw." She tried to convince herself, even though she felt otherwise. Cianne went to her bathroom and turned the faucet on. Splashing her face with cold water she looked at her reflection in the mirror

"It was just a dream." She said those five words again and again.

◉

"I was just defending myself," Tristan said out loud as he sat in his truck. That was the truth but he still felt guilty. It wasn't because he had gotten into a fight with Nick and his crew. It wasn't even because JC, the muscle head of the three, was in the hospital with a few broken ribs.

Tristan felt guilty because, when he was choking the life out of Nick it felt invigorating. So much so, that he hadn't wanted to stop. He hated Nick for what he did to Cianne, and getting his hands on the worthless bastard was something he had wanted since she confided in him.

It felt good to give in to the old Tristan again, but he knew that it was wrong.

Unsure of what he was going to do about it, Tristan got out of his truck and walked to Cianne's front door. He planned to surprise her with his presence and a lunch date but that was before daylight disappeared. The Dean of Kennecott University and a few other important heads wanted to meet with him after the altercation to discuss what had happened and to offer their apologies.

Tristan granted them their request to meet instead of following through with his plans with Cianne. He still wanted Nick to bleed. Even after the meeting, he needed time to calm down, so he went home and slept off his lingering aggression.

As he stepped up on Cianne's porch he noticed the house was completely dark with only a glimmer of light coming from the setting sun that shone through the open windows. Tristan knocked on the door several times before turning the knob. He pushed it open.

"Cianne," he called from the small foyer.

"Up here," her voiced sounded distressed as she called back.

Tristan ran up the steps taking two at a time, not even registering the fact that the almost complete darkness was not a hindrance at all. His movements were swift and light enough not to trigger the creaks her steps usually made when he walked up to them. Once at the top, Tristan pulled her shadowed figure close and held her tight. He nestled his face in the strands of her long silky hair before releasing a nervous breath.

"What are you doing here?" Cianne moved out of his hold and led him toward her room. "I thought you were coming back the day after tomorrow?"

"I came home early to surprise you." Tristan gently tugged Cianne closer so she didn't bump into the edge of her bookcase. "Careful," he said, as he helped her navigate through her dark bedroom. "Why is it so dark in here? Nothing happened, did it?" He waited for her response but when she didn't readily answer he said, "Did you foresee something happening to me?"

"No…well not something that's happened to *you*."

Tristan made sure Cianne was seated on the bed before going to the wall to flip on the light switch. He turned back to Cianne, who was visibly adjusting to the sudden bright light. She patted a spot next to her, signaling him to sit.

Cianne watched him as he walked over to her desk and took a seat in the chair instead of sitting beside her. She frowned but didn't say anything. "I was trying something."

"Trying what?" Tristan asked, as his eyes moved over her barely covered curves and smooth skin. He lingered over the sections of her that were covered—the parts he wanted so desperately to see and touch. When he realized that he was staring, he looked up only to see her head was tilted to the side and she was watching him with a big smile on her face.

Feeling a little embarrassed, Tristan looked away.

He hated being in Cianne's room. It was small, which made keeping a respectable distance hard and there were only two possible places to sit—the desk chair that was too short for his legs, or her bed; the bed that she slept in every night, wearing barely anything at all. The same kind of clothing she wore now.

It was hard enough being left alone with her, but to be alone with her in her bedroom was torture. Hell, being alone with her in any room anywhere was a problem. Keeping their relationship uncomplicated was becoming more and more complicated.

Sex was something Tristan felt Cianne had to be 100% sure of, with no coaxing from him. He had managed five months of self-restraint, a personal record for him. He figured he couldn't manage much more.

Cianne frowned. She knew that Tristan was trying to keep his distance. It was something she got used to over the past five months. Used to it, yes, but she didn't like it.

If he didn't want to sit next to her, he didn't have to. It wasn't as if she was a porcelain doll, that she'd break with the slightest touch, but it seemed he thought so.

So, fine. She sat back against her headboard and laid her hands on her lap. "Tell me about your trip?"

"Not much to tell. Just some business I needed to handle. I'll tell you all about it one day but not now," Tristan said, as he relaxed a little in the chair.

She silently prayed he got an ass cramp for trying to fit in her chair.

"Alright," she shrugged. He never talked about his trips and she never pressed the issue.

"Do you want to tell me what you were trying?"

Cianne exhaled. She knew she would eventually tell Tristan if he didn't drop the subject. However, she hoped to lead him in another direction. The problem was that Tristan wasn't easily diverted when he thought her safety or sanity was in jeopardy. His protective nature was a bit much, but she learned to deal with it.

"Something happened to me today after my run. I was looking at an old photo of my mother. This photo," Cianne pointed to the photo on her nightstand. "Hey, I almost forgot, my dad wanted me to tell you he needs to speak with you."

"Stop stalling," he ordered.

"Fine." Cianne rolled her eyes.

Tristan listened intently as she told him what had happened a few hours ago, without a single comment or question. All he did was shake his head or nodded every so often so she knew he was listening.

The retell didn't take long but with every word that spilled from her mouth, Tristan's blue gaze penetrated her inch by inch until she felt mentally naked. The worse part though, was when she was done, he said nothing.

"What are you thinking?" Cianne asked, after a few more minutes of silence.

"Did you get one of your headaches?"

Tristan's expression gave nothing away. Cianne wondered if he thought she was crazy now. If he finally realized she was a freak. "No," she answered honestly.

"Dizzy?"

"No, nothing like that, I was just lying here," she told him.

"May I?" Tristan motioned to her computer behind him.

Cianne nodded but wondered why he wanted to use her computer when they were talking about something she thought was…well serious.

The security screen loaded and Tristan typed something in the password field. 'Incorrect' flashed on the screen. She smiled but her smile fell when he tried again and managed to successfully sign into the computer.

Tristan glanced at her over his shoulder and smirked. Cianne raised her brows but didn't return the smile, which was hard because his smile had all but melted her.

She hadn't told him her password and had never used her computer in front of him. It kind of bothered her that he figured it out but she wouldn't freak. The only explanation for him knowing her password was that he knew her better than she thought and that was a plus. So, she quietly watched him navigate the internet from her bed.

"Were there any other people there, like around you?" he asked after a minute or so?

"Other than my mother," she said, "yes."

"Did you know any of the other people?"

"No, but," she started, "I may have known the person she was speaking to, sort of. But his back was to me the entire time, why?"

"One more question. You said you were outside. Have you seen or been to the place you saw before?"

"No," she answered curiously, "but it looked familiar."

Tristan moved slightly to the side and waved her over to look at the computer screen. Cianne got up from her bed and walked over to her desk. She looked at the image on the screen.

"That's where I was in my dream!" she exclaimed. "How did you know? Where is this?"

When he didn't answer, Cianne turned to look at him. His eyes were focused on the short kitty shorts she wore.

Again, when he realized she was looking at him he quickly turned back to the monitor. Tristan squeezed his eyes shut for a moment then scrolled down the page slowly allowing her to view more pictures and different angles of the location until a picture with a large sign came into view.

"Claremont University," she whispered.

"I don't think you were dreaming, Buttercup," Tristan told her, smiling.

He had never called her Buttercup before, but knowing she liked the nickname enough to make it her password, she guessed he was considering calling her by it now.

"How did you know my mother went to Claremont?" Cianne sounded surprised.

"Your father told me. He said you've been accepted," he admitted, "Claremont University was the only school that didn't make the top ten lists of colleges in the United States. I knew that there had to be a reason you would consider going there."

"Am I that transparent?"

"No, not really," Tristan said. He smiled up at her.

Cianne backed up and sat on the edge of her bed. "I didn't think I was dreaming either. I don't know what I did but I was trying to do it again. You would think that I wouldn't want to, being as I'm already the poster child for the unexplained. But I saw her and she was young and beautiful and…she was alive. I wanted her to see me but I guess I shouldn't provoke the freakish things that happen to me."

Tristan rolled the desk chair over to the bed and took her hands in his. "Why do you look at this as bad? Most people would love to do the things you can do."

"Everything was going so well these last few months." Cianne knew she was whining but didn't care. "Now this happens and who knows what's next."

Tristan caressed her hands which sent a surge of heat and emotions through her body.

"You act like this is a disease, Cianne, and it isn't. I'm sure we can figure it all out. Maybe learn to control these abilities so you don't hate it as much," he suggested.

"I don't want to figure them out or control it. I just want to be like everyone else." Cianne lowered her head. "I wish I could be like you, Tristan. You're always so calm about everything, nothing ever bothers you. That's why I love you—" Cianne covered her mouth. Her body went rigid when she realized what she said. "Uh, I meant—"

"Really?" he said, smiling. "You loooove me?" He playfully dragged the word love out.

Cianne bit at her bottom lip but soon felt his warm fingers brush over them. He then caressed her cheek with his thumb before he lifted her chin tenderly.

"Don't ever be afraid to tell me how you feel, Cianne."

He looked into her eyes and she noticed that his seemed lighter.

"I love you too," he breathed out. "I love you so much," he said softly. Then he pulled her into him and gently covered her lips with his.

When they parted, Cianne opened her eyes to see his gorgeous face still close to hers. His clear blue eyes revealed nothing, as usual. She wished he was easier to read. She wished she knew when he meant what he said, although she had no reason to mistrust him and he never spoke a lie to her as far as she knew. She just didn't understand how he could want her.

"You wouldn't say it if you didn't mean it, would you?" She hated the weakness of the question, the doubt in her voice.

"You know me Cianne. Do you really believe I would say those words without really meaning them?" He didn't let her answer. "Not only do I love you, I'm in love with you. I've never said those words to anyone before today because I've never felt this way about anyone else. My guess is that I never will."

"Then what's with all the mixed signals Tristan? I mean, you say that we are together but you never want to be close to me, like someone who's in love. We hang out all the time with our friends but it's rarely just the two of us. Why don't you ever want to be close to me?" she asked.

"I do want to be close to you, Cianne. Believe me, I do. But it's complicated." Tristan pulled his hands from hers and sat back in the chair. "It's just that with me once being active and you—"

"You mean sexually active?" Cianne interrupted. She had heard her friends use the term 'active' before.

"It's hard for me to be near you and not want to be *with* you. You're so beautiful and so…" He looked to the ceiling. "And so unbelievably sexy, Cianne." He looked back into her eyes. "I don't want us to do something you may regret later."

"I won't," Cianne said. She extended her arms.

Tristan took her hands and rolled the chair closer to her. She put her lips on his for a moment then pulled back to look at him.

"It's not easy for me to be near you either." She leaned in and kissed him again, this time more sensually, slowly. Holding the kiss, she took his hand and placed it on her bare thigh.

Cianne inhaled as the heat from his hand warmed her skin. It felt amazing. He squeezed her thigh and began to slowly move his hand up to her hip and around her back. She felt him pulling her closer.

This is it. This is really happening.

Cianne thought that it was going to happen until Tristan abruptly pulled away.

"Not a good idea."

That was all he said.

"Why is it not a good idea? You said you loved me."

Tristan sighed. "That's why it's not a good idea." Tristan took hold of her hands that were kneading his thighs and held them against his chest. "Because I love you Cianne, and I want you to be absolutely sure that you want what comes next and not just because I do. Can you tell me that you're ready beyond a shadow of a doubt?" He shook her hands lightly as if he wanted her to understand him and his words clearly.

Do I? Cianne looked at him for a moment before answering. *He could have me with a touch and a whisper. Tristan knew it.* He wanted her just as much as she wanted him but he hadn't taken advantage of her inexperience. *Instead, he wants me to think about it…to decide if I'm truly ready to have sex.*

Cianne was shocked by the high settings of Tristan's moral compass. Most of the guys she knew wouldn't care if she was ready or not. Tristan was a great guy. He was compassionate, smart, and one of the sexiest men she knew, but...

"No," she admitted, "I can't."

He smiled as he kissed the back of one of her hands. "And that's ok," he said, "because I can wait."

Chapter Sixteen

Cianne enjoyed several weeks without incident. The "thing with her mother" had become a memory that they never discussed again. Life had never felt so normal and Cianne loved it.

She sat quietly, staring at Tristan from the passenger seat of his truck as he drove up his long driveway. He was quiet and had been the entire ride from school. It took some time but Cianne learned to decipher the subtle changes in his demeanor, to determine his moods, because it was almost impossible to tell from his facial expressions.

Except when he was angry. When Tristan was upset, his eyes darkened. It was the only warning because his perfect lips would still stretch into an easy smile. It was a mask that hid something dark.

Cianne had to admit that she wasn't at all interested in seeing his "full out angry" mode.

Today, to her surprise, he actually looked somewhat anxious. His smooth handsome jaw was unusually tight, his eyes searched her out more than usual, and when she looked back at him he would look away.

Something was going on.

"What's on your mind?" she finally asked him.

"Nothing," Tristan offered an uneasy smile. He pulled his truck in front of the garage and turned the engine off then opened his door. He slammed the door shut, which was unusual, then walked around to open the door for her.

He never slammed a door the entire time she knew him. Whatever it was that was bothering him, she could tell he wasn't interested in talking about it.

"Are your parents home?" Cianne really wanted to know if his parents were inside.

She watched him struggle with the doorknob then followed him inside. She walked behind Tristan, toward the kitchen, not knowing if she should try to comfort him. He'd never been in this kind of mood since they began dating so this was new territory for the both of them. So, when he didn't answer her question right away, she dismissed it.

"No. They're out of town for a few days." He turned and gave her a smile she couldn't decipher. "So, you can relax."

Cianne didn't realize he knew how uncomfortable his parents made her. *Of course, he knew*. Why wouldn't he? Whenever they were around his parents, she didn't leave his side.

Tristan's mother was nice enough but Mr. Bertram hadn't warmed to her. Maybe he thought she and Tristan wouldn't work out. Or maybe he saw deeper than his wife and son. Maybe Mr. Bertram saw how flawed she really was.

Cianne pushed the thought away as Tristan led her into the dark kitchen. She felt it odd that it was the middle of the afternoon and the kitchen was dark. "Where are Martha and Celia?" she asked, as Tristan flicked on the light.

"Surprise!" an assortment of voices shouted.

Cianne jerked back, startled by the outburst. The room erupted with laughter.

"Happy Birthday Cianne," Tranae sang. She walked over to the entryway where Cianne stood with a frown on her face.

Cianne hugged her best friend. She hoped Tranae felt how fast her heart was beating. It would serve them right if she had a heart attack.

"Happy birthday Cianne," Brian said. "I've never seen someone that surprised in my life. We really got you."

"It's my birthday?" Cianne felt blood rush to her cheeks with the scare and she knew her face was getting even redder. She pulled her phone out of her pocket. February 23rd was stretched across the banner. Cianne searched for Tristan.

He had moved into the kitchen to give everyone space to greet her but was now moving toward her. She didn't know what he was thinking but she saw that his smile was gone and he was looking at her with his penetrating eyes.

"You really didn't remember your birthday?" Tranae asked her. She grabbed Cianne's hand.

"Do you need to sit sweetie?" Martha asked Cianne. Tristan and Tranae walked her over to a chair at the table without waiting for her answer.

"Maybe I should get her something to drink," Benjamin offered. He walked over to the table and poured some water into a glass. Tranae sat down next to her while Benjamin handed her the glass.

"Are you alright?" Tristan asked. He sat on the other side of her.

Cianne knew that Tristan was more concerned than he was letting on.   "Yes, I'm fine. I just have a lot on my mind I guess." Cianne smiled. She looked around the kitchen at the beautiful decorations. There were balloon bouquets, table cloths, and brightly colored dishes. Streamers and banners were hung from the ceiling with her name spelled out.

"The decorations are beautiful you guys, thanks so much."

"Everyone helped out," Tranae boasted, "Now open my present first." Tranae handed her a box.

Cianne gently undid the paper and opened the box. "Just what I wanted." She beamed as she held up the shirt. Cianne had considered buying it for herself a couple of days ago when they were at the mall but hadn't.

"Mine next," Brian handed her an envelope.

Cianne read the card first then showed everyone the gift card that was secured to it. "Thank you, Brian."

"This is a gift from the three of us." Martha handed her a box as she motioned to Benjamin and Celia.

"We hope you like it," Benjamin added.

Cianne placed her card on the table then opened the little black box that was handed to her. "They're lovely. Thank you so much." She put the earrings up to her ear, modeling them for her friends.

"They're white gold," Celia commented.

"We didn't know if you liked gold or silver more so we compromised," Ben told her.

Cianne smiled. "They're very nice, I love them."

An uncomfortable feeling had come over her when she noticed the gifts from the doorway. It was hard for her to accept gifts from others. The whole process of accepting presents was one she could do without. She never knew how to act when someone gave her something. Giving was much better.

As she graciously thanked everyone again, she noticed that Tristan had gotten up. When she placed her earrings on the table he was standing behind her, leaning close.

"Close your eyes," Tristan whispered.

Cianne shivered when his lips brushed across her ear. It had been the closest his mouth had been to a part of her body other than her lips, since that day in her room weeks ago. She froze momentarily, doing her best to hide the spark that danced inside her belly.

"Please," he added and took her hand.

Cianne stood and closed her eyes. She allowed Tristan to lead the way.

"I had my gift pre-assembled but I couldn't bring it in the house." He slowly walked her out of the kitchen.

She didn't know his house well enough to know where she was being led but she knew the others followed close behind. They all were full of hushed comments and excitement.

Several possibilities swirled around Cianne's head as she carefully put one foot in front of the other. She had no idea what Tristan could possibly have for her that needed to be pre-assembled. They had discussed buying bicycles and finding a nice bike trail to ride them on. She figured he forgot about it when he didn't mention it again.

The more they walked the more excited Cianne became. She heard a door open and had to fight to keep her eyes closed.

"Three steps down," he told her.

She held his arm a little tighter. His grip around her waist was sure and firm so she lowered herself down the three steps and found her footing on the floor. She was sure Tristan would catch her if she slipped. He led her a few more feet then made sure she was stable. Cianne felt his hand slide around her waist as he moved behind her.

"Alright you can open your eyes now," he said, close to her ear.

Cianne slowly opened her eyes. She saw the concrete floor first, then the shelving, and realized quite quickly that she was in his garage. It took only a moment to pinpoint her gift. All four of the garage doors were raised to let in the natural mid-day light to illuminate the white car with the largest red bow she ever saw on top of it.

"Oh, my god, you bought her a Mercedes!" Tranae cried from the doorway, "Oh My God."

He didn't!

"Do you like it?" Tristan asked her. "This is only what I picture you in but you can choose the make and model you want and my dealer will trade it out for you."

Thank goodness, he was standing behind her or he would have seen the look on her face. As he continued to tell her that she could take her time choosing another make and model, Tranae had the car door open and was already seated in the passenger seat. Brian was busy inspecting the outside of the vehicle.

"Tristan this is too much," Cianne said as she looked over her shoulder at him. "I can't accept this." She shook her head as she spoke. "Your parents couldn't have approved this."

"This is *my* gift to you Cianne," Tristan said softly. He leaned over her shoulder and wrapped his arms around her waist then rested his head on hers. "Do you like it?" When she didn't answer, Tristan turned her around to face him. His eyes conveyed his question.

Her answer was the uncomfortable silence that filled the garage.

Martha, noticing the awkward moment, was the first to break the silence. "I think it's time for cake," she said as she moved toward the door to go back inside the house. She waved for everyone other than Cianne and Tristan to follow.

Tranae gave Cianne a squeeze as she passed and whispered, "Keep it or I'll strangle you."

Tristan knocked before entering his bedroom. Cianne glanced over her shoulder at him before turning back around. She sat on the sofa with her back to him as she spoke on the phone to her father.

She doesn't look too happy.

He sat down on the sofa making sure to avoid the middle cushion where Cianne had her gifts spread out. He said goodbye to their friends and helped Celia clean the kitchen, now he just wanted to be next to his girl.

"It was very nice daddy. Yeah, I was totally surprised." Cianne spoke into her cell phone as she gave him a partial smile. Tristan winked in response. "Alright," she paused, looking down. "I understand, but I don't think that's—" Cianne leaned forward, resting her elbows on her knees. Her long hair tumbled forward, effectively covering her face. "Yes, but daddy—" She sighed.

Tristan stood, sensing that she needed some privacy. "Alright," he heard her say as he left the room.

"Everything alright?" he asked. He gave her a few minutes. Tristan strolled over to the sofa and took a seat beside her. Cianne had moved the gifts from the sofa and placed them neatly on the coffee table, so he sat closer this time.

When she turned to face him, she smiled but he could see the wet glare in her eyes. "You don't have to talk about it if you don't want to." He pulled her close.

Cianne folded into his chest and put her feet up on the sofa so that she lay snuggled against him. "You already know what's wrong." Her voice was rough and held an accusatory tone.

"I know something you don't," he said in jest, "that's hard to believe."

She frowned and Tristan immediately regretted being playful when she was obviously upset. He hesitated but attempted to give her comfort by kissing her forehead anyway.

"My father missed my birthday. *I* almost missed my birthday." She sniffed. Tristan rubbed her shoulder as she spoke. "My dad usually does all this for me, the gifts and the cake. He's never missed my birthday before, until today. And he calls from who knows where to wish me a happy birthday." She looked up at him and his stomach lurched at the sight of unshed tears that she was too stubborn to let fall. "But you knew he wasn't going to be here for my birthday and I didn't, because apparently, neither of you thought it was important to tell me."

"I'm sorry. I guess I just figured he spoke with you about his plans." Tristan wrapped a long string of her silky hair around his finger.

"He said you asked him about the car?"

"I didn't want to get you a car just for your father to tell me that you couldn't keep it. So, I asked his permission first.

That's all. Your father and I aren't a part of a conspiracy to keep things from you, Cianne."

◉

Cianne laid her head back on Tristan's chest. She tried to convince herself that her father not being with her on her birthday was alright but failed.

He traveled more and she supposed he was a bit occupied with his business but she still felt a little salty. Though, it wasn't as if he forgot like she had. Somehow it seemed much worse to forget your own birthday. However, Cianne refused to dwell on it. Besides, all she was able to think about was the beautiful car that sat in Tristan's garage.

It was actually hers.

"Tristan," she said. Her face, which rested on his chest, slowly rose and fell with every breath he took. "I really do love the car, but it's too much."

"There is nothing you need to do other than sign a paper or two saying that you accept the car as a gift and it is yours unconditionally, no strings attached."

She was aware of his touch. That he twisted her hair around his fingers only to let the strands fall to her back then recapture them.

"Are you in a position to be buying something like that?" Cianne wasn't certain how to say that she didn't want him using the money his parents meant for him, on her. Yet, when he laughed she felt foolish.

Maybe gifting cars was how rich people did things, but still. "I'm serious. It's a beautiful car Tristan, but it is not a girlfriend kind of gift. Especially not the kind of gift you give after only six and a half months." He smiled and the effect on her was immediate but Cianne quickly dismissed the feelings he stirred in her and managed an unyielding stare that demanded an answer to her question.

"Ok," Tristan said, laughing. He raised his right hand as if taking an oath, "I, Tristan Bertram, am in a position to buy something like 'that' for a girlfriend of only six and a half months."

His effort to convey seriousness was halfhearted, and a bit childish to her. "I'm so glad that I amuse you."

"You do." He grinned.

Cianne still felt uneasy about the expensive gift and he must have sensed it.

"Look, you haven't had a vision in a while. There's little chance of you zoning out while driving so I thought it was time you had your own car. I didn't want for this to be such a big deal."

It sometimes scared her how well he knew her. Cianne had never confided in anyone that she feared driving because of the visions. Not even her father. She told everyone that she just liked walking, that doing so kept her healthy.

"Tristan, it's a car. No, it's a Mercedes. My visions have nothing to do with this." She shook her head. "How exactly did you think this would play out?"

"Well, I thought you'd thank me and accept the gift I gave you graciously." He brushed her hair from her face so he could see her eyes clearly. "Just answer me this. Do you like the car?"

"Of course, I like the car. I love the car but that's—"

"Then it's settled," he spoke over her. "A car is something that I wanted to get you so…I did. It's yours so it would make me very happy if you keep it. But if you decide not to, for whatever reason, I can accept that too. It is yours to do what you want." Tristan shifted under her.

Cianne figured he was uncomfortable so she rose from his chest.

Tristan reached for something on the high table behind the sofa. When he brought his hand back, he held a silver heart shaped box. "This though," he said as he looked at the box, "I really want you to keep."

Cianne pushed herself all the way up until she was in a seated position. She looked at the heart shaped box then looked at him. His blue eyes melted her heart as they urge her to take it. She extended her hand and lifted the box from his. On the top of the box was the number 8 but the symbol was positioned sideways.

She traced the raised symbol with her fingers. "Forever," she whispered.

"Open it," he said to her.

Cianne opened the box as butterflies danced in her belly. "It's beautiful," she said, looking at him.

"It's one of a kind, just like you." Tristan took the white gold necklace with a diamond key pendant from the box.

Lifting her hair, Cianne moved forward so that Tristan could put the necklace around her neck. She dropped her hair and looked down at the key. Brushing it with her fingers, she took a deep breath. It was a shimmering example of the finest craftsmanship she ever saw. Cianne loved it and she loved him.

The realization that she had loved him for such a long time, sank in. She took Tristan's face in her hands and looked deep into his eyes. "I don't think I will ever be able to express to you how much I love you."

She pressed her lips to his and when he opened up for her she moaned with delight. She kissed him slow and deeply. When their lips separated, Cianne placed her hand on his chest and kissed a path from his lips to his ear. When she felt his body tense under her palm, she smiled.

"I will love you forever," she whispered breathlessly. Cianne kissed him passionately on the mouth again, stopping only to shower his lips with a collection of gentle kisses.

"Ci, please," Tristan begged her between kisses. "Honestly woman, you're torturing me." Another set of butterfly kisses caused him to whine in desperation.

Cianne slowly got to her feet. Her eyes were fixed on his as she unbuttoned her shirt. The cool key fell to the bare skin between her breasts, causing her to suck in a breath of air. Her long dark hair fell freely over her shoulders and down her back and arms as she lowered her shirt to the floor. Nervous and a little shy, Cianne covered her bra with her arms but when she saw the way Tristan watched her, when she saw the fire in his eyes, she smiled and dropped her arms to her sides.

Tristan watched as Cianne's beautiful hands slipped each button through the small openings of her shirt. He wasn't sure what shocked him more: the fact that she started taking off her shirt or that he did nothing to stop her.

God help me. I don't want to stop her.

What he wanted was to feel her bare skin on his. When she revealed her violet lace bra that her perfect breast fit snuggly inside, then smiled at him, he stood.

Tristan lifted her easily in his arms. He stared into her eyes and she wrapped her arms around his neck and placed her forehead to his as he carried her to his bed. Her body was warm and soft. Tristan shivered as her soft fingers caressed his shoulder and back.

He took his time removing her underwear. Not just because he wanted to savor the moment, but because he wanted to give her a chance to change her mind. "Are you sure?"

Cianne was bare to him. He gazed down at her, knowing that his imagination hadn't even scratched the surface of her full beauty. But even now, with his need boiling and the pressure on his restraint edging on unbearable, he would stop if she wanted to.

"Beyond a shadow of a doubt," she panted.

Tristan watched her face as he removed his clothing. Her stunning eyes kept him grounded and calm. He noticed when her composure faltered and was replaced with a hint of concern when he slid his briefs down his thighs.

With other women he'd been with, he was flattered by their apprehension regarding his size with swollen pride, but now he just wanted to assure Cianne that they were made for each other. He climbed on the bed next to her and pulled her close. Tristan reveled in the warmth of her entire body against his. He kissed her shoulder and neck before looking into her eyes again.

"Don't worry," he told her with his usual confidence, "I was created just for you."

Cianne gazed up at him lovingly. She placed her hand on his cheek and kissed his lips tenderly, showing him her trust.

Feeling like his dreams were finally coming true he slid his thigh between hers. Her heated center all but scorched his thigh, causing an animalistic hunger to suddenly surge through him. A hunger Tristan had never felt before this night.

Could he be gentle? Gentle had never been a concern for him. Sex had always been a driving need. As Tristan again searched her eyes for any doubt and saw none, he resolved to be gentle.

He could be anything for Cianne. He wanted to be everything to her.

Chapter Seventeen

The room was normal enough. As normal as a room could be. It was so normal that a person could completely forget when and where he or she was. Most of the people at Dorchester Psychiatric Hospital didn't much care where they were, or when, for that matter. But Bianca Prescott wasn't like most people. She cared.

Time was different for each of the patients in places like this as well. It went by fast or at a snail's pace. For Bianca, time virtually stood still.

Bianca peered out of the window, her mind far from where she stood. In her mind, she lay in a large bed, in a room that was so familiar it felt like home. Her hair was perfect, as it usually was. Her makeup was flawless and she wore his favorite flavor gloss on her lips. He liked for her lips to look wet.

Bianca knew everything he liked. His favorite books, music, color, even the way he liked to be touched.

In that familiar room, where her mind often took her, Bianca watched him as he slept. She had watched him many times like this before. She caressed his handsome face, her touch a bit rough but loving. He opened his blue eyes and smiled because he liked it rough at times. He gripped her wrist and pulled her close. He kissed her long and hard. Just the way she liked to be kissed.

"Ms. Prescott?"

Bianca opened her eyes then slowly looked over her shoulder at the nurse standing in the doorway.

"The doctor is ready for you now." The nurse turned and began to walk out, but stopped and turned back. "Are you ok Ms. Prescott?"

"I'm perfect." Bianca beamed. She folded her arms around herself as she thought of Tristan. "Everything is just so perfect."

The truck was virtually silent when Cianne started it up with the key Tristan had given her months ago. She would have taken her brand-new car but it was locked inside his garage. She didn't want to wake him but she really had to get home so she took his truck.

She checked the mirrors again before easing around the dimly lit private driveway. It was early, still dark out, so Cianne turned on the headlights as she made the turn onto the main road. She thought about turning on the radio but decided to drive in silence. She seldom drove at all and didn't feel entirely comfortable in the expensive truck, so the sound of morning traffic would have to do if she wanted to concentrate.

When she arrived home, she made a beeline for the kitchen. Cianne opened the refrigerator to find something to eat. Rising early always sparked her appetite. After reviewing her options, Cianne turned to look at the microwave. Three a.m. was flashing in digital green. She closed the refrigerator.

The desire for something to eat seemed to dissolve once she realized she would actually have to prepare it. She looked through the cabinets for a fiber bar or anything quick. Nothing appealed to her so she closed the cabinet doors and took a banana from the always stocked fruit basket on the table.

After eating the banana in record time, she threw the peel away. It would be impossible for her to go back to sleep so Cianne decided that she would get cleaned up first then cook if she was still hungry. As she climbed the stairs her thoughts went to Tristan and she found herself smiling. Laughing at herself, she stepped into her bathroom, turned on the shower, then stripped.

Cianne hissed as the cold key fell to her naked chest. She touched it, taking in a deep breath as the reality of everything that happened during the last six months washed over her.

"Am I dreaming?" she asked herself, as steam distorted her reflection in the mirror.

Feeling somewhat dazed, Cianne stepped inside the shower. When the hot water hit her skin, she closed her eyes as ripples of her recent lovemaking surged through her body. When the sensations subsided, she relaxed and moved forward, letting water run over her hair and face. Cianne exhaled as the spray of water soothed her, making the soreness between her thighs a secondary distraction.

"What?" A hint of irritation laced Tranae's tone. She eyed Cianne closely. Her disdain for the guessing game was written all over her face. "Wait…the necklace? He gave you a necklace too?"

Cianne pulled the key from under her tank top for Tranae to see.

"A Tiffany key…you've got to be kidding me." Tranae leaned in closer to inspect the diamonds. "He got you a Tiffany Key. Those haters are gonna be so jealous." Tranae's excitement bubbled over as she took a quick look at her watch. "You need to get dressed. We have to get to school. Hey, and wear something low cut in the front." Tranae stood up and paced the kitchen. "We're going to speak to everyone, even the shadows. You know, the people we don't usually speak to." Cianne shook her head as Tranae threw her finger up. "Brenda…" She smiled devilishly. "Is going to be sick with envy."

Cianne hadn't said a word during Tranae's spiel. Listening to her friend was somewhat of a treat most days. One of the many things she loved about Tranae, was her genuine friendship. Tranae didn't have a jealous bone in her body. Although, Cianne hadn't felt that much of her life was something to be envied. Tranae often told Cianne that she didn't see herself the way others did.

Finally, Cianne felt that she had something to be envied—Tristan, who loved her.

"I did *it*," Cianne admitted, unable to hold it in any longer.

Tranae instantly turned to face her then slowly sank back down in the chair. "Did *what* exactly?"

Tranae knew *what*, Cianne could tell, but she wanted "it" spelled out. Cianne scrunched her nose up as she bit on her bottom lip. "You know," she said, tilting her head, "*it*." Cianne waited and then, Tranae's eyes flickered with understanding.

Tranae's hand flew to her mouth as a muffled scream almost forced its way out. A high pitched muffled cry came out of her two more times before she was able to compose herself. Cianne offered Tranae a sheepish grin before she shook her head.

"How was it? Did it hurt? Did you cry?" Tranae asked.

"Painful," Cianne admitted when Tranae took a breath. "At first it hurt. The pressure coupled with my anxiety probably made it worse but I was so nervous. Then once he found a rhythm it felt…it was amazing but near the end, the pain started again. I wanted to just scream but—"

A tap on the front door caused both of them to jump with fright.

"That was the door," Tranae said, trying to whisper.

Cianne frowned. It was way too early in the morning for visitors. Tranae shrugged. They both got up from the kitchen table and walked to the front door. Tranae was the one to look through the window.

"It's Tristan," Tranae whispered again…then mouthed it.

"Why are you whispering?" Cianne asked. She reached around Tranae and pulled the door open.

Tranae shrugged again, "Damn if I know."

With her head slightly tilted, Cianne opened the screen door. "Hey," she said. Cianne avoided Tristan's eyes but she felt them on her. A wave of self-doubt cascaded over her. She knew that her face was flushed with color. When their eyes met she immediately looked down.

Last night was still fresh in her mind and she didn't know how she should act. Her face burned more as memories of what they'd done played in her mind. A muted but wondrous feeling pulsed in her.

"Can I come in?" Tristan asked.

The hood of the jacket he wore shadowed most of his face and he sounded strange but Cianne moved out of his way so he could enter, thinking nothing of it. She looked out of the door as he stepped inside. Parked next to his truck was her new car, minus the big red bow.

When Cianne turned around Tristan was standing in front of her with his hands in his pockets, the hood of his jacket still over his head. She wanted to kiss him but decided against it with Tranae glaring at them with a knowing smile. Kissing him would sort of feel dirty right now because she was just talking about, well, *it*.

"How's it hanging?" Tranae asked, sounding too upbeat. Cianne gave her a hard look. "What?" Tranae glared at her. "Sorry," she shrugged, as she walked to the door. "Are you driving me to school? Brian can't take me. He has to do something for his dad today."

"Um, yeah," Cianne said. She was about to tell Tranae to give her a few minutes but Tristan spoke up.

"Do you mind taking yourself, Tranae?" Tristan had already pulled the keys to his truck out of his pocket and was passing them to her.

"Sure," Tranae said, as she quickly grabbed his keys. "I get to whip the G550." She looked up at Tristan, "I'll treat her like my own." Tranae quickly opened the door and shut it behind her as if she had the devil after her.

Cianne shook her head. Her friend was a right nut.

"I'm still getting dressed." She knew her voice sounded shaky but she couldn't help it. Tristan made her more nervous than before. She hurried past him and jogged up the stairs. He was acting strange but so was she. To her, it felt as if their relationship had reset to square one, the nervous beginnings phase.

Cianne hurried to her closet. She wondered how long this awkwardness would last. The intimacy they shared should have made them more comfortable but it obviously hadn't, at least not for her. She was more nervous now and the butterflies that she felt whenever he was around seemed to have multiplied.

"I'm so sorry about last night," he said.

Cianne peeked out from behind her closet door. Tristan stood by her bed with his hands in his pockets, looking at the floor. He looked up briefly, long enough for Cianne to see hurt and shame reflected in his eyes.

Sorry…sorry about what? Did he regret…

She watched him as she walked over to her bed and sat down.

"I just wanted to be with you so badly that..." Tristan kept his eyes on the floor knowing if he looked up…if he saw the pain he caused her, he'd lose it. "I wasn't thinking clearly. I…," he tried to look at her then, but he couldn't.

Last night, he tried to be careful with her. Every motion, every movement he made was deliberate. He tried to think of her, even though such concerns were foreign to him.

Tristan thought about how being with her made him feel and how he had never experienced such ecstasy before last night. He thought about how intense and perfect making love to her had felt. So much so that he lost his focus. Near the end, he took her with abandonment. He'd been careless and greedy. He'd caused Cianne pain.

Tristan glanced over at her, seeing the sadness in her eyes. It was time to face the music. He pulled his hood off his head, exposing his face. He smoothed his hands over his short hair and sat next to her

"I heard you say stop. I felt you pushing me away and...I couldn't. I didn't want to," he said, ashamed. He looked her in the face. "I hurt you and I am truly sorry."

Cianne shook her head in disbelief. Words escaped her but her body was obeying her thoughts. She moved closer to Tristan, wanting to comfort him, but when she reached up to touch him he moved.

He moved so fast it took her a moment to catch her breath.

When Cianne looked up, Tristan was no longer sitting on the bed next to her. He was standing outside of her bedroom door, facing her. Her hand still hovered in the air where he had been sitting.

Nope, you're imagining things.

Cianne was about to mention how fast he moved but quickly dismissed what she thought she saw when she noticed the haunted look on Tristan's face. He had been so tender last night. The way he held her close, the gentle way he handled her. It was the perfect blend of agony and ecstasy...until the end. He had sped up, had become a bit wild. But she never *said* please stop.

She thought it, but the actual words never left her lips.

Tristan rubbed his head again, letting his hand slowly run down his face. She wouldn't even talk to him. Her silence had to be a refusal to accept his apology.

She doesn't want you here.

He sluggishly started toward the stairs but stopped when he heard the bed creak. Cianne's footsteps turned him around.

He wasn't sure how he closed the space between them so quickly but he lifted her off her feet and buried his face in her neck.

"I can't lose you," he told her. "I'll do whatever it takes for you to forgive me."

"Tristan, what we did last night was something I wanted to do." He placed her back on her feet. "I don't regret it and I don't want you to."

"I woke up and you weren't there and I thought…" He placed his hands on either side of her face and peered into her eyes. "I saw your tears." His gut tightened as he thought of what he would admit next. "And I didn't stop." He shook his head. "I don't know what came over me. I should have stopped."

"I never said 'stop', Tristan."

Tristan shook his head, he heard her. *I heard her.*

Cianne took hold of his wrist then pulled his hands away from her face. Tristan noticed how she looked at his hands instead of his eyes but he wrote it off as her usual shyness, even though his instincts told him differently.

"If you hadn't fallen asleep so fast I would have told you I needed to get home. We do have school today. Besides, I'm sort of relieved that you feel asleep. It would have been too embarrassing to talk to you. You know, after," she said, frowning.

He remembered holding her close, thanking her, and telling her how much he loved her but he could barely keep his eyes open.

Another first.

"How someone so beautiful could feel embarrassed about anything is beyond me."

Cianne shrugged then smiled. She lifted her head and looked him directly in the eyes. "I love you, ok?" Tristan nodded. "Now that that's settled, I have to get dressed." She kissed the back of his hands before going back to her room and into her closet.

"So, your first experience wasn't all bad then?" He followed, feeling once again like the luckiest man alive.

"God no. It was amazing."

He could see she was blushing before she turned away.

"How was it for you? I worry that I didn't measure up to what you're used to." She stuck her head out of the closet. Her brows wrinkled. "I wanted to be good for you."

"For me?" Tristan's mouth curled into a smile. He was astonished by her modesty. "You are so above my caliber and you don't even see it." He walked up behind her and turned her to face him. "No one, least of all me, is worthy of you, Cianne. You are exquisite perfection in every way. My heart, mind, and body are yours." Tristan placed his forehead to hers and lifted her right hand. He turned the ring he gave her one full turn, "forever."

He wanted to tell her all he was feeling but the truth was that he didn't really understand it. He felt connected to her on a much deeper level. What she gave him, her innocence, was… It was the single most precious gift a woman could give, other than her love. He wasn't worthy of such a gift, especially from Cianne. She was perfection, beauty personified, a radiant soul that lit the way to his salvation.

How could he tell her that she was his life?

Cianne threw her arms around his neck. "I love you, Tristan Bertram."

Tristan pulled her close, lifted her off the floor, then took her lips. His hands slid over the bare skin of her thigh. She only wore a thin yellow tank top with matching underwear, and he was holding her. He abruptly dropped her to her feet and took a step back.

"What?" Cianne squealed.

"Uh, unless you're ready for round two," he said, blushing as he looked down at his pants. "I…uh, it may be harder for me to be alone with you more than before, now that we've…" He wiggled his eyebrows.

Cianne laughed as she shook her head and waved her hands. "School, remember."

He rubbed his head as his face burned with embarrassment.

So much for my supreme control.

"I'll just wait downstairs while you get dressed."

It didn't take Cianne long to finish dressing and to get downstairs. Once outside, she stood on the porch for a moment, not knowing what to do. It took a few seconds to digest that she was the new owner of the beautiful new car that sat in her driveway.

Tristan grinned as he dangled the keys in front of her face. She sighed, then she took the keys and walked to *her* car.

"You sure you don't want to drive us?" she asked Tristan.

"It's your car so you should drive it." Tristan opened the passenger door and sat down.

Cianne huffed as she got into the car and started it up. The engine didn't purr like people often said. It barely made a sound. Cianne took several minutes to look at all the gadgets before she adjusted the mirrors.

This is really happening.

She took an exaggerated breath, sat up straight, then pulled off.

"We could ditch," Tristan said as he played with the car stereo. "We're probably going to be late anyway."

Ditching was something she had never done and the look on her face must have told him that it was out of the question.

"Alright." He lifted his hands in defense. "Don't look so worried Ci, I was just kidding."

"Only eight minutes late," Cianne said to Tristan in the vacant hallway just outside of the school office. She gasped as he pulled her toward him and kissed her. She frowned at public displays of affection, especially in school, but things were a little different now.

Before letting go of her completely, Tristan gave her a quick kiss on the cheek then winked at her before jogging away in the opposite direction.

Cianne sighed as she watched him disappear around a corner. She had only two minutes before the bell would signal the end of homeroom. She should have gone straight to her first class, and she would have but she wanted to see Tranae first.

As soon as Cianne opened her homeroom door she felt everyone's eyes on her. The entire class turned to watch her as she placed the late slip on her homeroom teacher's desk then walked to her seat. When she sat down the whispers began.

Cianne gave Tranae the most hateful look she could muster.

"I only texted Vanessa," Tranae whispered in her own defense.

Cianne immediately regretted not going to her first class to wait outside the door for the bell. *It would have been infinitely better than this*, she thought as she sank down a little more in her chair. Cianne pulled her long slightly damp braid over her shoulder and took the thin band off the end of the braid then began to unwind it. Once her hair was free she finger-combed through it, letting the wavy mass fall over her shoulders to cover her face. When the bell rang Cianne waited until everyone left the classroom before she got up.

"They're all talking about me," Cianne said, as she walked down the hall with Tranae. She glanced over at the third group of girls who she heard say her name since she left homeroom. They stood in a semi-circle looking over at her as they spoke in hushed voices.

Cianne walked faster. Her intentions to graduate high school drama-free had just dwindled away.

"Who cares if they're talking about you? What can they possibly say? They're just jealous." Tranae said loudly, daring anyone to oppose her. "Tristan fell for you. Some girls are bound to hate on you for that alone." She shook her head at Cianne. "Everyone isn't going to be happy for you dear."

As soon as the words left Tranae's lips, Cianne noticed that Sharon Graves and Diane Siedenburg were staring at her. They were Bianca's best friends and the look of pure hatred they were giving her would make anyone's skin crawl.

Tranae looked at Cianne, who wasn't paying attention, so she followed Cianne's gaze. "Problem?" Tranae asked.

Sharon, the shorter of the two, tapped Diane on the shoulder and they slowly looked away.

"You can't pay those two any mind," Tranae said, trying to keep up with Cianne. "You should be happy right now, considering what has happened in the last 24 hours."

"I *am* happy," Cianne admitted, as they reached the staircase leading to the second floor. "It's just that I don't like it when people talk about me."

Tranae looked at her as if she was stupid. "Oh sweetie, they were already talking about you. Do you honestly think that these bitches like you?" Tranae laughed as if Cianne had missed the punch line. "They smile in your face every so often but that's only to make sure that you feel some type of loyalty to them and not go after their boyfriends." Tranae caught her slipping bag and readjusted it back on her shoulder. "Look Cianne, you got the guy and he has a lot of admirers who are going to be shooting you dirty looks, which you should already be used to," she said plainly, "but who cares? Be proud and stop feeling ashamed of it. He isn't going around feeling bad that he took you off the market."

"I'm going to be late," Cianne said, as she started up the steps. She wanted this day to be over and that meant getting through it. "I'll see you at lunch."

"Everyone wouldn't be so shocked about you guys being an item if you'd showed some kind of affection in public before now!" Tranae yelled from the bottom of the staircase.

"And pull that damn key out from under your shirt!" she added.

By lunch hour, West Hills High had exploded with talk of Cianne and Tristan. Not so much that they were dating. Everyone had assumed that months ago even though neither of them had confirmed it.

But now, everyone's assumptions had been validated. The key around Cianne's neck and the car was the talk of the school. Even the faculty had been overheard discussing the news.

For years Cianne had avoided this kind of attention.

I can't wait for this day to be over, Cianne thought, as she leaned back on her locker. She avoided the curious looks from her peers. Tristan walked up just as she was debating if she was going to eat with him and their friends, or go home and apologize later.

"Hey you," he said, moving in for a kiss.

Cianne put her hand up on his chest before he could kiss her. She then looked around to see if anyone was watching them. A few freshmen were walking in their direction but no one she knew.

"Tranae was right." Tristan took a few steps back but kept his eyes on hers. "You don't want anyone to know we're dating."

I am going to kill Tranae.

"It's not that," she whispered. She watched the freshmen pass before she finished. "I just don't want to rub this, us…in anyone's face, that's all."

"So, you think showing me affection in public is rubbing it in the faces of people that we will most likely never see again once we graduate. Does that make any sense to you at all, Cianne?" he asked her calmly.

"I'm not worried about those people. It's a person you know very well that I'm worried about," she admitted. "I saw

Diane and Sharon today. They gave me the most venomous looks."

Tristan sighed. "Oh." He leaned on his locker next to her. "I never considered *that* could be an issue for you." His entire body went rigid as he pushed off his locker. "Did they say anything to you?" Tristan asked with deceptive calm.

"No, nothing," she told him. He relaxed on his locker again after a few seconds. "It's just that I know that they tell Bianca everything that's happening here and I don't want news about us to be something she has to hear about from them."

Tristan pulled her around by the waist to face him. "All I can say is that we can't live our lives for Bianca's sake. I've tried, and in the end, I realized that I was not only hurting myself but I was hurting her as well. But, if you'd rather we keep our torrid affair a secret," he said as he grinned, then his expression became serious, "I can live with that. I just don't want to live without you."

Cianne was grateful for how understanding and accommodating Tristan was about everything. She hadn't made one sacrifice for him. The least she could do was publicly claim him. Cianne leaned into Tristan, wrapped her arms around his neck, then kissed him. She had meant it to be a chaste kiss but when she heard a few students coming in their direction, Cianne turned it into a hot melting one.

One of the students who passed made a loud whooping sound while another yelled for them to get a room.

"Wow." Tristan smiled.

When they separated, Cianne was blushing. She watched as Tristan adjusted his sweat pants to hide what she awakened. She loved how she affected him.

"You hungry?" he asked. "I told Brian and Tranae we would stick around and eat with them today."

"I'm actually starving," she confessed. The two strolled toward the cafeteria, and for the first time in six months, Cianne pulled Tristan's arm around her shoulders. He held her close, showing anyone who noticed that they were indeed a couple.

Chapter Eighteen

It was February 28th, the last Sunday of the month, and Tristan was late for family dinner by nine minutes. When he sat down at the dining room table his mother gave him a half smile. Tristan knew exactly what that meant.

Though Leslie looked as calm as still waters, his father was furious.

A man who can mask whatever he is feeling is a man holding all the right cards, his father often said.

For his mother, Tristan decided that tonight he would be the agreeable one no matter how much his father tried to push him. "Good evening Mother, Father."

Mr. Bertram jostled the ice in his glass. "Is she worth it?" Leslie asked.

Tristan sighed. He tried.

"Oh, come on." Tristan's voice carried across the dining room, "Her name is Cianne. Cianne Baxter. You've known her for more than six months, and you're still choosing to refer to her as "She". As cold as you've been to her, I'd say she's earned the right to be called by her name. Don't you?"

"Tristan." His mother warned before turning to his father. "Leslie, please not tonight."

"It's fine mom," Tristan said. He held his hand up, feigning peace. "He wants to talk so we talk. Is she worth what dad?" He stared at his father.

Mr. Bertram placed his glass down. "Your future. Is *Cianne*," Mr. Bertram said, emphasizing her name, "worth your future?"

"Cianne *is* my future," Tristan said with confidence.

His mother's mouth gaped open but to her credit she said nothing.

He turned to her. "Cianne is my future," he said again, but softer.

"She's your future, yet we know nothing of her family, her upbringing. Where does she come from? What kind of name is Cianne anyway?" Mr. Bertram stood from the table and walked over to the liquor cabinet. The bourbon settled with the melting ice as he poured it into his glass.

"What you're really asking is what ethnicity is she and if her family has money, right Dad?" Tristan pushed away from the table and stood. His mother gasped at his sudden movement but he was too amped to have noticed.

Mr. Bertram laughed heartily. It was a condescending laugh that his father perfected over time. "My God, Tristan…a car," his father said. He took a sip from the cup in his hand. "You were with Bianca for years. Did you ever buy her a car?"

Tristan knew where his father was heading and it infuriated him. He clenched his teeth. "Bianca has a car."

"So, you're done with Bianca? We can just add her to the many broken hearts you've stepped on? You know, if you think just because you're honest with these young ladies that you aren't hurting them in the end, you're wrong." Mr. Bertram grunted, "Maybe it's time you're the one who ends up hurting. You've heard of karma Tristan, but are you familiar with the term gold-digger?" He took another sip from his glass.

Tristan moved so fast that he was on the other side of the dining room when the 'r' in the word digger was leaving his father's mouth. Standing mere inches away, he looked his father in the eyes. Mr. Bertram gave him a bewildered look as he took a few steps back, spilling some of his drink on the expensive wood flooring.

"Leslie?" His mother stood. She looked appalled by the accusation and at the same time, worried about what Tristan planned to do.

Tristan held his father's gaze, making certain that there would be no misunderstanding his words. "You're my father and I love and respect you. I have followed your advice on most matters and I'm in your debt for what you have done for me as a father, and now as a mentor. Nonetheless, you have no right to tell me who or what I choose to do for the woman I love. You don't get to insult or mistreat her. Don't ever assume you have that right." Tristan turned around and gave his mother a forced smile as he walked toward the dining room door. "My apologies Mother, could you please let Celia know that I won't be joining the family tonight?"

May I come in?" Mrs. Bertram asked as she tapped on her only child's bedroom door. She sat down on the bed next to his head. She lifted one of her legs up on the bed and left the other dangling off.

Tristan raised his head to acknowledge her then laid his head back on his pillow and continued to stare up at the ceiling. All the lights in the room were turned off except for a lamp on his nightstand that didn't give off much light.

The low sound of a thunderstorm hummed throughout the room. "Rain and Thunder?" she said, as she picked up the CD case and read the title. She turned it over in her hands then sat the case back on the nightstand. "I've never seen you like this before, Tristan. You have never given anyone, or *anything* for that matter, this much attention."

"Have you ever listened to the rain before? The way it sounds when it hits something…" Tristan turned his head to look at her. "It does relax you. Cianne loves this kind of stuff."

He knew his mother wasn't in his room to talk about the sounds of nature but he wasn't in the mood to discuss his feelings. He had seen fear in her eyes tonight. She was afraid of the person he was and who he might become. For a half of a second, when he was in his father's face, he was afraid too.

She sighed. "You know sometimes we confuse infatuation with love. Are you sure this is love you're feeling Tristan?"

Despite his reservations about speaking his feelings, he decided to. "I sometimes think my heart is going to stop when I hear her say my name. I mean, really stop." He laughed. "I want to know what she's thinking and how she feels, and all I can think of is ways to make her happy because I physically hurt every time she cries." Tristan looked at his mother. "I'm in love with her."

On the verge of tears, his mother kissed him on his forehead. "Falling in love can be glorious if it's reciprocated. Does she feel the same for you, Tristan?"

"That's the billion-dollar question." He smiled.

She smiled with him then kissed him on the forehead. "You bring Cianne over for dinner soon." His mother stood, then left his room.

It was the first day of Spring Break and the weather was beautiful. *Perfect for a morning run.* Cianne inhaled the fresh air that came in through her bedroom window. She dressed then grabbed her cell phone off her nightstand. When she stepped out on her front porch she waved to her car, feeling a bit silly that she wasn't taking it.

She pulled out her earbuds, inserted them in her cell phone, and when her music started she set off for Ridgeview Park, only a few blocks away.

Once at the park, Cianne stretched then set out for the trail just minutes after she left her house. Jogging this early in the morning would only be possible for two weeks, then Spring break was over and back to school. She wanted to take full advantage of her morning freedom.

Starting with a slow pace, she jogged for about five minutes before she accelerated to a brisk trot, with her music motivating her every step. Twenty minutes into her run she felt better than she ever felt, despite her lack of exercise these past months. She was just about to step it up a notch when everything around her started to spin.

Cianne stopped running. She made it to a tree a few feet away and used it to steady herself.

"It'll pass," she whispered, as she looked for the closest place to hide. She hadn't had a vision in months…nor had the dizzy spells beforehand been this bad. Barely able to stand, Cianne closed her eyes as she rubbed her forehead. She needed a minute.

"I thought I'd find you here."

Cianne looked over her shoulder and saw Tristan strolling toward her.

"Did you forget about our breakfast date?" Tristan smiled.

Cianne was just about to tell him she hadn't forgotten. That she wanted to get in a quick run before breakfast but her vision blurred and the ground moved under her feet. She swayed…

"Cianne?"

She heard the concern in his voice as she felt strong arms wrap around her waist. Cianne closed her eyes as Tristan steadied her. She was so out of it that when Tristan lifted her legs from under her, she thought she was falling.

It wasn't until he sat her on a park bench that she realized he carried her. When she opened her eyes, it took her time to focus and see that he was kneeling in front of her.

Cianne quickly covered her face as she fought the vision and the change that would precede it. She waited for her veins to darken, for her eyes to redden, for his look of disgust.

"Cianne, are you alright?"

She waited…and waited. When no vision came, she held her hands in front of her. *Nothing.*

"Um, I…I guess I should have eaten first," Cianne stuttered. She was confused that there had been no vision so she reached for an explanation. "I haven't run for a while, and I overexerted myself. I just need to sit for a moment."

Tristan watched her closely as he rubbed one of her legs. "I'll go get you some water."

"No, I'm fine really," she argued. Her head was still a little hazy and now that she knew there would be no vision, she thought that maybe the issue was simple. Maybe she pushed herself too much and should have started off slow and built her endurance up again.

"Let's get you home then," Tristan told her, as he reached to pick her up again.

Cianne pushed his hand away, "Don't be ridiculous. What…are you going to carry me the entire way?"

"No," he said with all seriousness, "just to my car."

"I can walk." Cianne slowly stood and took a few steps just to convince herself. She took one careful step after another until she was sure she could walk without incident. Tristan positioned himself close beside her as they walked to the parking lot.

Cianne tried to hide the fact that she was worried. Minutes later she was turning her key in her door. Whatever happened at the park had passed for now and she felt great, again.

Once she convinced Tristan she was alright, Cianne left him in the kitchen and went to take a shower. When she stepped out of the shower, wrapped in a towel, she didn't expect to find Tristan sprawled out on her bed, and in his hands, he had one of the books she'd been reading.

"What are you up to?"

Tristan flung the book back on the nightstand and smiled. "Nothing, I ordered some food for us." He sat up on the edge of her bed and pulled at the bottom of the towel. "What time does your dad get home?"

"Don't know," she said, grinning. "Wait, didn't you once say that sex can complicate a relationship?"

Tristan reeled her over to him and slid his hand under the towel and up her leg. Cianne's mind and body definitely wanted more, but she wasn't about to get caught with her panties literally down. Her father would be home any minute.

"What I meant was, that it complicates things if you're doing it with the wrong person."

"Oh, right." Cianne smiled but pushed his hand away. She grabbed her undergarments off her bed then wriggled out of his grasp and headed for the bathroom. Cianne knew he wanted her but the opportunity hadn't presented itself since her birthday. In fact, every time she thought they were going to get a chance to be intimate, something came up.

"Have you thought it over?" Tristan called out. His voice easily carried through to her in the bathroom.

"Some." Cianne tried not to smile as she came back into the room. She laid next to Tristan, who had spread out on her bed again. She placed her head on his chest, enjoying how solid and strong he felt. When his arm wrapped around her, she felt completely safe and utterly happy in love.

"Well, your answer then?" He rubbed her arm.

"Is…yes," she squealed with delight.

Tristan pushed up, causing her to do the same. He looked at her for a few seconds then took her by surprise with a loving kiss. "It'll be awesome, you'll see."

Cianne gave him an uneasy smile. "We still have to run it by my dad," she reminded him.

Tristan's smile faded. "What do you think he'll say?"

"I don't know," she admitted. "He can be protective at times then other times he's quite liberal. But I'm eighteen so I guess it's my decision ultimately. I just don't want to upset him right now. He's been looking so stressed lately, and with all the business trips he's been going on, I don't want to add more to whatever is going on with him."

"How about I stay for dinner tonight and we ask him together?" He stroked her wet hair.

"Alright, but if my dad says yes I have one condition," she bargained.

"Whatever your heart desires."

Cianne almost laughed, due to how serious he sounded. Then she realized he *was* serious. She mentally shook her head then said, "We ask Tranae and Brian if they'll go with us. I don't want to be stuck in the hotel all day while you're hanging with your father doing whatever business people do."

"I wanted it to be just us." Tristan pouted. He seemed to ponder her request for a moment then said, "But I don't want you to be alone when I can't be there either, so we can ask them if your father gives you permission to go."

Cianne gave him the brightest smile she had. "I am so excited! I've never been to Houston before. What should I pack?" She jumped up and went to her closet.

Tristan laughed. "You'll have five weeks to figure it out. Just remember when you start to pack that we're only going for the weekend."

Cianne felt as if the room, and everything in it, was spinning out of control. Or was it just her life that had spun out of control? She clutched her pillow tightly. In her head was a miasma of problems and her mind reached for solutions. It was just that she had none.

"Cianne," Tranae said softly.

She looked up to face her friend's judgmental gaze again. She had completely forgotten that Tranae was in her room. Her presence was easy to forget because she hadn't said much in the hours they'd been home, Cianne reasoned.

Cianne lay her face back down on her pillow. A single tear rolled over the bridge of her nose and down her cheek.

This pillow might need flipping over soon.

She vacantly stared forward. The squiggly image of her bookcase stood out. On it, books lined the shelves but there were no cutesy knick-knacks. In fact, her room was barely decorated.

I have nothing to even suggest that I'm a teenager.

New tears streamed down her face.

"Cianne," Tranae said with a hint of irritation. "He's just going to keep calling until you talk to him." She held the phone out to Cianne. "He's been calling all morning. You have to tell him something."

Do I?

Cianne moaned into her pillow. She couldn't bring herself to speak to him. Not right now, maybe not ever. She sighed, knowing that she would never be able to shut him out completely. To never see him again would destroy her.

"If you don't answer," Tranae said, putting the ringing phone on the nightstand next to Cianne's head, "he's just going to come over. It's after twelve; he's out of school for the day."

Cianne's head popped up as a new wave of fear assaulted her. "He can't come over," her voice sounded nasal. She grabbed the phone, wiped her face, and sat up.

Tranae, as helpful as ever, handed her a cup of water. Cianne took a few sips then handed the cup back. She took a couple of deep breaths then hit the send button on her phone.

"Cianne!" Tristan sounded frantic. "I've been calling since last night. Are you ok?"

Am I ok?

"Cianne, are you ok?" Tristan asked again, sounding more desperate than before. When she didn't answer, he cursed and said, "I'm on my way over there."

Cianne heard some rustling in the background on his end. The sound of his car door as it was slammed shut was unmistakable.

"No," she quickly said, "don't. I'm contagious. You can't get sick right now. The doctor said that I have a bad case of the flu and that I am very contagious. You can't get sick right now," she repeated.

"I can reschedule. I want to see you," he told her.

"You saw me yesterday," she sighed.

"Through your screen door, that doesn't count. And why is it ok for Tranae to be there if you're contagious?"

"She's already been exposed," Cianne lied. "Look, I'll see you when you get back. Tranae said she would stay here with me so you and Brian can go to Houston. It'll be fun for you two to hang out. Besides, you both got the time off from school already. It'll be just like it was before you and I started dating. Brian will like that." Cianne looked over to Tranae who was giving her the thumbs up signal. "Tranae has already cleared it with Brian, so you can't back out now."

Cianne felt sick to her stomach but was unsure if it was because of her "illness" or the lie she told.

"Fine, I'll go to Houston with Brian, but I need to see you. It's been hell not being near you," he said, "plus I have something I need to discuss with you, in person."

"Ok…tomorrow before your flight." Cianne couldn't hold back the tears any longer. Her voice cracked as she tried to control herself. "The doctor said I needed lots of rest if I want to feel better anytime soon."

At least that part was true.

"Alright then," he agreed, "you know how much I love you right?"

"More than life itself," she said softly. He told her that often. That was how much she loved him. *Enough to forfeit my soul if need be.*

"Without reservation," he said, matching her tone. "Get some rest and I'll call you tonight."

"Alright, see you tomorrow," she said, then sighed.

"Around five am," he said, sounding hopeful.

Cianne put her phone on the nightstand after she was sure he disconnected.

"So, you've decided then?" Tranae had laid down next to her on the bed.

"I don't want him to ever know what I've done." Cianne covered her face.

Tranae scooted closer and hugged her. Neither of them said anything else. Tranae and Cianne snuggled next to each other in silence. Eventually, Tranae fell asleep while Cianne listened to her friend's steady breathing. It relaxed her a little but not enough to fall asleep or to forget what unfolded last night, but it relaxed her just enough for her to keep her sanity.

Cianne went over it all in her head again.

It was around ten o'clock yesterday evening when Cianne couldn't take it any longer. Maybe it was because she had never been sick before, or it could have been that she wasn't able to keep any food down. Whatever the case, she had to see a doctor.

Her symptoms hadn't gotten better and she felt that maybe what she had might be some type of viral infection other than the flu. She had already missed two days of school and she didn't want to miss the trip to Houston when she had convinced her father to allow her to go.

Besides, she didn't want to still be sick next week. God forbid. She already had the perfect prom dress, a charmeuse print dress with a red strapless top, and the perfect pair of shoes. Cianne didn't want the flu ruining the sendoff party that signified her journey through school.

Tranae showed up right after school to take care of her. It was finally her turn, to help Cianne get better. Fully stocked with homemade remedies and store-bought medicines from Hammonds Drug store, her friend did what she could to make her feel better. In the end, nothing worked. In fact, Cianne felt worse and started vomiting more.

Because she was unable to keep anything down, Tranae suggested that they go to the emergency room. It had taken some convincing, but Cianne eventually agreed. The thought of not being able to go to Houston or her prom gave Cianne the push she needed.

The ride was short but seemed so much longer. Tranae drove while Cianne sat in the passenger seat, hoping that she didn't get sick again because she didn't bring a barf bag.

The emergency room process was foreign to Cianne, so Tranae had to help her through it. Getting registered was simple enough but the wait for the doctor was excruciating. When Cianne's name was finally called, she was placed in a room that was slightly larger than the intake exam room and it had a television with basic cable.

Tranae flipped aimlessly through the channels while Cianne lay on the bed trying not to hurl. If she hadn't already been sick with the flu, Cianne was certain she would be later, because the waiting area seemed like an invitation to a death sentence. It had been full of people who seemed not to care about covering their mouths, even though they were most likely spreading germs

Cianne wanted to scream, "For Christ's sake, you nasty, nasty people. Cover your mouths, please. And flush the damn toilet when you're done. It's basic hygiene you manimals!" as loud as she could. Instead, she just sat there with limited energy and a closed mouth. Besides, some of the people looked as if they weren't the type to take being yelled at calmly.

Plus, Cianne wasn't a yeller or screamer.

Inside the small room, it had been extremely cold but a nurse supplied Cianne with warm blankets that had just come out of the dryer. Yet, they still smelled a little musty. But after twenty minutes of freezing, she took the musty blanket up and covered herself with it.

It had taken another twenty minutes for the nurse to appear and request urine and take blood. Twenty minutes more for the test results. Around two-thirty in the morning, a doctor tapped on the door. When the door creaked open, a drowsy Cianne managed to sit up in the hospital bed.

"Morning, I'm Dr. Nolan," he said.

Cianne looked at the young handsome doctor. Earlier, the doctor who greeted her had been a woman who was much older and very curt, but this doctor looked like one of those television show doctors. One who's really hot but was usually a badass with a heavy dose of sympathy.

Cianne squinted. "Morning."

"Well miss Ci-au-ny." He butchered her name. "We have your tests back." He looked at Tranae who had awakened the same time as Cianne. She was giving the hot Dr. the once over. "Would you like to speak in private?" he asked, looking back to Cianne.

"Uh, no," she said, "Tranae's fine."

The question sounded routine but it still caused Cianne to worry. If she was dying, she wanted to have her best friend with her. Tranae must have felt the same way because she sat up and gave the doctor her full attention.

Cianne braced for the worst.

"No, no, it's nothing bad." Dr. Nolan smiled. He read her easily. "It's just that we have to ask before releasing any information to you with other people around." The doctor glanced at his clipboard. "As I've said, we have all your test results back." He paused, flipping the papers on the chart as if reading them for the first time. "Everything looks fine but it seems that your HCG levels are elevated." He flipped through a few more pages and began to read something.

HCG, Cianne thought, *what is that*?

"What's an HCG?" she asked.

Tranae stood up. Clearly, Tranae knew what the doctor was talking about. When Tranae covered her mouth, Cianne turned to Dr. Nolan, who was watching her. Any other time she would be flattered by the way he was looking at her, but not today.

Dr. Nolan cleared his throat then looked down at his pad after their eyes met. "Uh, it's a hormone produced by an embryo when—"

"Embryo? Wait…I'm not pregnant." When Dr. Nolan raised a brow, Cianne frowned. "I'm not pregnant. I've never missed a pill in three years…never…not once." She shook her head. "That test is wrong."

"It's pretty accurate," Dr. Nolan told her.

Cianne looked at his unwavering eyes.

After several seconds, he cleared his throat again. "Uh, the pill you're taking may not be strong enough. There's even a slight chance that that particular pill may not work for you. That's why it's suggested that you use an alternate form of birth control when using the pill." He pulled a pen from his breast pocket. "When was the first day of your last menstrual cycle?"

"The twelfth of this month," Cianne said confidently. "I haven't missed any. The test is wrong."

"Some women experience some bleeding in the first trimester. It can be light or as heavy as a normal menstruation. So, bleeding isn't uncommon. I assure you that the test is correct. Uh, now to really be sure of how far along you are we would need to have an ultrasound. I recommend it, being as you've experienced some bleeding."

"I can't be pregnant," Cianne said with disbelief. She felt her chest constricting as she looked at Tranae, who gave her a pained grimace.

Tranae walked over to the bed, sat next to Cianne, and held her hand. "Couldn't the test be wrong?" Tranae asked.

"Not likely." Dr. Nolan arched a brow.

Tranae looked at Cianne, who looked back at her with a blank stare on her face. "Alright." Tranae looked at the doctor. "It's an accurate test so what do we do now?"

Dr. Nolan lowered his clipboard. "First we see how far along you are. We usually use the last day of your menstrual." He held up a round plastic spin chart. "But in this case, that won't work. So, an ultrasound will have to be done. We can do that now or if you'd like, you can make an appointment with your OBGYN and they can set it up for you."

"Would the day she had sex help?" Tranae asked.

"Umm," he said, "well, not necessarily." He rocked back on his heels.

"What if it was the first and only time she's done it?" Tranae asked.

Dr. Nolan looked as if he didn't believe what Tranae had said, but when he looked at Cianne and saw the way she looked back at him, Cianne could tell he knew Tranae was serious.

"What was the first day of your period before you had intercourse?"

"February 8th," Cianne spoke up.

The doctor fumbled a little but managed to get the clipboard under his left arm to work the chart. "That would make you about twelve weeks which would make your estimated due date November 29."

Cianne thought back to when she was dizzy in the park. Those days when she was abnormally tired. Even those times she felt a little nauseated. She had dismissed it all.

God…I'm pregnant.

"I can refer you to an obstetrician if you like," the doctor offered.

"Can you write the information down for us?" Tranae asked him when Cianne didn't respond.

"Sure," the doctor said. He wrote a number on a prescription pad. "If you sign these, you're free to go." He handed Cianne the clipboard. She absently signed her name and handed it back. "I'd like you to take it easy for a few days and follow up with this OBGYN as soon as possible. Eventually, the sour stomach and dizziness will go away. Do you have any questions?"

"Cianne?" Tranae asked when Cianne didn't respond. Cianne shook her head. "No," Tranae said, speaking for them both. Dazed, Cianne watched as he handed Tranae a few sheets of paper.

Dr. Nolan offered Cianne an apologetic smile before moving toward the door. "I hope everything works out for you," he said before leaving the room.

A single tear fell from Cianne's eye. She shivered. She felt as though the exam room was even colder. Tranae wrapped her arms around Cianne just as she broke out into a full-fledged panic attack.

Chapter Nineteen

Cianne rolled over onto her side and blinked until she saw the time on her cell phone clearly. It was a quarter to four in the morning. Her eyes ached from all the crying and burned from the lack of sleep.

She woke several times during the night and she could only think about what she was going to say to Tristan when he got there. She buried her face in the pillow that was covered with one of Tristan's shirts.

What am I going to do? She thought as she rolled to her back and looked at her ceiling.

She heard paper crinkling underneath her, so she pulled it out. It was the pink instruction paper she received the night before from the emergency room doctor. Cianne read over it again before she tucked it under her mattress. She had never hidden anything from her father before today but this was different.

Her father never looked through her personal things but she felt better hiding it.

She sighed then rubbed her eyes a few times before sitting up on the edge of her bed. For some reason, she found herself lifting her shirt to look at her stomach. It was as flat as it had always been. Raising her hand up, she felt the urge to rub it but she lowered her hand before she could. She needed to get ready.

During the long shower, Cianne thought again of what she planned to say to Tristan. She was up half the night and still, she couldn't decide how to tell him she had messed up. It *was* all her fault she was in this situation. It was she who told him many times that he wouldn't need a condom because she was on the pill. She had decided long before her birthday that she didn't want him to use a condom.

Why should we?

She knew he was safe. He had given her a copy of his clean bill of health. He was clean and she was protected.

I thought I was protected.

Cianne fought another bout of tears as she towel-dried her hair and tied it in a loose floppy ponytail. Then she rummaged through her drawers for a nightshirt and a pair of baggy sweats. She pulled the shirt over her head and slid it down her torso.

Will he be able to tell?

Feeling self-conscious that Tristan would be able to see that she was pregnant, Cianne changed her shirt. She changed it several more times before finally deciding on a gray long sleeve thermal top.

According to one of the sites on the internet she and Tranae researched last night, it took on average four months for a pregnant woman to start showing. With her being about three months, she had to be cautious.

Cianne sighed as she took one last look in the full-length mirror then threw on some socks and went downstairs to the kitchen.

No coffee smell?

Cianne looked over at the coffee machine, wondering why no coffee was brewing. Then it dawned on her. She was up a lot earlier than her father today. He was going to need coffee so she brewed some and poured some cereal in a bowl. She opted not to add milk to her cereal because the thought of it made her stomach churn. So, she ate the cereal piece by piece.

Tristan arrived a few minutes after she finished drinking a cup of orange juice instead of her usual cup of coffee. He stood on the other side of the screen door with a smile so gorgeous it threatened to break her. He held up a small wicker basket.

"Do you feel any better?" He gave her a lingering look as he entered.

"Some." Cianne tried to smile.

He leaned in to give her a peck on the lips but Cianne offered her cheek instead. She had to keep up the charade.

"I brought you a get-well basket to help you feel better sooner," he said, lifting it a little.

Guilt stabbed at her chest as she took the basket and led the way to the living room. Cianne took a seat on the sofa and placed the basket next to her so he would have to sit on the other side of it.

"So, this is what you look like when you're sick."

His warm smile seemed to wrap around her, weakening her more. "Yeah," she said, looking down. "I guess it's a good thing I don't get sick too often."

Technically, she'd never been sick as far back as she could remember.

"What are you talking about? You look amazing." Tristan reached over and touched the side of her face. Being close to Cianne always provoked a battle for control between his darker nature and his gentlemanly side. It wasn't a contest though, not really. He would never allow her to see his dark side.

Touching her brought to mind his botched plan to seduce her in Houston. He wanted to do everything right this time. He needed to show her that he wanted to be with her always. He wanted more and was ready to show and tell her so.

It's crazy how I've fallen so fast and hard. I can hardly believe how tied up in knots Cianne Baxter has me.

Cianne closed her eyes and moved her face in unison with his hand as he rubbed her cheek but she pulled away suddenly as if she shouldn't touch him.

Damn flu, he silently cursed. Cianne took his hand and placed it on the basket that sat between them.

"I've missed you," he told her when their eyes met.

"I've missed you too."

He brushed his fingers over the back of her hand and he felt her shiver. That made him smile but she moved her hand.

"What's in the basket?" she asked.

Tristan hid his frustration. He wanted, needed to touch her, but he wouldn't push it. She controlled all the cards here. So, he reached inside the basket and lifted up the first item. "I brought you one of my t-shirts with my stank on it. I'm sure the one you have has lost my scent by now." Tristan moved some things around in the basket. "Celia made some chicken soup and bread for you. There are a few movies in here that I thought you might like. A few gossip magazines and some fresh oranges." He looked at her. "You know; I can have my doctor fly in from Baltimore to take a look at you. Dr. Bannerman is the best."

"No!" she said hastily. "I'm fine really."

"Ok…ok, no Dr. Bannerman." Tristan gazed at her lips. "I just want you to get better, that's all." The urge to kiss her was ever present. "What's this?" he asked, lifting his thumb to her bottom lip.

He touched the cut she created by chewing nervously on her lip. The contact brought things she shouldn't be thinking to mind. Images of them, naked and tangled together, flashed in her mind.

Cianne sucked in a deep breath, purging the hot images that had put her in this situation in the first place. She folded her bottom lip into her mouth and he dropped his hand.

The cuts on her lips were due to her anxiety. She started to bite on her lip early yesterday morning when Tranae asked her what she planned to tell Tristan. Cianne didn't give Tranae an answer at that time.

She hadn't decided then. But now, as she sat next to him, all she could think about was what Tristan promised her months ago. She looked at the ring on her right hand and sighed. Trust was what he had pledged and she had accepted on the condition that she would offer the same.

"Tristan," she started, "I have something to tell—"

"Ci," he cut her off, "You don't have to stress about that anymore. I've figured out a solution."

Cianne was definitely confused but she would listen.

"I know that you've been worried about leaving for college. You don't want to leave your dad, or me behind. That's why you haven't opened any of your acceptance packages yet." He moved the basket to the table and moved closer to her. "What I'm trying to say is that I don't want to be the couple who lives thousands of miles away from each other. So, I think we should move in together." Tristan spoke with his usual confidence. Giving her no time to respond, he continued. "I'll attend the same University you choose and we will get an apartment close to campus, that way we can be together."

Cianne was speechless. She hadn't really thought about college since they started dating. She hadn't given any thought to the possibility that they might go in separate directions after the summer.

"Unless you want to pledge a sorority or something," he said when she didn't respond.

"Uh…" She shook her head. Weariness and guilt consumed her. "No, I wasn't thinking of pledging." Cianne tried to hold back the tears, but she couldn't. They flowed with no regard to what she wanted.

Tristan kneeled in front of her and took her hand. With them at eye level, he pulled her into his arms and she rested her head on his shoulder. "Ci, it was just a thought—"

"You…" she blubbered, cutting him off, "you have everything planned out so neatly."

"No baby, it's just an option. We can figure out something else. It's not written in ink."

Cianne raised her head and looked at him. He winced as he rubbed her tears away, and she realized that she hadn't thought of them being apart because it was never an option for her. She would never let him go without a fight.

"I love that idea but…" Cianne stopped before she said too much. She couldn't tell him about the baby now. Not with him making plans for their future. "I thought you weren't going to college. You never showed any interest and you didn't apply to any."

"I applied to all the universities you applied to. I thought we could see which ones accepted the both of us and choose between those. If you feel strongly about a school that I, by some freak chance was denied entry, you can go and I'll do a gap year. I can reapply next fall. Though I don't think my acceptance to any of them will be a problem even though I applied late." He continued to wipe away her tears. "I just want us to be together but it's ultimately up to you. I'll understand if you feel it's too soon for us to take such a step like this. I just don't want to be any number of miles away from you if I have a choice in the matter."

Cianne felt exactly the same, but…. "We should talk about this when you come back from Houston."

It was difficult looking into his eyes with the secret she carried. So, she hugged him again. The absence of his intense and beautiful gaze gave her conscience a bit of relief, though not much. As she laid her head on his shoulder she lightly stroked the back of his neck.

"I can't think clearly right now."

That was the truth.

"Fair enough," Tristan said. He never pushed. They stayed linked together for a few minutes until Tristan kissed her cheek, separated from her then moved back on the sofa. "Did you eat already?

"Don't have much of an appetite," she honestly admitted. Cianne snuggled under his arm and her anxiety eased some. "You know what I would like to do," she said. "I'd like for you to hold me until you have to go."

It wasn't long before sleep took her.

Chapter Twenty

Cianne stared through her windshield at one of four large brick three-story buildings that made up the office park. She was parked in front of the building where her appointment was scheduled. She'd been fixed in the same spot since eight o'clock this morning. According to her phone, it was currently three p.m.

The receptionist at the Women's Health and Family Planning Center had given her an appointment for eight-thirty this morning. Cianne missed that appointment. Not because she was running late like she told the receptionist when she phoned from the parking lot.

She missed the appointment because she couldn't bring herself to actually do what she drove forty miles to do. Talk of college had come up four times during her phone conversations with Tristan since Friday morning. Cianne tried her best to sound upbeat when she told him that she loved the idea of moving in together after she thought it over of course.

What she had really been thinking over was what to do about her situation. In the end, she decided that Tristan's future was more important than her soul. She was also sure that his ideas for that future did not include the pitter-patter of little feet.

Not this soon anyway, if ever.

The tears started again. Cianne dabbed her eyes with a tissue and tried to fight the rest of the tears back. There was no point crying anymore. The truth was, she knew what had to be done when he left for Houston Friday morning. Tristan wanted college, an apartment, and her.

Cianne looked up and sighed when she thought of a new wrinkle in her mounting problems. She hadn't even considered what Tristan's parents would say about her situation. She knew what they would assume. A girl from a modest background dug her claws into their only son who will one day inherit all their money. Cianne was pretty sure Tristan's father already believed that she wasn't worthy of Tristan, and her getting pregnant would only confirm it for him.

Cianne glanced over at the building again. She found this place on the internet and chose it because they were able to schedule her on a Sunday, unlike the other places she called. The building looked clean, fairly new. The grass was trimmed and the grounds were pristine. Truthfully, she expected something else.

She imagined a dark, dank, dirty building that was in serious disrepair. A building that was so unsightly that she would be forced to change her mind about the abortion for fear of death or permanent injury from the unlicensed doctor. Like the ones, she saw on TV when a girl got into the same kind of trouble. What she saw here was the exact opposite.

Which meant that she had no excuse for why she still sat in her car at three-fifteen when her appointment had been rescheduled for three-thirty?

She tapped the steering wheel with her fingernails. "Come on Cianne," she coaxed, "It's now or…." She never spoke the last word. Instead, she just sat back and rested her head on the headrest, and went over everything again.

She was about twelve weeks pregnant and just turned eighteen years old. It was Tristan's baby and in every way her love child. A love she never imagined would be, a love that she didn't want to ruin. She had no idea how Tristan would react if she told him that she was pregnant. What would her father think of her?

Cianne pounded on her stirring wheel. She had none of the answers to any of her questions. But one thing kept repeating in her head.

Tristan deserves to know.

But this wasn't entirely about Tristan. It wasn't about her father or his parents. This was about her.

Can I live with the decision I'm about to make?

"What do I want to do?" she said aloud.

When she found out she was pregnant, her first thought was what it would do to Tristan. A baby *was* a big responsibility but couldn't she handle it? She was smart, generally a good person, and she had loving parents that taught her good morals. Maybe she could delay school for a few years and get a job. She would need help from her father, sure, but he loved her. It wasn't as if she did this to herself on purpose.

"I took my pills every day," she spoke again. "This wasn't meant to happen," she whispered, "but it did." She tapped the steering wheel again, cursing. "I can't do this," she said. "This is his baby too, a part of him. I can't do this," she repeated.

She had made up her mind. Everything was suddenly brighter, better. Cianne sighed with relief as she placed a hand over her belly for the first time, and in that instant, she felt what could only be described as a tickle in her abdomen.

Cianne tearfully laughed. *It's a sign*, she thought. To tell her she was making the right choice. Or, the baby was telling her that it was time to eat. She laughed as she wiped away her tears.

With her mind made up, she remembered that she drove past a little deli at the end of the business park. Cianne took the key out of the ignition and grabbed her purse before getting out of the car. It was a sunny beautiful day out and she could use a nice walk.

At the deli, it only took a few seconds for Cianne to order but a little while to get her food. She took that time to call her family physician to get a number for an obstetrician. She called the OB and took the first appointment available, Wednesday at 10 a.m. That allowed her a little over two days to tell her father that she was pregnant. She would tell Tristan over the phone. It wasn't ideal, telling him over the phone, but she had kept it from him long enough.

All she could do was hope for the best.

Cianne paid for her food and left the small bistro. As she walked back to her car she thought about what she had to do. She would quickly eat in her car, then be on her way. Once she arrived home, she'll call Tristan. The conversation would be mostly her explaining the situation and letting him know that there would be no strings attached. That she didn't expect anything from him, though she wanted his acceptance, love, and support.

When she was at her car, Cianne reached down to open her car door with the key but lost her balance and had to decide whether to hold onto her food or her keys. She quickly let the keys go to keep the fountain soda that was slipping out of her hand from falling. Cianne placed the drink on the roof of the car, and after making sure the cup was stable she picked up her keys and pushed the button to unlock the door.

Cianne pulled the door open and that's when she felt an arm wrap around her waist, hauling her back and off her feet. She bent forward to pull away but only succeeded in dropping her bag, the keys, and her purse.

She tried to scream as she reached frantically for her car door but a gloved hand covered her mouth. All Cianne could manage was a muffled squeal. She could feel herself being lifted from the ground and she had a strong feeling that if she was taken somewhere she wouldn't live long after that. She struggled, kicked, and pulled at the arms of her attacker but with no success.

"Grab the bags," a deep voice called out.

Cianne squirmed and twisted her body as she dug at the face of the person who held her but all she felt was a slick material. The grip around her tightened as the person back-walked with her in tow. When she realized that she was being pulled into a vehicle, she struggled even harder.

Her eyes widened when she saw a figure dressed in all black from head to toe jump from a van to the ground.

"Hurry up," the same voice ordered. Though, it wasn't the person holding her or the one outside of the van.

Cianne cried out as her body hit the floor of the van face down. She inadvertently bit the inside of her mouth. Her blood trickled out but was smeared over her face as one of her attackers gripped the back of her head and pushed her into the carpeted flooring.

Her scream died out as a heavy knee rested on the middle of her back, pinning her. Cianne grabbed and scratched at the gloved hand that pinned her. She continued to kick out with her feet and at one point she heard a husky grunt.

She figured that she managed to hit one of them, possibly the one who was instructed to collect her bags. Cianne felt the one who was pinning her downshift his weight. She pushed up just as the van door was being pulled closed.

"Help!" she cried. Cianne didn't get another opportunity to scream, kick, or hit at her attackers because the last thing she felt was a hard blow to the side of her face.

"Tristan," she whispered.

Tristan pushed the send button on his phone for the tenth time. Again, his call went straight to voicemail. He dialed again and received the voice message greeting again. He cupped his phone in his hands, rested his elbows on his knees, and began to tap his head repeatedly. He wanted to throw his phone against the wall but he couldn't. He needed it.

It was Sunday, eleven o'clock in the evening, and he hadn't heard from Cianne since early this morning. She sent him a text telling him to have a good day and that she would call him after five. He waited until just after six to call her.

"Tranae said she hasn't seen her since early this morning," Brian called from across the room where he sat on the arm of the sofa.

Tristan tapped his head a few more times with his cell phone. He needed to call Mr. Baxter. He wanted to call earlier but he didn't want to sound like a stalker boyfriend who has to call his girlfriend every minute when he's out of town.

"To hell with it," he said as he dialed.

"Hello?"

Tristan got right to the point. "Mr. Baxter, I've been calling Cianne for a few hours now and I haven't been able to reach her. Is she there?"

"Tristan?" Mr. Baxter asked.

"Yes sir." Tristan rubbed his head anxiously. He had no time for pleasantries. At least that was what his gut was telling him.

"I'm actually on my way home now."

"Can you call me once you get in? I'm a little worried about her."

"I'm sure she's just sleeping off that bug. I'll be there in five minutes and will have her call you."

"Thank you." Tristan hung up and returned to tapping his head with his phone. Something was wrong. He felt it. "I need to go home." Tristan stood up. He glanced around the luxurious bedroom suite as if he didn't know what to grab first. Then he began packing.

"I bet everything is fine man." Brian got to his feet and made his way through the double doors that led into Tristan's suite. "She probably forgot to charge her phone or something," he said.

When Tristan didn't respond, Brian left the suite.

Tristan was packed and speaking to the front desk on the hotel phone when Brian returned with his luggage in hand. "Several hours ago, I got this feeling I can't explain," Tristan told Brian when he hung up the phone. "Then, I could have sworn I heard Cianne call my name. It was as clear as you hear me speaking now. She sounded scared."

He picked up his suitcase and made his way out of the bedroom, then they exited the suite and quickly walked to the elevator. They rode to the lobby in silence.

Tristan reached in his pocket and answered his phone on the first ring as they walked to the front desk. It wasn't Cianne's number that appeared on his display screen. Brian spoke with the hotel staff while Tristan listened to what Mr. Baxter had to say.

"It looks like she hasn't been here all day. I've called her phone several times since speaking with you and just as you said, it goes to voice mail after several rings. Tristan, please hold on one moment, my house phone is ringing. It could be her," Mr. Baxter said.

"Sure," Tristan said into his phone. He tried not to focus on Mr. Baxter's conversation on the house phone until he heard Cianne's name. Then Tristan listened closely to Mr. Baxter's muffled words as he spoke into the other phone.

Who is he speaking to?

Whoever it was, Mr. Baxter's voice went from accusing, to explaining things, to sounding defensive, and then angry. When Mr. Baxter informed the person that he was involving the police, the conversation ended abruptly.

"Tristan, I'm going to report her missing," he sounded irritated.

"I'll be there as soon as I can."

"If I hear anything I'll call you," Mr. Baxter assured him.

Tristan hung up the phone. He looked out of the double doors of the hotel to see a car waiting with a driver standing by the open passenger door. Brian was already inside when Tristan got in the car.

"She's been reported missing," he said, looking out the window into the darkness.

Brian patted Tristan on the shoulder. "We have to stay positive man."

◉

The sound of vehicles as they passed by was the only sound Cianne could truly make out. A busy street or highway was close by. All she had to do was get out of this room and she might be able to make it to the road.

Cianne looked around the room with tired eyes. By the looks of it, she figured she was in the office of an abandoned building of some sort. She stood with a grunt then slowly walked over to one of two doors in the room. She pressed her head to the only thing that looked new, a metal door that separated her from her kidnappers, and listened for voices.

No sound came from beyond the door.

She turned and looked to the only other door. Cianne cringed but decided to just go for it. She walked to the other door. It was slightly ajar and the paint had peeled away from most of it. She cringed again as she pushed it open with her foot. Cianne expected to see a giant rat jump out at her, and she jumped back just in case. As soon as she realized that no rodents were going to attack, she crept into the filthy bathroom.

The room contained a sink that was broken and filthy, a toilet with a missing cover, and a space on the wall where a small piece of mirror still hung. Cianne looked in the piece of mirror. She lifted her hand to her face. She felt the bruise on the side of her cheek that was already purple. Whoever he was, he hit her pretty hard.

Cianne let her hand drop and focused on the task at hand. A four-pack of toilet tissue sat on the floor next to the toilet. Four rolls? That meant they were keeping her for a while, she guessed. Her eyes moved over the filth in the small room. She cringed once again as she decided that the need to relieve herself was much more important than her disgust with the state of the bathroom.

"Of course," she said, "no knob, no lock." Cianne tapped the door with her foot, trying to close it as far as it would go then quickly took care of business.

The bathroom was deplorable and she hoped to avoid using it again, until…well…forever. Problem was, she would probably have to go again in five minutes.

Cianne stepped back into the room, her cell for who knew how long. She looked up at the walls; her focus was on the spaces where the windows had once been. They had all been replaced by bricks and by the look of it they had been there for years. It would take her months to scrape away enough mortar to remove the number of bricks needed to create a space large enough for her to fit through.

Startled by a sudden noise coming from beyond the metal door, Cianne backed up to the dirty twin mattress that lay in the center of the room. She stepped on top of the mattress and continued to back up until she felt the floor under her and the wall to her back.

She heard footsteps, and they stopped on the other side of the door. The sound of the door being unlocked caused Cianne's heart to race. When the door slowly opened, a figure dressed head to toe in black stood just inside the door with a brown shopping bag in hand. The person stepped to the side and another person dressed the exact same way entered the room and sat a small foam cooler on the floor near the door. He watched her as he backed away.

Cianne didn't move. She just watched him as he exited the room. The first person who had entered the room kept his eyes on her the entire time. Cianne, who had been watching the person with the cooler, looked to the person who was staring at her. A black ski mask covered everything but the person's eyes. They stood there for no more than half a minute, watching each other before he sat the bag down near the cooler and backed out the room.

"Wait," Cianne said, stepping forward, "why are you holding me here?"

The figure held the door slightly open and glared at her for another second then abruptly closed it. The sound the lock made when it clicked, sounded like hope fading. She had a thought to run over to the door and bang on it again but she knew it would be no use. She had spent what seemed like forever banging on it already, with no results.

Cianne made her way over to the brown bag that was placed near the door and opened it. Inside she found the sandwich she had ordered earlier today and a small container of antibacterial wipes.

They want me to stay clean?

She almost smiled…almost. The last item was an envelope with her name typed on it. She tore the envelope open and read the note inside.

Cianne, trying to escape is useless. This building was chosen because of its location and design. But if you feel it necessary, then by all means try. You will be here as long as it takes. You will not be harmed as long as you do not attempt to get out when the door is opened. If you attempt to escape through the door when I come in, it will impact your food supply. When I enter, you are to back away from the door and stay back until I leave. When I return, I want this letter in front of the door. This will be as painless as possible as long as you do what you are told.

"Why am I here?" Cianne screamed. She crumpled the letter up and threw it at the door. She lifted the envelope and looked at it again. It was apparent they knew her well enough to know how to spell her name correctly.

Cianne walked the few steps over to the cooler, grabbed the paper bag then dragged the cooler over to the mattress. Once she got the cooler close enough she sat on the edge of the mattress and opened it.

The cooler was filled with a small bag of ice, water, and a few bottles of cola. "Exactly what every baby needs," she said, "empty calories." Cianne placed the lid back on the cooler and rubbed her belly.

Protecting my baby is my main priority and if that means doing what I'm told, I will.

She picked up the container of antibacterial wipes and cleaned her hands. Then she ate the sandwich she had purchased earlier. Once she finished eating she placed the trash inside the cooler and wiped the mattress down with a handful of wipes.

At this rate, she would use all the wipes within the hour, she surmised.

Cianne took off her sweat jacket and laid it over the stained mattress. Then she laid her head on her jacket with her eyes fixed on the door, wondering what Tristan was doing at that moment.

Chapter Twenty-One

As Tristan pulled his truck next to the mailbox in front of Baxter's residence, he felt the house didn't look as busy as it should. A single police cruiser sat in the driveway next to Mr. Baxter's vehicle. Another police car, unmarked, was parked on the street in front of where Tristan had pulled in.

It didn't escape him that Cianne's car was nowhere in sight.

Tristan hoped that she would be here, in her bed sleeping, when he arrived. That his constant uneasy feeling was just an overreaction from her not returning his numerous calls. The worst, he hoped, was that she was a little sicker than she thought. That maybe she had to return to the hospital.

Even with all the hope, the truth was that he somehow knew she wouldn't be here when he arrived. He also knew without a doubt that wherever she was, she was scared.

I feel it.

Brian opened the door as the truck came to a full stop. "I'm going to check on Tranae," Brian said as he got out of the truck then shut the door.

Tristan said nothing as he closed his driver side door and slowly walked to the Baxter's front door. He didn't knock. He just pushed the door open and stepped inside. A police officer, who stood just inside the doorway, turned to face him. Tristan briefly acknowledged the officer then started toward the kitchen. When the officer put out an arm to block his path, Tristan gave him a questioning look.

"Let him through," an unfamiliar voice came from the kitchen, "he's the boyfriend."

Tristan stared past the police officer and down the hallway but the person with the deep voice wasn't in sight. When the officer dropped his arm, Tristan walked toward the kitchen. As he entered the room he saw Joseph Baxter sitting at the table with a man about the same age, seated across from him. Joseph looked visibly shaken.

"What?" Tristan asked. He searched Joseph's and the stranger's eyes for the answer. "Where is she?" he demanded.

"I'm Detective Malone. I need to ask you a few questions. If you would please sit." The detective pointed to the chair across from him. "If you'll excuse us," he said to Joseph, "we can get started."

Joseph lightly patted Tristan on the shoulder as he got up then left the room.

Tristan sat in the chair facing the detective. He rubbed his hands over his head then placed them on the table in front of him.

The detective looked at Tristan for a long moment with an unassuming gaze, logging whatever he found interesting in his head before speaking. "When was the last time you saw Cianne?"

"About two days ago, before I left for Houston." Tristan looked at the detective. "Early Friday morning."

Tristan sat forward. His usual cool demeanor absent, replaced by anxiety and anger. The key was to remain calm and avoid losing his temper. Only, his calm threatened to explode into a five-alarm fire because for the first time that could remember, Tristan was afraid and frustrated.

He took a deep breath then asked, "Where is she?"

"Mr. Bertram, please calm down," Malone said.

The detective must have sensed the thin thread of restraint that held him together. Tristan sat back in the chair in an effort to appear calm. He needed answers.

"Did she seem upset?"

"Why aren't you looking for Cianne?" Tristan asked. When the detective didn't respond, Tristan sighed. This was the way the law worked and Malone knew more than he did…right now. He needed to answer the questions. "No, but she isn't feeling well, the flu or stomach virus."

"She didn't share any of her plans for the day with you?" the detective challenged.

"If she had I wouldn't be here looking for her," Tristan said abruptly. He made up his mind to cooperate but he couldn't sit still. Tristan tapped his foot on the floor under the table. He looked Malone directly in the eye. "Obviously, you know something I don't. You can continue this insufferable questioning or you can tell me what you know."

Det. Malone met his gaze then raised a brow, "Alright." Malone adjusted himself in the chair. "A vehicle was found in Palm Valley around six this evening with the driver's side door ajar…a white—"

"Mercedes," Tristan interrupted.

"Ms. Baxter was seen earlier today in one of the shops." Malone stood, lifted a glass that sat in front of him, and swallowed the remaining cola before placing it back down. "If you can think of anything else," he said, handing Tristan his card, "Let me know."

"So instead of finding her, you are here questioning me." Tristan huffed.

"I'm not altogether sure that Ms. Baxter wants to be found. Maybe she needed to get away for a few days. You should speak to Mr. Baxter." The detective strolled toward the kitchen archway.

Joseph was waiting in the hall and walked the detective to the door.

Tristan heard the Detective say that he would begin a search for Cianne but he was sure she would turn up on her own. The front door opened then closed a few seconds later. Tristan found Joseph with his head pressed against the door.

"What is it that you're not telling me?" Tristan demanded.

Joseph turned to look at him as he pushed away from the door. "Come in the living room and sit down Tristan."

Tristan followed Joseph into the living room. They were about to sit when they heard a knock on the front door. Joseph motion for Tristan to sit then excused himself. When Joseph returned to the living room, he was accompanied by three people.

Tristan stood as the people walked into the room. He wasn't sure why he stood but he somehow felt compelled to do so.

The first person who entered the room behind Joseph was a young man about the same age as Tristan, maybe slightly older. He was tall and dressed in a very nice black suit with a beige tie. The young man gave Tristan a scathing glance.

Tristan easily dismissed him and his attitude almost immediately.

Following the young man was a very petite young girl. She also wore a black suit. Her body was athletic but not too developed, telling Tristan she was probably in her early to mid-teens. Her hair was pulled back tightly in a bun, away from her youthful beautiful face.

When the final person entered the room, Tristan understood why he felt the need to stand. Only, her presence seemed to weigh the entire room down. The woman was mature, with the beauty and grace of someone of importance. She wore a tailored suit with high heels, and her hair was also pinned up in a bun.

There was something slightly familiar about her as she walked by without giving him a glance. Each of the three carried themselves with a hint of authority, but the woman had an air of royalty. She chose to sit in the chair instead of sitting on the sofa or loveseat, while the youthful teen stood to her left and the young man to her right.

Tristan stood until the woman took a seat then he sat on the sofa. Instead of taking a seat on the empty loveseat, Joseph sat next to Tristan. Doing so effectively separated Tristan from the strangers and he suspected that was Joseph's intent.

"Did you get what you were looking for from your local police department, Joseph?" the older woman asked. Her voice was smooth but strong and held the same commanding elegance as her appearance as if she was comfortable giving orders.

"Please, not now," Joseph said, then sighed. "It's after one in the morning and my daughter is out there somewhere, alone."

Tristan sensed that the woman would have disemboweled anyone else who would dare to speak to her the way Joseph just had.

"If any harm comes to her Joseph, I will hold you responsible." Her voice revealed no emotion but the threat was clear. "You have been stalling for months, flying to Canada to persuade me to give you more time. If she was with me like her mother and I agreed, this wouldn't be happening."

"Forgive me Sovereign, but should you speak so freely," the girl asked with a bowed head, "with the middling in the room?"

Tristan looked from the standing girl down to the woman who was now looking at him. From the expression on the woman's face, he was pretty sure she hadn't even noticed he was in the room. It was as if she had dismissed his very existence.

The woman carefully scrutinized Tristan, her expression never changing from the dignity it reflected.

…and what did the pixie mean by characterizing me as a middling?

He wasn't the outwardly vain type but he knew he was anything but ordinary.

"How long were you going to hide him from me?" the woman asked Joseph but kept her eyes on Tristan.

"I wasn't hiding him. I promised to give Cianne some semblance of a normal life. Being a normal teenager means dating." Joseph exhaled as he rubbed the bridge of his nose. "She was happy."

"*Is* happy," Tristan spoke up.

All eyes fell on Tristan.

The girl stared at him with a frown on her face, then she blushed and looked away. The young man peered at Tristan with disgust. The woman, on the other hand, grinned. Her broad smile was a mixture of curiosity and displeasure.

"Zeta, this is Cianne's *boyfriend*." The woman watched him as she spoke.

Tristan didn't miss how the word boyfriend came out as a hiss.

"As for his presence, Joseph feels the boy should be here and this is Joseph's home so we will try to respect his wishes."

"Tristan," Joseph said then sighed, "this is Vivian, my mother-in-law and Cianne's grandmother."

Tristan regarded the woman in the chair with fresh curiosity. He was pretty sure Cianne hadn't mentioned having a living grandmother or any other maternal relatives. She tilted her head slightly to the side as if she were allowing him to take his fill of her.

"Look, there is something the both of you need to know." Joseph sat forward.

Tristan had never seen the man so unhinged. He had a feeling that Joseph believed the detective was right about Cianne needing some time alone. So that meant that either the news he was about to share was bad or that Vivian was the cause.

"The detective said that Cianne was in Palm Valley today," Joseph continued. "She was there for a procedure."

Vivian and the young man beside her gave Joseph their full attention. Tristan looked from Joseph to the girl called Zeta, who continued to watch him.

Does she think I'm a threat?

"She had an appointment at eight a.m. but apparently, she missed it and reschedule for the same day at three-thirty p.m. The receptionist in the office said that Cianne sat in the parking lot for a few hours before finally calling and canceling the appointment altogether. She changed her mind." Joseph paused for a few seconds then turned to Tristan "She changed her mind, Tristan."

Confused, Tristan focused on Cianne's father.

"What are you trying to say, Joseph?" The woman demanded.

She was able to express her impatience, unlike Tristan who was still trying to work out on his own what it was Joseph was telling him.

"She made an appointment to end her pregnancy," Joseph said with grief-stricken eyes as he peered at Tristan.

Tristan felt as if the room was closing in on him. The air that would naturally enter and exit his lungs freely had abandoned him. He felt an intense pain with every hard-fought breath. Conversation erupted in the room around Tristan but he had no involvement in what followed Joseph's revelation. He didn't hear the several questions posed to him, nor would he have cared if he had.

All he could think of was Cianne.

Where is she? What is she thinking? Why didn't she tell me?

He had to find her…to talk to her.

When Tristan stood, a few things happened all at once. He moved to leave and a blur of motion and a light breeze blew past him. Tristan felt a hand pressed against his chest. He quickly realized that the girl named Zeta had moved to block his way.

How she had moved so fast was beyond him, but if she thought to stop him, she had another thing coming. Tristan grabbed the girl's wrist and spun her out of his path. Without missing a beat or her balance, she spun behind Tristan and placed her other hand on his shoulder then pushed him down. Tristan fell to one knee even though he fought to remain standing.

This girl is strong...abnormally so.

Tristan looked at his shoulder, at Zeta's right hand that held him down with what seemed to be little effort on her part. Centered on the back of her right hand was a most intricate tattoo that featured a black circle surrounded by a thinner outer ring. It resembled the birthmark on Cianne's neck but it was bigger. Around the outer circle were four beautifully scripted words that he couldn't decipher. Starting at her wrist was a set of knives that were crossed at their hilts, while the blades encircled the script. The tips of the blades ended at the base of her middle finger.

"Nice tattoo," Tristan said. He used his right hand to grab Zeta's wrist, but her hand only moved a fraction before she applied more pressure. He was unable to stand no matter how hard he tried, but he refused to let her get him down on both knees.

Still resisting, Tristan turned his head to look up at her. She gave him a peculiar look as if she was trying to figure him out.

Screw this, Tristan thought as his eyes narrowed. He took hold of her leg that was closest to him and swept it from under her. Zeta did one of the most graceful back handsprings he had ever seen, landing on her feet beside him, exactly where she was standing.

"Zeta," Vivian said as she stood and made her way over to Tristan.

He was prepared for another attack and didn't relax, even when he noticed that Zeta had returned to her standing position next to the chair.

Vivian circled him slowly, looking him over, he never took his eyes off her two peculiar escorts.

"How long have you known my granddaughter?" Vivian asked him.

"Four years," he answered as he continued to stare at his attacker, and the quiet young man.

"You're not being entirely honest, are you?" She stopped directly in front of him, face to face.

Tristan looked down at her, turning his focus from her entourage. "As I said, I've only known Cianne for four years." He relaxed a little. "I moved here four years ago," he said, then paused, trying to see the relevance, "But if you prefer a different answer then—"

"Is there a different answer?" Vivian interrupted.

"I would say that I feel as if I've known her all my life," he admitted.

Joseph, who had been watching them in silence, spoke up, "I guess you can't control everything, can you Vivian?" He chuckled.

Tristan wanted to ask her the relevance of her questions when he heard someone speak his name, in a low familiar voice.

Cianne?

She sounded sad…and tired. Tristan went to the large sliding glass door on the far side of the room and peered out into the darkness. Only, he moved so fast that Joseph stood up and gasped. Zeta moved to Vivian's side in a flash of speed. The young man, who stood by the chair, didn't move at all.

"What is it?" Vivian asked.

"I…" he said, then sighed, "it's nothing," Tristan continued to peer through the glass, searching the darkness.

I'm hearing things again.

It was the first step to losing one's sanity. He figured Cianne's voice was haunting him because he was lost without her. He needed to see her, he needed to hear her voice, so his mind was splintering from that need.

"Why would she try to handle this on her own?" Tristan asked no one in particular.

For the first time since he arrived, Tristan heard the young man curse. Then the young man spoke, but not in any language immediately familiar to Tristan. He spoke quickly; his tone was hard and angry but Tristan heard the underlined sense of distress in it as well. As the young man spoke, he looked from Vivian to Tristan several times.

Tristan listened intently, confused at what he was hearing. Alarmed, he turned to Vivian when the young man finished his rant. "What does he mean, I'm an abomination?" Tristan demanded. He looked at the young man, then faced the others, who stared at him as if he just said something inexcusable. "Who are the Coesen, and what does *he*," Tristan said, pointing to the young man, "want with *my* Cianne?"

Monday Morning

Warm air wafted through the window, causing the blinds to sway back and forth and make a tapping sound when they hit the wall. Night had slowly dragged into morning while Tristan waited for Cianne to call. The collective opinion was that she had been so stressed, so worried, and so emotional, that she needed time to be alone. That she would come home after she thought things through.

Tristan wanted to believe that, but he had an ominous feeling inside. A feeling he chose not to share with the others.

From the window seat just under her window, he looked over to her empty bed and imagined her there, watching him with her incredibly vibrant eyes. Instead, her pillows lay there untouched, but with her enchanting scent locked inside of them.

The blinds hit the window sill harder as the motion of the downstairs front door opening sucked the air out of the room. Tristan squeezed the items he held in his hands, Cianne's promise ring, and the necklace he gave her. She left them behind.

Come back to me.

Tristan placed the ring and necklace back on the computer desk where he found them. He refused to acknowledge for another moment, his thoughts on her reasons for leaving them behind.

I just need to speak with her, he thought, as he picked up his phone again and scrolled over his calls. He knew that no new calls had been logged but he went through the process anyway. Only Brian had called during the night to inform him of what he already suspected. Tranae knew about the baby but didn't know about the appointment.

It seemed that Cianne kept her plan a secret.

Tristan reached up and pulled the window down before he made his way downstairs to see who just entered the Baxter home. He knew who hadn't, so he took his time. He also knew it wasn't Vivian or her escorts from last night. He wasn't sure how he knew, he just did.

The two men looked up at Tristan as he entered the kitchen. Joseph, who stood at the kitchen counter, gave him a halfhearted smile as he poured coffee into a mug. Malone, the Detective from last night, stood just inside the kitchen entryway.

"Coffee, Tristan?" Joseph reached for another mug from the high cabinet.

"Thank you." Tristan took a seat at the table where Joseph placed one of the cups of coffee. He looked at Det. Malone.

"Now that both of you are here," Malone said as he pulled something out of his pocket, "I came because this was dropped off with the morning mail at the clinic your daughter went to yesterday." Det. Malone placed a large clear evidence bag on the table. "It's a ransom note, and I believe more than one kidnapper is involved."

Tristan knew something was wrong from the start. He felt it. He lifted his gaze from the evidence bag to Joseph, who placed his elbows on the table and his head in his hands. When Joseph looked up a few seconds later, his face seemed more vacant and hollow than it had been just thirty seconds before.

Keep your shit together.

Tristan repeated the phrase in his head over and over again until he didn't feel the need to beat the dining table to a pulp. Once he felt calm enough to think straight, he glared at the letter that was placed in front of him. He slowly pulled the letter to him and lifted it from the table. He read it out loud through the plastic:

I was told that no harm would come to me if I do what is asked of me. That being said, I am to request that three million dollars be available and ready to be traded for my safe return. My captor is aware the police are involved and would like to convey to you and to them that this transaction will go smoothly if their involvement regarding this matter is purely that of consultants. I am to tell you that once the money is received, my location will be revealed. I'm sor ——.

A jagged pen mark ran from the last word to the end of the page. That made the hairs on the back of Tristan's neck prickle. He placed the letter back on the table.

Of all the possibilities, he had not considered kidnapping. So, he was the target and she was just the means to get to him. He was to blame for her not being home with him, her family, and her friends. He was the cause for her suffering in the condition she was in.

It felt as if the world had just dropped from beneath him. He was to blame.

"Is this her handwriting?" Detective Malone asked.

"It's hers," Joseph said.

Tristan didn't see him take the clear bag but he watched Joseph as he flung the letter back across the table towards the detective.

"The paper it's written on is hers too." Joseph's voice cracked. "Why would someone demand that kind of money from me? If they knew me they would know I don't have that kind of money."

Malone looked to Tristan. Tristan looked over at the note again then back at the Detective's knowing gaze.

"Did you get something that would let us know she's alright? Do we have proof of life?" Tristan asked.

Joseph's brows creased as he regarded Tristan.

"I know a little bit about kidnappings," Tristan admitted sullenly.

The detective pulled another clear plastic bag from his pocket. This bag contained something thin, maybe it was a photo. The detective flipped the plastic bag over, noted something on the back, then handed it to Joseph.

Tristan kept his hands clenched tight to keep from grabbing the evidence bag from Cianne's father. He watched Joseph inspect the item, stretching the plastic over it to see it better. Joseph sucked in a breath and stiffened before he slid the bag across the table toward him.

Tristan sensed that Cianne's father was on the verge of a breakdown. They both were. He reached for the bag then held it up and peered at the image.

"As you can see, she is holding today's paper. Plus, the reference number of this picture has today's date," Malone said. "She seems to be in good condition considering the circumstances. Take that as a plus because neither of you can fall to pieces right now, you both need to be strong."

The picture was clear. Cianne sat on a mattress with a newspaper in her hand. Her legs were folded up to her chin and her head leaned slightly to the side; her long hair cascaded over her shoulder and down her leg. She wasn't smiling nor was there a frown on her beautiful face. Her eyes were clear, not sad or defeated like he thought they might be. Cianne looked calm, resigned.

Tristan focused on her eyes. Those green-blue orbs were as beautiful as he remembered but with less of a spark. She looked tired. The dark circles under her eyes confirmed that she hadn't had much sleep.

Tristan had to bite down his rage. He wanted Cianne. He wanted to kill the bastard who thought to take what belonged to him, to harm what belonged to him.

"We will get her back," Detective Malone said with confidence.

Joseph rubbed his forehead. "I can call her grandmother but I'm not sure how long it will take for her to get that kind of money together."

Tristan stood. He loosened his clenched fists and ignored the crescents his nails made from digging in his palms. "I can get it." As he dialed on his phone he stepped out of the kitchen without looking at either of the men. After a few minutes, he came back into the kitchen. "It'll be here by end of business today."

Malone choked on his gum.

Tristan knew the Detective was aware his family had money but maybe he didn't know how fast it could be put together. While a good deal of their wealth was tied up in some way or another, unlike most of the wealthy a good chunk of it was just sitting in vaults in banks around the world, waiting for short-term investment opportunities.

Joseph's eyes opened wide. "You have three million dollars available to you, just like that?"

"This is my fault. I will fix it," Tristan admitted. It was hard to look at Cianne's father. All of this, everything that had happened to her, was his fault. He sat back down.

"Umm," Malone spoke up, "I ah…don't know if giving them what they want will result in Cianne's safe return. Let's just try to focus on who may be responsible. Do you know of anyone who would want to extort money from you? We have to assume that someone knew that you could pull that kind of money out of the air like that. I mean, not many people can do that."

"If Tristan can get the money and is willing to pay…" Mr. Baxter looked at Tristan. Tristan nodded. "Then I think that we need to do what we can to get her back safely."

"Look, Mr. Baxter, I know that you are upset but the chances of getting her back safely even if they get the money are slim. We don't want to make them think it is easy to get money from you. We need them to make a mistake if we can, not pay them." He tapped the plastic bag in front of him. "If we make this easy—"

"I can't take the risk of pissing them off. If they want money, then that's what they'll get. I think that we can handle it from here Detective Malone." Joseph stood.

"You are going to hand three million dollars over to these pricks with no guarantees and you don't want the West Hills PD involved. You can't be that irresponsible." Det. Malone looked at Tristan.

"I just want Cianne home. I'll pay whatever they want to have that." Tristan stood too.

Detective Malone stepped in front of Joseph. "If you try to keep the law out of this it won't end well."

"It's what they want, so I am willing to take that chance," Joseph said, as he led the detective to the door.

Monday Night
Night two in captivity

Barking dogs replaced the soothing sounds of moving traffic as day dimmed into night. Frightened by every sound amplified by the empty building, Cianne had no other choice than to stay awake.

That first night, one of her darkly-dressed captors had opened the door, hurled a flashlight at her feet, then quickly shut the door. She kept the light on the entire night as she sat up in the corner clutching her knees to her chest, wishing that all this was one of her awful nightmares. That she was home with her father and that Tristan held her close.

By the time the sounds of traffic signaled daylight, Cianne was exhausted. She wondered throughout the night if she was alone in the building or if her captors stayed with her through the night. The thought of being alone in this place was a bit more frightening to her than they were.

No one had checked in on her since one of them had tossed her the flashlight. Before that, they came in after she ate to give her paper to copy a letter that one of them wrote that was to be given to her father. When she tried to add that she was sorry, the taller of the two had snatched the paper from her.

Cianne hoped Tristan would forgive her for everything that happened. Tranae would have told him by now that she was pregnant, and she was pretty sure the police figured out the timeline of her day as well.

She tried to imagine the conversation Tristan would have with his parents. She imagined him saying, "Mom, dad I need three million dollars to save the woman who ruined my life by getting pregnant."

He'll think I trapped him; that I am with him for his family's money.

Cianne shook her head to clear the wild thoughts she created. Tristan loved her, she knew that for certain. He may not be happy about her being pregnant but he might understand.

She had to stop worrying about that and focus on the situation at hand. Getting out of this cell was her number one priority. As she looked around the interior of the room again she realized the possibility of accomplishing her goal of freedom looked bleak.

At that moment, Cianne considered the possibility that she may not make it out of this alive. Most hostages she heard about were killed before the money even exchanged hands. She also knew that there was no way her father could get that kind of money, and it would be difficult even with Tristan's parents' help.

The sound of the bolted door being pulled open startled Cianne. A masked head peeked into the room to see if she was far enough away before he entered, she surmised. Once the person saw that she was far enough away, he entered the room and immediately shut the door behind him.

They never came alone and never let the door shut behind them.

Cianne assumed this was a man. Not knowing who they were was terrifying but she got the impression that all three were men. Men may want *other* things. Afraid, she moved further back hoping that he wasn't thinking of what had flashed in her mind.

When he moved his arm, Cianne actually jumped back. Her head met the hard wall and a whimper escaped her pursed lips. Her captor's eyes almost looked sympathetic as he stared at her for a moment. She was so scared that she didn't notice the bag he carried in his hands until he bent down and placed it on the floor.

He chuckled at her, then placed his finger over his masked mouth and slowly backed away until his other hand touched the door handle behind him. He pivoted but never took his eyes off her as he opened the door and left the room.

Cianne waited several minutes before she got the nerve to inspect the brown bag. The smell coming from it was simply mouthwatering. She opened the bag to find a plastic container inside filled with warm roast beef, mashed potatoes with gravy, and peas. It also contained two dinner rolls soaked with gravy.

Excited, she tucked the bag under her arm, reached into the cooler for the plastic spoon she had been given earlier, sat on the mattress edge, then dug into the potatoes. They were delicious, seasoned, and mashed to perfection. Cianne closed her eyes and moaned in satisfaction.

As she shifted to get into a more comfortable position on the mattress, the brown bag secured under her arm fell to the floor. Something inside made a low thud upon contact. Cianne placed the food on her lap and picked up the bag. She pulled out a bottle that read: Prenatal Vitamins. Cianne froze.

They knew. How?

She placed the food on the mattress then scooted away from it. Fifteen minutes passed before she lifted the container of food again and inspected it. She went over it a hundred times and still she couldn't figure out how they had known, let alone cared, that she was pregnant.

Is the food poisoned?

It took another fifteen minutes of smelling the scent of real food before Cianne concluded that it would be very unlikely that someone would go to the trouble of giving her sealed prenatal vitamins only to poison her with a roast beef dinner.

She took a small bite of meat and waited for a bad reaction. Five minutes passed before she convinced herself to continue. Once she finished the meal she took a vitamin. Then, for some reason she couldn't fathom, she hid the food container and the vitamins under the mattress.

Cianne went back to her corner of the room and waited. A few hours later the person returned, again allowing the door to shut behind him. It was odd but telling. Cianne took special notice of his frame and height. The closing of the door was also an indication that this was the same person who gave her the bag.

She hesitated at first but when he just stood there, she slowly moved to the mattress and pulled out the bag with the container, and placed it on the floor. She then backed up against the wall, giving him ample space.

He bent and picked up the bag.

An idea came to her then. Cianne held his gaze as she slowly lifted then placed her finger to her mouth and quietly made a hush sound, smiling somewhat to thank him.

He nodded as he did the same gesture with his finger. Then he backed away, leaving the room as he had before.

She realized then that her hunch was right—that he gave her the food and pills unbeknownst to the others and she was to keep it a secret. Cianne knew then that she may have a sympathizer.

Chapter Twenty-Two
Friday, four days in captivity

The days and nights seemed to slip away with no communication from Cianne's captors. The private investigators Tristan hired hadn't offered any useful information either. The fact of the matter was that the person or persons holding her left nothing that could be traced. There were no prints on the letter other than Cianne's and the photo was a dead end. There was nothing to go on and nothing stood out.

Tristan racked his brain trying to think of who would do this. He already knew the why. The problem was, money could motivate just about anyone to become a kidnapper; everyone was a suspect and that was the plain truth.

Four days had passed and with each day Tristan sank deeper inside himself. He couldn't trust anyone but himself, and he was starting to think that even he was becoming unreliable.

He was hearing things; he was hearing Cianne in his head.

Tristan looked at his watch again, something he did every few minutes now. It was about lunchtime, but he wouldn't eat. He had no good reason to eat. The image of Cianne starving on that filthy mattress with his child growing inside of her stayed with him at all times.

He wouldn't eat.

"Baby," his mother whispered. She touched his hand, her voice full of concern. "You look so tired, sweetheart. Won't you let me take you home so you can eat and rest for a while?" She rubbed his hand. "Tristan we're concerned about you." She looked over to his father who sat in their car. "Brian says that you haven't slept in days. We are all worried about Cianne sweetheart, but you have to take care of yourself, she would want you to."

Tristan glanced over at his father. He knew the man had pulled every string he had in his arsenal to find information on Cianne's whereabouts with no results. He then turned his gaze on his mother, who sat beside him on the Baxter's porch glider for over an hour. Tristan saw the pain of helplessness in his parents' eyes. It was the same pain he felt for his unborn child.

Tristan's eyes glossed over, and for the first time since he was six years old, he cried. "I'm dying inside," he choked out.

"Oh baby," his mother said as she took him in her arms.

Tristan laid his head on her shoulder. "I can't live without her," he sobbed.

"Don't say that Tristan. Cianne is coming home and everything will be as it should be."

His mother held him tighter but he felt nothing. He was numb.

Hours Later

Tristan grunted and opened his eyes as a bright light blinded him then flickered away, only to blind him again. It was then that he heard the tapping on the driver's side window and the muffled sound of voices. The flashlight was now pointed directly into his eyes again, so he couldn't see who held it.

In an attempt to find his bearings, Tristan held up his arm and turned away from the light. He looked out his passenger window to see where he was.

"Are you alright in there?"

Tristan ignored the question and looked at his surroundings.

Kennecott?

He wasn't exactly sure how he ended up at Kennecott University in his truck, in a virtually empty parking lot. Confused, but no longer able to ignore the man who continuously tapped at his window, Tristan started the engine and rolled down the window.

"I'm fine." He blocked the light with his hand when he turned back to the driver-side window. "I must have dozed off. I'm sorry."

"Do you have any ID on you?" the security guard asked,

"Yeah," he groaned. Tristan looked down and slipped his hand into his pocket and took out his billfold. When he looked up, the security guard pointed the light away from his eyes and took the ID handed to him.

The guard looked the ID over for a few seconds then took a pad from his pocket and wrote down Tristan's name and then handed the ID back.

"Do you need me to call someone for you?"

Tristan shook his head. "I'm fine," Tristan told him. "I'm actually here to see someone."

"It's nine o'clock at night," the guard said, "no one's here but night security. Have you been drinking tonight?"

"Not a sip, Officer. I'll catch up with my *friend* another time," Tristan said. "Sorry for the trouble,"

"No trouble at all," the guard said, looking Tristan over again. The guard shined the flashlight over the empty passenger seat, then in the backseat before returning it to his side. "You sure you are ok?"

"I'm fine," Tristan assured him.

"Drive safe," the guard said, waving as he turned to walk away.

Tristan didn't know how he ended up at Kennecott but he realized now that he wanted to question Nick about Cianne's disappearance. Though, he doubted Nick was bright enough to plan and execute a kidnapping without getting caught within a few hours. He must have had Nick in the back of his mind when he started out earlier after his mother's visit, with no real destination in mind.

Tristan pulled out of the empty parking lot and into traffic. He decided to just drive. No particular destination, just not sitting still. He would just see where he ended up.

He wasn't a religious man, but he prayed it would be where Cianne was being held.

Saturday Morning, May 14th
Early Hours

Cassius waited on the line for a response. His loyalty was unquestionable and under normal circumstances, he would never question his Sovereign, but he couldn't understand why she didn't order him to lay the city of West Hills to waste.

"Cassius," Vivian said calmly. "The Augur came to see me Sunday morning before all this happened."

Cassius didn't speak right away. He let what his Sovereign, Vivian Harper, said sink in. "She spoke?" he finally asked.

"Yes," Vivian confirmed, "she spoke."

The Augur had only spoken a handful of times in over a hundred years so Cassius knew the importance of her words, even if he wasn't privy to what those words actually were. "I understand," he said in a low tone, hoping his queen couldn't hear the wonder and awe in his voice. Overjoyed and ashamed, Cassius spoke again, "I meant no disrespect my Sovereign. I apologize for questioning your judgment."

Vivian excused Cassius' questioning, unable to muster the venom to chastise him. The fact that Oma, the ancient blind woman who was their Augur, had only spoken seven other times in her long life was too momentous to stress over the little things.

On that quiet Sunday morning, the frail-looking woman had arrived unannounced and cemented what Vivian had to do.

The Augur, or Oma, was the Coesen version of Prophesier and her words were more precious than the rarest of diamonds to their people. Vivian knew that Cassius wanted to find Cianne as much as she did. It was a comfort considering his history with Cianne's father, but Oma was specific when she said that 'the boy must be the one to save Cianne.'

The problem was, Vivian assumed that 'boy' was Whodai and that was why she brought him to West Hills a few nights past. To her utter shock, she soon realized 'the boy' was none other than Tristan Bertram.

"Cassius," she said gently, in a manner she rarely used, "how many this time?"

"We lost nine good men but it is done."

Vivian grimaced but would grieve for her lost soldiers later. Right now, she sat in a luxury suite a few miles from West Hills, waiting. "We can breathe a sigh of relief for at least sixteen more years." She looked over to the ringing phone on the table next to the couch where she was seated. "You finish up there, I will handle things here. I will contact you in a day or so." Vivian disconnected the call and picked up the ringing hotel phone.

The door to suite 12-1 was already open when Tristan stepped off the elevator. The hotel clerk told him there would be someone to greet him. There wasn't.

When he slowly entered the room he half expected to see Zeta or the nameless young man who had come to Cianne's house a few days ago. Instead, he saw Vivian, seated in the sitting area looking as regal as any queen.

She was fully dressed in an ankle length dark blue long sleeve dress as if it were four in the afternoon versus four in the morning. He closed the door behind him and walked over to where she sat. She motioned for him to sit on the sofa across from her.

Tristan decided to stand. *Just in case*. "I think that I may be losing my mind," he said as he looked down at his feet then nervously rubbed his hand over his head. "I…uh, I can hear her in my head."

Vivian tilted her head to peer up at him with a look of shock on her face.

"I don't really know why I came here," Tristan said, "I just…" He rubbed his temples. "I was sitting in her room and I heard her whisper to me. At first, I thought it was just my mind replaying the things she's said to me before, you know, but—"

"What did she say?" Vivian moved to the edge of the chair, giving him her full attention.

"She said that…" he started then paused, as he sat down across from Vivian, "that she hoped the baby had my smile. That she loved my smile." He cleared his throat. Tristan looked at his hands then said what he came to say. "I know that you're different, like Cianne. Whenever you're around I feel, I feel like I must…I don't know." He shook his head. "That I must submit to you." He looked at Vivian. "I want you to tell me if she's…"

Tristan sighed and looked away. He was unable to finish the question he drove here to have answered.

"You want to know if she is dead and if it is her spirit you hear." Vivian sat back when he gave her a mournful nod. She then took her time inspecting him. "How do you feel Tristan?"

Tristan, puzzled by the question, frowned. He knew what the question meant, but he didn't know what she meant by asking the question.

"Let's try this then," Vivian said impatiently. "Zeta." Before Vivian finished saying the girl's name, a blur of color filled Tristan's field of vision. The petite one called Zeta was at Vivian's side.

In sync with Zeta's lightning speed entrance, Tristan went on alert and flipped over the sofa to a standing position in back of it. He quickly read the room for the other escort but only the girl was there. He relaxed only when he realized that she was not going to move until she was told.

Tristan looked at Vivian who was still seated on the sofa. She had a look on her face that made him very uneasy. He wasn't sure if it was a look of admiration or contempt.

"Sit down Tristan," Vivian said; serenity had returned to her face.

He hesitated briefly before sitting.

"You are a definite anomaly."

Tristan was tired of being insulted by the woman. First, he was an abomination and now an anomaly. His look of confusion was replaced by one of annoyance.

"Have you always moved with the reflexes and agility of a cheetah and with the strength of an elephant?

Again, she had him confused.

"You come from good stock dear, I've checked…but not that good," Vivian said shrewdly. When she realized she was going to get nothing but a glare from him, she continued, "You have been improved Tristan, upgraded. Some would say, perfected. I bet you were always the best at everything, right?"

He'd always been fast. It wasn't until a few seasons ago while playing football that he realized he was much faster than the other players. He was so fast that he had to make an effort to slow down and take a few hits to keep the crowds interested. But that was just the way he was. He had always been what coaches called exceptional, for as long as he could remember.

"You've been checking up on me?" Tristan asked calmly. From the moment he met her, he sensed that Vivian felt some way about him, but to insult his family was rude. Yet, she had the answers he needed. "Why?"

"At present, time is brief so you will get the short version of what has to be done. The full tutorial will have to wait. As for your original question, yes…Cianne lives." Vivian sighed as if bored. "Zeta will explain some things to you," she said then stood, "and then she is going to tell you how to find my granddaughter." Vivian started out of the room.

Tristan's eyes followed her as she proudly walked by him. There was no way she could have known how to find Cianne and hadn't told him. "You knew how to find her all this time," he accused, his voice shrill.

Vivian stopped. At first, it seemed as if she would turn back and respond but she said nothing as she started out of the room again with her head held high.

"It's complicated, Tristan." A quiet voice came from beside him. "…and it is not our place to question." Her words were slow and precise with a subtle French accent.

Tristan looked over at the small girl who now sat beside him. He didn't even hear her move.

She reminded him of an adorable little devil. Just days ago, he was defending himself and now the girl who attacked him was being nice. Tristan moved over an inch, in case the sweet little angel decided to show her claws again.

"Complicated," Tristan sneered. His anger simmered. "If there is a way to find Cianne then I need to know now."

"I will tell you all I know but you need to listen to everything I have to say," Zeta insisted. "We…you and I, aren't like other people. Well," she said, smiling, "you are even more…special."

"What are you talking about?" Tristan's anger hadn't defused but he would listen, for now.

Zeta gave him an unreadable look, "Considering recent circumstances, and the fact that your Coesen was suppressed when she was just a little girl," she said, the last words slower than the rest as if she were thinking out loud. "We don't exactly know when she transferred to you. Your speed and strength have been seeping out just as her abilities have. That could be the explanation for why you didn't notice any changes in yourself."

Zeta lost him somewhere around the word Coesen. "My Coesen?" he asked, confused, "what circumstances?"

"Tristan," she said with excitement, "you are truly remarkable."

She held his gaze longer than Tristan felt comfortable as if he was some kind of lab experiment.

"Vivian, as you call her, is the Sovereign of a race of exceptional humans. We are known as the Coesen. We can trace our lineage to four amazing men. You are what we call a Protector. You are your Coesen's physical defense against any and all aggressors. You will be stronger and faster than the average person and most other things in this world. You will think and react faster than any middling or the fastest animals."

Tristan took a moment to process what Zeta told him. As farfetched as it all sounded, he knew that what she said was the truth. He *was* different, had always felt it. "What is a middling?"

"A middling is an average person without unique abilities. Your parents, Mr. Baxter, they are considered middlings," she explained. "You are connected to your Ward. Protectors can always locate their Wards, the Coesen who has transferred the gift to them."

Tristan considered this. "A guardian of sorts," he said. "Then Cianne is…"

"She is a Coesen," Zeta said slowly, for his benefit. "Was there ever a time when you felt overheated or warm when Cianne was near?"

Tristan thought back to all those times that he felt hot when they were in close proximity. "Yes," he admitted. He thought that warmth was because she made him that nervous.

"That was the synching process your bodies were going through," Zeta explained.

"Then what's wrong with me?" Tristan asked. "If we are synched then why haven't I got a clue as to where Cianne is?

And if there are others like you, who can do things, then why haven't your people found her yet?"

Zeta cleared her throat. "I don't know," she admitted, "but as her Protector, you are our best hope. As for you not being able to find her, we think it's because her abilities are bound...and perhaps because you two are lovers." She looked down nervously when Tristan met her gaze. "We think that because of your emotional connection to your Ward, you cannot focus properly...but we can't be sure."

"So, no Protector has ever been in love with their..." Tristan couldn't remember the name. He was tired and still very angry.

"Coesen," she reminded him as she looked away.

Tristan waited for an answer as he stared at her profile. After a moment of silence, Zeta looked at him then nodded. Wards, sovereigns, supernatural powers, Tristan had no time to be amazed about what he learned. All he wanted was to know how it all would help him get Cianne safely back in his arms.

"Little is known of the two relationships similar to yours but both unions ended in death. Any such union would be looked at as an—"

"An abomination," Tristan finished.

"Unlawful," Zeta corrected. "The thing is, your love for her may be clouding your senses but you are, as I said before, not a 'normal' Protector. Mainly that is because Cianne, as you call her, isn't a "normal" Coesen." Zeta hesitated then said, "Mr. Baxter has informed us that she has been having visions. You are stronger and faster than most middlings, meaning your abilities are somewhat present, even though they shouldn't be. Cianne is very powerful. Her abilities were bound when she was a child, but apparently, they seem to be trickling out on their own which is enabling your use of the entitlement she has given you. Understand that once her abilities are unrestrained, once her power is fully released, yours will be significantly enhanced as well. The scope of what you two are capable of is… Well, it is unknown."

"It's Zeta, right?" Tristan asked. She nodded. "All that's exciting but I need to know what I can do now. If my feelings for her are clouding my senses, then what do I need to do to find her?"

"No Coesen has had the ability to hear anyone's thoughts for some time. If you are hearing her, as you say you are, then she may be able to hear you as well," Zeta said.

"I said that I *think* I *may* be hearing her." He wasn't sure anymore. He wasn't sure of anything.

A low buzzing sound alerted Tristan of a text message. He immediately pulled out his phone. His pulse increased. Finally.

Kidnappers: Have my money. Ready for the orders soon.

Chapter Twenty-Three
Saturday Evening

"**D**amn it!" Tristan cupped the top of his head in his hands. His voice boomed throughout the hotel suite but no one seemed to care. In fact, he lost his temper several times in the last sixteen hours and no one complained.

Time was ticking away and he was no closer to figuring out how to communicate with Cianne telepathically. "We've been working at this for hours and nothing."

Tristan pounded his fist on his head. "FUCK!"

"We can't be sure she hasn't heard you." Zeta pointed out.

"I think if she had, she would have answered me by now." Tristan fell back against the sofa like a weightless blob.

"Maybe we are going about this all wrong. Cianne has been saying random things, right?" Zeta stood.

"Like she's talking to herself," Tristan agreed.

Zeta began pacing in front of the seating area. "Let's assume that she isn't aware that you can hear her. So maybe she isn't concentrating at all or maybe she's asleep. When you heard her, what were you doing?"

Tristan thought about the last time he heard Cianne. "I was driving around not thinking about anything really. More or less, I was trying not to think."

"Well let's try to figure out what she could have been thinking. What did she say?" Zeta turned to face Tristan.

Tristan sat up. "The first few times I just heard her say my name. Then she mentioned the baby." He thought about the way Cianne sounded. "Each time her voice was calm, relaxed."

"You need to fill your mind with thoughts of her. Only the happy times you shared."

He tried not to take offense but said, "All my time with her was happy." Tristan closed his eyes and let his mind wander to happier times. He first thought of the first time he sat with Cianne at Crimpy's Burger Shop, when he discovered that she liked him. Next, he thought of the day they were in her kitchen for the first time, and how he couldn't help telling her how he felt about her, even though every fiber in his being begged him not to put himself out there.

Tristan thought of Cianne's blue-green eyes and how every time he looked into them he felt powerless along with a sense of calm he never felt before. The moment she told him that she loved him…

"Cianne, where are you?"

Cianne sat against the wall with her knees pulled up to her chest, her head resting on her knees. This was her usual way of sitting and sleeping in her cell. She didn't feel comfortable lying on the nasty mattress, and she wanted to keep her eyes on the door at all times. So much so that Cianne was able to figure out the pattern her kidnappers worked by.

Before traffic got too busy in the early morning, one checked in on her and gave her food. No one looked in on her again until what she surmised was lunchtime. It was always two of them although one always stayed out of sight now. They usually brought her something edible but never very appetizing. Then she was either left alone or ignored until early evening. The one she named, Cook, came in then. He often secretly brought her food, good food, and sometimes he brought a nice home cooked meal.

Even though Cook never spoke to her, seeing him had become the highlight of her days. Only, something was wrong because not only had Cook not shown up today, neither had anyone else.

It was dark outside and Cianne was more frightened than ever. The dogs seemed louder tonight than they had been the past few days for some reason. Their barking and howling were scratching at her last remaining nerve.

Worried that her kidnappers now had what they wanted so they decided to leave her to starve to death, Cianne was on the brink of hysterics. She knew she needed to remain calm because there was nothing else she could do.

Tristan.

She attempted to find her calm by thinking about Tristan. She pictured herself in Tristan's bed with his face next to hers. She thought of his lips and the way he traced them over her cheeks, barely touching her skin. He always knew exactly how and where to touch her. His smell was a clean intoxicating scent that called to her soul.

She wanted Tristan.

Cianne looked up suddenly and shined the little flashlight toward the door. There was no one there. She pointed it to every corner in the room but no one was there.

Calm down...calm down, she thought. Only she couldn't. Her heart raced as her chest heaved in and out. *It was nothing. You're just scared and…*

"*Cianne, where are you?*"

Cianne jumped to her feet. This time she heard his voice clearly. Startled she began flashing the light frantically in every direction.

He's not here. You're going crazy?

Cianne sank to the floor. Tears slid down her face as she shook her head. This was it. She was going to die but, batshit crazy was taking over first. As much as she wanted to hear Tristan's voice again, she didn't want to hear voices that her mind created. A voice that, no matter how comforting, wouldn't stop and that scared her to death.

"Just stop!" she screamed aloud.

When the voice in her head, his voice, asked her where she was again, all Cianne could do was scream back mentally, *"I don't know?"*

"Cianne, you can hear me! Are you hurt?"

Cianne covered her mouth to keep her scream silent.

"God, I'm really going crazy."

"No Buttercup, you're not. Are you hurt?"

With a hysterical giggle, Cianne decided that didn't she care. So what if she was crazy? She forced herself to relax because hearing Tristan now was just what she needed. Cianne took a deep breath in…then she responded.

"I'm not hurt, out of my mind, but not hurt." What if it *was* him? Crazier things have happened to her. She was the standard for crazy, right? Besides, why would she conjure Tristan's voice just to ask herself if she was hurt? That made no sense at… *"Oh my god Tristan is that really you? If it is, I'm so sorry—"*

"Ci focus, what do you see and hear?"

Tristan had never been that short with her. Could it really be him? *"I'm in a room, a building. All the windows are bricked up. I'm near a busy street or a highway. I can hear lots of cars during the day."*

"Do you know who has you?"

"No, they all wear ski masks. There are at least three of them."

"Is there anything else you can think of that can help me find you?"

"It took us about an hour to get here from where they took me."

Cianne knew Tristan most likely knew where she was and what she planned to do before she was kidnapped but she couldn't confront that just yet. Not yet.

"The CD that was playing in the van played one full-time and by the time the car was turned off, it had looped and was on the second track again. Also, I think I could be near a kennel or something. I hear dogs barking and they get louder at night," she transferred. Cianne waited for him to say something else but minutes passed with silence. *"Tristan, are you still there? Please...please...please,"* she begged.

She wondered if she imagined the entire conversation. It was totally normal for a person to hallucinate in this type of situation. More minutes, minutes that felt like hours, passed with no word from him.

It felt so real. It has to be real.

Eventually, Cianne found herself smiling. It didn't matter if she was dreaming the whole thing or not, she spoke to Tristan and that meant her fractured mind could conjure him again. That gave her some peace.

"I have the drop location, I'm coming to get you."

Cianne's heart leapt into her throat. It was real...and Tristan sounded so determined that hope flared in her anew.

"I love you Cianne."

It was barely a whisper in her mind but she heard it. Tristan loved her, still. Not only that, she was able to hear him *and* he was searching for her. Cianne smiled as hopeful tears fell from her eyes.

"I'm going with you," Zeta said. She sat down in the passenger seat of his truck then slammed the door shut. Tristan heard the seatbelt click. "A guardian having a telepathic link to their host again." Her eyes widened as she glared at him. "Well, it's amazing. What all did she tell you?"

Tristan noted the time as he started the engine then pulled off. He looked at Zeta, feeling somewhat annoyed. However, he had no time to argue with her, which meant she was going with him.

"She said that she hears cars passing by all day so she may be near a busy street or highway. She also mentioned that a CD played all the way through and wrapped to the first two songs again. On average, we can guess that means we need to check a 40 to 45 minutes' circumference from the clinic."

"We are looking for abandoned properties near highways, about 45 minutes from the clinic?" Zeta listed all the clues out loud as if committing them to memory. "Where is the drop?"

"I was instructed to get on the interstate. I'll be given more direction as I drive." Tristan approached the on-ramp. "Call Mr. Baxter," he spoke to his hands-free phone.

'Calling Mr. Baxter,' a computerized female voice said through the speakers of the truck. The sound of dialing numbers filled the vehicle.

"Mr. Baxter, do you have a map?" Tristan asked when the line picked up.

"I do." There were a few seconds of silence then the brief ruffling of papers. "I have it, where do I go?"

Tristan explained all the information Cianne gave him to Joseph who had Vivian and another three of the "Coesen Guard" with him. Now all they had to do was figure out where Cianne could be before the drop, in case they were double-crossed.

"There are two possible places she could be, based on her description. It's a tossup between Mansfield Industrial Park which is off Clay Avenue, or some buildings located behind the cemetery off Seminole and Madison Avenue. Both are in bad parts of town, and both are close to the interstate," Joseph informed them. "Which one do I take?"

"I think we should wait to see what direction they want me to take. I can take the place closest to the money exchange while you guys take the other. If we don't, we could end up in the same place," Tristan advised.

"You're right, we'll wait for your call," Joseph said. "And Tristan, thank you for everything you're doing for Cianne.

And…and for your understanding with all of, well, this…" Joseph trailed off.

"Thank me when Cianne is home safe." Tristan disconnected the call. He drove about an hour before he got the message from the kidnapper to go to a gas station on a busy street. He pulled into a parking space at the designated place and waited while Zeta paid close attention to what was going on around them.

"This can't be where they want us to be," Zeta said, as she watched the busy storefront in the side view mirror.

"I guess they don't want us to know where we're going until the last minute." He surmised. Tristan wanted to speak to Cianne but he was pumped full of adrenaline and he knew that the telepathy thing only seemed to work when he was relaxed. Usually, he was a calm person but when it came to Cianne, he lost all his cool composure.

Tristan looked at his phone again. If he was counting the number of times he looked at the thing, he would be somewhere in the hundreds. When it finally buzzed, he was instructed to drive ten miles south and wait. Once Tristan got on the road, he called Joseph and advised him they were on the move again.

Zeta looked over the map she purchased from the Gas and Go. "It looks as if we are going to be within a few streets of the warehouses near Seminole and Madison," she told him. Then she called Vivian and advised them to go to the other location, Mansfield Industrial park.

Tristan drove, paying close attention to his surroundings. He passed a number of stores that lined either side of the street, and a good number of them were liquor stores. Why any area would need so many was a mystery to him.

At a red light, Tristan noticed a woman with light hair and gray eyes cross the street carrying a little cherub face boy with mischievous eyes that matched the woman's. The boy waved and Tristan waved back. He ignored the way his chest ached from the exchange. It made him think of the baby Cianne carried. It was up to her to decide to keep the baby or terminate the pregnancy.

The painful thought urged Tristan on. He drove slower when the GPS advised him that eight miles had been reached. He drove a few more miles, which led them to a less populated area. Tristan picked the speed up a little.

The kidnapper communicated that they should keep straight. Undoubtedly, they were being watched but he hadn't noticed any vehicles following them. Tristan continued straight until he was told to turn right onto another street leading to an unmaintained road lined with street lamps overrun with weeds. Dim light from a few working lamps gave the area an eerie glow but Tristan's sight was exceptional so he saw the details most couldn't. He slowed when he saw the entrance to an apartment complex.

Zeta looked at the GPS. "We are a few miles from the warehouse district."

Tristan followed the road until they reached a welcome sign. "An abandoned apartment complex," he murmured. Drifting slowly forward in the truck, he looked around at the boarded-up buildings and the overgrown grass. "She's here," he said to Zeta.

In sync with his remark, a few feet in front of his truck a masked figure stepped into the glare of his headlights. It took all the strength he had not to press the gas pedal to the floor and run the darkly dressed figure over.

Tristan was pissed but not stupid. He stomped on the brakes and put the truck in park.

"Get out the car!" The person in front of the truck yelled his instructions.

Tristan had his eyes on his side-view mirror and the other masked person who crept up alongside his truck. He did nothing when he felt the gun at his temple but he was too angry to be afraid. The need to fight reverberated through his entire body but Tristan pushed it down. He knew he had to stay composed until he had Cianne safe. He slowly removed his keys from the ignition and let them dangle from his fingers while raising his other hand for the gunman to see.

The darkly dressed figure who stood in front of the truck moved toward them with another gun raised. "Get out," the approaching gunman ordered. "I thought I told you to come alone."

"She's my bodyguard," Tristan said. He smiled bitterly as he got out of the truck. He felt a jarring pain as the butt of the gun connected with the back of his head. He stumbled forward but held onto the door of his truck to keep on his feet.

"Please," Zeta begged in an innocent tone.

Confused by the sudden change in her normally assertive manner, Tristan glanced over at her. She stood next to the passenger side door looking at the figure who stood in the glare of the headlights.

"I hid in the back of the truck; he wasn't aware I was with him until it was too late. Don't punish him for my mistake."

As much as Tristan wanted to beat the shit out of the kidnapper who hit him, the one beside him, he gave the one in front of him his full attention. He seemed to be the one in charge so Tristan labeled him Leader.

"You seem to be a magnet for beautiful women," Leader teased as he eyed Zeta appreciatively.

The asshole must not notice the youth of her face, either that or he didn't care, and that made Tristan angrier.

"Where's the money and hand over your phones," Leader ordered.

Tristan wiped at some blood that trickled from his head as he stood straight. He finally turned to look at the person who had hit him, silently promising to do much worse. But not now. "In the back seat," he said, tossing his phone to Leader. Zeta did the same.

Leader, the one giving the orders, walked over slowly after pocketing their phones. He passed Tristan and his partner to get to the back door of the truck. With his gun fixed on

Zeta's head through the window of the car, he took out two large bags and threw them to the ground.

"Cover the girl," Leader told his partner, "I've got Lover-boy."

The two men switched targets by adjusting their aim but didn't move. With his gun pointed at Tristan now, the leader bent down and unzipped one of the bags.

Tristan slowly looked around at the four-story buildings that surrounded them. He looked from building to building wondering which of them Cianne was in.

"You think I'm stupid," Leader said, as he zipped one of the bags back up. "She's not in any of these buildings." He stood and took his silent partner's place. "Now walk," he shoved Tristan around his open truck door and forward.

"You got the money, so tell me where she is," Tristan demanded, as he moved forward.

"Walk!"

Tristan looked back at the silent guy who was still aiming his gun at Zeta from the driver's side and noticed that the guy's hand was more than a little shaky.

"Not a really good idea to be nervous with a gun pointed at someone's face," Tristan said, as he took a few more steps in the direction he was told to walk.

Leader looked over his shoulder at his accomplice then shook his head. "Don't worry about the girl." Leader said to his silent partner. He motioned to the bags. "Just take those to the car and wait for me there."

It took the mute gunman two trips but he did what he was told while they all waited in silence in the high grass. The one giving orders motioned for Zeta to join them. She complied. Tristan and Zeta walked a few feet into a clearing between two tall apartment buildings, Leader told them to stop walking and to turn around to face him. They stood only a few feet away from the barrel of his gun. They both watched in silence as he pulled out Tristan's phone and started pushing buttons, all while still pointing the gun at them.

"I see you've erased all your calls. Smart," Leader said.

Tristan couldn't tell because the man's face was hidden behind a black cloth mask but he felt the gunman was smiling. "Where is she?" Tristan asked again.

"You got a lot of questions for a man with a gun pointed at him." Leader dropped both phones on the ground and crushed them under his foot. He cocked his head to one side as he appraised Zeta again. "You, Mr. Bertram, have great taste in women," he said. "I wish I'd met you under different circumstances sweetheart. The accent is very sexy."

Cianne was sick with worry. She didn't hear from Tristan and the more time that passed, the more she thought of the worst possible scenarios. As one such scenario flickered through her mind, she heard movement from the other side of her cell door.

When she heard the key in the door she jumped to her feet. She took a deep breath, allowing the realization that her nightmare was finally over. She dreamed of seeing Tristan for five days. Her excitement threatened to bubble over, so she held her breath as the door creaked slowly, then was suddenly pushed wide open.

The sudden boom from the door hitting the wall shocked Cianne. She gasped as the glare from a flashlight blinded her. When the light was turned away from her face, she lifted her small light. The person she saw standing inside her cell wasn't Tristan. Cianne quickly dropped her own flashlight and covered her face.

"I didn't see anything," she said, through her covered mouth. "I swear."

There in the doorway, dressed in the same clothing as her kidnappers, stood a man without a mask covering his face. Cianne knew that her survival depended on not being able to identify him. Frantic, she turned around so her back was to him.

"I'm not here to hurt you," he said, stepping further inside the room. He let the door close behind him. His tone was urgent and pleading. "I'm here to help. You need to come with me."

Cianne let her hands fall to her side as she turned and looked at him. She started mentally checking off all the things she learned about the three kidnappers as he secured his flashlight inside the strap on his shoulder. She also noticed that he had let the door shut behind him. This man was the one she called Cook. She took a step toward him but out of the way of the bright light, the flashlight gave off.

"Tristan," she said. "What happen to Tristan?"

Cook held his hand out for her to take. "I don't know, but we need to get out of here now." He moved a step closer.

Cianne moved a step back. "I'm not going until you tell me what happened to him."

Cook cursed then looked away. He seemed to be contemplating something then he looked at her. He turned, went to the door, opened it a little, and peeked through it.

"Ok," he said, turning toward her. "If I tell you what I know, will you go with me then?"

"Yes," she said.

He closed the door again. "Your boyfriend is at the exchange not far from here. But…" He looked as if he was fighting a private battle inside himself.

"What?" she questioned.

"He's planning to kill your boyfriend. He's planning to kill you both," Cook said, as he moved toward her again. "That's why I need to get you out of here." He grabbed her limp hand and pulled her toward the door.

"No…God no." Cianne felt her world tilt.

"Tristan it's a trap. They're going to kill us."

Chapter Twenty-Four

Cianne's words ricocheted in Tristan's head like a bolt of energized lightning. He made a dead run for the gunman. He was directly in front of the gun when it discharged. With unnatural speed, he turned from the path of the bullet and positioned himself to the side of the Leader. Tristan grabbed him by the arm. A loud roar escaped the delinquent's mouth as Tristan twisted the arm at an awkward angle. The gun dropped from Leader's hand and the man fell to his knees, cradling his broken arm.

Tristan kicked the gun away and placed his hand on Leader's shoulder, applying a crushing pressure that made it almost impossible for him to move. He quickly surveyed the area for the second masked man. What he saw was Zeta on the ground where he had been standing seconds before. Tristan pushed Leader to the ground then ran to Zeta.

Her body lay still on the crumbled grass beneath her small frame. Tristan turned her over gently, making sure not to hurt her more. "Damn," he growled, as he placed one hand under her neck and scanned her body with his other hand and eyes to find where she was shot. He felt her tremble so he looked back to her face to see her eyes open. Tristan looked from her eyes to his hand which was wet with her warm blood.

"I thought we were like superhuman or something," he said, grimacing down at her.

"We're humans with mods," she said, then tried to smile.

"Where were you hit?" Tristan asked. He searched her blood-stained shirt for the wound.

"It's not bad," she said. "Go find Zaria."

The angelic-devil is already going into shock, he thought as he patted his pockets frantically for his phone. She forgot who they were here to find.

"Asshole took our phones." Tristan looked behind him where he left the gunman. The area was empty.

"You can't let him get away. Catch him. He knows where she is." Zeta tried to push him away and sit up.

"I can't just leave you here." Tristan picked Zeta up in an effortless move, cradling her securely against his chest. Moving so fast that not one drop of blood seeped from her wound to hit the ground, he ran her to his truck. He raised his foot and kicked the bumper, creating a huge dent. The truck slid back a bit and the airbags deployed.

"This is Mary with Vecon, Mr. Bertram I show that your vehicle may have been in an accident," A vehicle safety representative spoke through his speakers.

"My friend is injured, please send help," Tristan said, as he placed Zeta in the back seat of the vehicle.

"I have your location. Emergency services are on their way…"

"Go," Zeta urged through clenched teeth as they ignored the operator.

Tristan looked around. This time he looked over the top of the buildings. He saw the large interlaced overpass of a highway. It had to be a little under a mile away. He looked at Zeta, still worried about leaving her unprotected.

"Go," Zeta pushed him away.

Cianne did her best to resist being pulled out of her cell when Cook grabbed her hand. He barely allowed her the time to grab the mini flashlight she dropped.

"Tristan is coming for me."

Cook managed to get her halfway out of the doorway, but with one properly timed yank, she managed to pull free and retreat a few feet back into the room only to have him grab her wrist again.

"We need to go. Please," Cook said, as he desperately pulled her along. "They'll be here any minute."

"I can't leave. Tristan is coming for me!" she screamed, as she continued trying to free herself.

"If I were him I would want you safe." He looked at her with pleading eyes that shadowed some emotion she couldn't read. "He would want you and the baby safe."

The sound of a vehicle screeching to an abrupt stop made both of them jump and turn to the door. Cook quickly pulled her out of the room and down a long litter-filled hallway. They passed a row of broken down lockers and a few boarded-up windows along the way.

It's a school, Cianne thought as she was pulled into a midsized room that looked like it was probably her captors' base camp. She shadowed Cook as he ran to a boarded-up window on the far side of the old classroom and peeked through a space between the boards.

"They're here." He grabbed Cianne's hand again and pulled her back into the hallway. "I need to get you to the bottom floor and out of the building. We're going to have to use the back stairs," he said, so quietly that she knew he was talking to himself.

Cianne could tell from the way he sounded that he really didn't want to use the back stairs. She realized that they were in real danger but she wondered what was the issue with the stairs.

As she kept pace with Cook, she couldn't stop wondering what happened to Tristan.

Cook was fast, and when he pulled her around a corner she stumbled, making her focus on what was happening with her. He slowed enough to allow her to right herself then returned to his quick pace.

His flashlight was bright and spanned wide enough for them to see a good deal in front of them. They whizzed by classroom after classroom, hurdled over debris, and avoided anything that would slow them down. Resisting was no longer on Cianne's mind. Getting out of this so she could get to Tristan drove her now.

When they made their way to the stairwell, Cook allowed her to stop to catch her breath before he pulled open the door that was barely hanging on two hinges. Debris, a strong stench, and filth filled what was visible of the stairs.

Cianne looked down the dark stairwell with only his flashlight as a beacon to guide them and felt a chill run through her. There was no way to tell how many flights there were to the bottom floor but she knew there was freedom beyond the darkness. Cianne pushed her shoulders back then looked at Cook. He looked back at her. The expression on his face scared her more than the thought of what they had to do. He squeezed her hand then let it go as they made their way down.

Cook went first, with her close behind. Cianne slipped a couple of times but Cook was there to steady her with a firm grip when she needed it. When they reached the bottom of the first flight, Cianne felt as if it hadn't been that hard. That gave her the confidence she needed to get down the next two darkened flights.

Just as she mentally patted herself on the back, a faint noise reached her ears. "Did you hear that?" Cianne questioned, then stopped.

She looked down at Cook who stopped just as she had. Her eyes squinted into the darkness that lay before them, beyond the range of his light. With them stopped, Cianne heard the sound clearer. She had no idea what it was but it sounded like it was getting closer.

"Go back," Cook whispered.

Cianne turned halfway around and was just about to take a step back over a small metal trashcan when she felt Cook's hand on her leg. Cianne turned her head and looked down at him. But he was focused on something down the stairs. She followed the direction of his gaze. She had to suck in a gasp of fear when her eyes focused.

"Back up, slowly," Cook whispered. He gave her leg a slight nudge.

Cianne couldn't move. She was frozen with fear as she peered at the scraggy dog that looked up at them from half a flight down. The dog's eyes, shadowed by dirty matted hair, glowed as they bore into them. Its lips were tight and pulled back, revealing pink and black gums with sharp teeth that could be clearly seen with the flashlight in the dark stairwell.

The hound watched them for a few seconds before its growl echoed through the hollowed space between them. Cook gently pushed at her leg again. Cianne carefully began to take a slow step up when another dog came up behind the first.

"Run!" Cook yelled.

Cianne turned and started up the stairs. She tried desperately to keep her balance as she tracked over bottles, paper, and broken furniture. Cook was right behind her with three dogs now closing in. She reached a door labeled "Fourth Floor" and pushed. Cook, who was right behind her, rammed his shoulder into the door to force it open enough for them to squeeze through. He slammed it shut just as Cianne was clear and used his body as a barricade. Winded and scared, Cianne backed away as the dogs barked and slammed into the weak door and against a tired Cook.

"You picked this bitch over your friends." A pained-sounding voice grunted.

Cianne whipped her head around to see two shadowy masked figures coming toward them from down the hall. She looked at Cook who struggled to keep the stairwell door closed as he peered at the two figures.

"What do we do?" she whispered to him.

"Run," Cook whispered back. His body was suddenly jolted forward by the pressure of the dogs that were determined to get at them. One of his feet slid on impact but he quickly recovered his footing and held the door closed. He looked to her. "Please run."

"Come with me," Cianne begged, as she shifted from one foot to the other.

"Run," he ordered.

Cianne was emotionally and physically spent from the whole ordeal, but she didn't want to leave him. She started to refuse but when he gave her a sweet smile and mouthed the word "please" again as he tilted his head to her stomach, she took off in the opposite direction from the two figures coming at them.

As she turned the corner at the end of the hall, Cianne heard a gunshot. She screamed and covered her ears.

Terrified, she looked to her right. *Nothing*. Then to her left. *There*. Cianne opened the door and closed it behind her. Once inside the room, she looked around for a place to hide. Her breathing was heavy and frequent as she frantically searched for cover.

Several old rusted cabinets lined the peeling walls. Cianne ran over to a row of cabinets and hid behind them. She tried to be as quiet as possible as her salty tears ran over her quivering lips.

The sound of heavy footsteps seemed to echo through her body as they got closer to the room she hid inside. Cianne held as still as she could and covered her mouth to assure that nothing, not even air, escaped.

"Where are you, you little whore?" a harsh voice called out from the hallway.

Cianne held her breath when she heard the sound of footsteps near the door. Suddenly, the sound of barking dogs and gunshots rang out through the corridors of the building. A dog yelped then started to whine. Cianne tightened her hand over her face.

"Don't come out," the man called out.

She heard the anger in his tone. He was very close now, probably outside the door of the room she hid in.

"The damn dogs can have you."

The footsteps hastily moved away from her. Three more shots rang out then there was only silence. Cianne peeked out from her hiding place after a minute or so. She pointed her small flashlight around the room then at the door. When she realized she was utterly alone, she ran out of the room toward where she left Cook.

Cianne turned the corner and froze. Just a few feet in front of her was a bulky lump of fur lying still on the floor. She crept forward slowly. As she passed the dog, Cianne saw that its chest moved up and down. It was still alive but it was bleeding out. The gunman had shot it.

She had to turn her head away when she passed the suffering animal then ran for Cook. He was slumped over just feet away from the door he barricaded. Cianne fell to her knees at his side. She turned him over and winced at the blood that trailed from his chest and mouth.

"Cook, get up." Cianne caressed his cheek. It was warm still but he didn't move. He wasn't breathing. "Cook, you need to get up. We have to leave," she hiccupped.

He was dead.

Cianne cried harder. She was alone. The one person who helped her from the moment she was brought here was dead because of her. He was…her friend.

Her pity party lasted only a moment before Cianne noticed something moving in the shadows. She turned her head and raised her light. *Dogs.* She fell to her butt but instantly recovered and got to her feet. Cianne ran as fast as she could with the dogs in pursuit. She burst through the door of the room she hid in and climbed the cabinets. As she pulled her leg up, sharp teeth caught her ankle.

"*Tristan!*" she screamed aloud and in her head, as the dog's teeth dug into her flesh.

Cianne tried pulling her leg free but the dog's grip was too strong. She kicked at it with her free foot but there was no use. It held on. The pain was excruciating as the dog tugged in an attempt to drag her from the cabinet. The other dogs snarled and chomped as they tried to climb the file cabinets to get to her. Cianne clung to the cabinet's edge with all her strength but it was metal and her hands were wet with blood and sweat.

The dog shook her ankle violently.

Cianne fought to hold on. She ignored the pain and forgot about kicking the other dogs away. She had to climb. The tip of her toe found the edge of a drawer so she attempted to pull herself up but her fingers started to slip. One finger, then another.

It's over. I couldn't save us.

"*Tristan...*"

Every paper, every bit of dust, every scrap of debris, flew up from the floor in a small cyclone near the door. A familiar scented breeze filled the room. Cianne sensed him before she actually saw him.

Tristan!

She felt a sense of relief but that feeling faded as she saw the dogs turn from her. Even the dog that had hold of her ankle released her and was the first to launch at Tristan. To Cianne's surprise, Tristan caught the animal by the neck with one hand then gave it a hard shake. A sickening snap of the animal's neck was heard over the growling. Tristan tossed the corpse in a corner of the room.

What the...

Cianne watched in horror as the rest of the dogs growled and barked while they slowly circled Tristan until he was surrounded. He stood completely still with his arms at his sides. Only his head moved as he tracked their movements around him.

Tristan looked...calm, focused, yet he hadn't even looked at her yet.

The scene that ensued was chaotic. A dog, one of the largest in the pack, leapt for Tristan's neck. The rest of the pack followed its lead. Cianne tried to make out what was happening but she wasn't able to focus on Tristan due to the speed in which he and the dogs moved.

How the heck is he moving so fast?

Her little light wasn't bright enough and her hand wasn't quick enough. At times, Cianne heard loud yelps and moved her light in that direction only to see a dog hit the floor or wall. More loud sounds from the dogs filled the room. However, Cianne never heard a sound from Tristan.

That worried her but a lone dog had separated from the skirmish. It clawed at the metal cabinet she had managed to climb up on. Her teeth ached with every scrape of its claws over the metal cabinet as it climbed.

Three drawers up, she said to herself as she tracked its progress. There were three more to go.

Cianne glanced at Tristan again, confused by what he was doing—the speed, the brutal way he fought. Another scrape alerted her of her own danger. She managed to drag her eyes from the chaotic scene to look down at the dog intent on getting to her. Its teeth were exposed and its tongue whipped from side to side. She was terrified as the animal repeatedly lifted then dropped its hind leg, feeling for something to step on so it could get to her.

Frightened, Cianne inched back as far as she could. She kept her eyes and her light on the beast as her free hand searched for something to use as a weapon.

Two more. One more.

At the precise moment, the dog found its footing, Cianne screamed. She beat the animal on its head as it stretched toward her with her mini flashlight. She looked to Tristan.

Tristan looked at her, leaving his body open for attack. Despite the dogs ripping at Tristan, he was inches from her in a flash and grabbed the dog that threatened Cianne, by the leg. Tristan slung the dog against the wall behind him. The dog hit hard enough to leave the bloody imprint of its body on the wall. The beast cried out then fell to the floor.

Without missing a beat, Tristan dispatched with the remaining dogs that followed him save one. Cianne's gaze landed, on the lone dog whose teeth were dug into Tristan's leg. She watched, transfixed, as Tristan pried its jaws from his blood-soaked thigh. Once his leg was free, Tristan straightened to his full height. He held the dog by its snout and lower jaw then gave a little tug. It was subtle, an effortless motion, but that tug ripped the dog's jaws apart.

The dog's lifeless body hit the floor with a sickening thud.

Oh My God… Cianne winced.

Cianne raised her flashlight and moved it around the room. In disbelief, she peered at the dogs that lay lifeless and scattered. She forced her gaze away from the carnage to look at Tristan. His clothing was tattered and bloody, but he didn't seem to be hurt too badly, as far as she could tell.

But he must be hurt.

She could see blood soaking through the fibers of his khakis and spreading outward. He stood perfectly motionless, his face impassive as she looked him over. His shirt was dirty and torn and exposed several gashes.

Tristan breathed in and out normally as if he had been relaxing just a minute ago rather than fighting off a pack of feral dogs. His hands hung at his sides as blood ran down his arm and dripped from a few of his fingertips. Cianne wasn't sure if it was his blood or dog blood. When their eyes met, Cianne had to close hers.

Am I dreaming?

Cianne opened her eyes slowly to find that Tristan was still there. He was real and he was there.

What *is she thinking?*

Watching her, Tristan wasn't sure if it was horror or shock that was reflected in the stunning eyes that stared back at him.

Seeing what just played out must have been disturbing to witness.

Is she scared of me now? He wasn't sure.

What Tristan was sure of was that she was safe now. He had Cianne and he wanted to touch her, to hold her.

He took a slow deliberate step forward. He didn't want to scare her any more than he already had. Another step.

Before he could get any closer, Tristan saw her eyes widen.

"No!" she screamed.

Tristan froze in place as he felt what can only be described as a surge of heat, encompass him. The sensation circled around then pulsed through him. He closed his eye as every muscle in his body tightened; intense heat penetrated every molecule.

Then it was gone.

Tristan swayed on his feet. He felt energized and tired at the same time. It was a feeling he was sure to never forget.

The sound of several small thuds behind him caused Tristan to open his eyes and turn around. In the doorway and beyond, lay several lifeless dogs. Dogs that looked unscathed. Dogs he hadn't killed, because the ones that attacked him were inside the room.

Confused, Tristan turned back to peer at Cianne. Their eyes meet for a split second before hers closed.

"Hell," Tristan cursed as Cianne fell forward. He moved like the wind as he caught her in his arms.

I love you, Ci. I promise I will do whatever I have to do to always keep you safe.

Chapter Twenty-Five

Intense light glowed all around Cianne as she floated in nothingness. It felt familiar and nurturing, though she couldn't remember feeling this way. However, she just knew that everything was alright. How she knew, she wasn't sure because her mind was a little cloudy.

Where she was…well, Cianne wasn't sure of that either. Yet, her instincts told her that she was safe inside the glow. The light grew brighter and felt warmer, and Cianne had to shield her eyes but she was too curious to close them completely.

As the brightness faded, solid ground replaced what she would describe as nothingness. She took a step forward and a room became visible. The faint smell of cinnamon, an aroma Cianne once loved, perfumed the air around her. Memories flowed over her, all of them of happy times.

It reminded her of…

Cianne didn't move as she realized where she now stood. Her heart swelled, and her hands itched to touch furnishings she hadn't seen in years.

"Home," she sighed.

It was the home she hadn't seen since she was a little girl. The foyer was just as she remembered, the walls…everything was exactly the same.

"Let's go."

Startled, Cianne turned around, then stumbled back as her father, a younger Joseph Baxter, strolled by her. He was close enough for her to touch as he headed for the front door. She raised her hand but didn't try to touch him.

He can't see me.

Cianne backed up until she felt the door of the closet she used to play inside, behind her. She had a clear view of the front door and could see the staircase behind her through a large mirror that was placed high on the wall across from the closet. The mirror reflected the stairs and everything on them.

"C'mon Buttercup, we're going to be late," her father called up the stairs.

"Coming daddy," a small voice came from the second floor.

That's me.

Cianne looked up at the mirror across from where she stood. She first saw the colorful sneakers that she loved so much when she was just eight years old. They were mostly white, with blue fronts, pink backs, and yellow sides. She loved those shoes so much that she slept in them until her mother put an end to it.

Cianne watched in awe as her younger self bounced down the flight of stairs with their beautiful mother following close behind.

"I'll see you later baby. Have a good day at work with daddy, ok." Kayla Baxter bent over and kissed the young Cianne on the forehead.

The elder Cianne sucked in a breath of air. She actually felt her mother's lips on her own forehead. Her hand rose up and touched the very spot.

"What are we having for dinner tonight?" Joseph, her father, asked. He kissed Kayla on the lips before she could answer.

Cianne had forgotten the love that sparkled in her father's eyes when he looked at her mother.

"It's a surprise," Kayla said, smiling. "Drive safe." She let her hand slide down his tie, straightened it, then pulled the front door open. The younger Cianne had been watching the exchange with bright eyes and a genuine smile. She smiled even brighter as she took their father's hand.

Cianne watched her father and younger self leave and her mother shut and lock the door behind them. She backed out of the way as her mother passed her to enter the kitchen. Cianne wanted to follow but couldn't move. The smells, the colors, her mother, everything was exactly the way she remembered.

She didn't ever want to move from the spot. She felt that if she did, she might be whisked away. A vague memory of another fold in time came to her—the college campus, when she had seen her mother and who she thought may have been her biological father. That time, Cianne had moved and everything had disappeared.

Can't move. Don't move.

But sounds from the kitchen caught Cianne's attention. She could only assume that her mother was busy moving chairs but the wall that separated the hall and the kitchen was in the way.

Move. You can't see her. But if I move…

While Cianne debated, something happened that she didn't expect.

"Are you going to join me in the kitchen, Zaria?" Kayla smiled as she stuck her head out of the entryway.

Cianne eyes opened wide. "You…you can see me?" she asked in amazement.

"Yes, I can see you." Kayla smiled brighter. "Now come on in the kitchen and have some cocoa with me."

Cianne's feet felt heavy as she walked slowly into the kitchen. She forgot about the decor that filled the space. The green and white curtains with the green leaves smack dab in the middle caught her eye first, then the green border that lined the four walls around the ceiling. She forgot the hunter green-accented containers and small appliances that littered the shelves.

Funny, the things you forget.

Cianne looked at her mother who pointed to the seat across from her. She sat down and wrapped her hands around the warm cup of cocoa that sat on the table in front of her, feeling nostalgic and a little sad.

Her hands were so cold for some reason, but the warm cup took the chill away.

"How are you, Zaria?"

Her mother's voice was gentle, and it wrapped around her like a warm blanket.

That name.

Cianne looked into her mother's dark brown eyes as they stared back into hers. "Zaria," she said, "I remember you calling me that."

"It was your name. It means, Princess and that is what you are." Kayla looked down at her cup. "You have grown into such a beautiful young lady." She smiled again.

Cianne watched her mother closely. Every movement and gesture Kayla made, Cianne logged to memory. Kayla took a sip of her cocoa, then placed the cup softly back on the table in front of her. Cianne didn't miss any of it.

"You're not sure if I'm real or not, are you? Or you think you may be dreaming." Kayla very slowly took her hand from her mug and with the same slow movement reached across the table and touched Cianne's hand.

Cianne held her breath and prepared to be yanked back to her reality. However, nothing happened when their hands touched.

"I'm real," Kayla said.

Cianne looked at her hand and back at her mother, "I know I'm not dreaming and I assumed that you were real. What I don't understand though, is how I'm here. And…" Cianne took her mother's hand in hers. "I just don't want to do or say something that will make me leave again." She wiped the tear that fell from her eye.

"Ah," Kayla started, "it seems that you have a little more control this time."

The memory of watching Kayla and a man conversing on a college campus rushed into her consciousness. So many questions came to mind but one found its way out first.

"You saw me that day?" Cianne asked with excitement.

"Yes. I saw you but I didn't know who *you* were at that time. I thought you were one of my mother's spies. Until…" Kayla smiled then said, "Until I found out that I was pregnant. Then I knew."

Cianne reflected on something her mother said minutes before. "So, *I* am doing this?"

Kayla raised a brow. "It's not me. Which means it can only be you." Kayla rubbed Cianne's hand gently with her thumb.

"How come dad or the young me didn't see me?" Cianne questioned.

"I think it's because you're blocking or diffusing your ability somehow. Apparently, you only want me to see you." Kayla took a sip of cocoa. "So," she said cheerfully, "why are you here Zaria?"

Cianne took the napkin her mother passed her and wiped her eyes.

If I am doing this, then how am I doing this?

She wiped her cheek and balled the tissue up in her hand. "I don't know," Cianne admitted, smiling a little.

"What were you doing before you got here?" Kayla asked, raising her brow. She let go of Cianne's hand and put the mug to her lips again.

"I can't remember," Cianne answered, a little confused.

Kayla sipped her cocoa and swallowed before she spoke again. "I couldn't actually Time Weave with ease until," she said, thinking, "well, to be honest, I was never able to Time Weave without total concentration. The fact that I can actually see and speak to you is amazing. Only few Weavers are able to communicate inside a thread of a Weave. Yet, here you are weaving and talking to me and you're not even trying." Kayla laughed.

"Weaving, through time?" Cianne frowned. "Is that what I've been doing? I can weave in and out of time?" Cianne gazed at her mother. What she was doing had a name and her mother acted as if it was something normal.

Kayla looked at her daughter's beautiful face. She was perfect, breathtaking, and very powerful. Yet the clueless expression on her face told Kayla that something was wrong. It was just a week ago that the zoo incident had occurred. Kayla had driven Cianne to New York a day later so 'The Four' could bind her abilities. But here her daughter was, and she was powerful, Kayla sensed that much.

"What else can you do?"

"What do you mean what else can I do?" Cianne asked, confused.

For whatever reason, her daughter knew nothing of what she could do. That wasn't right. "Tell me something first, how is your grandmother doing?"

"Fine, I guess," Cianne said plainly. "We don't talk really. Grandma Baxter still hasn't warmed up to me after all these years but dad says she will one day."

Grandma Baxter…and not one word about the generous and powerful Vivian Harper

Kayla realized then that Cianne had no real knowledge of her maternal grandmother. That would only mean… She took a deep breath. "Am I alive in your time?"

Cianne gave her a haunted look that seemed to last forever. "No," her daughter said finally. "You've been gone for about nine years now."

Kayla looked down briefly. It felt as if a brick had been pitched at her stomach but she pushed back her shock and looked at her daughter. "I'm sorry that I wasn't there for you. With all our abilities, there are some things we still cannot change or cheat. Death is one of those things."

Cianne couldn't believe what she heard. Her mother couldn't be the reason for the abnormalities inside her. "What are you telling me? That you are like…me?"

Kayla pushed her mug aside. "*You* are like *me,* sweetie. You are a Coesen. Like me, my mother, and our ancestors before us. We are human but we are different. Our people are modest in number when compared to other nations but we've been around for a very, very long time.

Most of our kind are born with dormant abilities that will never manifest. The ones whose abilities do manifest will have a single ability such as time weaving. Few have more than one. But you sweetheart, are the HALO. You have the complete birthmark, so it is believed by many that you will have more abilities than any Coesen before you."

There are others like me?

Cianne tried to grasp the information her mother just told her. Her mother was different and she inherited this…*these* things from *her*. Not to mention, her mother had just told her that she wasn't even normal for a Coesen. She always knew she wasn't like others, so what she now knew explained that but...

"Why?" Cianne asked, "Why am I different from others like us?"

Kayla took in a deep breath. "You're not different, but you are special."

Cianne shook her head in puzzlement. "Wait, is dad a Coesen?" Kayla shook her head, so Cianne went on. "Is he aware of all of this?" she asked,

"Joseph," Kayla said, smiling softly. "Joseph has been raising you." Cianne realized that her mother was speaking mostly to herself. "That sounds like what I would have wanted."

"How do you not know that?" Cianne demanded.

Kayla raised her hand and lowered it in a motion to calm Cianne. "It is nine years in your past but it's today for me. I only know what happened today and before. Time Weaving into the future is forbidden if you are gifted enough to do it. It is very rare for a Time Weaver to have that capability. Only one Coesen we know of could. We also believe that a Weaver cannot weave to a time they may not exist in." She sighed. "Time is a very sensitive thing sweetheart. Currently, Joseph knows nothing about our abilities, but if I'm dead and he is raising you, then everything has been explained to him."

Cianne thought about the time period she was now in. She didn't remember anything from this day, this year, except…

"This year is mostly a blur to me, but this is the year we moved and the year you…"

"Died," Kayla added. "It's alright, you can say it." Kayla stood up and walked over to Cianne and sat down in another chair so they were closer. "Now let's see what we can do about your memory." Kayla put her hand on Cianne's temple.

Cianne took her mother's hands in hers. "How can you be so blasé about what I'm telling you? You're not alive in my time."

Kayla smiled at her. "Death is inevitable and there is little we can do to prevent it. Besides, my number was up five years ago. Only then, love and an old friend intervened." Kayla raised her hand to Cianne's temple again.

Cianne was confused by her mother's willingness to accept her death so easily and even more confused about the comment about *her number* being up years ago, but as her mother's warm fingers touched the side of her head; she frowned and then relaxed a little.

"You can retrieve memories?"

"I am a Time Weaver. Memories are just motion pictures of a time past. I can replay them in your mind," Kayla told her.

"Wait," Cianne said nervously, "what will you be able to see?"

"Don't worry. Something inside you prevents me from seeing your particular thread of time. I have never been able to see your future, and even if I could somehow see your thread, I wouldn't be able to see past my own existence, so all your adult things will remain private." Kayla raised a curious brow and smiled. "Now hold still."

Cianne felt a warm sensation where her mother's fingers touched her head. Warmth spread through her body before the movie of her life began to play out at a fast pace. She saw moments of her life as a young child, then at school age. Then she saw herself playing with three of four beautiful women in a room that was completely white. Her mother was nearby speaking with a fourth woman, who was looking at *her*. For some reason, those women gave Cianne a sense of safety as they stared at one another.

More scenes flashed by and it almost felt as if she was reliving every moment all over again. Another memory Cianne had forgotten began to play out. She wore her favorite colorful sneakers and a purple outfit. The scent of animals and the sound of people calling her name frightened her. She was at the zoo and her head felt as if it were going to explode. There was a boy with her. He had crystal blue eyes that seemed to see right through her. She touched his hand and felt a wave of heat transfer from her to him. Just like that, her headache was gone and the boy, he stared into her eyes for what felt like forever.

But he looked away when…when he heard his name. An old man had called him. The man had called him…Tristan.

Tristan.

Cianne pulled away, breaking the connection. She gasped for air as the image of an eight-year-old Tristan was replaced by the image of him at nineteen, with blood dripping from his fingertips.

Oh God, Tristan.

Everything around her suddenly faded as Cianne was yanked away from her mother. She reached for her mother's hand.

"No…mom!" she screamed.

Their fingertips barely touched before Cianne was overcome by the bright light again.

Chapter Twenty-Six

At the hospital, Malone insisted that Tristan retell the events that happened the night he found Cianne, over and over again. But no matter how hard he tried, Tristan couldn't fit all the events together in one believable package. He knew the veteran detective wasn't buying it. Who would?

He needed to speak to Cianne before Malone did, to discuss what they were going to divulge and what they weren't. The problem was, Cianne wasn't speaking to him or to anyone else. Well, no one except for Tranae.

After rescuing her, Tristan stayed by her side the eighteen hours she slept in the hospital. But when she woke up she looked at him as if he was a stranger. She wouldn't speak to him, and his very presence seemed to bring her to tears so the nursing staff asked him to leave the room. Later he was informed that she wanted no visitors at all except for Tranae.

Now, she was home and Malone wanted her to fill in all the missing pieces Tristan didn't provide.

Outside Cianne's house, Tristan watched from his car as Det. Malone tapped on the Baxter's front door. The door was pulled open and Tristan watched Det. Malone step inside.

Malone stepped outside onto the Baxter's porch. He walked to his unmarked car with his head down but looked up and saw Tristan, who waved to him. Malone changed direction and headed for the kid.

"Nice car," Malone said. He took his time looking over the red Porsche Tristan leaned on.

Tristan's head hung low as he played with his keys. He smiled as he tilted his head to the side and looked up. "Thanks," Tristan said. He looked at the keys in his hands. "I didn't get to thank you for recovering the reward money."

The official report stated that when Malone arrived at the scene that night, Zeta was being treated by emergency personnel near Tristan's SUV. The only thing she was able to tell him was the direction Tristan had run.

Malone had taken a few officers with him and drove in that direction until he saw a random car sitting in front of an abandoned school. When he inspected the car, he found two large duffle bags in the back seat. The next thing he saw was Tristan carrying Cianne out of the building. He figured the kidnappers most likely had seen him and the two other police cruisers next to the car from inside the building and had gone in another direction.

"I'm just glad that things didn't turn out worse than they did. You know that it could have gone differently," Malone said. He knew he sounded more like a father than a cop.

"Right," Tristan said. He looked back down at his keys again.

It was clear the kid was suffering from the distance Cianne had apparently created between them. But that wasn't his business. "Tell me, did you ever locate that tracker I put on your truck?" Malone bent his head a little, making an effort to look Tristan in the eyes.

"Sorry," Tristan shrugged. "Guess it fell off. But," Tristan said as he raised his head, "with the reward money you earned for recovering the ransom you can purchase more for your precinct, ones that stick a little better."

"No reward necessary. I was just doing what I've sworn to do." Malone took a step closer to Tristan. "You remember anything else about Saturday night that you'd like to share?"

The only concrete information Malone had to go on was the identity of Peter Walters, the one Cianne called Cook. Nothing was found that connected anyone else to the case. Even the car he retrieved the money from had been stolen.

Everything about the case was strange and Malone couldn't understand how Cianne and Tristan survived two gunmen and over a dozen bloodthirsty dogs with only a couple of bites and a few scratches between the two of them. Furthermore, what happened to some of the dogs was another mystery altogether.

A few dogs were shot dead; seven dogs had broken necks and other assorted broken or dislocated bones. Six other dogs were found in the abandoned school with no apparent injuries. Yet, even weirder, every dog in a two-mile radius had died that night. According to reports from several veterinarians in the area, the causes of death in each case were unknown and the CDC was investigating the matter.

Plus, what was that little girl Zeta doing there?

All these questions needed answers.

"No. Everything happened so fast. It was just luck I guess," Tristan said, "us getting out alive."

Malone sighed. "Well if either of you remember anything."

"You will be the first to know." Tristan pushed off the car then headed toward the Baxter's porch.

Tristan sat in the Baxter's basement family room with the remote in his hand. He flipped through channels aimlessly without paying attention. Malone wasn't going to give up and it was apparent that he wasn't a man who was easily sidetracked.

Zeta found and removed the tracking device on his truck and destroyed it before they set out to meet the kidnappers but that information wasn't something he planned to tell the cops. The Detective could know nothing of the Coesen or their involvement, or both of their lives were forfeit.

He stopped switching channels to look at a commercial he liked then started channel surfing again. He did this until he heard Cianne's name on a news program. He sat up and watched the news report.

"Cianne Baxter was found Saturday evening in fair condition we're told, after being held against her will for several days at this abandoned high school." The studious looking reporter motioned to the school behind him. "A body was also recovered but police aren't releasing any information about that victim. Police say that Ms. Baxter was taken from a parking lot on the corner of Tollson and Richmond Avenue late last Sunday afternoon between the hours of two and five pm. If anyone saw anything, they are being asked to contact Det. Malone at the number you see here on the screen."

The screen panned to an anchorwoman who could have easily passed for a fashion model. "Gregory, we have been getting unconfirmed reports in the newsroom that Tristan Bertram, Ms. Baxter's boyfriend, and the grandson of the late Patrick Arlington, was the one who found her. Can you confirm that?"

"Not at this moment Robyn. The local PD are keeping details about the case hushed for now being as it's an open murder investigation."

"Thank you, Gregory, from our sister station WJY in Palm Valley," Robyn said. "In unrelated news, the CDC hasn't been able to discover what caused the deaths of over a hundred dogs in Palm Valley on Saturday night…"

Tristan turned the television off when he heard someone coming down the top floor stairs to the first floor. He ascended the basement stairs, taking two at a time. He knew it was

Tranae before he saw her. She half smiled but she could see he was disappointed that she wasn't Cianne.

"Hey," he said.

"Hey." Tranae waved back as she stepped around him.

"When do you think she'll be ready to see me? It's been two and a half days now." He followed Tranae to the kitchen.

She pulled several containers of food, brought to the Baxter home by their neighbors and friends, out of the fridge and made two plates. The local news featured the story which began the onslaught of flowers, cards, and casseroles. Now it seems the National News has picked up the story.

Tristan watched silently as Tranae heated both the plates in the microwave. "She just needs a little time to recover, that's all." Tranae grabbed some silverware and carried the food to the steps.

Tristan leaned on the wall facing the stairs. "She hasn't said more than two words to me since she's been back. She blames me, doesn't she?"

Tranae didn't answer his question. Instead, she gave him a sympathetic look as she carried the food out of the kitchen.

"If it makes you feel any better she hasn't said much to me either. I'm considering calling a specialist to come speak to her. I think it might be good for her to speak to someone not connected to all this," Joseph said as he entered the hallway from the living room. "I never got to thank you, Tristan." He walked slowly over to Tristan and half patted, half hugged him. "You have handled yourself very well considering that you have been dragged into our family's special 'issues', if you will."

Tristan smelled alcohol and noticed the glass filled with brandy in Joseph's hand. The liquid swayed to the rim of the glass but miraculously didn't spill over the edge. He never saw the man drink before.

"I didn't find out what I got myself into until right before my wife passed away." Joseph took a sip from the glass as he looked up the stairway.

Tristan could see the man was borderline drunk. He didn't blame him either. "Nothing could scare me off when it comes to your daughter," he admitted.

"Good, because Vivian is pretty damn frightening." Joseph chuckled as he took another sip. "Thank god I was married to Kayla before I met the woman. She drives me crazy. Her voice alone makes my eyelashes ache. I wonder how those kids put up with her." He paused, as if in thought. "Speaking of those kids," he said, then took another sip. "How's the girl doing? Zeta's her name, right?"

Tristan nodded. "I tried to see her yesterday but wasn't allowed. I was going to try again later today, but I guess I won't be seeing Cianne," he said, "so I have some free time now. You want to go with me? Your mother-in-law would love to see the both of us together again, I bet." They both knew that wasn't true.

"You're on your own. Just give Zeta my thanks and best wishes. See if she got the flowers I sent. Vivian may have tossed them out if she read the card and discovered they were from me." Joseph lifted the glass to his mouth as he walked to the living room. He turned back. "Can't you do that mind thing with Cianne? Ask her yourself when you can see her."

"She doesn't like it." Tristan shrugged. "I'll see you later Mr. Baxter."

Cianne heard her door open but she didn't get up or turn around. She knew who it was but kept her eyes closed to appear asleep.

"I know you're upset about all the secrecy but you shouldn't take the anger you have for me out on Tristan." Her father stepped into her bedroom. "I can't expect you to understand why I agreed to keep you in the dark about… But I guess it's time that I gave you these." She felt him set something on the bed behind her. "Your mother said that I should give them to you but only after you discovered the truth."

Cianne moved her arm up to her face to wipe her tears but still didn't turn around. She was so tired of crying but it seemed she had no control over it.

"I did what I did because your mother told me it was the way things had to be, and I believed in her. I still believe in her," he said as he left, closing her door behind him.

Cianne rolled over after she heard the door close. She looked at the three red leather journals for a moment before she picked one up. The Private Annals of Kayla Baxter-Eighteenth Year. The other two had the same wording but different years. Opening the cover of the Eighteenth year, Cianne saw a folded piece of paper inside. She put the journal down and unfolded the paper.

Dear Cianne,

It's kind of funny, me using your new name and actually writing it down on paper. The younger you have really taken to the change. I suppose that means it was meant to be. I'm not really sure what I should put in this letter and what I shouldn't. Knowing that I won't be there for you is torture but I am glad that I was able to prepare. You gave me that.

My Time Weaving ability has never worked on you. I wasn't able to see any of your future and that scared me. But the most amazing thing happened. After the zoo incident, I saw a glimpse of you through the eyes of a little boy. I don't know when you will be reading this so I cannot tell you too much. I didn't get a full picture but I saw enough to see that you will have the opportunity to be very happy.

What I must do, my decisions, they will haunt me even in death but I know that in the end that I will have done the right thing for you. Baby, being loved and loving someone with all your heart is what living is all about. You will no doubt have some tough decisions of your own to make and I'm sorry. I have to believe that if you were me that you would have made the same choices I've made. My belief in that will be my only comfort.

> Trust your heart baby. Choose love. I love you.
> Your mother, Kayla Baxter

Cianne felt a lump in her throat as she tried to fight back more tears. She folded the letter back up and looked at the journal. She turned the first page and began to read. By the time she finished the first book, she realized that she and her mother were very different but they were similar in many ways too. Both of them were trapped. Cianne finished the second journal and opened the last one. She sat up when she was halfway through.

March (date unreadable)

The guy who has been coming into the store, he smiled at me when he caught me looking at him. He's been to the store every day this week. He introduced himself last week and is such a hottie that I can hardly look at him. He always buys something then sits and read, sometimes for hours. Well, he asked me out. I told him I can't. I so wish I could.

Anyway, I've gone 30 days without Weaving. Vivian called today. She said it's not good to go so long, that I need to use it more often if I want to be better at it. She wants me to leave school to continue my training with Marcel. I told her I'd think about it.

Spring Break is coming. I plan to spend it here, with my homies. There's a party next weekend at Rochelle's. I swear if she plays that Vanilla Ice song more than once, I will scream.

April 20

His eyes are so pretty. The greenest blue eyes I've ever seen. He came to Rochelle's party. We hung out the entire time. Oh, almost forgot, he passed the test.

Anyway, I told him that I don't date. He said we could just hang then. I do like him but the only reason Vivian let me have this "freedom" I have now is because I promised to go through with the Tandot. I sometimes wish I could just run away from my prison guards (that think I don't know they're here), from Vivian, and the entire world. To do what I want and to actually date someone I choose. But I know they wouldn't rest until they found me. I like this guy a lot. He knows it too. (smile)

August 8th

I've been secretly dating "him" for four months now. He's so refreshing compared to the other guys I know. He's very mature and patient. Very patient. We never argue or fight like the rest of the couples I know. I asked him if it was normal that we don't fight. He says that my friend's relationships are different than ours because they're going through life not knowing what they want and he does.

He doesn't talk about his life before me but I don't mind. I'm not ready to talk about mine with him either. I love him and I know he loves me, even though he has never said the exact words. Only, I can't help but feel that every time he says goodnight, it feels like he's really saying goodbye. I don't know how long I will be able to hide our relationship from Joe and Dana or Vivian for that matter. I just know that I want him more than anything in this world.

December 27th

I spent the Christmas holiday with him at his nephew's estate. Richard was very welcoming and nice. He isn't that much younger than we are, family scandal is my guess. Richard is single. (Note to self: see if Richard is interested in being set up)

From what I could gather, they only have each other. We discovered that neither of us celebrates Christmas so we didn't exchange gifts. It's funny how much we have in common.

The Private Annals of Kayla Baxter–Nineteenth Year
March 5th

Vivian called, the Tandot victor has been decided. I don't know what I am going to do. I am so sick of the ancient rituals and ways. This is the 20th century. No one is walking around with copies of "Malleus Maleficarum" anymore so why haven't we evolved? I should be able to live a normal life. I want to marry for love. I need to talk to him.

March 9th

I explained the Tandot to him. Well, sort of, minus the mystical parts of course. I tried to explain it in a way that a normal person would understand. I know he doesn't want me to go through with it but he wouldn't tell me so. He just held me. I told him goodbye.

March 10ᵗʰ

I've decided what I'm going to do. I just hope he feels the same way I do.

Chapter Twenty-Seven

Tristan's visit with Zeta was short. She was happy to see him but the pain medication she was on had her a little drowsy. The bullet had broken one of her ribs and damaged some tissue but overall, she was pretty lucky. Tristan knew she needed her rest so he left after an hour, ending up at Brian's house. It was the first time he had seen Brian since he rescued Cianne.

When Brian opened his front door, Tristan was greeted as if he were a hero. The Williams family kissed and hugged him as he stepped inside the house, overjoyed that he was safe and wasn't seriously hurt. The love they expressed made Tristan feel a little better, but it wasn't what he needed.

He stayed for dinner and sat in his usual spot at the dining room table with Brian and his family. It had been a while since he last enjoyed a meal with his best friend's family but the conversation flowed as always. He'd known them for years and he missed them, not seeing them much since he and Cianne started dating.

After dinner, Brian led him outside on the patio and asked him what happened on Saturday night. Tristan told Brian the same version he told Det. Malone. Even Brian couldn't know the truth. Brian, satisfied with his response, quickly moved on to discuss everything that Tristan missed in the last week.

He told him how weird it was at prom without him and Cianne being there. Tristan even laughed a little when Brian told him that because of his absence that Francis Dennison, the class clown, was picked for prom king and how Dennison fell going up the stairs to the stage to accept the crown.

Tristan felt a bit like his old self when he got into his car to leave a few hours later. He was able to relax a little now that Cianne was safe but he wished she'd talk to him. He knew what she saw freaked her out but…

Maybe she didn't feel about him the way he felt about her.

He drove by her house before heading home and waved as he passed by the policemen who sat in the cruiser next to her mailbox. One of the officers waved back. Vivian also assured him that one of her Guards would always be watching Cianne. She had Coesen bodyguards now but she was unaware of that as far as he knew. Confident that she was safe, Tristan headed home. He was ready to sleep in his bed for the first time in over a week, instead of in the Baxter's basement.

Pulling into his garage he dialed Cianne's cell phone. He called her every night since they started dating, including every night she was missing, and every night since she started avoiding him.

"Goodnight," he said to her voicemail, "I love you."

Tristan stepped through the door that led from the garage into his house. The house was dark and that meant he was alone. As usual, his parents were out of town. He was grateful for their support and felt embarrassed that they witnessed his breakdown over Cianne's kidnapping and the aftermath, but was relieved when his father was called away on business hours after he rescued Cianne. Tristan was grateful no one was around to witness his dark state of mind. He was still in breakdown mode and would be until Cianne agreed to see him. He was a wreck.

He opened his bedroom door and headed straight for his bathroom. Still not in the mood for too much light, Tristan turned on a few accent lights, undressed, stepped into the shower, then pushed a few buttons on the shower wall. One button switched on some soothing music and the other button turned on the hot water that sprayed from all directions onto his sore body.

The dogs hadn't done too much damage. In the end, he had to get a shot, there were some scrapes on his hand and a few stitches in his thigh. Overall, he was just sore and tired.

Tristan stood still in the middle of the shower for over ten minutes before he felt sleepy. He lifted his heavy head and pushed another button on the shower panel. The soothing music that played was replaced by rock radio. He reluctantly opened his eyes and reached for his shampoo.

Sleep would come quickly tonight, he mused. That was good.

He stepped out of the shower and dried off. He wiped the mirror with his hand and looked at his tired reflection. Everything had changed so quickly for him and Cianne. If she would only talk to him, they could figure out how to proceed, together. Her silence was driving him insane.

He needed to know what she thought, if she had doubts about them and if she blamed him. What were her plans in reference to the pregnancy and did those plans involved him?

Tristan sighed. He had no answers and she wasn't offering any. He opened his bathroom door and walked through the cloud of steam that released into his room. He reached to turn off the bathroom accent lights as he walked out when he saw something that stayed his hand.

Cianne was lying in his bed.

He fell back against the bathroom door frame; his fingers rested on the switch but didn't flick the lights off. He thought about how tired he was so he closed his eyes and refocused.

Has to be a dream.

However, he wasn't seeing things. Cianne was lying in his bed sound asleep.

Tristan left the light on but cracked the bathroom door. Then he walked softly to his bed and slid in beside her. He studied her face, compared all her delicate features to the recorded version in his memory.

Her lips drew him in but he resisted. He had no desire to wake her. He watched her for a while, content. That was until she woke up and buried her face in his arm when she saw him staring at her.

"How long have you been watching me sleep?" Cianne peeked at him from under his arm.

"Not long, maybe twenty minutes or so." He had to speak low and slow to hide the emotions in his voice. "I cannot believe you are still this shy with me. Although, I must admit I'm flattered."

He pulled Cianne close and kissed her on the head. He wasn't sure if she was comfortable being this close to him after all she'd been through but he needed to hold her. He needed to be close to her. He wanted to smell the heavenly scent of her hair again, to touch her soft satiny skin. He nestled his face in her neck and held her for as long as she allowed.

"I was scared that I would never feel you holding me again," Cianne said, breaking the silence. She slowly pulled away. "I wish we could stay like this forever."

He saw the tears form in her eyes and had to force his body to stay relaxed. "I'm sorry for everything you've been through Ci." His throat burned as he spoke the next words. "Your life would be so much simpler if you would have kept ignoring me."

She caressed his jaw. "I could say the same thing."

"I'm sorry," he whispered in her ear, through her hair. He caressed her neck where her birthmark was with his lips, causing her to shiver.

Cianne looked into his eyes for what felt like an eternity to him. Then she gently pushed him back so that he was lying flat. His face burned as his body reacted immediately. He looked down and watched her short cotton nightshirt rise, exposing all of her thighs as she straddled him.

"We don't—"

"I've missed you." Cianne leaned forward and kissed him as she positioned his erection at her entrance. She slowly eased herself down, taking him inside her.

Tristan groaned as he penetrated her. Arching his back, he buried the back of his head into his pillow and savored the feel of her. He rested his hands on her thighs as she slowly moved. It was heavenly torture, the pace she set. His heartbeat quickened with every motion as sheer ecstasy flowed through every cell in his body. He opened his eyes, to see her loveliness, to remind him this wasn't one of the many dreams he stored away in his mind.

His eyes, deep blue in this light, burned through Cianne as he looked up at her. She enjoyed the pleasure and bewilderment she saw in his face. His body synced with hers in a way that branded her very soul. Having all of Tristan was the most pleasurable *and* life-shattering moment in her life and the only way to express the two extreme poles of helplessness was with tears.

However, her emotional response instantly changed Tristan's blissful expression to concern. Cianne watched him close his eyes tight as if he were fighting what he was feeling. She felt the pressure of his palms increase on her waist.

Tristan groaned as she continued to ride him but he looked torn, reluctant, and he moved to lift her off of him.

No, Cianne thought, as she caught hold of his wrists. How could he want this to ever end? *My tears aren't from pain.*

He had to hear her thoughts because she was unable to say a single word as her sheath pulsed around his erection. Cianne held tight to his wrists, wishing she could just show him what she was feeling.

Cianne was no match for him when it came to strength, but Tristan was fighting more than her. He fought himself as well. He tried hard to focus, to stop. Her tears were too much for him to bear. He applied more pressure to her waist in an effort to move her but he couldn't.

She had her delicate hands wrapped around his wrists and was somehow overpowering him. Tristan looked helplessly from his hands up to Cianne's face as her long hair rose up from her body like she held a static ball. Her beautiful skin was sheer with sweat. Her tears glistened like diamonds.

What Tristan saw next was both beautiful and frightening. The color of Cianne's eyes turned crimson with only a thin emerald green rim surrounding her unchanged pupils. Only that hadn't been the most significant change. He felt more. He felt the ecstasy of his pleasure coupled with a new overwhelming sensation of bliss.

Tristan moaned and panted as his body surrendered to the new sensations. His pulse quickened as his heart pumped harder and faster than it ever had. He had to briefly close his eyes to handle it as he thought he might die from the rapture he felt.

The bed literally moved beneath them, and as the bed shook he focused on Cianne. Her beauty radiated through him. At this moment, she was lovelier than he had ever seen her before with her red eyes and her hair suspended in the air.

Tristan managed to push up on his elbows. The sounds of his pleasure filled the room. Under her spell, he threw his head back as she rode him faster. His vision blurred.

So, close…

His hazy gaze caught sight of the large picture above his head that was shaking violently.

Just as their bodies reached a sensation neither of them had ever felt before, the picture frame exploded above them. Tristan held Cianne close, dug into the mattress with his heels, then pushed off the bed with his free hand.

Before a single shard of glass hit the bed, Tristan had Cianne pinned to the wall with her legs wrapped tightly around his waist. She fell into him as she cried out her release. Not at all fazed by the glass on the bed behind them, a gratified Tristan buried his face into Cianne's neck to muffle the snarl that escaped him as he joined her.

With one arm around his neck and her other arm between them, Cianne placed her palm over his heart which had already slowed to a subtle rhythmic beat. She looked up and their eyes met. He noticed that her eyes were almost back to their normal color.

He leaned forward and kissed her.

When their lips separated, Tristan placed his hands on her waist. He hissed as he separated them then he lowered her so that her feet rested on the top of his. He kissed her again before he lifted her in his arms and carried her into his bathroom.

Cianne sat curled up on the oversized chair in the sitting area with a blanket wrapped around her. Showered and tired, she watched quietly as Tristan pulled the glass-filled sheets off his bed. He then swept up the remaining glass that had landed on the floor and threw it in the small garbage can.

Every so often, he looked over at her with an uneasy expression that he turned into a smile when their eyes met.

What the hell is going on with me?

She could accept that she was a Coesen, that she had visions because of that, but did being a Coesen mean she would be a danger to the people she loved most in the world?

Cianne looked at the huge glassless print above his bed and sighed. She placed the side of her face on her knees so that she faced away from Tristan. Pieces of her wet hair clung to her cheek but she didn't wipe them away. She had too much on her mind to care what her hair looked like.

This is bad, very bad. That glass didn't shatter into little safety chunks like it should have, she thought. It splintered into shards of sharp projectile pieces.

"Ci," Tristan said, in a hushed voice. He was at her side, crouched next to the chair she sat in. "I know I've asked you a hundred times already, but are you alright?"

Cianne lifted her head and saw the worry in his eyes. "I'm fine," she mumbled.

Tristan moved his hands through a slit in the blanket and rested it on her stomach. He looked concerned.

"I think everything is fine, Tristan."

"I should have had that picture printed on canvas, not framed." He lifted her way too easily and cradled her in his arms. "In case I missed some glass I feel better carrying you. I'll sweep again in the morning."

He walked her over to the bed and gently placed her down. Cianne slid over to allow him to get in beside her. She waited until he opened his arms to receive her and when he did she got as close as she possibly could and nuzzled into his chest.

"I don't know what or how I…" she started, then paused. "I thought you were upset about the tears again. I just wanted you to feel what I felt…so you wouldn't worry. I don't know how I did it, it just happened."

"It was amazing," he said. Tristan laughed. "The picture was an accident, no harm done."

"An accident, no harm done?" She knew she sounded shrill but didn't care. "How can you be so blasé about what just happened?"

"It's nothing Cianne. We weren't hurt. Everything is good." Tristan rubbed her damp hair.

"Is it?" she asked. *Everything is not good.* The image she had of their first meeting nine years ago, the one he wasn't aware of, was not good. Then there was the baby she sprung on him.

"Everything is going to be fine," he said confidently, as he kissed her on the head.

How was it that he summed up everything that happened over the past few weeks as fine? How could he not care about her lying to him?

Cianne sighed. "I'm sorry." She couldn't avoid it any longer. "I should have told you I was pregnant as soon as I found out. It was wrong to keep something so important from you." Cianne looked up at him. "I didn't want to see you because…because I honestly didn't want to face you. I wasn't sure how angry you were with me. I had to prepare myself for the worst possible reaction from you. I was scared. I still am, but my need to see you overcame my fear of what you might say to me," she admitted.

"And I thought you were freaked about the dog thing."

"Yeah," Cianne said. "We need to talk about that." Cianne could tell Tristan was different the night he rescued her. He was definitely like her, a Coesen.

Tristan winced. "Do you trust me?" he asked her.

Cianne looked into his eyes as she agreed with a nod of her head.

"Then let's hold off talking about that right now. I promise you everything will be clear very soon. About us," he said quietly. Tristan tenderly placed his hand on her belly. "I want this baby Ci, and I want us to raise our baby together." He moved from under her and pushed up on one arm. "I should have been more careful. I wasn't thinking. I should have used protection." Tristan looked into her eyes and took a deep breath. "I respect your right to choose and I don't want to upset you by telling you what I want but I wouldn't feel right letting you choose without telling you how I feel."

He leaned back and reached out to open his nightstand drawer. He pulled out a little black box then held it between them. "I know this isn't the ideal place to do this but it feels right." He smiled nervously. "I've run a thousand ways to ask you this over and over in my head but I can't seem to put the words together just right." He rubbed his head. "I just know that I don't want to live without you, Ci."

Cianne sat up and looked from him to the box. She had fantasized about this moment so many times over the past few years that it didn't seem real. She wanted this, she wanted him. "I love you so much Tristan," she said tenderly. "I don't want to live without you either but I can't say yes. Not right now."

Tristan stiffened then looked away but lifted his head and smiled. "I'll wait then," he said with a shrug. He placed the box back inside his nightstand. He then wrapped his arms around her and pulled her closer.

Cianne wrapped her arms around his neck. That was just like him. No fuss, no drama. He'll wait. "Thank you," she said. "I just need to—"

"It's not the right time," he interrupted, "you don't need to explain. I told you once that I will take whatever you have to offer and I meant it."

She kissed him softly on the lips. Tristan returned the kiss with more vigor and Cianne melted into his embrace as he locked his fingers in her long hair and moved closer to her.

Remembering the glass falling down on the bed burned away any resurging passion she may have felt. She needed to know how she did what she did, so she would never do it again in that type of situation.

"I think you should get some sleep," she transferred.

Tristan pulled back slowly. "You're right, we have a big day tomorrow. Tranae told me about the OBGYN appointment."

She looked at him, amazed. "You want to go to the baby doctor with me tomorrow?"

"Of course, I want to go, if it's ok with you."

Cianne smiled big. "I'd like that very much."

Chapter Twenty-Eight

Cianne stood in the cold dimly lit room while several men spoke the words that would likely haunt her for as long as she lived. "Where are you, you little whore?" Each man said, one after the other. None of them sounded like the voice of the one who gave the orders.

It had been almost two weeks since Tristan rescued her and the police were no closer to finding the ones responsible. She listened closely to the last man recite the words and shook her head when the detective looked at her. The voice was familiar but it wasn't the one she heard that first day or that awful night. Tristan squeezed her hand. Like her, he couldn't ID anyone positively.

Det. Malone led the two of them through a maze of desks to get to his office. Cianne sat in the chair that faced Det. Malone. Tristan sat down in the chair beside her.

"Officer Perkins," Malone called out when he saw the officer walking past his office. The officer gave Cianne and Tristan a nod as he stood in the doorway. "Officer Perkins has transferred here from DC. He's devoted to finding out who is responsible for your abduction, Ms. Baxter." Malone popped a piece of gum in his mouth then offered some to Tristan, then to Cianne. Both declined.

"Thank you," Cianne said to Perkins. The Officer smiled then left them alone with the detective.

"It's not easy trying to remember a voice from a stressful situation such as yours," Malone said, turning back to them. He opened his desk drawer. "Peter Walters," Malone looked at her, "you knew him as Cook. His sister lives near the abandoned school where you were held." The detective handed Cianne a photo.

Cianne looked over the picture. It was Cook. "He was trying to help me."

Tristan took the picture from Cianne and looked it over. "I've seen this guy before." Tristan looked at the detective, who was about to speak when something outside the office drew his attention. He followed the detective's gaze and saw two familiar faces. The men moved toward the elevators on the other side of the office.

He tilted his head to one side then straightened it with understanding as he looked back to the detective, then back to the men by the elevator. Tristan said nothing as he stood.

"Now Mr. Bertram," Detective Malone said as he stood up, "There's a wrong time and a wrong place and this is it."

"What's wrong Tristan?" Cianne asked, also getting to her feet. She reached for his hand but he avoided her touch and simply touched her shoulders.

"I'll be right back," he said. He made sure he sounded calm and he added a smile for her benefit.

"What's going on?" Cianne asked.

Tristan heard her ask the question as he exited the detective's office. He walked briskly toward the elevator where the two men stood with their backs to him, waiting for the elevator. With a chime, the doors to the elevator opened. Tristan moved into action. He made a dash toward the men, tackling both of them to the floor. He rolled over on the muscled one of the two, hitting him with two quick blows to the face.

As the taller one tried to stand, Tristan, kicked his feet from under him causing the man to fall face first to the floor. The tall guy grunted then shrieked in pain. Tristan got to his feet swiftly then stomped on the big guy's groin. The sound of the man's scream satisfied him enough to move to the taller of the two.

He wanted Nick to suffer the most. Tristan stood over Nick, who had just rolled over from his face plant. Tristan stomped him in the face with the heel of his shoe.

Everything happened so fast that by the time two officers tried to subdue him, Tristan had done a lot of damage. He slung the officers off him with ease. Nick had curled up in the fetal position with his hands over his head as Tristan continued his attack.

It didn't take long for them to be surrounded by officers. A few tackled and pinned Tristan to the floor.

"I'm going to kill you! Both of you!" Tristan yelled. His eyes were on Nick as the police officers struggled to keep him down. He heard someone yell for a taser but he didn't care. Someone else grabbed him from behind, putting him in a headlock.

"Tristan, please stop!" Cianne screamed.

He faintly heard her but he was determined to reach Nick. The officers were getting rougher as he continued to struggle toward his target who still lay on the floor in a ball.

"Think of what you're doing and how it affects her." A calm voice said next to his ear.

Tristan craned his head back as far as it could go to see that Officer Perkins had him in a headlock. It was Perkins who mentioned Cianne and how his attack affected her. He looked at Nick who was pulled to his feet by two other officers. Then he looked to Cianne. She looked terrified.

He stopped his struggles then lifted his hands up as a sign of surrender. One by one, the officers slowly released him.

"Place your hands behind your back please," Officer Perkins told him.

Tristan allowed Perkins to place plastic ties around his wrist.

As Tristan sat in Malone's office with his hands still secured behind his back, he looked through the open door at Cianne. She was seated on a bench with a female officer who spoke to her and Mr. Baxter. Tristan winked and she managed a half smile for him but looked away when Officer Perkins handed her a bottle of water.

"Let's see," Malone said to Tristan, as he walked into his office, "you broke his nose and two of his fingers." Malone leaned down and cut the ties around Tristan's wrist. "But he isn't going to press charges."

"Really," Tristan hissed. "That's because the son of a bitch is guilty."

"Guilty or not, neither you nor Cianne could say that his voice was the one you heard. With no evidence, no prints and the only vehicle we have is one that was stolen days before the kidnapping, we can't do a damn thing until he or his friend slips up."

"So, he gets to walk even though you connected him to the Cook guy." Tristan shook his head in frustration. "I mean Peter. Nick has harassed Cianne in the past." He stood. "You can't let him get away with this!"

"All can be explained away as inconsequential." The detective rocked back in his chair.

"Inconsequential?" Tristan yelled. He slammed his fist on the detective's desk.

A few officers outside Malone's office heard the loud noise that Tristan's fist made as it connected with the desk. They were prepared to restrain Tristan again but Det. Malone waved them off. "You got lucky Mr. Bertram. You got your girl back unscathed, your money and your life. Mr. Carter and Mr. Cruz aren't pressing charges. I'd say you're pretty fortunate. Don't make me regret letting you walk out of here." Malone put a piece of gum in his mouth, dismissing Tristan's aggression. "Mr. Carter and his friend are on our radar so I doubt they will try anything else. I figure you're both pretty safe now."

"Do you know she can't hear a dog bark without recoiling? She can't sleep unless a light is on in the room or I'm with her. Cianne barely wants to leave the house because of him and you're saying that nothing can be done about it because we can't place his voice at the scene?" Tristan asked in a low tone.

"Not without evidence."

"Alright," Tristan said with his usual calm as he turned to leave.

"Don't do anything stupid," Malone called out to him. He looked at the spot on his wooden desk that Tristan had struck. "Damn it," he said as he rubbed his finger along the large crack that spread from one end of his desk to the other. "How in the hell…" He looked out his door at Tristan, with a curious look on his face.

The school and all the seniors were adorned in their school's colors. Blue, white, and silver covered everything. Graduation day for West Hills High School was here. It was a bright calm day with the temperature at a spicy 85 degrees at just ten o'clock in the morning. The auditorium filled quickly with family and friends. A stream of happy chatter hovered over the crowd as everyone found a seat.

Tristan held Cianne's hand in his as they sat in the fifth row from the stage. He looked over at her and smiled. She returned the smiled and squeezed his hand. He knew she would be happy that he was able to get Sterling Basle to switch seats with him so that he could sit next to her. He wished he was able to walk across the stage with her, but he knew it wouldn't be possible. She would be called to the stage before him.

He turned around and looked through the crowd of spectators. When he saw his parents, he turned back around to face the stage. He hadn't seen much of them since the incident at the police station and wasn't ready to deal with his father's scornful looks just yet.

After a few minutes, the speakers made their way to the podium to say words of encouragement and well wishes to the senior class. Some of them were known to Tristan, and some he didn't know, but every one of them said basically the same thing, and that was that the seniors were no longer children. That they would have to go into the big scary world alone, with only the lessons they've learned from their families and their twelve years of schooling.

When it was time to call the senior class to the stage, loud clapping echoed throughout the building. The Principal and some VIP whose name Tristan hadn't logged to memory, took turns calling each student's name to come up and accept their diploma. Every so often when the name of a popular student was called the clapping and yells from the crowd were louder and took longer to settle.

When Cianne's name was called, the crowd clapped and yelled. He watched in awe as she smiled and accepted her diploma. It still amazed Tristan that she was his.

Cianne followed the student in front of her back to her seat. Tristan proudly watched her from his spot near the stage, almost missing the principal call his name.

The crowd erupted with screams and yells as he made his way up the stairs to the stage. People were yelling all sorts of things from, "you're a hero" to "I love you." He laughed when Mrs. Grey, one of the counselors, blew him a kiss.

The speaker had to give the crowd a few minutes longer than normally allowed to settle down before he impatiently called the next name. After the last student's name was called a final farewell was given, Tristan and Cianne tossed their caps in the air.

◉

At the end of the ceremony, everyone crowded into the halls, the parking lot, and the school lawn to take pictures or to say their goodbyes. Cianne kept close to Tristan as people stopped him to talk. She held onto his hand most of the time, and when they weren't holding hands, Tristan had her pulled close with his arm around her waist or her shoulders.

In time, they slowly made their way through the maze of people to a clearing. As they walked past friends and strangers, Cianne noticed that a beautiful older woman dressed in a black jacket dress with gold trim was watching her. She thought the woman had a familiar face so she smiled. The woman smiled back but was quickly swallowed up by the crowd.

"Hey Cianne," Vanessa called from somewhere in the crowd.

Cianne squeezed Tristan's hand. *"I can't do this."*

"Yes, you can. I'm right here." Tristan looked down at her and smiled.

"Cianne," Vanessa appeared in front of them. She, like most of the graduates, had taken off her robe in the summer heat. "How are you?" Vanessa asked, giving her a look of pity.

"Good Vanessa, thanks for asking. How are you?" Cianne asked.

"Aren't you all hot in them robes?" Vanessa asked. Before Cianne could respond Vanessa gasped, "Wow!" She reached for the cords around Cianne's neck. "You guys got every honor cord they have. What are they all for?"

Cianne leaned back to avoid being touched. Vanessa held her hand in the air for a brief moment before pulling it back. She gave Cianne and Tristan an apologetic look.

"The black and gold are for National Honor Society, the red is for Science. Blue is for Student Council, green is Math honors. The purple is for English and the yellow one that she has and I don't is for Community Service. And this one," he said, holding up the green cord he wore, "she doesn't have, is for Business."

"You guys really are nerds," Brenda said as she rolled her eyes.

Cianne hadn't noticed Brenda when she walked up with Vanessa. She nervously looked down when Brenda's eyes met hers.

"Are you guys coming to Alex's party—," Vanessa started.

"We still have some more people we need to say goodbye to. It was nice seeing you geeks, um guys, but we have to go," Brenda said. She stepped in front of them and took Vanessa by the arm. "It was especially nice seeing you Tristan," she said seductively, as she pushed Vanessa away.

Cianne felt something on her hand so she looked down. Brenda was gently brushing her fingers over Cianne's. She looked up to see Brenda walking past her with a compassionate smile on her face. Cianne had never taken Brenda for the caring type but…

She smiled back.

"See, that wasn't too bad, was it?" Tristan kissed her cheek.

"Not too bad," she admitted.

"Wait, I think I spoke too soon. My parents and your dad are walking this way and they have cameras in their hands," he said, laughing.

"Did they see us; do we have time to get away?" Cianne pouted playfully. Somehow, she was feeling a lot better.

"No. I think I made eye contact." He looked away and pretended not to see their families coming toward them.

"Cianne," Tranae called out.

Cianne looked around the mass of people until she saw Tranae fighting to get through the crowd with Brian and both of their parents. "I guess we can pose for a few pictures for our parents. They were cheated out of the prom pictures; this is the least we can do." Cianne bent her head and touched one of her long curls. "How do I look?"

"Amazing as always." Tristan squeezed her hand.

"Is my baby bump showing?" she whispered. Cianne ran her hands down the front of her robe then back up to her curls.

"Remember what the doctor said. You may not show for a few more weeks." Tristan pulled her hand away from her hair.

She felt so uncomfortable with herself lately.

"Smile, everything is going to be ok, I promise," Tristan told her telepathically as their family and friends reached them.

Cianne put a big smile on her face. She wanted to believe that everything would be fine. That they would live happily ever after, but somehow, she knew that her troubles were just beginning.

To be continued in…
The Awakening of the Halo
Head on over to my website www.SheaSwainWrites.com for
Upcoming Releases,
Character Dream-casting
And sign up for my Newsletter
THANK YOU
and
Please consider leaving a review!

Prologue
October 12th

Bored almost to the point of changing her nail polish a third time, Tranae decided she may as well see what was going on outside. She walked out of her bedroom, jogged down the stairs, and left out of her house.

Tranae glanced across the street before the smell of burnt rubber and the unmistakable chatter of curious spectators filled the air as she approached the intersection of Roland Road and Ridgeview Park Lane. She lazily strolled along the sidewalk, her attention split between the gathered spectators and the text message she was sending her best friend, Cianne, about all the commotion, because she was missing it.

At the end of the street, several police cruisers, three emergency vehicles, and at least one hell of a wreck littered the impassible junction.

"I wonder what happened?" Tranae asked herself. She let the hand that held her cell phone fall to her side as she slid her way through the group of spectators to get a better look.

A car accident wasn't much of a surprise at this particular intersection, but the several loud popping sounds that she heard following the crash tugged at her curiosity. Tranae didn't care for the macabre but the crash, the strange sounds, and the large number of people she saw walking by her house were enough to spark her interest.

This was so much more exciting than changing her nail color. Due to her current parental imposed imprisonment, she couldn't go to the spa to get it professionally done.

Tranae peered out over the police barrier, taking note of all the police, emergency medical techs, and firemen. "So reckless," she dragged the words out. "Someone must be hurt bad."

"Looks like it," someone close by offered.

Tranae didn't look to see who spoke. Her attention was focused on the metallic silver SUV sitting just inside the police barrier, with its roof caved in due to a large palm tree resting on top of it. The car looked familiar.

The make and model is kind of popular, she told herself in an attempt to dismiss her fears. There's no reason to stress. *Still.* Tranae scanned the scene from left to right, trying to see through the emergency workers who were huddled together in groups.

"It looks pretty bad."

Tranae looked over her shoulder at the man who spoke. She eased pass him.

"Excuse me," the sneered as he stepped aside, "no need to be rude."

Tranae paid the man no mind because her attention was directed beyond a huddled group of EMT's where there was another vehicle. It was totaled and it was a vehicle she was certain she recognized, despite the damage. Tranae's stomach knotted, curiosity made way for panic. She hurried around the length of the barrier, closer to where the huddled EMT's were frantically working. She needed to see who it was they were working on.

"I've got a pulse over here," a female paramedic yelled out.

In a state of utter panic, Tranae fixed her eyes on the female paramedic. When she jumped up, allowing a gap in the huddle, Tranae saw what she feared most. The scream that rose from her lungs caused everyone within earshot to look her way.

Chapter One
Present-June 2
Four Months Earlier

Tristan parked the borrowed truck under a large tree at the end of the busy street. He looked at the dashboard and noted that it was a quarter after one. The sun, which looked to be at a high point in the afternoon sky, wasn't able to penetrate the tree's shade. But even hidden under the leaves it was still about 90 degrees. It was a hot day but it was business as usual on the city block filled with vendors, residents, and children. For Tristan, the heat had never been an issue, and just like the people around him, he had business to take care of.

He reached for the bag on the passenger seat and pulled out a bottle of water. He had about an hour before his meeting so he decided to look in on an old friend whose apartment was in clear view from where he sat.

As Tristan began to drink his water, he saw his friend's image appear in the rear-view mirror. He watched Jason Cruz, also known as JC, walked right by the truck he sat in, turning every so often to glance over his shoulder.

Tristan made no attempt to move or hide that he was there, watching. He drank his water as JC strolled across the street and continued down to the far end of the block. He saw JC look around again before stepping into an apartment building, sure that JC hadn't seen him.

Jason didn't see him this time or the two other times he sat parked in the very same spot. "You seemed spooked," Tristan chuckled in a low hiss to no one. "Being spooked should be the least of your worries Jason."

It had only been two and a half weeks since he saved Cianne from the hell JC and his friends put her through to extort a large sum of money from him. Two and half weeks since she was left alone to defend herself from a pack of feral dogs that he had to kill with his bare hands to save her. It had been two and a half weeks since he found out that Cianne had supernatural abilities and had somehow inadvertently given him the strength and speed to protect her.

JC should be on edge. He along with his buddy, Nicklaus Carter, a college student Cianne once tutored, had literally gotten away with kidnapping and murder. The third accomplice, Peter Walter, a.k.a Cook, a name given to him by Cianne for the home cooked meals he brought her when they held her captive, realized early on that the kidnapping for ransom scheme was wrong. For five days Cook secretly made sure Cianne ate, and in the end, he tried to help her escape but lost his life in the process.

The police have nothing to link JC or Nick to Peter or the crime other than they knew one another but Tristan knew they were guilty. "Cook" had botched the kidnapping for Nick and JC so one of them shot and killed him.

Tristan owed Peter his life for helping Cianne and the baby she carried inside of her. His baby. She would never be the same because of them and if something had happened to her…

"Shit," he cursed at the thought.

Tristan put the top back on his water. He dismissed all thoughts of Cianne's mortality. She and the baby survived their ordeal. It was time to look ahead. He would do whatever it took to keep them safe. There were just a few loose-ends to tie-up. He focused on the apartment building JC went into.

SHEA SWAIN

CHAINED
to the
DEVIL'S
SON

PROLOGUE

SUMMER OF 1976

The sound of the gunshot was deafening as it shattered the calm night.

They were driving to Alabama. Had been driving for a long time when Evelyn's mother, Pearl, asked her father, Harland, to stop at a motel they were approaching. Only her father didn't stop. He continued driving so long after her mother's request that even the signs to direct them to food and fuel grew scarce. With nothing to occupy her mind, Eve fell asleep.

When Eve woke, her mother was urging her father not to pull onto a dirt road that looked deserted but for the beat-up mailbox that stood out like a beacon off the main road. They were just going to ask for directions or maybe use the phone; at least that was what her father said.

Eve listened quietly as her parents' debated what to do. Whether to knock on the rundown farmhouse door or to chance driving further because they were clearly lost. Her mother spoke of her unease. Having been raised in the South, she warned them that they needed to be ever cautious.

Harland was of a different breed. He had been raised among gentler white folk who seemed more apt to spear you with words rather than a sharp knife. He believed in the power of words, wholeheartedly. Harland Jones also believed that most people were well-meaning organisms who when given the facts were reprogrammable, at least that's what he often said.

Eve's father ended up winning the debate on whether to knock on the old farmhouse door or not. Eve fought a grin when she saw the handsome smile he always flashed when he won an argument. It was rare for her father to win one against her mother, who was a thinker by trade. He even offered Eve a wink as he gracefully slid from their vehicle and climbed the cracked stairs. He walked with that same grace before knocking on the tattered screen door.

Eve could barely see the girl who opened the door, and for a moment, it seemed as if the girl was going to allow her father to use their phone. Then, Eve heard someone yelling from inside the house. She tensed when a fuming man with stringy dark hair shoved the girl out of the way and pulled the screen door open wider. The man began yelling at Eve's father, who held up his hands in defense and seemed to speak calmly, which was his way.

Eve couldn't make out what was being said, so she rolled down the car window. The word 'nigger' was said a number of times by the man. She heard that word before, but it didn't have the sting it had on this man's lips. Eve's father must have felt the same because instead of arguing with the crazy-eyed man, he just shook his head and turned around.

Eve didn't even hear when her mother got out of the car, but she did and was ushering her husband down the porch stairs and toward the car. Her parents' slow trek back to the car didn't hold Eve's attention. Instead, she looked back to the door of the house, only to find that the angry man had disappeared back inside.

Eve settled back in her seat but kept her eyes on the dark house. She wanted her parents' to move faster. She had a bad feeling in the pit of her stomach and wanted to get away from this house as fast as they could. Her heart sped up as she silently willed them to move faster, to run if possible. The walkway wasn't paved and her mother was wearing heels. So while they tried to maneuver over the pebbles, neither her father nor her mother saw the angry man stepping back into the doorway with the long gun in his hands.

Eve did, and she screamed for her parents' to turn around. She screamed for them to run, but there was no time for either of them to react before the man took aim. Eve watched in horror as her father's chest exploded outward. She held her breath as her father slowly dropped to his knees. She saw the shock on his face and the sorrow in his gaze as he locked eyes with her briefly before falling to his back.

Mommy! Eve's panicked gaze immediately sought out her mother as she prayed that what she was witnessing from her family's car was just a nightmare.

Eve's ears rang from the loud blast, but she heard her mother scream as she frantically tried to stop the bleeding from her husband's chest wound. Wide-eyed with terror, Eve's young mind tried to process why this was happening. Shaking with fear, Eve watched through teary eyes as the girl from the house came to the doorway again. The girl was screaming and pointing when a boy rushed out of the darkened doorway and ran toward the man who now towered over her mother with the gun still in his hands.

"Mommy!" Eve shouted to her mother. Her mother didn't answer as she cried out for him, her father. Eve watched helplessly as the man raised the gun and slammed the handle down on her mother's head.

Jason Ray Shaw, aka Junior, tried to ignore being shaken awake, but it was useless because Sadie Shaw was determined. He groaned then rolled over and opened his eyes to see his sister's beautiful but worried face looking down at him. Though she was five years older at seventeen, she relied on him for a good deal of support. Clearly his sister needed him right now. She was crying, her brows were pinched, she looked freaked, and she was shaking him as if he was still asleep.

"Wake up, Junior. Dad…doing bad, bad," she said as she continued to shake him.

With a curse that would make a saint's ears bleed, Junior moved Sadie aside, slid out of bed, and pulled on his worn jeans then his socks as best he could. Sadie said a bunch of words but she wasn't making any sense, her crying jumbled everything. *God, my life is shit.* Not because of Sadie. She was his special girl. The doctors said retarded, but to him she was just plain special and he loved her just the way she was.

No, Sadie wasn't the problem.

As Junior followed Sadie out of his room he heard the tell-tale signs that his father was drunk again. The sounds of shotgun blasts were a constant here at home sweet home. The neighbor's dog was probably on their property again, and his sauced father was trying to shoot the damned thing... again. Seeing no reason to rush but wide awake now, Junior ranked Sadie's frantic pulls and urging low as he made his way through the hallway and down the stairs to the first floor of the house. It was only when he heard screams that he stopped dead in his tracks.

"Help them," Sadie cried as she pulled at his arm.

A second later, Junior was shoving Sadie behind him and running for the front door with no idea what awaited him. He pushed through the open doorway and stopped to take in the scene before him.

He saw… Junior blinked then blinked again. "What have you done?" Junior yelled. Cefus Shaw swung around with the gun aimed at him. Junior held up his hands and took a step back. "Pop?" Junior said softly.

Cefus' eyes were absent of any recognition or humanity. Junior saw this side of his father before. He endured many beatings that followed his father's drinking and this, what he saw, was that look. Junior gazed pleadingly into those hard, unsympathetic eyes enough in his short life to know that there would be no compassion. Would this be the night the old man ended it all for him? As he did often in times like this, Junior thought of his sweet, innocent sister.

Sadie was the only person in this world that Junior cared about. If he took anything his father ever said to heart it was, 'Blood boy'; the old coot would say 'it's all you got in this world.'

"Pop," Junior said again, cautiously.

As if jarred awake, Cefus lowered the shotgun a few inches, now aiming at Junior's chest instead of his head. Recognition flashed in Cefus' light glazed-over eyes before he blinked. "What the hell you doing sneaking up on me, boy," Cefus hissed before turning back around. With his father's focus away from him, Junior took a calming breath then looked past his father.

A woman was lying beside a man who had a huge hole in his chest. Junior immediately felt sick as pain and empathy slammed into him for the strangers. *Cefus done did it now*, he thought as he took a measured step closer. Junior was turning his gaze on Cefus when he saw *her* out the corner of his eye.

In a station wagon that had one of those wheeled storage moving containers attached to it was a girl. Her face was streaked with tears. Her eyes were pinned on the man and woman lying unmoving on the ground. Her mouth was wide as her screams filled the night. He hadn't heard her until now.

How did he not hear her?

Cefus heard her, and he was about to shut her up, permanently.

Junior moved; later he would wonder what propelled him to do it, but there was no time to dissect his actions now. He ran down the gravel walk as fast as he could, blocking Cefus' view and the barrel of the shotgun that he aimed at the car window where the girl was howling.

"Get the fuck out of the way, boy, for I fill you with holes." Cefus' words were slow but not slurred. That bastard wasn't as drunk as Junior originally thought. His father was a hell of a shot which explained why he actually was able to hit that man dead center in the first place. Cefus being sober…

"You need to think right now, Pop," Junior said. He shook his head when he noticed Sadie coming out of the front door. Sadie understood and quickly went back inside. "If you shoot that shotgun one more time, the Wilsons will have the law out here again. How you gone explain this," Junior motioned to the dead man. He only heard one shot so he assumed the woman may still be alive. "These aren't dogs, Pop."

"The hell they ain't," Cefus said, motioning with the barrel for Junior to move out of the way. "Niggers and dogs are one in the same. Now move your ass, boy."

"Sheriff Gifford won't be able to sweep this under his hat if you harm the girl. She's not a man, Pop. They won't see her as a threat like they might her parents'." Junior realized the girl had gone silent, but he couldn't check on her just yet. He was trying to reason with a man of many faces, and both their lives were on the line. The drunk, the punisher, the racist, on rare occasions the apologetic father, and now the murderer was staring at Junior as if he were a stranger.

Junior heard the gun cock. *Will he really shoot me?* The thought to appeal to the father in Cefus, the father he had never been, popped in Junior's head. "I'm your son, your blood." Cefus actually grinned, and that grin said none of that mattered. "You say that's all we got is each other, Pop."

That got Cefus to slowly lower the shotgun with a sigh. He stood there with his eyes on the girl in the car then he looked down at the woman lying at his feet. Cefus seemed to think for a moment then his eyes lit up. Junior's stomach churned because that look was one of his father's scariest, and by the way, Cefus was peering down at the woman's thighs, exposed by the rising hem of the dress she wore…

Junior could almost see the cogs in Cefus' depraved head turning. It was then that Junior realized that he should have let Cefus kill the woman and the terrified girl. That would have been more humane because now he and Sadie weren't the only prisoners of Cefus Shaw.

Available Now

INVIDIOUS *Betrayal*

SHEA SWAIN

Prologue

April 8th, 2012

Ian Howl cradled the delicate, unconscious, girl in his arms as he swiftly made his way through the maze of a mansion to get to the garage. Her head rested on his chest and his arms supported her back and legs as he held her close. The swell of her feminine curves against his body felt all too consuming; the warmth of her skin was like a sweet yet biting burn. Tapping down on his ill-placed desires, Ian forced himself to focus on the present: their escape.

He ignored the hulking guard that sat in the security room who called to him as he rushed by. Turning a corner, Ian glanced over his shoulder to see if he was being followed. He hoped for a confrontation-free getaway, but the odds were against them.

Gently, he lowered the arm that cradled the girl's legs so that they slowly slide down his body until he balanced her on the balls of her feet. Holding her close to his chest, he placed his thumb to the security scanner on the wall. He vaguely thought of her bare feet touching the cold floor, but it was something he couldn't help right now. He needed to get her out of there and a chill was the least of his worries.

Three heartbeats later, the door that lead to the massive garage swung open with an air-locked *swoosh* that brought his hope soaring to new heights. They were almost free.

Ian noticed his car was blocked in, so he grabbed a random set of car keys from the wall hook and pressed the door unlock button. The headlights of a beautiful Porsche flashed, but the vehicle was in the rear of the garage and several cars surrounded it. The third set of keys he tried unlocked a luxury sedan that wasn't blocked in and was close to the garage doors. Ian had eased the girl into the passenger seat of the sedan and was securing the seatbelt around her when he felt a heavy hand on his shoulder.

"Where do you think you're taking that car, kid?"

Ian turned his head around to see Brad... Or was it Brent? He didn't remember the guard's name, but Ian knew the guy was built like a defensive tackle. Striking first would surprise Brad/ Brent. So he grabbed the hand on his shoulder and pulled the guard into his elbow, targeting his large, beefy face. The guard stepped back, holding his gushing nose. Ian spun around; he thrust the base of his palm upward into the man's shocked, bloody, face causing him to stumble back again then fall to the floor. The guard didn't get back up.

"Please," the girl whispered.

Ian whipped his head around to see that she was still unconscious and strapped in the car. Rushing to the driver's side of the commandeered vehicle, he hopped inside and started the engine. The automatic doors to the parking garage opened when the car tripped the underground sensor and they barreled down the path toward the front gate of the property. Luckily there were still party guests inside because usually those sensors only allowed vehicles with an installed security plate placed under the hood to pass through without human intervention.

Again, the underground sensor allowed the vehicle to pass through. The large main gates had opened, but they were not in the clear yet.

Ian didn't floor the gas pedal until he was clear of his uncle's property. He wasn't being followed, but he continued to check the rearview mirror, knowing their absence would soon be reported.

The girl moaned, pulling his gaze from the road.

Her long dark brown hair was matted to her head, practically covering her delicate face, so he brushed some of it away. Bruises covered her body but her dry lips, puffy red eyes, and the darkening hand prints on her throat were the most obvious. She was in bad shape, and Ian feared that the thin sheet wasn't enough to keep her naked body warm.

"Help me," she moaned.

"I'm taking you to a hospital," Ian told her. He fought the bile that rose from his stomach. Disgust and shame assailed him, but right now he couldn't think of his role in what had happened to her. He had to get her medical help, but he didn't know Howard County, Maryland, all that well. The only time he even came to this part of Maryland was when he visited his uncle.

Ian brushed the back of his hand over her bruised cheek and was about to place it back on the steering wheel when her eyes popped open, jarring him a little.

She didn't move right away. She just looked at him with a hollowed gaze as if her mind had to reboot. Then those chestnut-brown orbs changed from confused to feral in a flash. Before he could react, she was screaming, "No hospital! No cops!" over and over as she kicked at him and pushed at the passenger door with her hands. Ian grabbed at her feet, but his hand slipped and she nailed him hard on the side of his head with her foot.

"All right, no hospitals!" Ian yelled her as he slammed his foot on the brake, causing the car to skid along the nearly empty road. The force of the sudden stop propelled her forward and the side of her head collided with the dashboard. Her body went limp.

"Shit!" he yelled as he slammed his hands on the steering wheel. Ian pulled the car off to the side of the road, took his cell phone out, and dialed his father's cell. The phone rang several times, then the voicemail picked up. He listened to his father's commanding voice, but he disconnected before the taped greeting ended.

"Damn it, Dad, this is important!"

Ian glanced up at the rearview mirror, peering out into the quiet darkness, lost in thought. The weight of his cell phone in his hand made him find his focus again. He turned the phone over in his hand twice before shutting off the power. Ian stared at the cell phone in his hand for a long moment as he unconsciously rubbed at a spot under his armpit.

"They will be looking for me, us."
He glanced at the girl then felt under his arm again. As long as she was with him, they would find her.

Available Now

About the Author

Shea is a woman in love with the idea of love so it's no wonder she writes Romance Novels. The East Coast native is a romantic to her core and reads and watches anything with a love story. She especially likes binging on the Hallmark Channel around Christmas time.

She enjoys meeting people and chatting, collecting Barbie dolls, toys, and is addicted to The Sims games. Shea also loves music and has mentioned that she writes better when she has movie scores playing as white noise in the background.

This new and exciting author writes Adult Romance in the sub-genres of Contemporary, New Adult, Paranormal, Sci-Fi, and Erotica. Come…Taste A Sample.

Connect with Shea Swain

Website: www.SheaSwainWrites.com
Email: SheaSwainWrites@gmail.com

Coesen Definitions

Words in italics are defined

Coesen: In the *Ilterian* language, the word *Coesen* means the combination of two or more items, particles, or organisms. The Four Originals adopted the term for their classification that defines them as a race of human-hybrids who originated from a single tribe on the continent of Africa. Most are born with birthmarks behind their left ear. Each tribe has a variation of this mark that they are born with. Some *Coesen* are born with an ability. It is present at birth but doesn't manifest until the age of puberty. Most are born with a single ability. A very small percentage are born with two.

Breed: The child of a Coesen and *Middling* coupling. Most of these children do not carry the birthmark of a full blooded Coesen. The law on the books state that Coesen parent and Breed are to be sentenced to death, the human parent's mind is wiped cleaned. 98% of Breed children are born with no abilities but may still carry the birthmark. If they mate a Coesen, their children may or may not have abilities.

Child of Jai or Pet: Jai of the *Arkean* tribe conceived a Breed with a man named Shaw. Even after her descendants couple with only Coesens, each are born with the physical features of a Caucasian.

Middling: Term to define a human with no *Coesen* blood.

Protectors: A Coesen who is chosen by the *Source* and is infused with power during the *transition* stage to keep the Coesen's Ward safe. They sense when their ward is in danger and is able to locate them at all times. These Coesen are stronger and faster than any living entity on earth with exception of one person, *Caleb Scott.* In history only two

Middlings have been chosen by the Source. It is believed that Middling aren't capable of surviving the transformation.

Transition: A Coesen abilities become active when they go through puberty. This process is called a Transition.

Transference: When a Coesen is chosen by the Source to be awarded the abilities to become a Protector.

The Halo: A Coesen whose prophecy states will bear a full halo birthmark and have all the abilities known to Coesen.